THE VAULT

THE VAULT

THE HYBRIAN SERIES BOOK ONE

L. WOOD

To all the strong women out there who get knocked down but get back up again. My dear daughter and mother—and all of those closest to me—you are inspiring.

CHAPTER ONE

I held the top of my forearm underneath the scanner jutting from the gym wall. The red light shining over the inked lines on my skin changed to green as my name and time appeared on the screen. Like everyone else, I had a small barcode tattooed on the top of my left forearm that was easy to scan and didn't cover any accessible veins. It made tracking when and where we went easy.

I spotted two of my friends and headed in their direction, barely noting the other Jects that were often replaced. The ones we had lost vanished, and their names were rarely brought up. Ject was our label because we were subjects to their trials, and I didn't know how long ago that name was patented. Newcomers were in their teens or rarely in their early twenties, and no one remembered where they came from.

"Good morning, sunshine." Liam discreetly nudged me when I reached him.

"Good morning, buttercup," I teased as my gaze drifted from his tousled brown hair to his taut grey T-shirt and black sweatpants. *Did I seriously just check him out?* He had arrived nine months before me, and we'd been friends ever since. I quickly averted my eyes and said good morning to Travis.

A whistle sounded and everyone silently started their warm-up laps. Our bare feet padded against the soft gym floor as we jogged. Our scheduled days started with a 5:00

a.m. alarm that summoned us to conditioning. It had gone by fast this morning but still left me exhausted, like usual.

I headed for the women's showers opposite of the men's on the other side of the gym. I walked through the door and was greeted by the sentinel in her blue uniform. My arm moved under the scanner like it was second nature as I wondered what the meaning was behind the red *01* on the sentinel's sleeve.

I quickly showered and changed into a fresh grey shirt and pair of black capris. I caught my pale reflection in the mirror on the locker door as I closed it and wondered who I had to thank for the uncontrollable golden-blond hair, light brown eyes, and dimples people mistook as adorable and innocent. My hair was still soaked, but I put it up anyway before heading to breakfast.

Maya followed as I carried my tray with two hard-boiled eggs and yogurt to our usual table where Liam and Travis sat.

Travis perked up with a grin that lit his eyes. "Look what the cat dragged in."

"Oh, shut it." Maya's deep brown eyes narrowed underneath her thick lashes as she sat next to me.

"His ego's hurt because he couldn't keep up this morning," I commented.

Travis raised an eyebrow and laughed from across the table. "I did excellent, just like I do every day."

"You'll catch up soon." Maya winked as Liam grinned next to Travis. "Tired of being the youngest?" Maya went on, her eyes sparkling.

Despite Travis being the youngest, he was the tallest out of the four of us. Maya had turned nineteen recently and had arrived a few months prior to him—that had been two years after my arrival.

"There's no catching up to do. Besides, being the youngest doesn't make me any less victorious." Travis's smile fell as he leaned in, lowering his voice. "I've been wanting to ask you guys. How have your injections been lately?"

"We shouldn't talk about this here—we could be sent to detainment." I bit the inside of my cheek and glanced around. We weren't allowed to talk about our injections or anything that happened during our treatment. Otherwise, we would be locked up.

"Mine's always been white, but it was grey the last few times. I don't feel any different, though," Travis continued regardless, his crisp blue eyes eager for information.

Maya looked at him curiously, and so did I.

"Harper's right. We shouldn't be discussing this." Liam leaned over the table, towering over it at his taller-than-average height. "Mine changed, but I feel the same. Now, laugh." His chestnut eyes shifted to the left and my eyes followed. A sentinel was walking in our direction and the sight of the radio, baton, and gun hanging from his belt made me shudder. Maya and Travis also caught on, and the four of us started fake laughing. The sentinel eyed us as he passed, but he did not stop.

Why did their injections change, and why had theirs been white? Mine had always been clear blue. My heart began to race harder the more I thought. What if the change in the serum was the reason Jects randomly turned violent and soon after, disappeared? That couldn't happen to my friends.

Breakfast passed, and we parted ways to our treatments without another word about our injections. The clock outside Dr. Susan Cole's office read 9:05 a.m., and the green light on the fob reader indicated her door was unlocked. I knocked and opened the door, scanning my arm once inside. Dr. Cole sat at her mahogany desk, her red glasses pushing up her narrow nose and bringing out her freckles. Her grey-streaked auburn hair was tied back in a smooth ponytail, and her pale skin showed a hint of sun exposure—something I lacked.

"How are you feeling this morning, Miss Harper?" she asked without looking up from her notes.

"Fine." I walked over and sat in the exam chair, like I did every day.

She pushed back her chair and stood, making her way over to me. "How has training been?"

"It'd be better if I weren't the guinea pig." My hard glance was interrupted by the penlight she shined into my eyes.

"Adam is there to progress your skills and help all of you. Your training is going to be vital." She removed her stethoscope from around her neck. The faint dark circles underneath her eyes extended to her nose.

"Vital for what? You never—"

Her hand flew up to quiet me as she listened to my heart and lungs.

She pulled her stethoscope away when she was finished, and I leaned back into the chair. I held out my arm and turned it over out of habit as she walked over to a stainless-steel table in the corner holding diverse blood-collection tubes and other medical supplies. Adjacent to it was another table with two different-sized centrifuges and other alienated-looking machines.

After five years of being their test subject, I still had no clue why they were taking my blood or working me like I was enlisted in the army. I had arrived when I was fourteen, which was the youngest of any Ject that I'd known, and it was rare to be there that long. Liam had arrived nine months prior at age fifteen, and he was also an exception. Our bodies were mature enough to be experimented on, and we were old enough to be trained in combat. For all I knew, there could've been a war raging above us.

Dr. Cole walked back over with supplies to obtain a blood sample. She inserted the needle, causing my blood to flow into the tube like water filling a glass. I had grown accustomed to the pinch and was no longer squeamish of needles. I held a piece of gauze where she had poked when she was finished. She walked over to the refrigerator, her flats barely audible on the floor.

I glanced down at my already-bruised arm. Bruises constantly littered my body from both treatment and training, but the longer I'd been there, the quicker they'd healed. They still took a week to disappear, but they didn't linger for two to three weeks, as they once had.

Dr. Cole walked back over, carrying a syringe filled with clear blue liquid. I wanted to ask why mine was different, but it would get my friends in trouble. I held out my other arm and she began to inject, turning my veins to a sapphire blue as it trailed up my arm and branched out. The injections hadn't changed the color of my veins until after a year, and I had deduced that it was my body taking to their so-called treatment.

Dr. Cole held out a cup of water along with three pills. One was vitamin D for the lack of sun exposure, and the other two were supposedly essential vitamins. I threw my head back, tossing the pills into my mouth and washing them down with the water.

"How come you never talk about what you plan to do with me—with us?" I asked, breaking the silence. She paused to face me, and I noticed her green eyes were duller.

"As I've told you before, my dear, patience. You will soon learn your purpose and the reason behind all of this. One day you will understand." She walked over to the door and opened it. "It's time for you to go."

I bit my lower lip, standing to obey. Like the five years of being held against my will were supposed to make me patient.

As I left, I looked up at the clock outside her office: 9:40 a.m. Treatments sometimes took a couple of hours; she would occasionally take me to the exercise room to monitor my vitals while moving. Sometimes, they would be cut short, like today.

CHAPTER TWO

With their exposed metal beams and ducts, the open ceilings made me feel small as I headed to the commons. A half-wall splitting two large areas greeted me. One side had a ping-pong table and other miscellaneous games, with deep blue chairs and a sofa lining the light grey walls atop the espresso-colored wood floors. The opposite side had black leather chairs and sofas sporadically placed, with burgundy walls and soft beige carpeting. Mahogany bookcases encased most of the area and lined the half wall, creating more of a separation. The commons was one of the few places that wasn't all white and grey, and I welcomed the warmth of the carpet on my bare feet before grabbing a book to read.

A few other Jects were sitting around, keeping to themselves as they waited to see their doctors. An older man sitting in the corner stuck out with crimped dark brown hair washed out with greys. He was the only one allowed to wear what he wanted and normally wore argyle sweater vests and dress pants. His name was Frank, and I usually saw him in the commons and occasionally in the cafeteria. He never had training or conditioning, and I assumed that most of the time he was in his room. No one knew his story, and he wouldn't talk about it.

Who knew what this place had done to him? *And if I never leave, I may end up just like him.*

Unfortunately, an opportunity to escape hadn't presented itself in the last five years. The place was a sealed vault. But someone had to have been working on the outside to keep it running, and the food and supplies had to have come from somewhere.

I had been reading for about an hour when someone sat in the chair next to me. I glanced over and saw Frank eyeing the book in my hands. It was usually pleasant whenever we engaged in conversation. I had attempted to talk with him a few times before, but I caught him in his off moments. His rashness masked his inner kindness, causing other Jects to avoid him.

"Again?" He looked from the book to me.

"There's so much to this book." I closed *To Kill A Mockingbird* and laid it across my lap. "Have you read it?"

"Ah, yes. But I prefer something else. More of a-ah . . . non-fiction and science . . . if you must." He didn't have a stutter, but more of a hesitancy, like he often briefly forgot the word he needed. Frank's grey-blue eyes dropped and then rose back up to meet mine, glistening. "It is a beautiful day outside, isn't it?"

"Lovely." I smiled gently, not knowing if he was being sarcastic.

A little over a month ago, I had overheard two workers talking about the relentless rain and the blooming pink peonies in their bushes. I knew what spring was, but I barely remembered the smell of fresh rain, cut grass, and flowers. My senses of the outside world had dampened over time without my memories. The workers, doctors, and the singular trainer all appeared to have theirs intact.

"It's a daunting world sometimes. We are, uh, fortunate to have beautiful days."

"Yeah, I guess so." I didn't know how to respond.

The sentinel stirred in the corner—a movement that was barely noticeable. If I'd stood as long and still as they did, I would've been antsy. The sentinels left Frank alone, besides the occasional escort from room to room. They actually left all Jects alone if we were behaving, but they watched over our every move like hawks, anticipating our faults so they could dive in and intervene as they deemed necessary.

"Have they been treating you well?" I joked.

"Them?" He glanced at the sentinel. "Ah, yes. They leave me be. Merely statues watching an old man in his park." Frank's lips curled into a smile as he stood. "Chess?"

"Certainly. I need to learn how to beat you—it's only been three years." I chuckled.

Frank and I hadn't started to connect until two years after my arrival, and it had started with him teaching me how to play chess. I guess chess hadn't been a game I played before the Vault; I had no clue how to play at first. Frank had laid out the rules of the game once, and after that, I had been on my own and learned each time I lost a piece.

"Beating me will be an exceptional triumph." He smiled.

* * *

Lunch passed, and so did the allotted time when we were required to read. Adam went straight into sparring after picking our partners, and thankfully, he put me with Liam.

No one knew who taught Adam how to fight, and Liam had told me he had been the trainer since he had arrived. He was skilled, tall, and brawny. Maya had once asked how old he was and had been shocked when he replied that he was twenty-three; he wasn't typically one to answer questions. Maya also cracked jokes about how hot he was—despite him being a total jerk—and found his minor Scottish accent attractive.

Our sparring entailed pacing in circles with calculated attacks and counters. We wore gloves, shin guards, and head-gear. Even though headshots were against the rules and the gloves were so thin we could feel most of the blow, it ensured that you learned how to block faster.

I moved into the circle with Liam and began. Training alongside him had improved my fighting skills immensely. He was the oldest Ject at age twenty and the best fighter. It wouldn't be long before he surpassed Adam. He never hit hard enough to hurt, just enough to know I should be moving more quickly to block his attacks.

"Remember, if your target has longer arms and legs, you have the advantage if you get in their pocket." Liam stepped closer, his natural smell of sage and vanilla overpowering the sweaty gym stench. He demonstrated how he wasn't able to extend his right arm appropriately to perform a full-impact punch. Up close, I was able to pack more power behind my punches and receive only partial blows if the opponent was bigger. "Adam has length and attacking his left side will force him to use his right."

"Easy for you to say." I laughed in my head at the advice he'd given me multiple times. Adam regularly paired himself with me when we had an odd number, and it was always brutal. His weak side—his right—still overpowered my strong side. My quickness was my strength, and I tried to use that to my advantage.

"You're getting there, sunshine. You're one of the best at fighting." The corner of Liam's mouth twitched right as he attempted a roundhouse kick. I sidestepped it and went for a low left uppercut, which he deflected.

"Not a match for the best yet." I smirked.

After sparring for a while, Adam had us go through takedowns, pairing me with a newer Ject to help catch him up. Once we were finished, he had us actually fight. There were three ways to end the match: pinning, passing out, or tapping—which was only allowed in painful situations. The last one seemed like the best way out, but it was the least favorable option. Adam wasn't a fan of tapping out, but he had to honor it. The next day, though, he would make sure the person who had tapped would be paired with him during training, and that was brutal.

Not everyone fought every day. You could go days without fighting or fight multiple days in a row. There were days Adam would even make you fight one against three.

Today, Liam and I were able to catch a break. Maya went last and was paired with the same guy she had done takedowns with. Though he wasn't a novice, he still lacked experience in applying his technique during a fight, and she was able to pin him after an intense minute. She would be reveling in her glory for the rest of the evening.

Maya walked over, grinning from ear to ear as her long, silky, black hair swayed in its ponytail.

"Good job," I praised.

"It does feels good." Her alluring laugh turned most heads, even in the Vault.

"I feel like you had older brothers." I started toward the showers.

"Yeah," Maya grunted as she followed. "I bet I was the rebellious little sister."

"I'm sure you were the one putting them in chokeholds." I imagined Maya roughhousing with an older brother or two.

I quickly showered and headed to dinner, wearing a fresh pair of grey shorts along with a white tank-top and grey pull-over, our nightly outfit. I grabbed a tray with medium-sized portions of brown rice, green beans, and pork from the kitchen window before heading across the white and black tiled floor to our table, where Travis sat alone.

"Where's Liam?" I sat across from him as Maya sat next to me.

"Being high maintenance today," Travis mocked. "He was still showering when I left."

The guys usually beat us to dinner—they didn't have to deal with the maintenance of long hair. It was unusual for Liam to take long showers unless he just finished fighting, but I also understood needing to take a moment to decompress.

Maya began gloating to Travis about the fight, and the two started bickering. Travis had been in a match against the same Ject a couple of weeks ago and lost. It hurt his ego when he lost to anyone that wasn't Liam or me, and even Maya—they just squabbled like siblings.

"Am I interrupting something?" The corner of Liam's lip half-heartedly tugged upward as he sat next to Travis with his tray. Something in his expression was off, but I couldn't place it.

"It's about time! Did you do your makeup also?" Travis teased.

I raised an eyebrow at Liam when he met my gaze. He quickly averted his eyes and laughed.

"No, just making sure my hair looked good." He ran his fingers through his wet, disheveled brown hair, smoothing his expression.

Maya ended up talking about her fight for the rest of dinner and exulted in the techniques she used. Around six twenty we started toward the commons, since we had to be back in our corridors by eight fifteen and in our rooms at eight thirty. The evenings in the commons were recreational, and we were able to talk and stay as we pleased. We were also allowed to head to our rooms early if we wanted, as long as we scanned in.

I sat down on the firm blue sofa, watching Maya and Travis pick up a game of ping-pong. Around me, the usual automated routine continued. The newer Jects stuck to themselves on the library side, afraid to move or ask questions with the hovering sentinels. A few other Jects that had been there for a couple of weeks would make acquaintances, but it was usually severed when one of them vanished.

"My bet's on Travis." The couch sank next to me as Liam sat. It took me a second to realize he was talking about the ping-pong match I was vacantly watching.

"Really? Why do you say that?" I looked over at Liam, who wore grey sweats and a white T-shirt.

"He's been on fire lately." His brown eyes shifted from the game to mine.

I paused. "Are you okay?"

"Well, besides the lack of sun, peachy." He lounged back. "But who needs sun with you here, sunshine?"

"All right, *Travis*," I mocked; that was something he would have said. "That's not what I meant." I looked back at the game, knowing Liam would keep avoiding the question.

Liam was the sanest, despite being trapped the longest. He was my anchor, and I couldn't fathom the thought of him disappearing. Same with Maya or Travis. The three of them were my best friends, but I was the closest to Liam. Our relationship had been genuine from the start.

"I'm okay, I promise." His words were soft, as if he could hear my thoughts. Out of the corner of my eye, I saw his hand move and felt its warmth on my back. He quickly lowered his hand before the sentinel noticed, and I looked up to meet his gaze. Other than fighting, training, or the shared high fives, we were not allowed to have physical contact with anyone.

"Yes!" Travis cheered, causing Liam and I to look up in unison to see the ping-pong ball bouncing on the floor behind Maya. "Game point!"

"We'll see about that." Maya never gave up easily. They were both so competitive that they butted heads but also got along great at the same time.

I looked back at Liam. His face hid any ill emotions. I had just opened my mouth to tell him I knew something was going on when Travis let out a shout of victory.

"Hah! I win." Travis raised his paddle.

"No, that was my point. It hit the side, not the top." She pointed to a spot on the edge of the table. "Right here."

"No, it didn't," Travis said. They both turned their heads and looked at us.

"Sorry, missed it." I shrugged, happy I didn't see the play.

"Didn't get a good look. Re-play?" Liam looked back to me. "Want to go play Scrabble while they sort this out?"

"Yes, please," I groaned as Travis and Maya went back to bickering.

When it was eight fifteen, I walked with Maya back to our corridor. Despite there being a sentinel on the inside and outside of the heavy door with its small window, I still had to scan my arm for it to open.

I let Maya take the lead as she walked through the last steel door in the corridor and plopped on top of the white comforter on my bed. Each night we sat on my bed and talked until the very last minute. She was different from most of the other Jects, which was why we became close. While everyone had stayed clear of me, she came over and sat outside of my room. I would beckon her to leave, but she had been stubborn and never listened. She'd wanted answers, but I'd never had any.

CHAPTER THREE

"Hi there. Are, uh, you ready for a rematch?" Frank's voice had its normal rasp.

I looked up from my chair, glancing over at the sentinel. We played chess often, but not during our scheduled reading time.

"Oh, don't worry about them. They don't care to, uh, deal with a fickle man like me." The wrinkles on his cheeks creased as he smiled. "You seem to be the only one."

My friends gave me incredulous looks from their spots next to me. I shrugged, feeling like I couldn't refuse his offer, regardless that this time was scheduled for reading only. I stood, following him as he limped his way to the chessboard.

"See, I told you." The sentinel didn't intervene as he started laying out the pieces.

"We won't get in trouble for this?" I whispered, glancing at the sentinel.

"Pshh. I think I scare them." He winked.

"I think they're afraid of your wits." I let out a quiet laugh. If anything, they would be afraid of him going insane.

"Honors?" He waved toward the chessboard and I moved a pawn.

"How are you?" he asked as we continued to play.

"I'm doing well," I replied in a cheerful tone.

"And your friends?" He glanced over to where they were sitting. I laughed to myself as I saw Travis's long body sprawled out on the couch where Liam and I normally sat, while Liam had moved to the chair next to Maya.

"Good, for now." I looked in their direction, my body slowly sinking under the invisible water that threatened to drown me. There was one thing I wanted more than getting out and remembering who I was: I wanted them to be safe and free. I had hope, which was both powerful and dangerous.

"You care a lot for them." Frank moved his king, taking out one of my knights. "They are, uh, lucky to have you."

"I do care, but I can't give them what they want. What they deserve." That was not lucky.

A hint of sorrow flashed across his face but dissipated as he looked back down at the board. He remained quiet for the remainder of the game, and of course, he won.

The other Jects had already left, and I glanced at the clock, which read 2:03 p.m. Normally, one of my friends would have grabbed me, but I guess they didn't want to interrupt. I said a quick goodbye and rushed through the arch. As I scooted around the corner, I collided with something solid. A hand reached out, grabbing my arm. I looked up to see Liam grinning as I silently cursed.

"Do you have to be hiding right around the corner?" Annoyance rose in my cheeks at how amusing my clumsiness was to him, but luckily, no one was around to witness it.

"You know the phrase 'watch where you're walking'? Well, you're not supposed to be actually watching your feet." He laughed.

I stared at him, suddenly becoming aware of the heat radiating from his hand on my arm, and swallowed.

"We're going to be late." I tugged out of his grasp and started down the wide hallway toward the gym with him in tow. "Why didn't you go with the others? I'm sure you don't want to do ladders again."

"And leave you to do them all alone?" He pushed open the gym doors. "Plus, we aren't late."

He waved me in front of him and I scanned in, seeing we

had a minute to spare. We had swiftly walked over to Maya and Travis when Adam whistled.

Something was off. There were two additional sentinels behind Adam that I didn't recognize. We normally had three: one near the entrance and two outside or inside each of the showers, not five. I glanced at Maya, who shrugged as we started jogging.

"What's going on?" Travis whispered to Liam behind us.

"I'm not sure," Liam replied, keeping his voice low.

An abnormal eeriness laced with apprehension filled the room as we finished our last lap.

"You have five minutes to stretch." Adam glanced down the line before talking with the sentinels again. I took a deep breath and began stretching; he rarely let us stretch.

"There will be no pins or tap-outs today, and the main rule is no longer in play. Fight to unconsciousness or fight to death." Adam's stern voice rippled through the gym after our five minutes were up. A shiver ran through me, causing the hair on the back of my neck to rise. The tension in the air built even more.

Adam walked over to the other sentinel by the entrance and gave an order we couldn't hear. The sentinel pulled out his radio and mumbled something into it. No one moved as an unsettling minute passed. Three more sentinels showed up, one steering Frank to a chair in the corner. Anger rose in my chest at the sight of him. He looked confused and misplaced. They could've ordered him to his room or left him with a worker; he didn't need to see this.

"Liam, you're up." Adam beckoned Liam forward. My heart stopped and my entire body went numb.

"Liam . . ." I managed to get out, though it felt like my airway was collapsing. He paused to look at me.

"It'll be okay, sunshine," he reassured.

I glanced at Travis and Maya, both equally pale. My hands turned into fists at my sides; I couldn't let Adam hurt him. I went to take a step forward, but Maya put her hand out in front of me, her eyes filled with warning. The sentinel near the men's showers noticed and strode across the gym to stand behind me.

"Sorry, brother, you're not fightin' me today." Adam's Scottish accent was barely audible as he took a step to the side, revealing the two sentinels looming in his shadow. "But you will be fighting them, and they get to keep their arms."

My entire body began to burn as the two sentinels stepped into the circle. Liam faltered as agitation flashed across his face. He was a skilled fighter, but the odds were not good against two sentinels with guns.

"They'll only use their arms when they see fit. Of course"—he glanced at me—"if anyone intervenes, the sentinels have orders to fire. The square is your boundary." He pointed to the large square outside of the circle. "Fight," Adam ordered, his word hanging in the air.

"This is going to be fun," the blond sentinel commented in a husky voice, moving to the left of Liam, herding him between the edge of the square and the second sentinel.

The second sentinel darted forward. Liam managed to dodge him, but took a blow in his side from the blond sentinel's fist. Liam evaded the next few attacks until one of the sentinels was able to grab his shirt and throw him down.

Adam watched on the other side with vigilant eyes as his chest puffed tightly, like he was holding his breath. His dark green eyes flicked over to me, meeting my cold expression. The sound of a body hitting the ground returned our attention back to the fight.

The second sentinel took Liam's place on the ground. They continued fighting as Liam held his own. The way Liam fought was beautiful and dangerous, each move fluidly precise and practiced.

The fight started to turn against him, and he was blocking fewer hits. A ghostly hand wrapped around my intestines, twisting with each blow Liam received. I took a step forward and felt a hand on my arm. I looked over to see Travis shake his head and glance at the sentinel behind me. The sentinel had mimicked my step, preparing to stop me if I took another.

I retreated and looked back at Liam as his eyes met mine. I don't know what he read on my face—worry, anger, fear, or all of it. His eyes narrowed and he sprang from the ground, pouncing on the blond sentinel. Liam wrapped his arm around his neck and grabbed the sentinel's chin. He invertedly pulled as the sentinel's body fell limp to the ground.

The second sentinel stilled, fully grasping what had happened. He went for his gun, but Liam quickly disarmed him and turned it back on him, firing. The sentinel's body hit the ground with a thud and shook violently as blue sparks emitted from the tiny slug sticking out of his chest, barely visible.

CHAPTER FOUR

My gaze shifted to Liam, who gripped the gun with shaking hands and grimaced as he stared at the body, an overwhelming amount of guilt displaying on his face. The imaginary hand clenched around my intestines loosened. He might feel guilty, but he was alive, and this wasn't his fault. Just because it wasn't a real gun didn't mean they weren't going to kill him, despite my feeling that this might have been a scare tactic.

They put a lot of work into our treatments and controlling us, so I suppose it made sense not to carry lethal weapons. Maybe we weren't so expendable after all, and death was never their intention. But if that was the case, why was Adam doing this?

Liam's hands stopped shaking as he pivoted, aiming the gun—taser—at Adam. The other sentinels drew theirs. I now understood why Liam's face faltered when he learned who he was fighting—he wanted to fight Adam.

"I would think twice about that." Adam was still frowning as his eyes moved in my direction.

I became fully aware of the ruffle of air at the base of my neck as the sentinel behind me raised his taser.

Liam scowled, slowly lowering the taser and setting it on the floor. Adam walked over and picked it up. He gazed down our line before looking back at Liam, nodding for him to get in place.

Liam gave Adam a fevered glare and slowly trudged toward me with a limp. He gave the sentinel behind me a low growl as he backed off and took his place in line next to me. Two sentinels walked over to the bodies with solemn expressions before carefully carrying them out of the gym. *Huh.* They did care about each other, but it took one of them dying to show any expression.

"No." The harshness in Liam's voice drew my attention to him. His lips pressed together and his bloodied hands curled into fists as his eyes locked onto something to my right. I had failed to realize Adam now stood a few feet away, staring at me.

"Let's see what you have today." Adam turned and started toward the middle of the ring. "You'll be fightin' me."

The sentinel who was behind me moved to position himself behind Liam as another stood near my friends for additional security. Travis was furious, and Maya's face was beet-red as her eyes remained fixed on Adam.

"Promise me you won't do anything stupid," I said, not as a question to Liam. "They need you too."

Liam took a deep breath, understanding what I meant. A few moments passed before he spoke. "Fine. But you have to promise to keep this ticking." He gently poked me in the chest over my heart.

I nodded and took my stance in the middle of the mat. I guess I would find out whether I could become a killer to save my own skin if it came down to it.

My hands clenched and unclenched as my mind began to run over scenarios. My only tenable options were to get knocked out or to knock him out.

"Ready?" Adam asked as I entered the circle. I unwillingly nodded. "The gym is our boundary."

I glanced over his shoulder at the weapons wall holding bo staffs, tonfas, and daggers that we occasionally practiced with.

"Yes, those are in the boundary," Adam said, knowing what I glanced at without having to look. I just had to get past him and to the weapons to end the fight. He never carried a taser or a belt with armaments over his athletic shorts. "Begin."

As I waited for his attack, I noticed sweat already laced his brow and dampened the collar of his long-sleeve shirt. Normally sweat drenched him after a fight, not before.

He must have decided he'd waited long enough and attacked. His knee jerked, catching my attention, but I realized his fake quick enough to block his punch and deliver a kick to his knee. He twisted his leg so most of the force went to the back, barely buckling his knee. He found an opening under my block and punched me in the gut, causing me to stagger backward.

Adam was fast, but so was I. He attacked again, and I avoided him completely. I attempted to counter, but he hoisted me over his shoulder and slammed me into the ground. I lost my breath as spots formed in my vision, blurring Adam as he stood over me.

He reached for my shirt, but I swung my leg straight up, kicking him in the face. I managed to catch my breath before turning onto my hands and swinging my leg underneath his, taking him out. I got to my feet and went to bolt toward the weapons when a hand grabbed my ankle and tripped me. My hands went out just in time to prevent my face from smacking the ground. I felt my body being dragged backward and rolled onto my back, knowing that I was defenseless on my stomach.

He grunted as I kicked at his arm holding my ankle, but he did not budge. He climbed on top of me, frowning as his legs pinned my arms at my sides. Was he actually sad about hurting me? His face quickly hardened. No, it was pity and revulsion.

Adam raised his fist and it quickly came down, colliding with the side of my cheek. My vision started to blur, and I strained my head backward in pain as blood pooled in my mouth. I was trapped, no matter how much I squirmed. All the experiments and strict schedules to see how I compared in a death match against Adam? Maybe this was a test, and if I didn't pass, I was never meant to leave. My friends . . . I would let them down.

My knee slammed into his back, causing him to lighten his hold just enough that I could pull an arm free. I punched him in the jaw, giving me the advantage to get out from underneath him. I backed away from him and we simultaneously stood.

"I thought that was too easy," Adam quipped.

We attacked and counter-attacked back and forth, each delivering successful blows. I managed to keep his left side occupied, forcing him to attack with his right. I tried to stay in his pocket as much as possible and was losing stamina fast. He realized that too and picked up his pace.

I tried to take out his legs as I had earlier, but failed. It ended with a hard kick to my shoulder. I hooked my leg behind his and kicked his foot out while putting my palm to his chest, shoving him to the mat. He lay there stunned and out of breath.

I had no time to gawk at my takedown and ran as fast as I could to the weapons wall. My bare feet hit the ground in slow motion. Just as I reached the wall, Adam's body slammed into me, causing me to fall along with a few tonfas. *Crap.* Hands wrapped around my neck and pushed me against the matted wall.

The gym around me started to fade to black as Adam's hands gripped tighter. If I passed out, I was sure he would keep choking me until my heart stopped. Part of me wanted to let the darkness take over, but adrenaline and anger rushed through me, tugging at the back of my mind as ringing sounded in my ears. I stomped on his foot with my heel, and he keeled over, leaving a small gap between our bodies. My knee rammed into his chest, jerking me free.

I grabbed a dagger and turned it on Adam. He dodged it, leaving a minor gash in his arm, the dull edge not sharp enough to do real damage. He swung around me and was able to knock the dagger out of my hand, now standing between the wall and me.

I went for the dagger at his feet. Instead of picking it up, he slid it across the floor. I kept my momentum going and collided with him, knocking him into the wall. I staggered back from the blow before attacking again. In return, he side-stepped me, spinning me around and pushing me against the wall.

"Just please give up," Adam murmured. "It's the only way to get through this." Why did he want me to give up? I thought he liked the challenge. Red danced along the rim of my vision. If he thought I was just going to roll over for him, he should guess again.

"Never." My rogue voice shocked me.

I attacked, sending him to the ground with me on top. Screams sounded as I landed punch after punch, but I drowned them out. Blood spattered from his face as he resisted less and less.

Two sentinels clamped onto each of my arms, pulling me off as I yelled at them to let me go. A moment passed before I noticed the limp, battered body in front of me. I stopped resisting as the ringing dimmed in my ears.

Adam had been unconscious for who knows how long. The gym was bleakly quiet and the screaming had stopped.

It was then that I realized they had been coming from me.

CHAPTER FIVE

No one had won a match against Adam. Liam was the only one who had ever come close. I wasn't given any consequences for beating Adam to a pulp besides being monitored more closely by Dr. Cole and the sentinels. She had prescribed three days of complete rest, and I would return to everything tomorrow. Maya had avoided coming to my room the last two nights, and I should have visited her, but I couldn't bring myself to leave my room willingly. My emotions raged as my body ached, which made me want to stay trapped in the room I loathed.

Keeping my head down, I walked into the cafeteria as all eyes were on me, probably shocked I was still around. My blond hair was thrown into a messy bun, and I sported a look that said I had just gotten done with a brawl, my bruised face already turning green. I gnawed on my cheek as I walked straight to the food window and picked up a tray.

"And the champion emerges." Travis came out of nowhere, putting an arm around me before quickly dropping it, his comical side more compassionate. "I knew you had it in you."

"Thanks." I slid my tray down the line and grabbed a turkey sandwich, apple, celery, and a small container with peanut butter. My stomach grumbled. I wanted to scarf it all down after barely eating the food Dr. Cole had sent to my room the last two days.

"Glad to see you're walking, sunshine."

I spun around to see Liam, my heart racing. I missed him

like it had been two months instead of two days. We had both fought to our potential deaths, which, after much thought, I theorized to have been a show. If they wanted me dead, they wouldn't be helping me heal.

"I could say the same to you." I examined his bruised cheeks and cracked lower lip. As his eyes searched mine to see if I was truly okay, I noticed a dimness to his.

"Where have you been? Did they keep you in Dr. Cole's office?" Travis interrupted our silent query.

"She's been in her room." Liam kept his eyes on mine.

"No, she never . . . wait . . . how did you know that, and why didn't you tell me?" Travis looked from me to Liam.

"Maya told me." Liam glanced at Travis, then back to me. "Did she talk to you at all?"

"Umm . . . no. Is she upset with me?" I glanced at our table and saw Maya using her palm to roll an apple in circles on the table.

"Why do you say that?" Liam asked.

I hesitated, knowing I sounded weak. "Because I lost control." Disappointment pounded at my chest. I wasn't going to let this place make me lose myself and stoop to a low level. My humanity and friends were the two vital things that I needed. "She didn't visit either."

"She'd be patting you on your back for that fight!" Travis paused and turned to Liam. "But if she knows that Harper's fine, why are her panties in a wad?"

"What do you mean?" My head shot up.

"She hasn't been herself since the fight. She's been distant," Liam calmly said.

My throat tightened as worry washed over me. I wondered if somehow she was upset with me, but to be distant with them didn't make any sense. I started toward our table.

"Harper, wait!" Liam called, but I kept going.

"Hey." Maya didn't look up as I sat across from her so I could see her better. I waited for a response, but she said nothing. Liam sat next to me while Travis sat next to Maya, and I started ripping apart my sandwich but didn't eat.

"Maya, are you okay?" I watched her for a reaction.

"I'm fine!" she snapped as she stopped rolling her apple and set it on her tray, her face slowly softening. "I'm just happy you're alive. Now, Travis, are you going to pick on her for tearing at that like a mongrel, or do I have to?" I didn't eat my sandwich like a normal person and always ripped off pieces as I ate. Travis always picked on me for it.

Travis's shrug told me that he was just as confused. Maya's attitude had flipped like a switch.

"Look at that lip! How do you even plan on eating?" Maya exclaimed in her normal mocking voice. Was I reading into it too much?

"It won't be easy," I cautiously said. My right eye was swollen, I had a fat lip, and bruises painted my face.

From there, we had our normal lunch banter—with Liam chiming in once in a while—until the fight was brought up.

"No one's ever beaten Adam! Liam's been close, but I don't think he ever had Adam that scared, right, Maya?" Travis grinned, not noticing Maya stilling at his words. "And when you—"

"Travis," I shushed. Maya's hands gripped the edges of her tray while she blankly stared at her uneaten food. Travis noticed and immediately closed his mouth. "Maya, what's wrong?" I shot a worried glance at Liam, who was quietly watching her.

"I said I was fine!" Maya stood, flipping her tray and sending her food flying. She stormed out of the cafeteria as everyone watched. A sentinel reached for his radio as another ordered everyone to go back to eating their lunch.

I nervously looked at Liam and Travis as I pulled a tomato out of my hair. She had her tantrums, but not like this. I stood, running out the cafeteria doors. I didn't see her in the hallway, so I ran to the commons, but she wasn't there either. If this was the rage right before vanishing, I needed to find her and not let her out of my sight. I wasn't going to let them take her.

"Harper!" Liam shouted down the hall, attempting to hide a limp as he and Travis jogged my way.

"I can't let them take her." I held back the anguish threatening to burst in my chest.

"We have to be careful with what we do." Liam glanced at the sentinel in front of the women's corridor, who was eyeing us. "We can't draw more attention to her than there already is, but we still need to keep eyes on her."

"She's not in the commons." I tried to slow my heart rate, knowing that panicking wouldn't help.

"Well, we're in a box—she can't go far," Travis joked without luster.

"Check her room, but make sure to get to the commons on time. We'll meet you there."

"I'll meet you at the commons, but I don't have to stick to the schedule today—I'm supposed to be resting until tomorrow. I'll find her." I turned and went to the girls' corridor.

The ivory privacy curtain around the steel toilet was drawn, and her white comforter was neatly made on her bed. Empty. When I got back to the commons, I spotted Travis on the couch. I still scanned my arm, even though I didn't plan on staying.

"Any sign of her?" Travis asked.

"No, nothing." I sighed.

"Where's Liam?"

Travis shrugged. "I'm not his mother. He doesn't tell me everything he does, although he probably wouldn't tell his mother everything either."

I rolled my eyes at him, not wanting his wittiness right now. Liam strolled in and grabbed a book.

"Anything?" I asked as he sat down.

"She's in the gym with Avery," Liam whispered.

"Avery?"

Travis softly whistled. "The smokin' hot relief trainer, but if you thought Adam was bad, give her one day. If it weren't for her looks, I'd rather have Adam back."

"Adam's not training?" I didn't think Adam was the type to hide out after a beating, even a bad one. His injuries must've been severe. He was our trainer, and not a Ject; the bruises I'd seen on him didn't heal as quickly.

"Nope, you got him good." Travis thought my fight had been a victory. I thought otherwise. He must have read my face or seen the look Liam shot him, because his brief joviality vanished.

"Why would she go see Avery?" I asked.

"Beats me," Travis said.

"Maybe she needs to blow off steam?" I was surprised the sentinels hadn't made her come to the commons, though.

"Maybe." Liam started to say something else, but a sentinel walked over to us. He didn't need to tell us to be quiet; his glare conveyed the message. I went to get up, but, when the sentinel walked away, Liam warned me it was a bad idea. "Less attention," he muttered. I grabbed a book and began absently reading the pages; I would let Maya cool down before we talked.

When the clock read one forty-five, I decided it'd been long enough. I laid my book on the table next to me and stood. Liam and Travis warily glanced at the clock and followed me out the door, ignoring the sentinel's glare.

Maya wasn't in the gym when I entered. A tall woman with deep-red hair was throwing punches at a bag. Her last punch toppled over the bag, along with its stand. Her blue eyes landed on us. She picked up the bag and walked our way.

"Where else would she be?" I turned to Liam.

"I don't know," he replied flatly. The tall, blue-eyed woman had already cleared the distance between us. I needed to find Maya, and had no time to talk to her.

"Hello, boys." Disgust and anger filled me at the way she eyed my friends like candy. Her eyes landed on me, her smirk fading. "Ah. You must be Harper. For winning, it sure looks like you lost." She let out a rugged chuckle.

"And you must be the temp." I was blunt, eyeing her back. She couldn't have picked a tighter workout pullover and leggings.

My comment stopped her laughing as she stared me down. She tried using her height as intimidation, but failed. If she were a better fighter than Adam, then she would have been training us instead. Although, she did remind me of a girl version of him—minus the slight Scottish accent.

I heard a door open as Maya walked out of the women's showers, hesitating when she saw us. I stepped around Avery as Maya started toward us with her head down. She stopped walking when she was about five feet away and looked up.

"Maya, is everything okay?" Liam's voice traveled from behind me as she kept her eyes on me, her face reddening.

I stared back at her. "Maya?"

"Yes."

"Can we talk?" I took a step closer.

"Why can't we?"

I lowered my voice. "You're not acting like yourself."

"Like I said, I'm perfectly fine." She attempted a smile.

"We're worried about you, and—"

"We?" She snorted. "You guys don't need to worry about me. I see things clearly, and I can take care of myself."

I frowned. "What do you mean by that?"

"Just that it's going to be okay." She put a hand on my shoulder. Her lips hardened in a straight line as she focused on her hand touching me.

"Maya?" I held my breath for her response as her hand started shaking.

"Things haven't been fair, and I'm sick of it." Her eyes shot to me as she dropped her hand. "There are favorites."

"Yes, very annoying favorites," Avery chided next to Maya.

"You've always been the favorite. Adam always chooses you," Maya cackled.

"Really, that's why you think he fought me?" Yes, Adam chose to fight me, but it wasn't because I was the favorite. "He tried to kill me! Maya, this is nonsense."

"Nonsense was being your friend!" Her hands balled at her side. "You even have your own doctor, while the rest of us share."

Liam stepped forward but halted when Avery whipped out her taser. Liam swallowed, and I realized that this taser was different. It was a gun.

She had to have snuck it in. After finding out they used tasers, I had checked with Dr. Cole, and for once, she gave me information, confirming the sentinels didn't carry real guns while watching us. I assumed this meant they had guns, but weren't allowed to carry them.

"I'm sorry you feel this way, Maya. Can we please talk about it?" I tried to keep my voice calm.

"You don't get it, do you? Next to you, I am nothing. And you're so hung up on yourself that you don't see any of it!" Maya fumed.

"Maya, this isn't you talking."

"I want you dead." She breathed.

I was speechless. My eyes felt hot and my face felt numb, like I had been smacked.

"Ouch." Avery grinned. She had never even met me before today—why does she hate me so much?

"Maya . . ." Liam stopped talking as Avery pointed the gun at me.

"You always come to her aid," Maya scoffed. "I hope it breaks you when I take your precious sunshine away."

"Maya isn't feeling well. I think Harper should leave and let Maya get some rest." Liam held out his hands, palms facing Avery, who turned the gun back on him.

"I want to see how this plays out." Avery flashed her teeth.

Maya darted toward me, but I was too slow, receiving part of her attack to my stomach. I hunched over in pain. She attacked again, but this time I was able to deflect her and counter with a kick. I didn't want to hurt her and was only going to counter her attacks while Avery held Liam and Travis at gunpoint.

"Maya, we don't have to fight," I huffed.

"Yes, we do." She went for my legs and effectively took them out, causing me to fall. Maya went to position herself over me, but I kicked her off, sending her to the ground. I couldn't let her get that position. We both stood just as the gym doors slammed open.

"Stop this right now!" A familiar voice echoed through the gym, and Avery quickly stowed her gun. Dr. Cole walked in with three sentinels at her side, and peeking around her from the hallway was Frank. "Avery, what on earth is going on?"

"Girl drama," Avery said, as if she had done nothing wrong.

Dr. Cole opened her mouth, but she was interrupted when Maya grabbed me and positioned a switchblade at my neck.

"Dr. Cole, nice of you to join us, but I suggest you leave, or your pet suffers." Great. Avery must have supplied her with it. I felt warmth trickle down my neck as she applied more pressure. Out of the corner of my eye, I saw Liam creeping closer.

There was worry in Dr. Cole's voice, but she remained calm and authoritative as she spoke. "Maya, this is not like you—"

"I'm sick of people telling me this isn't me." Maya dragged me with her as she slowly inched away from Dr. Cole.

"We can give you anything you want, tell you anything you want to know. No one has to get hurt." Dr. Cole eyed the blade at my throat.

Maya's hand shook at my neck. "This is what I want. It ends now."

I felt the increased pressure, along with a sharp pain as the gym muted around me. Liam darted forward, his mouth opened as if he were yelling, but I couldn't hear anything. He wouldn't reach me in time. I felt a small jolt of energy go through me, causing Maya to hesitate as her hand and entire body froze. I seized the opportunity to disarm her and switch spots. I dropped the blade and kicked it away. She thrashed violently in the chokehold I had her in as she suddenly became aware of her new situation.

"Maya, stop. Please stop," I pleaded, but she didn't listen. I tightened my grip until she passed out. I slowly dropped to my knees with her in my arms. I was vaguely aware of the trickling warmth on my neck as I gazed at Maya. What had just been an indignant, raging, and unrecognizable woman, was now my peaceful, unconscious friend lying in my arms. "What did they do to you?" I whispered.

I felt a hand on my back as vanilla and sage mixed with the copper scent in the air and knew it was Liam. He removed his hand from my back and gently took Maya from my arms, his face filled with pain. I didn't want to let her go, worried about what was going to happen to her.

"Harper, I've got her." Liam put his free hand on my neck. "Apply pressure to your neck, now." I brought my hand to where his was and replaced it. It wasn't bleeding quickly enough to kill me then and there, but I would lose consciousness and bleed out if it didn't stop.

I heard Dr. Cole's hazy voice as blurred figures approached us. "Take her to detainment until we transfer her and take Harper to my office. Keep pressure on her neck." I felt a hand replace mine. I thought the haziness was due to the flood of emotions surging through me, but now I was certain it was due to the blood loss. My body started to sag and weaken.

"What do you mean by 'transfer her'?" Liam asked sternly.

"Transfer her to where she can't harm anyone else for now. Maya will be well taken care of." Dr. Cole turned to

Avery and then someone else. "Take her gun and make sure she doesn't leave."

"Where exactly is she going?" Liam's strong voice started to fade as the gym closed in around me. His face turned to shock as he faced me. "Harper!"

Everything went black.

CHAPTER SIX

I woke in Dr. Cole's office, unaware of what time it was. I threw my right hand to my neck and felt a bulky bandage. I glanced at her digital clock on the wall; it was 12:02 a.m. I was about to pull out the IV catheter in my arm when a voice stopped me.

"That needs to stay in; you lost quite a bit of blood," Dr. Cole said through the dimly lit room from her chair. "You need to rest and heal."

"No, I need to find Maya." I sat up and brought my legs over the edge of the bed. They felt like Jell-O, but nothing hurt. Must be some decent pain meds. I yanked the IV catheter out, disobeying her as blood spilled on the concrete floor from the IV line.

"Please, lie back down. You have been through enough the past few days." Dr. Cole made her way over, clamping the IV line shut. Just hearing her voice infuriated me.

"I've been through enough the past few days?" I squeaked. "Never once in the last five years have you ever said that. Not through broken bones, being held against my will, or mine and my friends' agony . . . never. Something awful is happening to my friend and you're responsible! You're responsible for all of this! I won't let you hurt her."

"We are not going to hurt her. She will be okay." Dr. Cole wasn't fazed by my outrage.

"By disposing of her like the rest of the Jects that vanished? The *experiments* that failed?" I understood where my anger was coming from, but I couldn't rein it in. My blood started to boil as my hair stood on end.

"In time, you will understand."

"Why don't you enlighten me now?" My voice was harsh as I ignored the minuscule amount of blood trickling from my arm where the catheter had been.

She stared at me with fervent eyes, not saying a word.

"That's what I thought." I stood, my legs almost giving out beneath me. I reached for the bed to steady myself and felt a pinch in my neck. Dr. Cole set a syringe onto a tray and eased me back onto the bed.

Her voice was unusually soft as she whispered her next words. "Your genes aren't the only reason you're a good Ject. You're stubborn, but also resilient and caring, like your father." And just like that, everything was black, again.

* * *

I was in the field I'd dreamt about multiple times. It was normally beautiful, but this time the sky was charcoal grey and the air reeked of iron. My veins were glowing blue, and my hands were sticky, covered in dark crimson. My feet mindlessly moved forward until suddenly freezing to the ground.

A small sunken pit sat a few feet away. Leaning forward, I peered over the edge and gasped. Maya and Travis were covered in the same crimson as their lifeless eyes peered up at me. Next to them lay a lifeless man with short black hair whose skin matched the earth he laid on, a woman with blond hair and fair skin, and another man facing down in the dirt. Something felt familiar about them, but I couldn't place it as my heart throbbed.

Tears swelled in my eyes and ran down my cheeks as I backed away. My foot struck something large and I tripped, falling to the ground. Water seeped through my black dress as the sharp smell of burnt copper flooded my nose. I looked up to see what I tripped over, feeling like a rock had crushed my airway.

Liam's motionless body lay in front of me. I slipped on the wet grass as I crawled to him. He had multiple stab wounds to his chest, and his hands appeared burnt. I felt my hand firmly grasping something and glanced down to see myself gripping a knife. It was not water that soaked my dress, but blood. Not just Liam's, but everyone's in that pit.

I dropped the knife and cradled Liam's head in my lap as a pain I had never felt punched me in the chest. It was not physical pain, but it raged through my entire body nonetheless.

My eyes flew open as I abruptly sat up, grabbing at my soaked shirt. A sigh escaped my lips when I realized it was just sweat. I tried to slow my panting as I looked around my room, more than happy if I were never to dream again.

I pushed back the comforter and climbed out of my bed. I went over to the steel sink to wash up, splashing cold water over my face before looking in the mirror. I toyed at the damp bandage on my neck and suddenly became aware of my aching body and throbbing headache. Everything that had happened yesterday came rushing back.

Maya. I had to get to her. I shut off the water and glanced at the clock: 8:30 a.m. Was it our day off? And who had put me in my pajamas?

I put on black capris and a grey T-shirt and rushed out the door. No one was in their rooms, which was odd for a day off. I paused at Maya's opened door, only to see she wasn't there.

The sentinel standing on the other side of the door eyed me as I rushed past her, heading to the cafeteria. Liam and Travis were sitting in their normal spots, staring at their trays. I jogged over to them, fully aware of everyone's eyes on me, again.

"Where is she?" I asked, but they just looked at me with red-rimmed eyes. I put my hands on the table and looked at Liam, pleading for good news. "You have to know something."

"I'm sorry, Harper. When she didn't show up to conditioning this morning, I searched everywhere before the sentinels ordered me here. I checked detainment." He glanced at Travis. "He found me and went with me. There was no one there, but I saw Dr. Cole."

"What did she say?" My voice trembled.

"Not much. Just that Maya is okay but no longer with us for now," Liam answered.

"What does that mean?"

"That those bastards have her locked up somewhere, that's what it means." Travis slammed his fork into his untouched eggs and pushed his tray away. For years we had dreaded losing one of us, and the day had finally come.

"We will find Maya and find a way out of here," Liam reassured.

I didn't eat anything at breakfast and decided to head straight to Dr. Cole's office. I knocked, fighting the urge to break down her door. I entered as soon as I heard her mumbled words to come in.

"How did you sleep?" Dr. Cole sat behind her desk.

"Straight through. I think I had a little assistance." I walked over to her desk, not bothering with scanning in. "Unlike you."

"You're awake earlier than I thought you'd be." Her green eyes looked up at me from behind her glasses, the bags under her eyes suggesting she hadn't been sleeping.

"No thanks to the alarm. I gather you had something to do with that?" She didn't deny my assumption. "I'm kind of looking for someone."

"As I told your friends, she is safe and unharmed. Just not in this facility anymore." She stood and walked over to the chair. "Now, come sit. I need to check your neck and change the bandage."

I reluctantly walked over to the chair. Maybe if I complied, she wouldn't kick me out right away. "Yeah, and we don't know what that means."

She began examining my neck. "All you need to know is she is safe and well cared for."

"You and I have different meanings of safe and cared for." I was growing impatient. "You control everyone down here and talk directly to the suits. You think that—"

"You don't know what I think," she sternly cut me off, but at least I was getting a reaction. Her face flattened as she cleaned my wound and applied a new bandage. "The suits" were men wearing expensive suits, and they only talked to Dr. Cole. I've only seen two.

We both stayed silent until it was time for my injection.

"What does this do?" I asked, surprisingly calm. When she didn't answer I pressed on. "Are they the reason we become violent, like Maya?"

Nothing. I wasn't getting any information. She reached out to hand me the cup containing my pills, but I smacked it out of her hand and the pills went flying.

"Out! Get out. Now." She gritted through her teeth, not caring if I took my pills. I didn't move. She walked over to her desk and picked up her phone. "I need two sentinels to my office, now." She couldn't force me out, but they sure could.

"You have no idea how wrong and repressive this is." I stood, slowly walking to the door. Her face went from irritated to something more questionable. A hint of hurt and maybe guilt? I put a hand on the door, lowering my head as I remembered something else. "Did you know my father?"

"What do you mean?"

"You said something last night about my father." My eyes moved from the floor to her.

"I'm sorry." She lowered her head. "You must have misheard me." The sentinels showed up, and I decided it wasn't worth fighting them. I left.

"Harper." I stopped walking down the hall and turned to see Dr. Cole approaching me. She put her hand up to the sentinels who followed, ordering them to stay. "I forgot to inform you to stay out of conditioning and training, but you can still return to everything else tomorrow." Her eyebrows creased as her eyes narrowed. "Do you know why Maya hesitated?"

"What?" What kind of question was that? "If you mean hesitating to slice my throat like a baked potato, probably because she's my best friend."

"Did you feel different in that moment?" Her brow raised.

"That I wanted to hurt her in return? No. The only thing that's making me crazy right now is that Maya's gone and you won't give me answers!" My sanity was being questioned, but it was hers that should be.

"Okay. I will see you tomorrow." She didn't wait for me to reply as she headed back to her office.

CHAPTER SEVEN

"Harper! I see you didn't pass on the sausage." Blake grinned as he flipped his sleek black hair out of his green eyes. Travis shot him a warning look from across the table. I doubt Travis had talked to him before Maya's disappearance a month ago.

"I see you didn't either," I gibed back as Travis and Jeremiah laughed. They were serving sautéed Brussels sprouts with turkey sausage for lunch, which was unusual.

"See, I told you she can handle herself." Travis winked at me. His jokes had become less frequent when Maya vanished, and it was hard to see that part of him fade.

"I think we figured that out before we ever talked to her." Jeremiah pitched in as he ran a hand over his shaved head. He had become friends with Blake about two months before Travis started talking to them, and despite his perpetual scowl, he was a genuinely nice guy.

"Oh, now you're just sucking up, Jer," Blake joked.

I tapped Travis's shoulder, directing his attention to Liam as he walked in and headed toward Ellie. Her beautiful long, bright-blond hair looked like it had seen days at the beach and not a basement. She sat alone looking like an innocent schoolgirl with high cheekbones and a button nose. A quick flash of white paper left his hand and transferred to hers. He continued toward the food line and grabbed an apple before slipping out the door. The sentinels disregarded him because it was our day off.

"I should talk to him." I went to stand up when Travis

held out his hand. I was about to protest when I saw what he was looking at. Ellie had stood to take care of her tray and then left. "Okay, I'm finding out what's going on."

"I don't know if that's a good idea," Travis warned.

"Yeah, that man seems sly. He probably snuck a doctor's key so they can have some privacy." Blake chuckled. My anger at his remark must have shown, because he quickly clamped his mouth shut.

"Harper . . ." Travis went to object, but I was already in pursuit. I looked over my shoulder as Travis stood to follow.

"Just give me a minute . . . please?" I asked, holding up a finger.

Last week I had attempted to talk to Liam at dinner. He had been sitting alone at a different table and I'd set my tray down next to him.

"I don't really want to talk, Harper. I'm sorry," Liam had said before he took his untouched tray to the return window and left. Each time I tried to talk to him lately, my heart sank deeper as my anger rose. Liam would throw out the "not now" or "I have to go" card, though it was not like he had anywhere else to go.

I had started losing my temper a couple of days after Maya was gone, and as time passed, it was assumed my stress caused it and not the injections. All this time I had known that losing one of us would emotionally break us, but I had never thought it would break us apart. The only person I saw Liam talk to was Ellie, a new Ject who had arrived a few weeks ago. He had been helping her out during conditioning and training also.

I followed Ellie out of the cafeteria while maintaining distance so she wouldn't notice. She headed down the empty hallway before suddenly turning down another. My brows furrowed. There were only cleaning and maintenance closets down there, or so I thought. I peeked around the corner and saw a flash of blond go through a door on the left. I had explored as much as I was able to and knew that these doors were normally locked.

I quietly jogged over and caught the door before it closed. I bit my lip, hesitating as irritation twined my gut. I didn't want to know if they were hooking up and should probably leave, but another part of me was curious.

A small gasp sounded from behind the door as Ellie realized the door was being held open. I heard murmuring but couldn't make anything out. I took a deep breath and pushed the door all the way open.

"Seriously?" I huffed as I took in what I saw.

Ellie had her back against a rack of cleaning supplies, lips locked with Liam's. They pulled away from each other and turned to look at me, her hand on his chest. Ellie's bright blue eyes and Liam's brown ones were filled with shock. Our eyes briefly met before I looked at the placement of his hands— one on her shoulder and one at the back of her head. He quickly dropped his hands, backing away from her. I could feel my face redden as I curled my fists at my side.

"At least be more careful if you're going to risk hooking up." This was absurd. "And put your stupid hand somewhere less awkward than her shoulder." I waved my hand at Liam and left, storming back down the hall.

My blood was boiling. I shouldn't have been so angry. It was fine if they hooked up—as long as they didn't get caught. I didn't want Liam to go to detainment, although his attitude lately made it tempting. It didn't make sense why he would ignore Travis and me but talk to her. Maybe it was the fact that she had never known Maya like we did, and her modelesque body was an added bonus.

"Harper!" Liam jogged to catch up to me. "Please wait."

"I don't want to hear it." I picked up my pace and headed for my room, where he wouldn't be able to follow me.

"Please, it's not what you think." He caught up and tried to stand in front of me, but I walked around him. "Harper!"

I stopped and faced him.

"So you mean you weren't kissing her? It's fine, Liam." I started walking again. "Who knows what else was about to happen," I murmured.

"No—well, yes, but no. Please just stop so I can explain," Liam said, sounding concerned about what I thought. "Sunshine." His hand softly wrapped around my arm. I stopped, yanking away; he had lost the privilege of calling me that after not talking to me for a month.

"Don't touch me," I hissed.

A slight pang throbbed in my chest as his face filled with hurt, but it quickly disappeared.

"You think you can just ghost us and get cozy with some new Ject without us being upset? You left us when we needed you the most." *When I needed you the most.* "Not to mention how stupid you're being. You don't have to worry about me turning you in. I wouldn't do that," I added bitterly. After the incident with Maya, they were watching Liam, Travis, and me closer than ever.

A sentinel rounded the corner and noticed our interaction. It just looked like an argument, and he'd probably tell us to split it up.

"What's going on here?" The sentinel closed in on us.

"Everything's fine. I got it under control." The new voice gave me goosebumps as I turned to see Adam emerge from the gym and lean against the door. The sentinel nodded and left. "I see there's some tension between you two—more than in the last month."

Liam flinched and opened his mouth to say something to Adam but closed it when Ellie walked around the corner, freezing. Liam shook his head at her, and she paled while looking between the three of us. She swallowed as she turned around to leave.

"Ah, I see," Adam spoke without his usual mockery.

"You have no business to make assumptions." Liam squared his shoulders as he faced Adam, who stayed relaxed against the door. All of his bruises that had been visible had healed at a normal rate and were gone.

"Who said I was making assumptions?" His mockery was back. "It's clear you tossed your friends aside for new meat."

Liam's nostrils flared as he stepped toward Adam until he was only an inch from his face. "And if you were smart, you'd shut up."

Normally, Liam would back off, knowing an argument would make the situation worse. Adam pushed off the doors and loomed two inches taller than Liam, standing his ground.

I squeezed my arm in between them and pushed Liam back. "You should do the same."

"You're sticking up for him?" Liam looked at me, bewildered.

"No. Just apparently still protecting you, even if it's only one-sided," I said more harshly than I intended. He didn't need to get in a brawl and get in trouble. Adam was surprisingly quiet as he went back to lean against the door.

Liam frowned, momentarily distraught. "You don't think I care about you?"

"I don't know what to think. You weren't the only one that lost Maya." I could feel my heart beginning to race again. "It's like we lost you too."

Liam was silent, and I sighed before starting toward my room. Liam turned me toward him, resting his hands on my shoulders. The simple gesture should have been comforting, but right now I wanted nothing more than to be far away from him. I was surprised when Adam didn't intervene and prosecute the no-touching rule.

"I said, don't touch me." I spoke before Liam could and moved my arms up between his, knocking his hands off my shoulders. I took a step back, throwing a sidekick with enough force to push him back without hurting him. Liam didn't say anything as he staggered back, his face filling with sorrow. I wanted to keep fighting and had too much built-up anger that needed to be released. "Can we train?" I faced Adam, who raised an eyebrow. "Please?"

"You don't have to ask me twice." Adam smiled—a normal, simple smile—before turning and heading into the gym. I wasn't supposed to train, and I'm sure he knew, but I didn't care.

"Harper, come on. Don't do this." Liam followed in distress. "Can we talk? If not now, after dinner?"

"When Ellie isn't around?" I retorted.

"No." His strides were longer than mine and he was right on my flank. He lowered his voice. "So we're alone."

I stopped to face him.

"What? To talk? No, thank you. You haven't talked to me in a month, and now that I caught . . ." My voice trailed off. I was aware Adam had his assumptions, but I wasn't going to confirm them. "You casted Travis and me away. Maybe it needs to stay that way." I turned and met Adam in the center of the mat as he stretched.

"I'm not leaving you alone with him."

"Just leave the girl alone, would ye? She clearly doesn't want anything to do with you right now." *Huh.* Adam was defending me.

"So you can try to kill her again? I don't think so." Liam raised his voice as Adam pressed his lips together, holding something back.

"Adam's right. I don't want anything to do with you. Please leave." Tears began to swell in my eyes from anger and grief. I turned so Liam couldn't see.

"Did you want to stretch first?" Adam surprisingly asked.

I couldn't get much more out than a "no," so that was all I said before we started going through combos. I avoided looking at Liam as he backed off and left. The childish anger inside of me took over, wanting him to feel abandoned, just like I had. It had only been a month, though it had felt like a lifetime. We had never fought, not even once, and I knew that in a couple of hours I would regret my actions.

After the shockingly friendly one-on-one training, I felt better but decided to head straight to my room after my shower. Thankfully, I didn't run into anyone who would try to talk to me. Quite a few girls were in the corridor, but I imagined it would clear out in the next hour for dinner. Our doors remained open during the day, and we were allowed to hang out in them on our infrequent days off. Even though we weren't supposed to, I took my chances and shut my door. I was exhausted and wanted to turn off my brain, so I decided to take a nap.

I woke to the sound of my door opening and glanced at the clock nailed to the white wall. It was only six. I was expecting a sentinel to scold me for closing my door, but was surprised to see Ellie. I was even more surprised to see her shut the door behind her. She had a death wish.

"What are you doing?" I quickly climbed out of my bed. "Get out."

"I wanted to talk," she said with empathy, but she was the last person I wanted empathy from.

"I don't." I walked over to the door and opened it. "Out."

She didn't oblige. "I'm trying to help. You need to talk to Liam. He needs to—"

"You think you can walk in here and tell me what to do?" My voice rose as the previous anger began to rise again. I walked around her so she now stood between the door and me.

"You don't understand. He's—"

"Oh, I understand." I cut her off again. "You better leave before you regret ever walking into my room."

She frowned, taking a small step back. "He would never intentionally hurt you."

"Yeah, well, he abandoned us. Last I checked, family was supposed to mean everything."

"You're . . ." She shook her head. "He cares and is worried about you."

"If he cared about me, he wouldn't have ignored me when I needed him. You need to leave." I took a step toward her.

"This was a bad idea," she said, toying with her hair.

"You're just figuring that out?" I stared at her fiercely.

She inhaled sharply before whispering, "It's not worth jeopardizing everything."

What? Worth jeopardizing their relationship? I was about to lose it. I turned around so I couldn't see her anymore, closed my eyes, and tried to breathe. She was treading in dangerous water.

"Listen, I need to tell you—" Her hand landed on my shoulder, and I lost control.

I turned around and felt an energy surge through me. I slammed my hand into her chest as blue sparks bolted down my arm and out of my palm. She flew backward out the door, landing on the ground. She was still, but her chest rose and fell.

I glanced down at my hand, confused. There wasn't any evidence of what had just happened—no burn marks on my palms or her chest. Did I just imagine it?

A sentinel arrived with her taser drawn as she bent down to check Ellie's pulse. "What happened here?"

"She barged in here with questions about the Vault, demanding answers and wouldn't leave." I figured the truth would be worse for everyone. "So when she put a hand on me, I made her leave."

The sentinel looked at me disapprovingly but bought it as she radioed it in. I was surprised she hadn't heard us arguing. They took Ellie away, I assumed to a doctor, and ordered me to stay in my room.

Later that evening a sentinel stopped by to inform me she was fine. *Yay.*

CHAPTER EIGHT

A few other Jects emerged from their rooms, curious—just as I was—when our doors unlocked in the middle of the night. The main lights were out, but small, hidden lights in the ceiling corners were lit.

"They're working on the systems. I need all of you to report back to your rooms immediately," the sentinel threatened from around the bend.

I was about to round the corner when Ellie almost ran into me head-on.

"Holy crap." Her blue eyes were wide as sweat laced her brow. "Sorry, I didn't mean to run into you. I—"

"What's going on?" I cut off her babbling.

"Liam has a plan to escape, but we need to get out of here first." She glanced behind her.

"What are you talking about?"

"I tried to tell you earlier, but we are running out of time now. We need to meet up with him."

"Liam planned this?" I pointed at the lights above us. "How long has he planned this for?"

"Since before I got here," she whispered.

I could feel my agitation. "And he told you?"

"Yeah. I don't remember, but I must have worked on electronics. I picked up on the mechanisms of their readers and locks quickly. He caught me tampering with one." She went to reach for my arm but hesitated and lowered her hand. "We need to get past the sentinel."

I swallowed the bitter taste seeping into my mouth, questioning whether I should trust her. "Leave that to me."

Moments later, Ellie was searching for the fob in the pockets of the unconscious sentinel I had taken down. I had gotten close while tricking her into thinking I was groggy and simply asking questions. She'd kept her guard up, but it hadn't been enough.

"If the power is out, shouldn't the door be open?" I knelt next to her.

"The corridor doors and other main doors are on a different circuit. Even if that shuts down, they are wired to lock and can't be opened until overridden. So we need the fob, and promptly in case that happens."

My jaw dropped. She was well-rehearsed in the electrical aspect. I reached for the sentinel's sleeve, where the fob was attached to a retractable line so we couldn't steal them. I had to yank hard twice before it ripped out and held it up to Ellie.

"Huh." Ellie grabbed the fob and taser. "Do you mind if I keep this? I don't think you need it, after what you . . ." She trailed off.

"I'm not sure what I did." She was talking about zapping her across the room, and I wasn't sure I could do it again if I tried. "But yes."

I grabbed the sentinel's baton and radio. I turned off the radio and clipped it to the band of my shorts. After we exited the door, a few Jects bolted. A Ject with caramel-colored, shoulder-length hair lingered behind Ellie, who followed me as we trekked down the hall. Her name was Chloe, and she had arrived about a month and a half ago. She must have thought we were her best option to get out; she was probably right. A noise sounded from inside the commons, and I put up my hand to stop my two followers.

I prepared for an attack while Ellie held out the taser with shaking hands. Chloe also prepared for an attack, hands curling into balls as her soft brown eyes narrowed. I held my breath, but no one stepped out. I met Ellie's glance, asking me what to do. Honestly, I had no idea.

"I'm giving you the option to come out with your hands up. If not, I'll have to settle for shocking the crap out of you." I recognized the voice immediately.

"Travis," I said in relief.

"Harper?" He questioned as I cautiously rounded the corner. He let his guard down as soon as he saw me and gave me a giant hug. "I was expecting a mob of sentinels, but I guess you're pretty close to one."

I stepped back from his hug, keeping my smirk at bay. "Speaking of sentinels, where are they?"

"Liam set a distraction. We have to move." Travis wore grey sweatpants with elastic around the ankles and a plain white T-shirt, indicating he had probably been in his room and must've been filled in on the plan. If I hadn't run away from Liam earlier or sent Ellie away, I would have known. But that didn't change the fact that he should have told me weeks ago.

He noticed Chloe as she and Ellie came out from around the corner. I assumed Chloe wasn't a part of the plan, but when he didn't say anything, he must have accepted her tagging along.

"What distraction?" I kept my voice low as we started walking past the commons.

"A fire in the cafeteria," Ellie answered.

"Great. He's sleeping with you and telling you everything," I murmured, my agitation short-tempered. "So he's talking to you now?" I questioned Travis.

"He told me six hours ago. He didn't tell us because he was trying to protect us, but we don't have time to discuss it. We need to keep going and stay sharp." Travis picked up his pace down the hallway.

"Why didn't he come back to meet you?" I wanted to make sure Liam got away after setting the fire.

"He's going to meet up with us somewhere else," Travis answered.

"Blake, Jeremiah?"

"Blake got knocked out. Jeremiah couldn't leave him," Travis said flatly. He would have stayed with them if the plan didn't include finding us.

We came to a sudden halt as we rounded the corner toward the gym. Multiple Jects and sentinels were circling each other. One sentinel spared a glance at us but was too occupied in a standoff to stop us. I looked at Travis; he was trying to figure out a way around the mess.

"Follow me." Instinct took over as I ran, knowing we couldn't stand there any longer. I opted for the hallway opposite of the gym. A sentinel raised her taser off to my side.

"Duck!" I wasn't sure who she was aiming at until the slug ricocheted off the wall above my head.

I dove diagonally at her next shot and swiftly stood up out of my roll into a sprint. I was able to get to her before she could fire a third shot and knocked her to the ground as her taser slipped out of her hand. Unfortunately, my baton was lost in the process. She shoved me off her and onto my back as I groaned; this floor wasn't as forgiving as the one in the gym.

She was quick to her feet and grabbed the baton at her belt. She raised her arm and swung. I prevented the blow by grabbing her wrist with both hands. I glanced over to where the others were, wondering where my help was, only to see they were caught up with two other sentinels. Travis held his taser up in submission, while Ellie had already placed hers on the ground.

I averted my attention back to my current threat and twisted my hands to bend the sentinel's wrist backward, causing her to cry out in pain as she dropped the baton. I kicked her feet out from under her and quickly retrieved the baton. Without hesitation, I delivered a hard hit to the side of her head. She was out. I felt a little guilty, but she had crossed the line.

I faced the others to see Chloe eyeing Ellie's taser on the ground. She wouldn't be quick enough, and Travis wouldn't be able to ready his taser in time. To my left lay the taser that had belonged to the sentinel I just fought. I dropped the baton, launching my body on the ground to grab the taser and firing at the closest sentinel to me. I went to fire again, but the taser was empty. The other sentinel looked at me, causing enough hesitation for Travis to lower his taser and shoot. The sentinel fell to the ground.

"Are you all right?" Travis ran over and helped me up as I dropped the empty taser.

"Great." I grinned, pushing my hair out of my face. *How was I enjoying this?*

Travis let out a small laugh. He thrived on this kind of stuff, but I didn't. They had trained us to fight, to be their soldiers. Oh, the irony, to finally be able to use it against them. I walked over and grabbed the baton, telling myself not to lose it this time.

A fight was still ensuing, and I paused, wanting to help. Travis grabbed my arm and shook his head. "We have to go, or else we won't get out of here and be able to help them." I nodded in agreement.

I followed Travis as we headed to the doctors' offices, stopping in front of one of them. He knocked two times fast, then two times slow. Nothing. He tried again, but there was no response. He swore under his breath.

"What's wrong?" I kept my eyes on both ends of the hallway.

"Liam's supposed to be here," Travis whispered.

"We're sitting ducks out here." We had to keep moving or find a spot to hide. "What about that fob, Ellie?

She pulled the fob out from her bra strap, where she'd shoved it earlier, holding it to the reader. The light remained red. "That's what I thought. Travis, do you have the tools?" Ellie asked from behind me.

"Yes." Travis pulled out a small flathead, hand-sized wire clippers, and a mini screwdriver from his sweatpants pocket.

Ellie handed me her taser and rubbed her sweaty palms on her shorts. She took the tools and walked over to the fob reader. "It'd be easier to hack into it if I had a computer. I could use the connection between the buzzer on the desk and the fob reader." She pulled on a few wires. "Yes," she hummed as the red light turned green.

A small noise echoed from around the corner. "Get inside," Travis ordered as he pushed the door open.

"One second." Ellie was working on snapping the case back on. "I can't leave it off; it will give us away."

Travis waved me in, but I stayed. "I'll wait."

He paused for a moment and then nodded. I walked over to take his spot holding the door open. I was prepared to pull Ellie inside and smash the fob reader, but that would only buy us a small amount of time.

"Got it!"

"Good, let's go." I opened the door up for her as she grabbed the tools from the ground and slid through, with me right behind her.

We remained silent as small thuds came closer, passed, and then disappeared. This office was subpar to Dr. Cole's, but had lab machines and supplies that compared with her slightly outdated ones.

"Here." I gave the taser back to Ellie.

"Now what?" Chloe asked, clutching a taser in her hand. She must have gotten it off one of the sentinels in the hallway, and I regretted not doing the same.

"I'm not sure." Travis's voice carried a nervous edge to it, but he maintained his composure. "Liam was supposed to be here to let us in, and he knew the rest of the plan."

I took a deep breath. "Where was he going when you last saw him?"

Travis ran his hand through his shaggy blond hair. "He was already out of our corridor when the doors unlocked. He was supposed to set the fire and get our doors unlocked—thanks to Ellie—and then he had one more thing to do before meeting us here."

"He had to shut down the server so they couldn't communicate outside of their radios." Ellie slouched over the back of the chair.

Less than a minute had passed. "I'm going to go get him."

"Harper, you can't leave." Travis walked over and blocked my path to the door.

"We can't leave him behind." I exhaled.

"We aren't leaving yet." He took a step closer. "He asked me to get you out of here if he couldn't."

"We also look out for each other."

"That's what I'm doing."

"A few more minutes, that's it." I went over to the desk and set the baton down before reaching down and twisting the dial on the radio. We might be able to figure out the sentinels' whereabouts and listen for any signs of Liam.

". . . the offices. Jects could be hiding in any closet or room." The radio buzzed with a deep monotone voice. Something about it sounded familiar, but I couldn't place it.

"Yes, sir," a raspy voice responded. I glanced at everyone in the room, and each one of them had the same *oh crap* look I currently wore.

Two quick knocks sounded at the door, making my heart skip a beat while my body went into defense mode. Two slow knocks followed the first two. Out of the corner of my eye, I saw Travis twitch; he had used that same knocking sequence. We heard the unlocking click of the door as the handle turned. I willed the electric energy from earlier, but nothing came.

The door slowly opened and my breath released at the sight of a familiar face. Liam shut the door behind him, holding a taser and fob. His eyes scanned the room before settling on me, wearing the same plain white T-shirt and sweatpants as Travis.

For a brief moment, I forgot about how upset I was at him. All I felt was relief and contentment. I ran to him, wrapping my arms around his neck. He stiffened at first and then relaxed, returning the gesture and squeezing tightly. My head rested on his shoulder, and I soaked in his sage and sweet vanilla scent overpowering the fresh springs body wash.

Ellie cleared her throat. "Sorry to interrupt, but were you able to shut the communication system down?" Her voice was friendly but topped with urgency.

I hastily backed away and blushed, looking at the ground after our long embrace. The thought of him and Ellie in the closet came to mind, despite pushing it back. My cheeks began to redden with anger and embarrassment as heat coursed through my body. I felt Liam's eyes on me, but I kept mine fixed on the ground.

"Sorry I'm late." I felt his eyes shift off me. "Yes, I was able to shut it down, but our way out isn't clear anymore." He sighed. "They're coming through a door with a two on it and we need to get by it."

I flashed back to when Maya and I had wandered the Vault. We'd snuck behind a worker into an area with a mysterious solid door painted with a red 02.

"That's not all." Liam frowned. "They have real guns."

"How do you know?"

Liam looked at Chloe, who had asked. "The barrel of the taser is wider. If you look closely at the tasers, the front sight is also red."

Chloe and Ellie looked down at their tasers, examining them. I knew what a standard gun most cops had looked like, but, like most of the other Jects, I had assumed they carried their own version of a gun up until the day Liam shot one. They hadn't ever had to shoot one that I'd seen.

"Our way out is blocked?" Ellie's voice wavered.

Liam glanced at Ellie with veracity and compassion. "Yes."

I walked back over to the desk, setting the radio next to the baton and leaning over it. "Ellie, I take it those tools you had were meant for a different door?"

"Yes—for our way out if the fobs didn't work, which, apparently, they already turned the one off." Ellie crossed one arm over her chest and raised her other hand to her lower lip, grazing it with her finger.

"And chances are this one will be, too." Liam turned the fob over in his hand.

"The shutdown of the communication system was to the outside? And that was going to keep our path to whatever is out there clear." Travis answered his own question as the rest of the plan came to light.

"And you're sure that was the only way out?" Chloe asked.

"I—"

"No," I interrupted. "There's possibly another way behind the cafeteria." Everyone stared at me in confusion, even Liam.

"There's nothing back there but the kitchen and a locked pantry," Travis responded. It wouldn't surprise me if he'd snuck back there looking for food.

I went to respond, but the monotone voice coming from the radio interrupted me. "How many Jects are unaccounted for?"

"We believe seven, sir," replied a female voice.

"What of the three I inquired about?"

"Unaccounted for."

The radio was silent for a few seconds. "Names of the others?"

"We are still working on it. We should have the names in a few minutes."

The man speaking into the radio held down his talk button, causing static before speaking. "Don't—"

"Doc." *Doc?* A new voice spoke in the background behind the mystery man, and then the radio went silent.

A moment later, the man spoke again. "Code fifty-five. If they're close to the elevators, stop them, no matter what—except Harper. Bring her back, alive."

"Yes, sir," the female responded as other *yeses* filtered through the radio.

"What?" Ellie began laughing hysterically as her eyes watered. "They'll kill us?"

"Well, yeah. What else do you think they would do to us for trying to escape?" Travis said as I grabbed the radio and clipped it back to my shorts, struggling to process what I'd just heard.

Ellie glanced at me, raising her eyebrow and mumbling, "But not you. The murmurs I heard . . . your friend was right."

I was already repressing the anger building inside, but her words caused me to explode. I walked heavily at her, balling my right hand into a fist with full intent on using it. "You have no right to speak of Maya!"

Liam stepped in front of me and put his arm out, his palm landing on my chest. "Harper . . ."

"I'm sorry, it wasn't meant like that," Ellie choked out.

"She wasn't even here!" I waved my hand at her. "She doesn't even know Maya. Or me."

"She's just scared." Liam held his position, eyeing me. "We need to get out of here."

I snarled at Liam. "And follow the person who ignored me the last month, and when some stranger gets in his pants, he can't help but stick up for her? I don't think so."

He was baffled. I took the opportunity and shoved past his arm, but he was too quick and caught my elbow. He pulled my back against his chest and wrapped his arms tightly around me.

"Let go of me!" I yelled, forgetting about our current situation. I was fixated on Ellie, who backed away, eyes failing to hold back a couple of tears. The familiar rage from when I fought Adam returned, even though she was afraid of me and not a physical threat.

"I know what you're going through; you have to fight it." Liam spoke softly into my ear. "You're stronger than it."

"Let me go!" I yelled again, fighting his hold. I had no clue what he meant, but he would say anything to keep me from kicking the crap out of his new girlfriend.

I was just about to elbow him in the stomach when Travis walked in front of me, placing his hands on the sides of my face. "Hey, it's okay. Breathe."

"Sunshine." Liam's breath wisped against my neck. I felt a small thrill inside my stomach, calming me enough to look at Travis right in front of me. His eyebrows drew together as he looked directly over my shoulder at Liam. He wore the same look we all had when we'd realized Maya was changing.

Travis released my face when I relaxed, but Liam didn't move. Was it happening to me? Were these the violent fits of rage that had happened to Maya and the others who'd disappeared?

We were finally escaping and wouldn't get a chance like this again. I wouldn't let my temper ruin it. Despite the distance between us the last month, we were a family. I relaxed as Liam slowly released me. I walked over to the door—instead of at Ellie—and put my hand on the handle.

"Long story short, Frank had taken me to his doctor's office a while back. We had gone through the pantry door and down a small hallway." The plaque on the door leading to the immaculate office had read *Alan H. Roulings*. Dr. Roulings himself hadn't been there, and I was surprised they let Frank go there on his own. Frank had explained that his barcode tattoo worked on the pantry and the office fob readers, doubling as scanners, but his tattoo did not work on the other doors. I had tested mine on the reader at the pantry door on our way back through, but the small light only turned red, which earned me a glare from the Sentinel in the kitchen and a brief glance from Frank.

"There were other doors in the hallway that led to the office, but only one looked promising as an exit," I continued. "It had a punch code system, a fob reader, and a *01* on it."

"Ellie, it seems you know your stuff and can get us through." There was no way to escape—unless you had Ellie's skills.

I needed to get my emotions under control, especially if everyone was going to get through this alive.

CHAPTER NINE

"You're not taking the lead." Liam ignored my protests, leaving me behind him, with Ellie on my heels. Chloe was next, and Travis took the rear. Our bare feet were quiet against the pewter floors as we went past the other offices.

When I realized I had left the baton back on the desk, I internally punched myself. Travis tried to give me his taser, but I declined it.

A door suddenly opened between Liam and me.

"Eight all clear." The sentinel's mouth parted when he saw me, his hand freezing on his radio. I quickly disarmed him using a roundhouse kick, sending it across the hallway.

"Not clear." I grinned. He reached for his taser, but Liam was already on it, tasing him before he could pull the trigger. Chloe quickly fired her taser at the other sentinel who had emerged from the room, sending him to the ground next to his partner. Liam picked up one of the sentinel's tasers and handed it to me.

The lack of sentinels we encountered surprised me as we reached the cafeteria. I imagined they were covering the pantry, as well as Liam's planned exit. The steel doors were propped open and the smell of crisp, burnt paper filled the air. Liam quickly peeked around the corner.

"The hall is clear, but there's at least one in the kitchen, maybe more," Liam murmured to me and looked down the line at the rest of them. Travis gave a nod and a wink as Ellie side-eyed him, questioning his ease at the situation.

Liam quickly strategized a plan and checked his taser for ammo as we did the same. I had four slugs.

We stayed low, using soft, swift steps over the abundant ash-covered ground. It was slick and everything was soaked, indicating the sprinklers had gone off. Liam and I jogged to the kitchen door while the others jogged to the window, black soot sticking to the wall above it.

We heard shuffling as we got into position. Liam held up two fingers, and I nodded. There were at least two sentinels. Liam wanted to lure them out, but there wasn't much around to make noise. Besides some ash, the cafeteria had already been picked up earlier that night. He settled on hitting his taser on the metal leg of a nearby table and quickly retreating behind the door.

We couldn't hear the sentinels speak, let alone move anymore. The door slowly started to open when my hip let out a static noise. The door shut quickly.

Stupid, stupid, stupid! I'd never turned off the radio.

"There are Jects in the cafeteria. Do not have a count." The sentinel's voice from the cafeteria didn't echo through my radio. Now that I think of it, neither did the one from earlier. They must have switched channels.

Instead of charging out, they waited. Backup was coming, and we were going to be trapped. I dashed over to the door as Liam's hand slipped off my arm in a failed attempt to pull me back. Ignoring him, I put the taser in the back of my shorts, thankful for the strong elastic band. Travis gave me a dismayed look. I glanced away, knowing that his disapproval didn't matter either right now. I unclipped the radio and opened the kitchen door a crack, sliding the radio through.

"Please don't shoot." I managed to make my voice crack, showing false fear.

I raised my hands above my head and entered the kitchen, letting the door close behind me. The sentinels stood in the middle of the large restaurant-style kitchen. Steady hands with black thumbless gloves pointed tasers directly at me, their real guns at their hips. Their utility belts had a few extra things, including sets of heavy-duty handcuffs. Experience radiated off them from the way they carried themselves.

"What's your name?" a bald sentinel asked.

"Harper." My lips deceitfully trembled.

"What are you doing in this section, Miss Harper?"

"Hiding."

They both examined me as the other, dark-haired sentinel crept around to my side. I eyed him cautiously, not wanting him to see the taser concealed underneath my loose tank-top.

"And why did you not report back to your room?"

"Why would I want to go back there?" I glanced back to the bald sentinel. "It's a prison."

"Are you alone?"

"Yes." I held his glare without falter.

"Check her and radio it in to Dr. Roulings." He advanced toward the door. "I doubt she's alone if he suspected her to be leading a group." *Dr. Roulings?* That was the office Frank had taken me to, and the office we were going to pass.

The dark-haired sentinel reached for the cuffs, but I quickly grabbed my taser, shooting him. I whirled around to see the other sentinel face me just as Liam barged through, taser drawn.

"Lower it," Liam demanded.

"I wouldn't think about trying anything. It's three against one." Travis grinned as he stood from behind the stainless steel counter, taser in hand. He must have slipped through the serving window.

The sentinel set his weapon on the floor and raised his hands in the air. Travis looked at Liam, who nodded back in a silent conversation. Liam fired, and the sentinel's body shook until the disc's charge ran out.

Liam put his taser in the band of his pants before grabbing the sentinel's gun, along with ripping the fob out. He sighed as he held it in his hand for a moment—blankly staring at it—before releasing the magazine and counting how many bullets were left.

Something in Liam had changed, and I cringed at the ease with which he held the gun. When he had killed the sentinel a month ago, the guilt had almost destroyed him. He would do anything to protect his friends, and apparently, that included dismissing us.

Chloe rushed through the door, dropping her guard once she realized the situation was under control as Ellie trailed behind her.

"If they're going to shoot, may as well shoot back." Travis knelt and grabbed the other sentinel's gun.

Liam started toward the pantry door and tried the fob reader from earlier, as well as the sentinels', but both failed.

"Let's see what you can do." Liam nodded at Ellie.

Travis held out the tools Ellie had given back to him earlier, and she snagged them on her way by.

"Right. Let's pray I can do this." Ellie's voice wavered as she leaned over the fob reader, the four of us standing guard. "This one is more secure than the other one, but I think I can . . ." A snapping noise made me turn my head. "There." She had the cover off.

Twenty seconds later I was taking a pan and smashing the reader. My teeth clenched at the sight of Dr. Roulings's office as we ran past. Ellie started working on the next fob reader to the door with the red *01*.

Pounding raged from the door behind us. They had arrived, and she still needed to unlock the punch code panel. I took a step forward and held up my taser, along with the others.

No more than thirty seconds passed before we heard a saw. Travis leaned toward Ellie and patted her on the back.

"Now's the time to shine. Shaking like that won't do you any good." Travis did have good intentions of calming Ellie, but his attempt failed.

Liam assessed the door in front of us before retreating to Ellie's side, placing a hand on Ellie's shaking hands. "Hey, you can do this." She glanced up at him. "You're one of the most brilliant people I know, and that's including my memories I don't remember." He smiled, which in turn made her relax.

My breathing began to pick up as I quickly looked away, focusing down the hallway. They clearly had a connection.

The sawing became louder the closer they were to cutting through the door. Liam swiftly walked back over to us. My heart began to race in anticipation; they would be through that door at any moment.

A clicking noise came from behind us.

"Go, Ellie!" Travis shouted as the door slid open into the wall and began ushering her and Chloe through. What Ellie had done was skilled, and being able to do it without previous memories was even more impressive. She was a vital part of this escape, and I was letting my vexation cloud my opinion of her.

Red lights from the ceiling began to flash, and a loud pulsating alarm sounded as the door Ellie had just opened began to close.

"Go!" Liam pushed me through the door, and I turned and grabbed his arm, pulling him with me. He rotated himself so he was able to squeeze through, barely making it.

I sighed in relief after he made it through and took in my surroundings. The décor had completely changed except for the flashing lights against the scarlet walls and the alarm that rang more quietly. It looked like a hallway from a nice hotel, with small buffet tables holding vases with fake yellow and white flowers.

We walked tentatively along the tan carpeting and came to the middle of a split in the hallway. Straight ahead led to a dead end with an elegant-looking maple coat rack, and to the right was an elevator with a screen that flashed red. Ellie rushed over to it as I followed. The word *OFF* flashed on its display.

"What does that mean?" I asked, already knowing the answer.

"It means that they had a fail-safe we didn't know about."
She swallowed. "I can't access the elevator. It's completely
controlled from somewhere else now."

"So how do we get it open?" Chloe approached us.

"Even if we do, the elevator won't move." Ellie clasped
her hands together and brought them to her lips as they began
to shake.

"Ellie." I looked at her and forced my voice to soften.
"We'll get through this. Stay with us, okay?"

Ellie nodded. I didn't know where my kindness was
coming from. For a moment, I felt like my old self, before
Maya was taken. Less hostility, less anger, and no jealousy.

"Either way, it's our only option. They normally have a
ceiling hatch, and we can climb up the shaft. Travis, help
me." Liam walked over to the elevator and tried to pry it
open with his hands.

It wouldn't budge. Liam grunted in frustration as he hit
the elevator door with his fist. My teeth ground together. He
normally had more self-control, even in stressful situations.
He backed away and looked in my direction. His outraged
face dropped as he pressed his lips together and turned his
back to me.

"What are they waiting for?" Chloe's brown eyes were
locked in the opposite direction. "They should've started
sawing the next door by now."

"They probably have a faster way to get through." Ellie
half-heartedly shrugged.

"Look for something to pry the door open." Liam turned
back around, all signs of his frustration vanishing.

"I have an idea. Stand back." Travis aimed his gun and
fired at the elevator. The bullets ricocheted off the elevator
door and to the ground by his feet. "Shit!" he hollered as he
jumped back.

It didn't even dent the doors. I walked back to the dead
end, seeing nothing besides the empty coat rack, when a vent

big enough for a person to fit through caught my attention. They didn't think that one through.

"Guys!" I pointed to the vent in the ceiling as the four of them rushed over.

"Great, we have to climb through vents?" Travis sighed.

"Claustrophobic, are we?" Chloe taunted. "How do we get up there?"

"I'll lift you." Liam walked over and stood under the vent. "Back up," he added, pulling out his gun and firing. His second shot hit the screw and the cover swung open. "We have to hurry."

Liam and Travis worked quickly to hoist Chloe up. Next went Ellie, me, and then Travis. The three of us headed down the vent while Travis finished pulling Liam up just as the door opened and footfalls echoed through the hallway. We hastily crawled through the tight space.

The sound of tearing metal reverberated through the entire vent, and I reached my hand out, but wasn't quick enough. Ellie landed on the floor below, slowly sitting up and freezing. The sentinels aimed their weapons at her. I braced my hands on the other side of the tear and prepared to jump.

"Harper, don't." Travis's hand gripped my ankle.

"Get her out of here," Liam ordered before I heard a thud. I glanced behind me as Travis urged me forward; Liam was gone.

"I'm not leaving him!" I wasn't about to leave Ellie—what made him think I would leave Liam?

"If you go down there, Liam did all of this for nothing. He needs us to get out." Travis's grip loosened.

I held still, looking down through the torn hole. Liam had already fought his way to get to Ellie. His gun and taser were no longer on him, so I assumed they had been knocked away.

Liam glanced up, catching my eye and nodding for me to go. Goosebumps rose on my neck as I froze. Fierce marmalade eyes held mine as his thick brow furrowed. His body appeared larger, his biceps threatening the seams of his shirt and broad shoulders stretching the collar. He bared his sharp canine teeth and faced the sentinels in front of him.

"Travis, Liam . . . he . . ." I stammered.

Travis swallowed, not needing to see what I was talking about. "I know. We need to go."

"Get out of here!" Liam's words came out in a growl as Travis shoved me forward.

I'll be back. If all of us were caught, no one would be able to get help. I climbed over the hole and continued crawling.

"Liam!" Travis paused behind me. I looked back to see him dropping his taser.

Chloe was already at the end and had knocked the vent door open. Brisk air and a strong metallic odor struck me as I climbed out onto the top of the elevator after Chloe, squinting. The elevator shaft had dim lights, barely lighting both an outdated and a new structure. Long-rusted bars stood adjacent to new, sturdy ones, and it appeared that they had built a new elevator inside the old shaft.

"Now what?" Chloe looked up at the thick cable ascending into a ring of fog. I scanned around us as Travis climbed out.

"There!" I pointed to a rusty ladder on the wall.

"Who's up for an arm workout?" Travis droned.

"Let's go." Chloe climbed onto the ladder, wasting no time.

I followed, and the ladder weakly shook when Travis started climbing behind us. None of us spoke as we made our way up the ladder at a quick pace, making sure not to grab a rusted-through rung.

It felt like we had climbed eight stories without seeing a single door when a loud thud resonated from below. I spared a glance to see a small, lit-up hole in the elevator car as inaudible mumbles filled the shaft; the hatch on top was open. My eyes widened as a creaking noise soon followed and the cable behind us started moving.

"Faster!" Travis exclaimed, but we didn't need his command to go.

I started to pant as my palms became slick from sweat. When I reached up to grab the next rung, it snapped at its joints. Travis tensed below in preparation to grab me, but I caught myself as I slid down a rung. Unfortunately, my taser wasn't so lucky. My heart raced even faster at the double echo from the rusted rung and taser hitting the approaching elevator—that could've been me.

"I see a door!" Chloe huffed.

There was a dim light above the door, which helped illuminate the area as we began searching for something to pry it open.

"Will that work?" Chloe pointed at a flat bar on the other side of the doors. It was attached to the wall, but was completely rusted through a few feet up, and would make a great lever.

Chloe and I climbed out onto a sturdy beam. She took the far side as we both gripped the bar and pushed. I spared a glance at the approaching elevator, wondering if they had slowed it down because they didn't want to kill us—or me.

The bar finally broke, and I turned to face Travis. Together we crammed it between the two doors. He pushed at the far end while I pulled at the closer end, slowly prying open the doors.

"Keep it here." Travis let go of the bar and gripped the edges of the doors. The pressure released from the bar as he pulled, snapping it in half. It sliced down my left hand. I winced, dropping the other half and grabbing the wall to stabilize myself.

"Are you okay?" Chloe peered over my shoulder.

"What happened?" Travis dropped his hands after managing to open the doors so they stayed on their own and were wide enough for us to fit through.

"Yeah, I'm fine. Let's get out of here." I squeezed my bloodied hand, using the tips of my fingers to apply pressure to the cut. The elevator was almost to us.

CHAPTER TEN

We crawled through the doors and shielded our eyes from the fluorescent light above. Travis and Chloe pulled out their weapons, and I was seriously regretting losing mine. Simple piano music filled the room, and big square marble tiles lined the floor with white walls leading to an enclosed vaulted ceiling.

No one manned the large desk on the opposite side of the elevator, and a toilet flushed in the bathroom to our left. If that was security, I doubt they would be taking a bathroom break if they knew there was a jailbreak happening.

We took off through the single door to our right and ran aimlessly down a hallway with bright white walls. We passed a couple of custodial closets and ran until we reached a promising door. Behind it, a wide-set staircase led upward, and we took it until we reached the first level.

I hastily pushed open the door that led to another hallway with similar tiles, but the walls were blue. A silent alarm was triggered, and red lights began flashing when we reached the lobby. Huge block letters spelled out Westbrook, Inc. on one wall, while double glass doors and tall, dark windows covered the entire wall next to it. Our exit.

We started toward the doors when two men appeared in front of us, tasers drawn. The three of us froze, putting our hands up. They weren't sentinels but must have been guards, with their black pants and short-sleeved white button-up shirts. Shield patches were placed on their chests and left sleeves, while radios were clipped to their chest pockets. A semi-circled desk took up the most of the wall opposite the glass doors. It sat just behind the hallway, so we couldn't see it when we took off toward the exit.

"We have them in the front Lobby." One of the guards spoke into his radio. "Slowly put down your weapons."

I glanced at Travis, who held his gun in the air as Chloe started to put her taser down. My lip swelled as I bit down on it, willing the static I had accidentally used against Ellie forward. Nothing. I took a deep breath.

"My taser is tucked in the back of my shorts." I took a step forward, lowering my arm. They tightened their grips on their tasers, and I tossed my hand back into the air. "I'm going to step closer and turn around so you can watch me remove it."

I took a few steps closer and turned around while giving Travis an implying look. Travis understood and, while their attention was on me, he lowered his gun and fired. I turned to see the two guards drop to the ground, both holding their shoulders. A pang of guilt struck my chest; a part of me hoped they would recover, regardless that they'd known about the Vault.

"Nice shot," Chloe exclaimed.

"Yeah, that's where I meant to shoot them," Travis gloated sarcastically as we ran straight toward the exit. We were almost to the door when bullets started flying around us.

"Go! I'll hold them back." Travis turned around and started shooting toward the emerging sentinels.

I grabbed his shirt. "You're coming with us!"

"I'll catch up."

"We aren't leaving you, Travis!" Chloe spoke as I pulled Travis behind a pillar. Bullets whizzed by, yet they still were missing, and I doubt the sentinels were that inexperienced.

"If I don't hold them back, we'll all get caught. Go get the cavalry." He looked between Chloe and me.

Chloe grabbed my arm and pulled me toward the door.

I didn't fight her like I should've. I was starting to lose my composure and was getting rattled. As she pushed through the door, a slug flew over my shoulder and struck the taser in her hand. She immediately dropped it as it sparked.

Chloe finished opening the door and we ran out—almost to freedom, but it didn't feel right. We made it down two short flights of paved steps before my feet stopped moving. A mildly cool breeze hit me in the face, but the air itself felt warm. There were a few green trees planted in the small patches of grass at both ends of the bottom of the stairs.

I didn't recall if I lived in a city, nevertheless been to a city, but I was familiar with them: the massive crowds, the tall skyscrapers whose windows glistened in the sun, the lights shimmering so bright at night that you couldn't see the stars, and the smog and litter scattered about. I knew that cities could be both beautiful and squalid. It was like seeing a picture or reading about it and then turning it into reality. The only noises I heard were buzzing cars and music in the distance; there was no one in sight. My eyes focused on the sky, trying to see the stars, when I felt a tug on my arm.

"Come on, we have to go." She seemed less affected by our surroundings than I did. Then again, she had only been in the Vault for a month and a half.

I spared a glance at the building behind us. The glass was tinted black, unbroken by the flying bullets from inside. At the top, I could barely make out lit white letters spelling out Westbrook, Inc.

I turned with Chloe and started running down the empty sidewalk, passing multiple closed buildings and empty parking garages. We turned down a dark alley. There wasn't litter on the ground, and the windows stretched along the sides of the buildings as rectangular patches of grass lined the sidewalk. We reached the other side and turned the corner.

"We have to split up." I grabbed at Chloe's arm to get her to stop.

"Isn't that the worst thing to do?" Chloe panted.

I looked at the other end of the alley. "They'll be right behind us. I imagine they don't want to shoot us out here, but to be safe, we need to split up."

She went to protest, but I cut her off. "One of us needs to get help. If both of us get caught, then everything we just did, what the others did, was for nothing."

I felt my composure coming back. They knew this city better than we did. Even though we were fast, they still had the advantage. She knew she had to make a decision quickly and nodded in agreeance. "Follow me."

"This isn't splitting up," Chloe commented. I rolled my eyes as I took her across the street to another alley.

"Go this way. They won't see you and will only follow me."

"What? No! You being the bait was not a part of the plan."

"They won't kill me, remember?" At least, I hoped they had been missing in the lobby on purpose. "Plus, I make good bait." I winked.

After some hesitancy, she took off. I started jogging down the road, knowing the sentinels would be exiting the alley at any moment. They gave themselves away when they did as one of them shouted my position, and I took off in a full sprint. I looked back and grinned when both of them passed the alley that Chloe had gone down. I weaved around buildings and down multiple streets, running toward the music in the distance.

I managed to lose the sentinels and slowed to a jog. A tear ran down my cheek at the painful irony. I would have given anything for my friends to escape, even if it meant that I had to be left in the Vault, and yet, there I was.

There was commotion at the end of an alley. My jog slowed as I entered but promptly stopped when a sharp pain pierced my foot. I put my sweaty hand against the dirty brick wall to steady myself, pulling my foot up to rest on my knee. An amber glass shard was planted into the heel of my foot. I grabbed it, took a deep breath, and pulled as blood trickled down my foot. It was less than an inch, so it should be fine.

My foot stung and caused a slight limp as I continued to the street. I've had worse injuries and was not going to let a small piece of glass slow me down. My goal was to find somewhere more populated and find the police.

People rushed by, most not even batting an eye, while a few eyed me questioningly before scurrying on. I looked like a crazed barefoot lady wandering the streets at night in pajamas. Hopefully, they would ignore what they saw. I wanted to talk to the police, but not because someone called them on me.

Street lights and bar signs lit up both sides. Some buildings were tall, while others were only a few stories, but most of them had either a bar, restaurant, or store at the bottom. The crowd started to thin out the farther I walked. A yellow cab caught my attention as it stopped behind a parked motorcycle in front of a small bar, Mel's Pub, with a green-lit clover shining above its door. I didn't have money, but maybe I could get away with a cab taking me to the closest police station.

Music rang out the pub's doors as two men came out, nearly running into me. A man with dirty-blond hair and a clean-shaven face had his arm hung around his friend. The other guy mumbled an apology and helped his intoxicated friend into the cab. He pulled out his wallet and handed money to the driver as I quickly walked by, not wanting to draw attention. I would try another cab.

A dark figure leaning against the wall in front of me caused me to slow back down. He was wearing a suit and held something in his hands. He leaned off the wall and started walking toward me. I turned down an alley to avoid him but came up short when I realized it was a dead-end with multiple dumpsters and colored graffiti-splattered walls. The eerie presence of a person behind me prompted me to turn.

The man stepped into the light in the middle of the alley as the smell of vomit wafted toward me. I sighed in relief when I noticed he was holding a brown paper bag covering half of a liquor bottle. He wasn't from the Vault.

"Stay back," I warned as the man kept advancing. He didn't listen as he stumbled forward.

"What's a pretty thing like you doing out here all alone?" He bared his shiny teeth, grinning as he looked me over. "You know, I could set you up with a nice room for the night, and help get you cleaned up. I'd give you cash for some fancy clothes or recreational use—if you keep this between us?"

He was oblivious to my threat and daggering eyes. I knew enough to know he wanted more than to *help* me. His staggering posture proved he was not a threat, and I didn't have time for this.

"That's a good girl." His sly mouth grinned as I walked in his direction.

I went to walk around him, but he stepped in front of me. His expensive watch glimmered in the light as he lifted his hand and went to bring it to the collar of my tank-top. I scowled and snatched his hand before he could get close. I grabbed his wrist and put him in a standing armbar before buckling his legs and sending him to his knees.

"Ouch . . . let go!" he grunted.

His perversions made me sick. I felt the rage begin to boil under my skin and red started to take over my vision. I doubted this was his first attempt. I let go of his arm and threw a solid kick to his stomach, sending him to his back. I grabbed his shirt and lifted the upper half of his body off the ground. I cocked my arm to throw a punch but lowered it when I realized someone was watching me.

I looked up to see a man, appearing to be in his early to mid-twenties, step into the light from the shadows. I let go of the schmuck and he hit the ground with a thud, whimpering. I stood up to face the man as he walked uncertainly toward me, realizing he was the one who had helped his friend into the cab.

Below a black buzz cut, his hazel eyes swirled with green

and grey and his sharp cheekbones were visible underneath his shadowed stubble. His dark blue jeans and brown boots matched his plain blue shirt, which hugged his chest and sturdy shoulders.

My cheeks flushed when I realized I wasn't the only one staring. He looked over my rust-stained, blood-splattered tank-top before his eyes shifted from my sliced hand to my foot, which I had absent-mindedly shifted my weight off of. I unconsciously closed my hand into a fist to conceal the cut and stood tall.

I was barefoot, covered in grime, sweat, and blood, looking like I had just come from a crime scene. He should think I was crazy.

But the look he gave me was guarded yet concerned. He glanced at the pig on the ground and then back to me.

"Are you all right?" His voice was rough and edgy, yet warm.

I raised an eyebrow. I didn't know how much he had seen, but I knew he'd watched me kick the guy right before I almost punched him, and he was asking *me* if I was all right? He took a step forward, and I mimicked him, but in the opposite direction.

Noticing my hesitancy, he took a step back and relaxed his posture. "I'm not here to hurt you. I saw that man follow you into the alley"—he pointed to the man on the ground— "and I wanted to make sure you were okay."

"I'm fine, but my friends need me." I moved to go around him.

"Wait—I'm a cop. If you or your friends are in danger, I can help." His eyes locked on to mine and I froze. "I can show you my badge." He reached into his back pocket and pulled out a wallet, flipping it open. Inside the flap was a golden badge encircled with *City of Portland, Oregon*, with *Officer MacLand* engraved at the bottom.

"Portland?" I whispered. I hadn't had a chance to think about exactly where I was since stepping outside the Vault.

If this were home, it should have felt natural. Instead, I felt like an outsider and didn't know where I was going, let alone where in Portland I was.

"Yes, Portland." He slowly put the badge back in his pocket. "Are you okay, ma'am?" *Ma'am.* I had never been called that before.

"How do I know I can trust you?" I asked.

"Have I given you a reason not to?"

"Have you given me a reason to?"

The corner of his mouth briefly twitched, hiding any traces of a smile. "I showed you my badge. All I want to do is help. I'm not arresting you for punching this piece of work," he said, his voice turning bitter at the last few words, "but I am going to have someone come down and take him in for questioning."

"Fine. You can point me in the direction of the police station." I eyed him as I walked by him. He wasn't in uniform, and who knew if his badge was real.

"Many blocks that way." He followed me onto the street and pointed in a general direction, smirking.

An annoyed grumble rose from my throat at his unelaborated directions. "I don't have time for this."

"What's your name?" he called out as I walked away.

I turned around slowly. "Harper."

"Officer MacLand." He took a few steps toward me, holding out his hand.

I eyed his hand and hesitantly shook it, surprised at his gentle grip. "Is that supposed to make me feel better, Officer MacLand?"

"Only if it helps to know my name. You can call me Miles." He studied my reaction.

"So, Miles, are you going to tell me *exactly* where the police station is?" I asked.

"I did point toward the precinct"—he shrugged—"but I think it's a good idea if I take you there and you can tell me what happened."

"So you can supervise me." I chewed my lip. He wasn't going to tell me where his station was, and anyone else would have called the cops or ignored me. He mentioned someone was going to come to question the scumbag—maybe I could hitch a ride with them.

"My friends, along with others, are being held captive in a building called Westbrook." I held my breath, unsure if trusting him was the right decision.

"And that's where you came from?" His eyes didn't leave mine, searching for any trace of prevarication.

"Yes."

He glanced down the alley and then back to me. "I can send someone to check it out while we wait here until my colleague shows. Then I can take you to the precinct where you'll be safe."

"One person? They have an army!" I shook my head.

"You have my word that I will have someone check it out, and they will radio if they find something." He sounded sincere, but I had a feeling that it wouldn't help.

"I need to show them where they're being held." A few seconds passed, and I narrowed my eyes at his lack of response. "What?"

"We can't send anyone inside without a warrant."

"What? How does sending someone there help if they can't go in?" If the replacement guards or sentinels even answered, they would tell them everything was hunky-dory. I couldn't take them on alone. "We need to get one right now."

"I'll call my captain and we'll work on it."

I paced while he was on the phone, disregarding the throbbing in my foot as I slightly hobbled back and forth. Moments later, another cop showed up and she ushered the drunk man into the back of the car. I was offered a ride to the precinct, but I didn't want to be in the same vehicle as that guy and was fine with walking—if Miles would give me real directions.

"You're not walking with your foot like that." Miles

strode over to the sleek, navy blue motorcycle that was parked in front of the bar I passed earlier.

"I'm not sure riding on a motorcycle with you is any better." It almost looked metallic grey in the night.

"Your options are limited if you want to get to the precinct." Miles removed the lock from the helmet and held it out.

I hesitated, then grabbed the helmet, secretly not wanting to walk anymore. The exhaustion was catching up to me.

"You look like you've been through hell. We'll get a doctor to look at you before we head to the precinct."

"No," I said defiantly. "Let's just get to the precinct."

He cocked his eyebrow at me, then sighed and rubbed the back of his neck in frustration. Something told me people usually listened to him and didn't tell him off. "Fine. The precinct it is."

Leather and pine filled the helmet as I slid it over my head. It was loose, but my hair took up some of the space. He sat on the motorcycle and waved me on. I thought I saw him sneak a grin when I hesitated. If I had survived in the Vault, I could muster up the courage to get on a motorcycle with a stranger, now that I knew he truly was an officer.

"Put your arms around me." He raised his voice so I could hear him after I climbed on. Not exactly what I wanted to do, but I didn't want to fall, either. I complied and leaned forward, wrapping my arms loosely around him.

I swayed backward when he took off, tightening my grip. His abs constricted under my hands as a small chuckle rumbled through his chest and up his back. I rolled my eyes and took a deep breath as I peered over his shoulder.

CHAPTER ELEVEN

"You can sit here. I'll be right back," Miles said, leaving the room.

Must be he didn't think I was completely crazy, or else he wouldn't leave me alone on the main floor in a precinct. I sat down in the black office chair, guessing it was his. Desks with scattered papers and computers on top sat throughout the large room around me. Miles emerged a minute later with a cup of water and a small first aid kit.

"Here you go." He sat against the desk as he handed me the cup. I accepted it and chugged, not realizing how thirsty I was. "Let me see your hand."

I held out my hand and he laid it on his lap, palm up. I had been prodded and poked by multiple doctors, but having my hand resting on his leg made me feel uneasy—and something else I couldn't explain. I wasn't used to contact unless it was by a doctor or the small gestures from my friends.

He began cleaning and bandaging my cut.

"Aren't you going to question me?" I asked, wondering why he wasn't interrogating me.

He stopped wrapping my hand as his hazel eyes peered down at me. "I'll hear your statement when you tell Captain Shaw. Now, let me see your foot."

I hesitantly rested my foot on his leg. "You seem to know what you're doing."

"These are pretty nasty cuts, but, unfortunately, I've dressed worse." He examined my foot a little closer. "This one will need a few stitches." Sure enough, the first aid kit had suture and needles.

"Are you a paramedic, also?" I asked.

"No. I imagine you would fight me if I tried to take you to a hospital right now, but we'll have to get you looked at tomorrow."

I grinned at his accuracy. I didn't want to waste time talking to doctors and had made it clear I wasn't going to get checked out. Tomorrow, I would get out of it again.

"Is anyone else here?" I scanned the empty desks and the door behind him, half expecting a swarm of sentinels to barge in.

"There's an officer at the front desk, one roaming the grounds, and one downstairs. A few more are on patrol." He picked up a syringe. "This will burn, but will help numb your foot for the stitches."

"I don't need it." Even though it was in a sensitive area, it was only a few stitches. He eyed me doubtfully and I sighed. "You say you have dressed worse, so it should be quick. Plus, that stuff burns worse than the stitches itself and makes the process take longer."

Miles stared at me a second longer before setting the syringe down and stitching up my foot. He had just finished wrapping it when a man in dress pants and a burgundy button-up shirt walked in. His black tie was just as sleek as his hair, and broad triangular cheekbones framed his face, blending in with his tall frame. Despite his fit figure, his face showed signs of age, which led me to think he was in his early forties.

"Captain." Miles stood and waved at me. "This is Harper."

"Hello, Miss Harper." His tired brown eyes eyed me up and down as I stood from the chair. "I'm Captain Shaw. Shall we step into my office? I want to hear everything that has happened to you and see what we can do to help." He led me to a windowed office with opened blinds. "Have a seat. We will be right in."

I sat in one of the two smaller chairs across from what I gathered to be the captain's chair on the other side of the desk. The two of them talked for a few minutes before coming in. The captain sat in his chair, while Miles opted to lean against a beam between two of the windows with his arms crossed. The captain asked me if it was okay to record my statement, which was fine by me. Everything I had to say was the truth and needed to be heard.

I started at the beginning with what I remembered. I explained who the Jects, doctors, sentinels, workers, and suits were, along with the few files I'd gotten a glimpse of that had *Alcorp* on them. I tried to explain the best I could about how we couldn't recall our memories before the Vault. I explained our daily routine, the treatments, the injections, Jects disappearing, and training. I mentioned that they took Maya, a close friend, but I didn't explain the details of our recent fight. I explained who Liam and Travis were, even Ellie, and how they helped Chloe and me escape but left out the change in Liam. I needed the captain to believe me and not think I was mixing up reality with a movie.

After half an hour with no interruptions, I had managed to sum up most everything I could think of that was essential. I tried to include only what was necessary, expecting to answer more in the follow-up questions. The entire time I spoke, Miles remained quiet in the background while the captain sat back in his chair, occasionally tilting his head and humming.

Stagnant silence filled the room when I was done. I sat there quietly, fidgeting with the bandage on my hand as I waited for questions.

"Thank you, Miss Harper." The captain's Adam's apple bobbed. "Is there anything else you would like to add?"

"Umm, no I don't think so." Wasn't he going to start asking me questions?

"Okay, then. This concludes this statement." He leaned forward, pressing the button on the recorder and stood to usher me out the door. Miles stayed put, watching me as I walked out. "We will be out shortly." He shut the door and the two of them talked. Minutes passed until they emerged.

"Thank you for your statement. We will look into it further," the captain said as Miles came over and stood at my side.

"Aren't you going to do something right now? They could be hurt, or worse!" I exclaimed.

"I'm sorry, but there is nothing I can do at this time. An officer went by Westbrook and didn't find anything suspicious. We have to wait to speak to a judge and get a warrant for the next step. We can't go barging into places; that's not how the law works. You'll stay in holding tonight until we can sort things out tomorrow—later this morning."

"No!" The fact that he didn't express an ounce of concern infuriated me. "I will find someone else who can help." I turned to leave.

"Miss Harper, I can't let you leave." The captain spoke, but it was Miles who caught my arm. "I was not asking."

I glared at Miles, who removed his hand—he was lucky I didn't break it—and scowled at the captain. "What do you mean?"

"What I mean is that you appear to be a public threat, have admitted to being associated with multiple assaults, if not murder, and committed assaults yourself, and . . ." He looked down at my arms and didn't continue. I knew what he was thinking. My bruises looked suspicious of drugs. On the contrary side, I had already said in my statement why I had them. They would be completely gone in a few days, but they didn't know that; I had left my quick healing out of the statement.

"This is ridiculous! You can't lock me up again!" Even though they were considered our rooms in the Vault, they were just glorified prison cells. "What about my friend, Chloe?" If they found her, they had to believe me.

"We will put an APB out for a woman with that name

and her description. And we will start a search on a missing-persons report with your name and appearance." The captain's voice was hoarse.

"An APB?" I asked.

The captain pinched the bridge of his nose. "All-points bulletin. In other words, officers will be on the lookout for her."

I was about to question the subject more, but the captain was nodding at Miles. The two had locked eyes in a silent conversation.

"Let's go, ma'am." Miles stared at the captain for a second longer before turning to me. I swear I saw his eyes grey slightly.

"Please don't do this. They need me!" I pleaded, stepping back from Miles as he approached.

"Resisting will only make things worse and impede you from getting out sooner," Miles whispered as he closed the gap between us and grabbed my upper arm. His hand felt hot against my arm, despite the blood whirling through my body. I contemplated fighting back, but I knew that attacking an officer and a captain was probably not the brightest idea.

I needed them on my side.

CHAPTER TWELVE

Miles ushered me through the precinct's main hallway. When we were out of sight of the captain, he let go of me. He probably thought I was insane, but who could have blamed him? I was in pajamas, with dirt and cuts all over, claiming I had been held captive for five years in an underground vault with twenty or more others who came and went. If it was the same world as it was before the Vault, then I would have thought I was crazy too.

Same world. Was it the same as it was five years ago? It seemed like it. In the back of my mind, I could never shake the thought that they had been training us for something significant, although I never understood why they never trained us with guns—probably due to lack of trust. Was what happened to Liam the same thing that had happened to the others, or was that what they were trying to control?

"Here." Miles's voice broke my train of thought. "You can use the restroom if you need and wash up." He gestured toward the women's bathroom and leaned against the wall.

"You're letting me go to the bathroom, alone?"

"I have orders to bring you to holding; it wasn't specified that we couldn't stop along the way." He leaned his head back and crossed his arms. I had started to open the door when he spoke again. "Oh, and there are no windows in there." A half-cocked grin spread across his face.

As much as I wanted to leave, I had no choice but to cooperate. I used the restroom and took some wet paper towels to wash up. It took a few minutes to scrub most of the grime off my face and the parts that my pajamas didn't cover. I rinsed my hair in the sink, avoiding getting my bandage completely soaked. My hair was still greasy as I threw it in a bun, my clothes were still dirty, and even though I scrubbed, some dirt still littered my skin. I frowned at myself and left.

Miles pushed himself off the wall when I walked out and silently led me to the holding cells. He paused at the top of the stairs before continuing to the elevator, and I couldn't help but wonder if he despised them.

"What's it like out there?" I asked as we reached a propped-open metal door.

"What do you mean?" He looked at me curiously.

"I guess, like, is the world the same as it was five years ago?" I fumbled for the words to describe what I meant. "Is there a war going on . . . or an invasion of some sort?"

He cocked his head as his lips pursed together, trying to figure out what to say next. "Well, technology is always changing, and as far as a war, if you mean on U.S. soil, no." His lip twitched. "And invasions, as in aliens? No . . . not yet."

"Not yet?!" My eyes widened.

He chuckled. "No, there are no aliens. Just theories and beliefs, so far." He winked, but his playfulness faded when he saw the seriousness in my face.

His green-hazel eyes lingered on me. I quickly turned and walked through the door to avoid his stare. There was an empty desk to my right and three large, empty cells lining the back cement wall to my left. Each cell was wide, but shallow, and had huge benches along the back wall. No toilets or sinks, just holding cells. The first cell was the only one that had a small cot. They weren't as clean as my room and looked a bit grungy.

"The first one." Miles walked around the desk and grabbed keys from a drawer. I walked into the cell and turned to face the opening, waiting for him to walk over and shut the door. Instead, he grabbed the chair from behind the desk, placed it in front of the opened cell door, and plopped down.

"The officer on duty will be here shortly. There was no one in holding, so he took a break, and the drunken man from the alley was taken to get checked over first."

Good. I might have lost my temper if I were in the same room as that filthy dirt bag. I felt awkward standing, so I walked to the back wall and sat on the bench. I pulled my legs to my chest and rested my chin on my knees. This was a waste of time. I hoped Chloe was having better luck.

"So, you mentioned you can't remember anything before the Vault?" Miles leaned forward, resting his arms on his knees.

"Why are you asking? I thought you didn't believe me." I meant to make my voice sharp, but it faltered.

"I never said I didn't."

I held his stare. "Yes, that's correct."

"But you still remember the concepts of what you experienced prior?"

"Yes."

"So, it's like a coma—how some people wake up and can't remember family or friends, but still understand basic ideology, how to function, and what they learned."

"I was not in a coma for the last five years. I am *very* aware of what happened to me."

"That's not what I'm saying." He sighed. "I'm just trying to understand you, that's all."

"Understand me?"

"You're different, you aren't on drugs, and you're constantly checking over your shoulder."

My eyes narrowed. He was right on all accounts, but if he believed that, then why was I in a holding cell? I opened my mouth to say something, but an officer with short black hair and bronzed skin strode in.

"Officer MacLand!" The short stalky officer cheerfully said.

"Hi, Steven." Miles stood; he wasn't as thrilled.

"It's your weekend off. I figured you'd be passed out somewhere with Brandon." Steven laughed.

"Someone has to be responsible." Miles walked over to the cell and closed it. "I'll see you later."

"It sounds like it's your day off?" I wouldn't think his co-officer would suggest that he should be drunk at this hour if he had to work.

"Not anymore. I have a new case to follow up on." He walked over to Steven with the chair and set it down. "Take it easy on her."

"Yes, sir." Steven smiled, but his voice was absent of sarcasm. Miles left the room, and Steven moved the chair back behind the desk and sat down, leaning back and putting his hands behind his head. "So, what did you do to have him come down here on his Saturday night that he had off?"

I paused, wondering if I should just ignore him. "They didn't tell you?"

"Pshh. It seems like I was told a roundabout story. They told me they were holding a suspect with possible drug use. Don't get me wrong, you look like a mess, but Officer MacLand would have called an on-duty officer to come to get you and also wouldn't have bothered the captain."

He sat up, went to the other side of the desk, and jumped up to sit on it. "If Mac doesn't think you're guilty, then I don't either. He has the best intuition."

He fidgeted on the desk. "It's a shame."

"What is?" My head perked up; I didn't see how having a good intuition could be a shame.

"Let's just say there was an incident. Miles got stuck here and is insanely good at being a cop, despite being stubborn."

"What happened?"

He laughed. "Man, you're a curious one, aren't you? I've already said too much; he'd kill me if he knew I was talking about him."

I frowned. He lowered his smile and put his hands out. "Whoa, not literally. Now, why don't you get some rest? You look beat."

I didn't know much about Miles, but something told me that he was dangerous if you pissed him off.

* * *

I woke in alarm to a gunshot echoing through the building. It wasn't right outside the door, but it was close by. I sat straight up on the cot and looked at Steven, who was already standing with his gun out, speaking into his radio.

"Jim? Dale? Do you copy?" No one responded. He swore and pressed the button again. "We have a 10-32, Central Precinct! 10-32, 10-19!"

"What's going on?" I strode over to the bars.

He dropped his hand from the radio and brought it to his gun. "Miss, I need you to get in the far corner and crouch down." His earlier ease of conversation had disappeared.

"Holland, en route." A female voice sounded over his radio.

"Let me out! I can help."

"Miss, that's not going to happen. I need you to get in that corner." He seemed to be deciding whether to stay or go check things out.

Steven walked toward the door and peered through its small window. I walked to the corner of the cell and crouched down, hoping it would help him calm down. He slowly opened the door and hesitantly walked through, only to be tossed backward. He slid past my cell and collided into the wall between my cell and the desk. He let out a gasp as he slowly tried to right himself, his gun no longer in his hand. He glanced up at me, his face filled with horror.

"Are you—" My head cranked toward the door when I heard multiple footsteps entering.

My hands clenched the cold metal bars, causing my knuckles to turn white. I squinted, trying to distinguish if I was seeing clearly as terror crept up my spine. Three figures dressed in black towered over us with orange cat-like eyes. They looked like men mixed with beasts, each having similar features. Their nostrils flared, and the bone structure was altered, with jutted-out cheekbones. My eyes dropped to the hands of the one in front as he held them outward, sharp claws protruding from where his nails should have been. Fangs flashed as he sneered at me.

They looked similar to Liam; I wasn't hallucinating.

The beast's eyes shifted to Steven as he knelt, wrapping his clawed hands around Steven's neck.

"No hard feelings, as we appreciate your service. You're just in the wrong place at the wrong time." His voice sent shivers down my spine, despite his benign words.

He pulled out a syringe and plunged it into Steven's shoulder, knocking him out cold. With unexpected gentleness, he laid him on the ground. The color drained from my face as I backed away from the bars and retreated to the opposite corner. The beast stood up and reached his hand in his pocket, pulling out a second syringe that was larger.

"I'm asking you to please cooperate—we don't have much time. It will be painless and over quickly if you do," he said as the other two walked over to the cell door. The one lifted his foot and kicked the cell door open, breaking the metal lock. As soon as they entered, my hair stood up as if someone had rubbed my body with a static cloth.

My heart was pounding, and sweat trickled down my neck as my hands began to tremble. I needed to calm myself down and regain control. Fear and panic clouded my judgment, and I needed to lose every ounce of it if I was going to make it out of this. I closed my eyes and took deep breaths.

My eyes shot open. They reached out to grab me, but I jumped onto the bench at my side and grabbed the arm closest to me. Shocking myself with a burst of power, I flipped off the bench while twisting his arm and slammed my elbow into his back. He growled in pain and turned to face me. The presence of someone behind me caused me to reposition myself so I could see both of the beasts.

One of them advanced too quickly for me to dodge, flinging me into the bars. I winced, feeling the sharp pain ripple down my back and extend down the nerves in my leg. I prepared to take a fighting stance, but they were already at my sides and pinning my arms against the bars. I fought back to no avail as the one with the syringe advanced until his boastful face was a few inches from mine, his hot breath making me shiver.

He opened his mouth to say something but shut it when a gun went off. He looked at the beast to my right.

"Check it out. See if West has it under control." He grabbed my arm to replace the beast that left. I could feel their claws dig into my skin with the slightest movement. "Doc may be proud of your strength and courage, but he wants you returned promptly." My palms began to sweat, but not from fear—from anguish. They had probably found Chloe, and I was everyone's last hope. "No hard feelings to you, either."

The beast raised the syringe and planted it into my shoulder. Static jolted in waves of energy throughout my body. His eyes widened, dilating his cat-like pupils. Blue hazed my vision as bolts of electricity illuminated off my skin and sparks flew where the beasts made contact with my skin.

Another gunshot sounded before muffled fighting took place in the background. The blue haze faded and the ends of my hair stood down. The grips on my arms released as the beasts collapsed to the ground. The air was crisp with an electrical charge. My legs wobbled beneath me as my vision began to blur. I reached for the bars, gripping them for support as I braced my head against them.

A pair of brown boots stood in the doorway. I blinked repeatedly, trying to make out who the figure was. I started to panic as the figure took a step closer but quickly calmed down when I saw storm-grey eyes flecked with green staring back at me. Everything around me became unrecognizable. I swear I heard him say my name as my legs gave out and blackness engulfed me.

CHAPTER THIRTEEN

I winced as I swung my legs off the hospital bed. Pain radiated down my back, and my head dully throbbed. I was about to stand when a young officer with flat blond hair and sapphire eyes strode into the room carrying a cup of coffee.

"You're awake. They weren't expecting you to be awake for a while." The officer briefly stepped back out into the hallway and came back in. "The doctor will be in shortly."

"Where am I?" I asked as he walked to the foot of the bed. His badge was similar to Miles's, and I realized I recognized him—he was the same guy Miles had helped into the cab last night.

"You're in the hospital. You were unconscious when—"

"Clearly, but how far am I from Westbrook?" The room was filled with morning light, which meant I was running out of time.

He frowned. "I'm sorry to hear about what happened to you. Officer MacLand is getting a warrant as we speak. We'll be searching the building soon."

I rested my head back. At least there was some good news. It only took an attack on the precinct for them to believe me.

"Miles? He was there." I remembered seeing him before I blacked out.

"Yeah, he found you passed out. Said you must've knocked the two men out before he got there." He arched an eyebrow. "You must be tough to take on two men like that."

"Did he see how?"

"You don't remember?" He must have mistaken my

apprehensive look for confusion. "The doctor did say they gave you a high dose of sedatives."

"Yeah, everything seems blurry," I lied. I remembered exactly what happened and how it had felt: the static, my hair sticking on end, and the rush of energy that had filled my veins. It wasn't even close to what I'd felt when I sent Ellie flying.

"I'm Officer Kovar, by the way, but you can call me Brandon, seeing how you're already on a first-name basis with my partner." His sapphire eyes lit with amusement. "And that's not common with strangers."

"Harper," I said, even though he would have already been told that. "How come no one was sent straight there after the attack?"

"There's no proof that the attack was tied to Westbrook."

"I'm not proof?" My jaw clenched.

"I fight for the law, but that doesn't mean it always makes sense."

"What about the . . ." I said, realizing I didn't know what he knew, "men? Did you guys question them?"

"They were gone when backup arrived. Miles got you out of there in case more were coming. By the time he and another officer went back in, they were gone." His phone began to ring. "Excuse me." Brandon stepped out of the room just as a doctor wearing a white lab coat with chin-length ink black hair and piercing dark eyes walked in.

"Hi, Harper. I'm Doctor Kim," she said in a kind voice. "If you don't mind, I'd like to examine you and make sure everything is all right now that the sedative ran its course." A doctor had never asked me if it was okay to examine me; they just did it. I slowly nodded and she ran through a quick physical. "Everything sounds and looks fine."

"Excuse me, doctor, I'm sorry to interrupt. I just need to inform your patient about something." Brandon strode in and looked from Dr. Kim to me. "Officer MacLand has the warrant. I'm going to meet him at Westbrook, but there's another officer who is stationed right outside your room. The hospital security is also monitoring this floor carefully." He finished shoving his phone into his pocket and went to turn around.

"I'm coming." I pulled off the black thing on my finger and ripped out the IV catheter in my hand. Blood started to seep out, but I covered it with my other hand, accidentally getting blood on the fresh bandage wrapped around it. They must've changed Miles's bandages when I was out.

My legs almost gave out when I stood, but I righted myself. The sedative must have had some lingering effects, not to mention the dull ache in my back and the flash of pain in my foot on impact.

"What are you doing? You need to lie back down!" She rushed over as Brandon raised an eyebrow.

"You said it yourself: I'm fine. I'm going with him." I looked down at my pale blue hospital gown.

"You haven't been released yet." Brandon glanced at Doctor Kim.

"I'm pretty sure you can't do that. And I am not releasing you yet." She turned off the machine, which had started beeping when I pulled everything off.

"No offense to either of you, but I'm going. I can either go with him, or I'll sneak out of here." I looked at Brandon. "Plus, you said it yourself, I'm tough. I can handle myself."

Brandon sighed. "I was warned you might be stubborn."

"You can't possibly be thinking about letting her go with you." Doctor Kim waved her hands.

"Well, if her story is true, I'm pretty sure she could escape if she wanted. Unless you sedated her or tied her down," Brandon said matter-of-factly.

Doctor Kim took a deep breath. "Fine. I was only going to keep you today to monitor you."

I went to step forward, but paused, looking down at my hospital gown again.

"I'll go find some spare scrubs around your size," Doctor Kim said.

She came back with maroon scrubs and a pair of white slide-on shoes. I declined the shoes, but she insisted. They were a little big, but it still felt like my feet were being suffocated. I wasn't used to wearing anything on my feet.

When we arrived at Westbrook, there were already a couple police cars and a familiar navy blue motorcycle parked out front. People wearing dress clothes were filing out of the towering building and scattering throughout the sidewalk. The building looked like it had last night, except the front doors were propped open. Miles spotted Brandon's patrol car and headed in our direction, wearing the same clothes from before, but with a gun openly holstered to his belt. His lips pursed when his eyes landed on me in the backseat.

"This oughta be fun." Brandon sighed as he got out of the car.

"What is she doing here?" Despite the car doors being shut, I could still hear his muffled voice.

"What, no hello?" Brandon smiled, but it quickly faded at Miles's glare. "She threatened to attempt to escape if I didn't let her come. I told her she had to stay in the car."

Miles shot me a glance before looking back at Brandon. "Everyone's almost out. How are you feeling?"

"Supporting a minor hangover, but hanging in there." Brandon rubbed his head.

"Good day off, huh?" Miles sighed as he glanced my way. "I guess now that she's here, I'll talk to her. You can let her out."

Brandon walked over to my door and opened it. I quickly climbed out with no intentions of getting back in. Miles did a once-over of the scrubs I was wearing, but didn't comment.

"We got a call from the north precinct. They found a girl named Chloe whose story matched yours. She's over there." He pointed to a spot where an officer stood near a patrol car. I took off and squeezed by the officer.

Chloe immediately hugged me when she saw me and whispered, "I thought they got you." She still wore her smudged white tank-top and grey shorts, but had a black blanket wrapped around her shoulders and a pair of shoes.

"Are you kidding? I had to put those sprints to good use." I got a laugh from her before she frowned. "I'm going to try to convince them to let me go in."

"Me too." We both wanted revenge, even though we could go without seeing that place again. I nodded and strode back over to Miles.

"We're going with you. You'll need help finding how to get down there, and we know the layout. I can trace every inch of the Vault"—I paused—"besides the men's corridor."

"Your instructions will do just fine. We're not putting civilians in danger." Miles was firm.

I grunted. "How can you call us civilians if you can't find records of us?"

His brows furrowed. "Not happening."

"When you find what we say is down there, you're going to need our help to navigate it. And besides, if you think we're crazy, then we won't run into anything and aren't in any harm's way."

"You know I could make you get back in the car and stay there, right?" He raised an eyebrow.

"That's not happening either." I grinned.

He stared at me. "Fine, but you will stay behind me." He looked at Chloe, who had followed me over. "And so will you."

"You didn't put up much of an argument." Brandon turned from him to me. "Man, you've got to teach me how to do that."

"If you didn't bring her, we wouldn't be in this situation." Miles side-eyed him. "But she's right. We could use her help with finding and searching this place." He hadn't said "if it's there." *Good.* Someone had to be prepared.

Miles convinced the captain to let us come. There would

be two small groups going in, and Chloe and I were stuck with the Captain, Miles, and Brandon. They gave Chloe and me bulletproof vests to wear, and I ended up kicking my shoes off, despite my injured foot. I didn't want them slowing me down.

Captain Shaw looked over the blueprints he had been given, along with the access codes and a security badge to all levels. Chloe stayed at my side, with Brandon behind us and Miles in front as we made our way through the building and to the elevator. The captain seemed tense, as if this were a hassle and not a threat, as he led the way. Miles was composed but slightly on edge. I assumed he believed me after those beasts attacked last night.

"Is this it?" The captain pointed to the elevator when we got there. The desk that had been there before was no longer there, and no music played.

I nodded, and Captain Shaw scanned a badge and punched in a code from the paper. A humming sound rang as the cables moved the elevator car before the doors quietly slid open. He stepped in while Miles put a foot in front of one of the doors to prevent it from closing.

"It says we are at the lowest level—the basement." Captain Shaw stared at the blueprints.

"Trust me, it's down there." I pulled on the collar of the vest. "The sentinels took the elevator up after us. There has to be a way to make it go down."

"Brandon." Miles waved him over to take his place while he stepped in next to the captain. He bent over to examine the buttons closer. "Six, five, two, B." He hovered his fingers over each one as he said them. "They're significantly worn compared to the others. Captain, what's on those floors?"

The captain shuffled through the papers. "The second floor is offices while six and five are restricted access labs."

"Any other elevators?"

"Yes, three. This appears to be a janitorial elevator," the captain answered.

"Get in." Miles began pressing the buttons. "If the janitors use this elevator more than the researchers, you wouldn't think two of the three would go to labs that only allowed certain personnel."

The captain gave Miles a speculative look when the elevator didn't move. Seconds, later the corner of Miles's mouth twitched as he pressed the emergency stop button. No one questioned him when the elevator began to move and the display showed a downward arrow.

CHAPTER FOURTEEN

Chloe and I shared a glance. We were about to be in the place that had stolen our memories and trapped us into their own order. Shock spread across the captain's face as he drew his gun. Miles and Brandon slowly drew theirs as well, aiming at the ground with their fingers off the triggers. The captain radioed for backup to be on standby and informed them on how to get where we were.

My heart skipped a beat as soon as the elevator stopped. Seconds that seemed like minutes passed before the door opened. It was pitch black—even the emergency lights were off. They pulled out their flashlights and the fluorescent lights bounced off the familiar scarlet red walls and tan carpeting.

"Holy . . ." Brandon's mouth gaped open. In the shadowed light, I could see the captain was just as shocked, but Miles's face remained blank.

"Keep your eyes and ears sharp. Brandon, take the rear," the captain commanded.

Miles pulled out his phone and turned on its flashlight. "Take this." He shoved the phone into my hand. Our eyes met for a moment, his face flickering with apprehension before turning away.

This place should have given me the chills, but it felt familiar and infuriating at the same time. Chloe was tense next to me as anxiety radiated off her.

I expected the solid door at the end of the hallway to be locked, but the captain opened it with ease. A flashlight flickered across Dr. Roulings's door; his plaque had been removed.

"What is it?" Chloe asked, noticing my frown.

"His name. It's not on the door anymore." I pointed the phone light at the door.

"Whose name?" Miles asked.

"Dr. Roulings. I'm pretty sure he ran this place, but no one ever saw him, or at least I never had."

"I'd never heard of him until last night," Chloe said, cringing.

Miles attempted to open the door, but it was locked.

"Mac . . ." Brandon warned as Miles aimed his gun and fired at the lock. Miles slowly pushed open the door as the captain let out a sharp sigh.

It was empty, not just of people, but of any signs that this had been someone's office just yesterday. Random papers littered the floor and the desk was empty, the pictures were crooked on the nails, and the computer was gone. It looked ransacked and not used.

"We have to keep moving," Miles said as everyone looked at the remnants of the office.

"Let's go," the captain said.

We entered the kitchen, which appeared to be the same; they hadn't bothered cleaning up the soot that was caked everywhere. The only things missing were the two sentinels we had tased on our way out.

Our group slowly advanced, making our way through the Vault. It was silent and still. The other doctors' offices were the same as Dr. Roulings's—ransacked and emptied. Only a few pieces of outdated lab equipment remained. I wanted to run to the corridors, but Miles advised that we should clear each room as we went to make sure no one would come from behind us.

After we cleared the gym, I couldn't take it any longer. I needed to see if Liam and Travis were locked in their rooms—if Travis didn't get away. I sprinted, regardless of my name being sternly yet discreetly shouted.

I reached the already-cracked steel door and dragged it

open just enough to fit through. I heard quiet footsteps catching up to me, but gathered who it was and slid through. I didn't know which one was Travis's, but I knew Liam's was around the bend. He had a small picture of a dove on his wall that he had coaxed the sentinels into letting him have. Liam managed to earn respect and trust from most people, and the only reason I knew he had one was because Travis had mocked him for it.

My optimism diminished as I aimed the light into the opened rooms, finding each one empty. I eventually spotted a beautifully painted red dove against a white canvas, but no one was there. The bed was made to look like a person could have been sleeping in it, but the comforter was just fluffed up with a pillow underneath. I walked over and blindly stared at the painting hanging above the bed. They'd taken him, and now I had no clue where he was. I felt pressure starting to build in my chest, crushing everything inside me, the same feeling I'd had when they took Maya.

"Freedom, hope, strength . . . and determination," a voice spoke behind me.

"What?" I absently answered, unsure of what Miles meant.

"The painting." His deep voice was gentle. "The dove represents freedom and hope, where red usually symbolizes strength and determination."

"Oh." That made sense; Liam was strong and determined to get freedom for all of us. I stood up on his bed and grabbed the painting off the wall before sitting down. I was racking my brain for ways to find them, but I had no clue where to begin. Footsteps entered the corridor, and soon beams of light moved along the walls outside Liam's room. Miles took a seat next to me, making sure we weren't touching.

"We'll find them." His eyes were on me, but I kept mine on the painting. I wanted to believe he was a man true to his word, but I couldn't shake my helplessness and my worry about his promise being reneged unintentionally.

Captain Shaw went topside to call in what he'd found. There wasn't cell service in the Vault, and that explained why Dr. Roulings hadn't called to alert the others with a cell phone after Liam shut their communication system down. When the captain came back, he explained that he was going to have the building shut down for the rest of the day and tomorrow. He wanted every inch explored and the corporation to explain what we'd found. There was a mention of finding proof to tie a specific person or group to this before any arrests could be made, but surely there was plenty of proof.

The captain asked Chloe and me if we wanted to wait outside or at the precinct, but we opted to stay. If anything, we could help answer questions. We wandered the tarnished offices and rooms trying to find any leads to where they would have gone, but nothing turned up.

The investigators found that the other exit led to an abandoned building on a vacant street near the Willamette River. It sounded like it was the main entrance, with secure locks, a desk, and coat racks, along with small lockers on the inside. They believed the entryway had been made from the Shanghai Tunnels, and its skeleton could have been used as a building foundation for the Vault.

Brandon filled us in on what the Shanghai Tunnels were, also known as the Old Portland Underground. They were old tunnels underneath the city built in the 1850s that had connected makeshift shacks and basements of hotels and bars that led to the river docks for ease of moving supplies. He dove into details of how they had also been used to find suitable sailormen and for other illegal transporting and abductions. Though it seemed interesting, the story didn't engulf me; my mind was elsewhere.

"Captain, you should see this." An officer beckoned him to follow but paused, glancing at Chloe and me.

"They can come," the captain said.

We followed the officer to the main hallway and stopped in front of an open door.

"There's another main door to this area; this one appears to be a connector." The big metal door with a red *02* on it had completely slipped my mind. I shivered as we walked through, entering an area that had a wall covered with empty, clear display cases.

"Are those finger scanners?" I pointed to the small oval scanner next to each encasement.

"They appear to be," the officer answered without turning around.

That would explain the holes in the thumbs of the sentinels' gloves.

He led us through two more doorways where the metal doors were recessed into the wall. The ground was cold against my feet and my nose wrinkled at the smell of metal and copper. It felt more secure than our side—if that was possible. They didn't bother painting the walls white and everything was pewter to dark grey.

Rooms were lined up like our corridor, but a separate, partially glassed room was near the entrance. It looked like a control room. Inside were a few people I didn't recognize. Chloe and I stayed out while the others went in.

I made my way over to a room and peeked inside. There was a single bed whose legs were chained to the ground with a pillow and comforter tossed on it. A privacy curtain was pulled back, revealing a toilet, sink, and shower in the corner. Surprisingly, the walls were painted a pale blue; it somehow managed to look clean.

Chloe turned from the room she had peered in and looked at me, disturbed by what she saw. We silently headed back over to the control room as a tall woman with black flats and slacks walked out. Her curly black hair shone against her youthful, sepia-bronzed skin.

". . . basis of this investigation." She walked with the same confidence that she carried in her voice.

Miles's eyebrows furrowed when he saw the despair on

my face, making me feel like an open book. He sucked in his lips before waving us in front of him.

"Who's that?" Chloe whispered to Brandon, who followed behind us.

"Agent Katrina Foster. She's with the FBI." Brandon didn't elaborate further as Agent Foster led us to a large lab, ten times the size of Dr. Cole's office. The filing cabinets were emptied with their drawers ajar, and tables seemed to be missing computers and equipment that had probably been taken. On the left side was a glass-celled room with a solo cushioned exam chair with leather restraints.

Agent Foster walked over to the glass wall and tapped on it. "Bulletproof, just like the rest of the glass in here."

If that had held the things that attacked me last night, it only made sense. Those beasts could easily break glass with one punch.

Chloe came over and grabbed my hand, surprising me with the contact. She was starting to figure out what was unraveling in my head. This was our next place to be sent . . . where the other Jects were sent . . . where Maya had been sent. They were prepared, which meant they'd known what we were changing into, and I believed it was on purpose.

Frustration rivaled in me. I gently squeezed Chloe's hand before letting go and walking over to the glass. I slammed my fists against it, letting the anger run loose as my chest tightened and my hair stood on end. Reflecting off the glass in front of me were two vibrant blue eyes. I leaned back, realizing the eyes belonged to me.

I kept my fists against the glass and closed my eyes, taking deep slow breaths. I knew everyone was watching, and had to calm down. After a few breaths, I opened my eyes to see the reflection of my light brown eyes. I needed to get out of there, regardless of whether I had just imagined that.

I turned, nearly bumping into Miles. I'd been so focused on calming myself down that I hadn't realized he was standing right behind me.

"Let's get the two of you out of here." Miles stepped aside and waved me forward.

We left with the same group we went in with. Once we got to the lobby on the main floor, a well-dressed man with an officer was waiting for us. The man, wearing a tailored dark-blue business suit and burgundy tie, strode toward us while the officer stayed put. His black hair was slicked back and his face was freshly shaved. Something about him told me to run the other way.

"Captain Shaw, I apologize we could not meet sooner." The man held out his hand. "I'm Harrison Smith, CEO of Westbrook." The captain merely glanced down at his hand and then back to the tailored man.

"Mr. Smith." The captain's voice was hard. "I am showing these two ladies out, and then I have questions for you." Captain Shaw went to walk past, but Harrison spoke quickly.

"I know you are wondering if Westbrook is involved with any illicit activities. I can assure you we have no such occurrences or allegations. I am just as perplexed as you and your colleagues. I knew there were possibly tunnels and an old subway station below us, but I had no knowledge that the old shafts connected to our building. I searched the records from when we purchased the building twelve years ago, and nothing was found."

Subway station? It looked nothing like a subway station!

"And I suppose you know nothing about the holding cells down there, or the elevator, either?" Captain Shaw asked.

"Of course not," Harrison scoffed. "The security footage has already been turned in."

"We will review that closely. Now, if you excuse me, I will be back shortly." The captain ushered us past him.

"I know you," I whispered and turned around. "I don't really know you, but I recognize you."

"I'm sure you do. I am widely involved in the community and often at public conferences." He flashed his white teeth.

"I've seen you in the Vault," I recalled.

Harrison raised an eyebrow over my shoulder, but the captain didn't respond.

"You're a suit." I smiled inwardly; the captain was going to let me talk. "I see right through you. I know who you are and you know who I am," I sneered. "That means you must also know what you turned us into." I had to believe that I was changing in some way I didn't understand.

"I am genuinely concerned about her health." He tilted his head to the side, eyeing me up and down.

I ignored him and continued. "You will be caught and you will pay. Tell Dr. Cole I say hi." I turned to walk out the door but paused and spoke over my shoulder. "Oh, and tell Dr. Roulings I'll be meeting him soon."

I could hear a part of the conversation behind me.

"She is the most psychotic person I have ever met." Harrison's voice rattled in my ears as I pushed open the door.

"Don't confuse psychosis with enmity." Miles's deep voice floated through the door before it shut.

CHAPTER FIFTEEN

Miles and Brandon returned to the car damp from the rain after doing a perimeter sweep of the log cabin. Chloe and I grabbed our new duffle bags, which were full of clothes we had bought at an outlet store on the way, while they grabbed the groceries. Miles had implied that work was paying for it, and I hoped he wasn't lying.

The captain had wanted us to stay somewhere off the grid, seeing how they weren't afraid to attack the precinct. Miles explained that the cabin was self-sufficient and supplied its own power and water. It was an hour's drive from the city, and we had arrived late in the afternoon.

Midway to the house, I stopped before closing my eyes and tilting my head back. Warm droplets landed on my face as the smell of evergreens and rain filtered through my nose, relaxing me.

A moment later I forced my eyes open; the three of them were staring at me. Chloe was grinning from ear to ear as she skipped over and linked her arm through mine. Her movement took me off guard, but I strode with her toward the cabin regardless. She was not as used to the no-touching rule in the Vault as I was. When I first briefly met Chloe after conditioning one day, she'd seemed shy and nervous. I had noticed in the last twenty-four hours that I had pegged her wrong.

The inside of the cabin was quaint, and the woodwork was beautiful, with its exposed log walls. A musky odor filled the air from the lack of inhabitance, but not from being dirty.

The living room connected to the kitchen and had a small TV with a DVD player, along with a green rug situated between the furniture.

"It used to be the captain's family hunting cabin. Seeing how no one except him hunts anymore or uses the cabin, it works perfectly for a safe house." Miles set the bags on the small island.

"Man, you bought enough food to feed an army." Chloe walked over and picked up two loaves of bread.

"Brandon is like feeding an army," Miles joked.

"Hey, a man's got to eat." Brandon leaned against the counter.

He reminded me a lot of Travis, with a little less joking, and Chloe was starting to remind me of Maya, except less edgy and less wild. That explained the fairly comfortable feeling I had about being with them, but I still couldn't shake the aching in my heart. I was going to be safe while my friends were still out there under Dr. Roulings's control. No amount of arguing about staying in the city had changed Miles's mind. They said I was stubborn, but he was worse.

"Are you taking the car back to the city?" I asked Miles. He planned to head back to assist with the investigation.

"No. There needs to be a car here, so I'm going to be dropped off. We're all going to meet the captain later so you guys aren't left here alone."

Brandon was going to stay to keep an eye on us instead of an FBI agent. Apparently, their hands were full, and the captain had allowed it even though it was technically out of their jurisdiction. He now believed my statement and was going to help Chloe and me while the FBI managed things.

Our room was down a hallway next to the bathroom and had a bunk bed, along with a separate twin. When I grabbed my duffle, I felt something hard. That was odd—I had only bought clothes. I opened the duffle and pulled out the red dove painting, my jaw dropping. Someone must have grabbed it from Liam's room.

I gently hung it on a nail across from where I would sleep. I held back tears before setting aside charcoal-colored athletic capris with orange lining, a vibrant multi-colored workout tank, and a bright pink sports bra. I'd wanted something that wasn't plain grey, black, or white, but had no clue what to get, so I'd gotten similar-style clothes. Chloe had helped pick out a couple pairs of jeans and nice shirts for me also. Shopping for shoes was the hardest part; I didn't want any.

The hours passed slowly until we were piling into the black car. The sun was almost down, and with the grey clouds, it was getting dark quickly.

"Is this your car?" Chloe asked Miles as he turned the key.

"Nope, it's mine," Brandon chimed from the passenger seat.

"Oh. Why's he driving then?" Chloe tugged at her seatbelt to loosen it.

Brandon grinned at Miles. "Yeah, Mac, that's a good question, isn't it?" Miles's eyes rolled in the rearview mirror as Brandon turned in his seat to face us. "You see, he can be a bit of a control freak. But I do admit"—he turned back around—"he is a great chauffeur on the weekends."

"If you didn't constantly get drunk, you wouldn't need one," Miles interjected.

"I'm not drinking now, am I?" Brandon smirked.

Miles's tone lightened. "Trust me, you guys don't want him driving. This is his third car in two years."

"For a cop, I'd think you'd have a better track record," I teased.

"Hey, I am not a bad driver. Just a deer magnet." Brandon defended himself.

"Deer in the city?" Chloe laughed.

"There can be deer in the city, and I'm not always in the city," Brandon countered.

We shared a few laughs, and shortly after, silence filled the car until we arrived at a vacant parking lot to an abandoned factory. Rust coated the metal towers and pipes surrounding an old brick building that was five stories tall with shattered windows. The captain was already waiting outside a black SUV. Must be they liked black vehicles.

Miles got out and leaned into the open driver's-side window. "I'll be back in a few days. Brandon knows how to get a hold of me." He stood up and glanced at Brandon, who was already walking around the front of the car. "I'll make sure I don't have a tail when I come back. You do the same." Brandon nodded and climbed into the driver's seat.

When we got back to the cabin, I decided to head to bed. Chloe came in shortly after and we stayed up talking. She was hesitant to ask but wanted to know what I knew about the Vault. I didn't want to talk about it, but I knew she was curious, so I did. She asked how many years my friends and I each were there for, and even questioned what had happened to Frank. I honestly had no clue and wasn't sure if I wanted to know. She too admitted that she was worried she could have ended up like him.

* * *

A day had already passed, and I lasted an hour sitting on the deck the next morning before I couldn't take being trapped in my head. The guilt of being there was eating at me. I decided to go for a quick run and tiptoed back inside, careful not to wake Brandon, who was sleeping on the couch. There was another bedroom off the living room, but he wanted to be on guard. He'd been staying up late, but couldn't possibly be awake 24/7. I left a small note on the counter saying I left for a run at seven thirty and would be back shortly. They would probably still be asleep when I got back.

I had run for about twenty minutes when I decided to turn around. On my way back, I heard rushing water and followed the noise to a small stream. The stream weaved around lush vegetation and its water danced around rocks. I told myself I could spare ten minutes to let myself enjoy the beauty and climbed down onto a rock sticking out of the water. I bent down and reached my hand out, letting the cool water rush around it. A surge of energy traveled down my arm and to my hand as blue electric bolts sprang from my palm and into the water.

I gasped, quickly pulling back my hand. The majority of the energy dissipated but still lingered. *What was that?* I touched the water again, but nothing happened. I closed my eyes and reached for the energy that had grazed the surface of my chest. I felt it rise and willed it to my hand. When I opened my eyes, the bolts were back.

Electric blue eyes stared back at me in the reflection of the water. They faded quickly and returned to their normal brown hue as the bolts vanished from my palm. The other times I had felt this energy, I'd been angry. When I felt the water, I wasn't angry; it felt tonic. I continued downstream, exploring my new ability, and was able to produce small sparks from my hands. Could Liam do this?

I was so engulfed in attempting to summon it that I had not realized how far I had traveled from the path, and the sun had risen quite a bit. *Crap.* I followed the river back upstream and stopped once I recognized the area I'd come through. Once I reached the path, I started in a sprint downhill toward the cabin.

"Harper!" Chloe called as soon as I was out of the forest. She ran to me from the back deck and hugged me, almost knocking me over. "For crying out loud, I thought they caught you!"

"No, I'm fine. I just went for a run." I glanced over her shoulder and saw Brandon emerge from the side of the cabin, relief flooding his face. He stopped walking and pulled out his phone.

"They aren't happy with you." Chloe pulled away and briefly glanced at Brandon, who was already dialing. "And wow, you are red." We had lain out in the sun yesterday, and my Vault-dweller skin wasn't fond of it.

"Well, I'm fine. They'll live." I noticed her skin was slightly pink, but nothing compared to mine.

"I'm not worried about them. You should've seen Miles. Definitely the last man on earth I'd want to piss off, and that's including Adam."

"At least he's . . ." Her words gravitated back to me. "Should have seen? As in, he's here?"

"Yeah. He'll probably be back any minute." She glanced at the woods behind me.

I glanced behind me. "He's out there?"

"He went out there as soon as he got here. He said he'd try to find a trail to follow." She sheepishly smiled.

"When did you get the note?"

"Brandon woke me up around eight. He waited a little longer before he called Miles." She tucked her shoulder-length hair behind her ear as Brandon joined us.

"What time is it?" I asked before Brandon could lecture me.

"Ten thirty." Brandon glared at me for a moment. "Come here." His face relaxed as he hugged me. I appreciated his concern, but decided I'd had enough hugs to last me a month or even a year. Despite Chloe's constant hugging, I wasn't completely used to it, and Brandon had just met me two days ago.

"It can't be ten thirty already!" I pulled away. I couldn't have been gone for three hours.

"What happened to your short run that you knew you weren't supposed to do anyway? Are you all right?" Brandon asked.

"I'm fine—just lost track of time. Sorry." I felt bad for worrying them, but I didn't feel bad for going for a run.

"All right, let's go sit. Mac is going to be . . . concerned."

I had a feeling *concerned* hadn't been Brandon's first choice of word.

CHAPTER SIXTEEN

"Where did he get that?" I asked as the hum of an engine roared, and Miles appeared at the edge of the forest on a red four-wheeler.

"The shed." Brandon pointed to the other side of the cabin at the run-down shed.

"Oh." I hadn't realized anything like that was in there.

Miles parked the four-wheeler short of the deck and quickly hoisted himself off. Along with his scowl, he wore a dark-brown leather jacket, which opened up to a sea-green T-shirt.

"He's livid." Chloe gave me a sympathetic arm squeeze and got up to go inside.

"He took most of it out on me already. Maybe you can use some of that secret charisma you got going on him," Brandon said as he winked and followed Chloe inside.

I stood. Had they seriously just left me alone, and why did it feel like I was about to be reprimanded? We weren't in the Vault, and I wasn't a child. I was prepared to stand up for myself, but as Miles strode up the stairs, a lump formed in my throat. He stopped on the first step and stared at me. His eyes scanned me, and I was positive he noticed my lobster sunburn. He finally took a deep breath and walked up the rest of the way.

"Brandon said you looked fine. Are you okay?" He was holding back. I swallowed and nodded. "You think it's okay to go for a run alone after you were specifically told not to go anywhere without Brandon?"

I glanced at the knots in the wood at my feet before glaring at him. "I'm not sorry I went for a run, but I am sorry I lost track of time."

"'Lost track of time?' You don't even have a watch!" His voice rose as he pointed at my wrist. "You can't just run off without someone with you. Those . . ." He put a hand on his hip and rubbed the back of his neck with the other. "People are after you."

"I can take care of myself." If only he knew what I was doing.

"You disobeyed direct orders." He started pacing. "*SNAFU.* You're so perverse."

"What does that even mean?" I guessed the last part insinuated my lack of listening. "You know what, I don't care. I can come and go as I please. I'm not a prisoner." I turned to go inside but stopped when my hand reached the doorknob. I didn't want to be in tight quarters, and I was not about to shut myself in my room like a child. I dropped my hand and brushed past him, striding down the steps.

There was nowhere to sit, but a small tree in the backyard caught my attention. I had no memory of climbing a tree, but a small urge made me feel like trying. I walked over and jumped up to reach a sturdy branch. After hoisting myself up, I found a perfect spot to sit two branches up. I guess climbing the tree was still childish, but at least I felt better outside.

The tree started shaking, and the next thing I knew, Miles was standing on a branch diagonally below me so his face was level with mine. His jawline twitched through his stubble, and his fresh scent of pine and leather mixed with the tree's earthy smell.

"Seriously, you had to follow me up here?" I grunted.

"Situation normal, all F'd up," Miles calmly said.

"What?" I looked over at him.

"SNAFU." He sighed. "You're not a prisoner. We're just trying to keep you both safe. And I know you can take care of yourself. It's just dangerous, as you've seen." His dark hazel eyes held mine.

"What have I seen?" I averted my gaze from his.

"I'm guessing the same thing as me."

"I don't know exactly what I saw, but it wasn't human." I looked up to study his face for a reaction, but it didn't change. I may as well get on with it because he wasn't going to. "I haven't seen anything like it before, except . . . a friend."

"Your friend?" His hazel eyes lightened.

"Yes. He stayed back to help another Ject. The last time I saw him," I said, his cat eyes and animal-like features flashing across my mind, "he looked different. I thought I had imagined it until later that night, when those . . . beasts attacked the precinct." I shuddered at the memory of being pinned against the cell bars with their hard grips.

"I saw them too." He searched my face for something else.

"Did you see anything besides that?"

He studied me a little longer. "You don't just lose track of three hours."

Warmth radiated from his arm only inches away, and I slid my hand over, not wanting to unintentionally zap him. I held out my far hand from Miles with my palm upward.

I took a deep breath and focused. Despite our fight, his presence had the opposite effect on me than I thought it would have. My head was clear of everything else as the energy built and my chest fluttered. I summoned the electricity that dully pulsed through my veins, and it danced along my fingertips as small sparks appeared.

After a few seconds, the sparks disappeared, along with the energy. I pulled my hand back to my chest, afraid to see the revulsion on Miles's face.

"That's what I saw." A comforting smile formed at the edges of his mouth. "Except there was more. It surged all around you in a blinding hazy-blue dome. If you were outside, it would have been seen a mile away—like lightning in the dark sky." He held my gaze. I was at a loss for words as my heart slowed at his calm and benevolent response.

"I'm afraid of what it is," I admitted.

"We're often afraid of things we don't understand." He held out his hand for mine, which was holding the branch. I pulled my other hand away from my chest to support myself and hesitantly gave him my previously injured hand. Goosebumps rose on the back of my neck at his contact. "At least it seems to be in good hands."

My hand was only wrapped to hide the quickness with which it was healing, but I couldn't bring myself to pull it away.

"Your neck. What happened?" Miles began to unravel the bandage.

"An unfortunate mishap. I don't really want to talk about it." The small scar where Maya had put the switchblade to my neck was something I wasn't ready to open up about. He didn't pursue it any further as he continued to unwrap the bandage.

I jumped at the sound of the back door slamming, almost losing my grip.

"Easy." Miles's hand shot out to steady me, and he quickly retreated it once I was stable.

Brandon walked out holding his phone as he scanned the backyard. "Mac! The captain's on the phone." A couple of branches swayed, shaking the leaves as Miles dropped to the ground. "What were you doing up there?" Brandon glanced up at me and then grinned at Miles, who grumbled as he grabbed the phone. "Never mind. Don't answer that."

At least I didn't have to explain that I had no clue how my hand was healing so quickly. I climbed down and stood next to Brandon while Miles talked on the phone just out of listening range. The back door opened again and Chloe walked out.

"I see you're still alive." She smirked as she came to stand next to us.

"He's not so scary after all," I replied. He had a big heart; he just hid it.

"If only I knew your secret." Brandon winked at me.

My heart skipped a beat; had he seen what I did in the tree?

"You just have to be Harper," Chloe jabbed.

"I guess so. There's only ever been one other girl who could tame that man: his grandmother." Brandon shook his head. He couldn't have seen what I had done, or else he wouldn't have been so calm.

Miles walked back over, handed the phone to Brandon, and pulled him aside.

"The captain just wanted an update." Miles read the question on my face when they returned. We hadn't received any news on them pinpointing a specific person, or any leads about where our friends were. "I'll also be staying until tomorrow."

"Well, I'm going to go shower." Part of me was thrilled to have him stay, but another part of me was agitated, because it was to keep an eye on me.

"Harper?" Chloe ran to my side as I started toward the cabin. She looked down, rubbing her palms together. "I was thinking, before you showered, could you please help me train?"

"What? I thought you wanted nothing to do with any of that?" I questioned her.

"Umm, well I want to be ready. While you were out there, I couldn't help but think, what if they had come for us and captured you? I want to be prepared." She looked down at her hands.

"If you want, but I'm not the best teacher." That was Liam's territory. I felt a slight pang in my chest at the thought of him.

"You taught well during training, and are amazing at fighting. I'm screwed if they attack." She thought more highly of my teaching skills than I did.

"You don't give yourself enough credit. You put up multiple good fights when we escaped." I gave her a reassuring smile as Miles and Brandon hovered behind us. "I guess I could use a good fight anyways." I winked at her.

She happily ran inside to change and came back out wearing athletic shorts and a loose tank-top, which I assumed were the only workout clothes she had picked out.

"Are you guys going to full-on fight?" Brandon asked as we found a flat, grassy area. He wasn't thrilled.

"I have to see what her strengths and weaknesses are. Then we can learn and adjust." Liam had always done that with me, but, after five years together, he'd already known what mine were.

"Mac, you don't think this is a good idea?" Brandon stared at Miles, hoping he would agree.

Miles shrugged. "It can't hurt to be prepared. Just be careful." He stared at me when he said that last part. I didn't see myself getting angry or in a life-or-death situation with Chloe, so I shouldn't have to worry about zapping her.

I bent down and took my sneakers off before tossing them aside, catching a few smirks as I did.

"Old habits die hard." Maybe one day I would get used to shoes.

"Screw it." Chloe took hers off also.

"You ready?" I looked at Chloe as her laughter faded and her lips pursed. "What's wrong?"

"There's no boundary." She pointed to where a ring normally would have been in the Vault.

"There's no boundary out here either." I thought of Adam; he had said something similar in the match where I'd almost killed him. I hate to say it, but he had been right and was always grooming us for the outside world.

She nodded in realization. "Okay, let's start."

I advanced on her, going for the typical chokehold. I got my arm almost wrapped around her neck when she slipped an arm between mine and pushed it down. Her leg swooped out in an attempt to get me off balance, but I easily dodged.

This time I attacked with a punch. She had barely dodged it when I attacked again but with my other fist. She missed her block, causing a light blow to her body. She tottered backward and grabbed her stomach. I gave her an apologetic nod, asking if she was okay. She nodded and smiled. She knew I was taking it easy and was nowhere close to the unnecessary training that Adam had inflicted.

We went back and forth, keeping her mostly on defense until I pinned her. I stood up and reached for her hand to help her off the ground. I would increase the level the more we trained until she was ready for me not to hold back. Hopefully, by then, she wouldn't need to fight.

"That was good. We need to work on utilizing your weak side and speed. I use my speed to my advantage, but there are a lot faster and stronger"—I glanced at Miles—"things out there." The images of the unbelievably strong and quick beasts emerged in my head. I wanted to tell her, but now wasn't the time. I had freaked her out enough today with my run.

"Remind me why I'm here?" Chloe and I turned our heads to Brandon, who looked flabbergasted.

"Because I trust you." Miles grinned and patted him on his back.

"What? You don't think you're a better fighter?" Chloe mused. "Let's keep this training going. We learned how to disarm someone, but never learned how to shoot." Chloe grinned, eyeing Brandon's hip, where his gun was.

"Nope." Brandon waved his hands.

"Come on, please?" Chloe took a few steps toward him. "Mac, some help?"

Miles shrugged. "It might be a good idea."

"Not with our work guns, it's not." Brandon's voice rose. I thought Miles would have been the hesitant one, not

Brandon. But, after seeing what Miles saw, maybe he thought a little differently about things now.

"We don't have to. There's plenty here." Miles headed to the cabin.

"I thought you said those are in case of an emergency." Brandon followed right behind him as Chloe and I tagged along.

"The captain won't mind. Plus, the majority of them are mine." Once inside the cabin, Miles walked over to the area between the living room and kitchen. He pushed aside part of the green rug and opened a hatch that led to stairs.

CHAPTER SEVENTEEN

Miles emerged from the hidden cellar with a huge black duffle that you could fit a body in and carried it outside with ease. He dropped the bag on the grass and knelt. My eyes went wide when he unzipped it. There were several handguns and a few rifles, with multiple boxes of ammo.

"You knew about the cellar and the guns?" Chloe asked Brandon.

"Yeah." Brandon shrugged. "What's a safe house without a good hiding spot and protection?"

Miles handed us eye protection and headgear while Brandon walked inside to find things to use as targets.

"This is such a bad idea," Brandon said under his breath when he came out with cardboard boxes and water bottles.

"Have either of you ever shot a gun?" Miles looked at us as we both shook our heads no. We had only shot the tasers. "I'll show you how they operate, and after we're done, you'll clean them."

Seemed fair enough. Miles walked through how to properly use and hold each gun and made sure we knew all the safety rules. They were very similar to the tasers the sentinels had, except less modern and more deadly.

"I'll have you shoot three handguns, ten rounds each." His head shot down toward one of the bottles. His right hand, which held the gun, twitched at his side. He looked like he was about to lift it to shoot, but instead, he turned to Brandon. "Do you mind showing them?"

"Not at all." Brandon kept a straight face as he took

the gun and shot it using the same technique that Miles had explained: a steady stance with both hands on the gun and relaxed shoulders. All three of his shots hit the center of a water bottle.

"Any questions?" Miles asked. Chloe and I shook our heads. "Okay, who's up?"

"I'll try." Chloe beamed.

Miles handed her one of the guns and took a step back. She took a couple of shots at a different water bottle and missed both times.

"You're trying too hard. Relax," Miles advised her before she shot again.

"You don't seem very chipper about this." I moved closer to Brandon.

"Just confused." His eyebrows furrowed.

"With what?"

"With Mac. I mean, he's all for people having guns for protection and knowing how to use them, but he's not one to go out of his way to give lessons, especially to strangers who are—" He stopped talking.

"'Who are' what?" I raised an eyebrow at him, but he didn't answer. "We're going to grab some water; we'll be right back," I yelled to Chloe and Miles, knowing that it would be hard for them to hear me with the headgear on. I turned away from Miles's sharp glance and mouthed at Brandon to follow.

Once inside, we pulled our headgear down around our necks. I grabbed four water bottles from the fridge, handing two of them to Brandon. "All right, talk."

"Mac's going to kill me." Brandon waved the water bottles in the air. "The security footage of the attack on the precinct is ironically missing, and no one could identify their attackers. The FBI agent you met, Agent Katrina Foster? Her superiors are questioning whether it's been a waste of resources, despite everything they've found. Harrison Smith lawyered up—which was to be expected—and is saying the delay in their research cost them hundreds of thousands of dollars. Agent Foster's rebutting and has been working with Mac to find solid evidence that can hold up in court. The captain told him to take today off, which is why he wasn't in uniform this morning."

"How could there not be evidence? We're evidence!" I tried to wrap my head around what he had just said. Miles had filled me in on what the other officers had seen the night of the attack. I understood how Steven wasn't able to identify the beasts—I wouldn't know how to either—and the other two hadn't seen what hit them. The one had heard a noise and readied his gun, but barely remembered it going off as something struck him from behind.

Brandon looked down at the water bottles in his hand. "They can't find either of you in our system—or anyone you've mentioned—and are questioning your credibility. There's nothing on that abandoned place, even with all the equipment left behind. They can't specifically tie it to Westbrook or a person, and are saying it could be a bunker from World War II or an unethical experimental lab during the mid-twentieth century."

"With all the lab equipment?" Some of it had to be newer.

"It sounds like a cover-up." He let out a sigh.

"By who? The government?" I didn't get a response.

The entire Vault was evidence, but how could you fight the FBI, if they were the law? I felt defeated, and the defeat instantly spiked to anger as my hands clenched the water bottles at my side. Why hadn't Miles told me?

"Hey," Brandon said, gently slapping one of the bottles on my shoulder, "we're fighting for you guys. You have a captain and an FBI agent on your side; I don't think they can sweep this under the rug. Let's get back out there before Mac thinks we ditched his training session."

I put on the headgear and took a few breaths to calm down as I followed him outside. Miles shot us a questioning glance, but I ignored it. Chloe was on her last gun, and when she shot her last bullet, she squealed with triumph as the bottle ripped off the nail and flew away from the tree. She handed the gun to Miles and walked our way.

"You're up." Chloe brushed past my shoulder.

"That wasn't too bad." Brandon smiled.

"Pretty decent, huh?" She grinned.

I took a deep breath and walked over to Miles. I took the gun, trying to hide my anger and irritation. He studied me, but I disregarded him. I steadied my feet and aimed. Miles stepped in after I shot a few rounds and helped. My aim improved, but it still wasn't great.

After we were done with our lesson and cleaning the guns, I showered and ate lunch outside with the others.

"I have to run to the store; did you want to come with me?" Miles stood and reached his hand out to take my plate after I finished. I didn't realize he was specifically talking to me at first.

"Sure." I stood, grabbing my own plate. "I'll follow you in."

His jaw twitched as he looked at me before turning to the others.

"Do you guys need anything while I'm out?" he asked as he took Brandon and Chloe's plate.

"Ice cream! And popcorn!" Chloe practically danced in her chair.

"You can't go wrong with either of those." Brandon laughed.

"What kind?" Miles couldn't hide a small grin at her excitement.

"Umm." Chloe tapped her chin. "Make it a surprise."

Miles nodded and I followed him inside.

"I'd put jeans on." He eyed my athletic shorts.

"I thought it went well with my Oregon shirt." My joke fell flat as I tried to hide my irritation about him keeping things from me.

"We shouldn't have any issues. I'm a decent driver." His

lip curved upward into a smile that was inviting yet daunting. If I were to smile like that, I would just look weird.

I wasn't sure what he meant until I realized he had probably brought his motorcycle, and thought about asking if we could use Brandon's car. But I could use the thrill as a distraction, and quickly changed into jeans and tossed on a grey jacket before following him out the door. He unsnapped a second helmet hanging on the back of his motorcycle and handed it to me.

"When did you get a second helmet?" I asked, recalling that the first night we had met, he'd only had one.

"It's been in my closet."

I wondered if he'd purposely brought it for me or if I was reading into it too much.

He shrugged his jacket off. "You should wear this."

"No, I'm okay." I held up a hand. "I'm plenty warm in my jacket."

"It's for protection." He kept his jacket held out.

I sighed and took it, not wanting to argue. I put on the jacket and was instantly greeted by its comfort and leather-mixed-with-pine redolence. I rolled my eyes at my fluttering stomach. *Get a grip; it's just a man's jacket.* I had only met him a few days ago and was acting like a freshman with a crush on a senior in high school. I guess I really wouldn't have had the chance to know what that felt like.

The ride was exhilarating, and the energy surged through me like a current of contained, electrical adrenaline.

"Have fun?" Miles smiled at the joy in my face as we got off. I almost lied, but then realized I didn't need to.

"I felt the energy rush through me, like when I touched the water on my run. The water seemed to lift the energy." My smile quickly faded as I remembered he hadn't been entirely honest with me. "We should hurry."

I brushed past him, trying to shove down my anger the best I could. My temper had been better since escaping the Vault, but sometimes it was still hard to control my emotions.

I had every right to be mad, but my anger felt like it was about to burst. Miles took the lead inside the store as I silently followed, not knowing what we came for, besides ice cream and popcorn. Soon we were on our way back home, and the ride wasn't as enjoyable after my mood had darkened.

I lay in bed later that night, staring at the dove painting. Freedom. I'd just had ice cream while watching a movie, a result of being free, and yet I didn't feel liberated. My friends weren't free, and I was trapped in a safe house. Despite being irritated with Miles, it felt better with him around. It almost made it easier to forget, but the guilt still crushed me.

If nothing happened soon with the investigation, I would sneak off and search for them on my own.

* * *

My nose wrinkled at the smell of coffee as I quietly made my way outside to the porch. They hadn't supplied us with any in the Vault, and, to be honest, I was all right with that. Coffee didn't smell appealing to me. Miles was on the swing with a coffee mug in hand, wearing a black T-shirt and grey sweatpants. Even in what should have been a vulnerable state, he still managed to look impervious.

"You're up early," I noted.

"I could say the same to you." He took a sip of his coffee and slid over, gesturing to the spot next to him.

I would have preferred sitting in a chair by myself, but talking from across the porch might wake Brandon or Chloe.

"Coffee?" he asked.

"No, thank you." I shivered as the thought of warmth sounded good on this chilly and foggy morning.

"Are you cold?"

"I'm fine. It's summer, right?" I smiled.

He grunted. "Sure. Doesn't mean it's always warm at six in the morning."

"I'm used to seventy-two, no matter the season or time of day," I said flatly.

"True." He glanced sideways at me. "Our run will warm you up."

My eyebrows pinched together. "What?"

"What else would I have bought these clothes and sneakers for yesterday?" He looked down as he swirled his coffee mug. "Can't have you running off again, so I figured we'd go together. I'll come up every day and we can run." He peered over at me. "Do you have the phone on you?"

"No." Miles had bought Chloe and I each a phone yesterday.

"You should always have it on you, even if you're just sitting out here."

"Fine." I guess it made sense if they needed to get a hold of me, but it wasn't like I could call anyone quickly enough if it were a true emergency.

"When I finish this, we can go." He took a big sip.

"I'll go change." I snuck into the bedroom and grabbed the phone along with clothes to take to the bathroom. When I was done, I met Miles outside. He was stretching on the grass, his coffee cup nowhere in sight.

"You drank your coffee fast," I commented.

"Just my morning ritual."

I stood next to him and started stretching. "Do you add anything to it?"

"No." He shook his head. Brandon usually added a pinch of sugar and creamer, while Chloe apparently loved coffee, too, but added a lot of both. "Ready?"

I nodded as I finished stretching my hamstrings. We started jogging at a steady pace for about fifteen minutes until we came to a clearing. Fog floated across the large open space, with muted-grey pine trees lining the edge in the distance.

"It's breathtaking." The darkness and fog should have felt eerie, but it was scenic, like we were in a movie.

"I figured it's the perfect place to practice." Miles stepped next to me.

"You want me to practice, with my power?" My eyes widened. "Here?"

"Why not? No one is around and there's plenty of space." He looked at the field as he put his hands in his pockets.

"I don't know." I wasn't sure if practicing my power in front of him was a good idea, whether it was because I could hurt him or because it would be embarrassing. "Why do you want me to practice?"

"It seems like you need to release energy, and you should learn how to control it to protect yourself." He cocked his head to the side. "I promise I'm only trying to help."

Normally, I would question an ulterior motive, but I had faith in him—even if he wasn't filling me in on everything. I shoved that aside; now was time to focus on my ability. I was more relaxed when he was around, and releasing the energy was cathartic.

"I'll try it." I walked out farther into the clearing, excited yet nervous I would fail.

Miles followed but stayed a good distance back at my request. I closed my eyes and took a deep breath, calling forward the static that dully hummed in my veins and burned in my nerves. Hot, prickly energy flowed to my fingertips, and I opened my eyes to see blue radiating from each finger. I turned to Miles, beaming. The static fluttered until I could feel myself straining to keep it going. It was like holding something heavy, when your arms become so fatigued that you start to lose it.

The energy became easier to call as I kept practicing, but began to fade as time passed. After what felt like an hour of practicing, I was exhausted. The fatigue from yesterday's adventure didn't help, either, and Miles intervened when he noticed my exhaustion.

"I'm in uncharted waters here, but that looked like decent control to me." The corner of Miles's mouth curved upward into a smile. How could a stranger's smile seem so familiar and slow time? I guess he wasn't really a stranger anymore.

Miles started walking back toward the cabin.

"Why didn't you shoot yesterday?" I followed, relieved he didn't start jogging.

"Brandon loves to show off, so I figured I'd let him."

I shot him a glance but wasn't going to question his odd answer. Brandon didn't really want us to shoot yesterday, so I doubt he would have wanted to show off.

Miles sighed when I didn't respond. "I can't show how to hold a gun properly. I have nerve damage in my right arm. Anything ninety degrees or higher, my arm tremors." He stopped walking and held his right arm straight out. Sure enough, his whole arm started trembling, most of it affecting his hand. He looked up from his hand to me and quickly lowered it, rubbing his shoulder.

"Does it hurt?"

"It's acceptable." He smiled and started walking again.

"Is that why you're no longer in the Navy?" *Crap.* I quickly threw my hand over my mouth. "I'm so sorry. That was not supposed to come out." Brandon had accidentally mentioned it in conversation the other night, and I guess my exhaustion made me more of an oaf.

He let out a small chuckle before his eyes glossed over as if his mind were replaying a memory. "Yes." His voice was hoarse but softened. "I see you've talked to Brandon."

I nodded and didn't let any other rash questions or comments slip out of my mouth the rest of the walk.

CHAPTER EIGHTEEN

The sun soaked my skin and clothes as I lay next to Chloe on the blanket covering the deck. This had been our ritual the last few days after training and showering. Thankfully, my fair skin didn't burn as easily after my first sunburn a week and a half ago, when we'd first arrived. The peeling and raw skin had healed quickly, and I had stopped wearing fake bandages a few days ago on my hand and foot.

"Hey, guys, can you come in for a moment?" Brandon shouted out the glass sliding door and was back inside before Chloe and I could even turn our heads.

Chloe looked at me and I shrugged as we went inside.

"Okay, they're here." Brandon pulled his phone away from his ear. A few beeps went off and he handed me the phone. I went to put it to my ear but stopped when I saw Miles's face on the screen.

"Oh, hi." I blushed as Chloe peeked over my shoulders. I leaned my arms against the counter to give her a better view. Miles's growing scruff peppered his sharp jawline, and he had dark circles under his eyes. He'd been more exhausted each day I saw him the past week. "Are you okay?"

I was still angry with him for hiding things from me, but I felt bad that he was burned-out trying to help Chloe and me. Brandon had told him that I knew, and Miles had said he was trying to wait until he had good news to go with it before saying anything more. Good news had never come.

"I just have a couple of questions for you guys. Mostly you." He was in his uniform, and in the background, I could make out the desks from the precinct. "You mentioned you had a friend named Travis in the Vault, right?"

"Yes?" I squeezed the phone tighter. I had also told him my friend who I saw change was Liam.

"And I believe you mentioned a Frank, also?" He had listened that night I gave my statement—I hadn't mentioned Frank since then.

"Yes? Are they okay?" My foot tapped on the ground.

"A blond teenaged male and an older gentleman came into the precinct last night, asking about you and Chloe." His lips moved, but my brain took a moment to process what he'd said.

"And they're okay? Travis is okay?" I finally blurted.

"Yes, they're both okay," Miles said.

I looked at Chloe. "He made it out!"

"Harper?"

I recognized the voice and quickly looked back down at the phone. "Travis!"

"Hello." A quirky grin outshined the bags under his eyes as he waved to us. "I hear you two have been living it up?" *Same old Travis.*

"I'm happy you're okay! What happened? How did you get away?" Relief washed over me at the sight of him.

"You know me; I don't let people decide what I do," Travis boasted, and I decided not to mention the fact that he had been imprisoned in the Vault for almost three years. "So, really, where are you guys? Boss over here tells me you guys are safe, but wouldn't tell me anything else."

"Yeah, we're okay and somewhere we wouldn't be found. They came looking for me when I was at the precinct." I cringed at the thought. "Honestly, I didn't think the police believed me until then. Or even if most of them do now."

"Well, screw them." Travis's face became serious. "Did they hurt you when they attacked?"

"Not really." I remembered the jolting pain of being thrown into the bars and them pinning me. "You know me"—I forced a wink—"I don't give up easily in a fight. Miles showed up too."

"Have the cops been treating you good?"

"Yes, they both have been exceptional," I answered, glancing at Brandon. "You need to meet this one here; you guys are too much alike."

"Are you and Frank coming here?" Chloe asked Travis from behind me.

"I don't know what the plan is. I just wanted to make sure you guys were okay." Travis shrugged. "Anyways, Frank says hi." He quickly turned the phone and a very tired man with rustled hair popped up on the screen. Frank looked worn, and the wrinkles at the corner of his eyes were more prominent. "Here's Boss, he wants to talk to you guys." Travis handed the phone over to Miles.

Miles's mouth remained flat as he got up and walked off. "It's evident you know them, but do you trust them?"

"Yes." How could I not?

"Both of them?" he questioned.

"Yes. I trust Travis like family and Frank, yes. He's been nothing but kind to me, and he's been a prisoner too. Who knows what they did to him all those years?" He'd always had a haunted cloud filled with the past hovering over him.

Miles rubbed the back of his neck and sighed. "Okay."

"Does that mean they're coming here?" Chloe exclaimed. She was thrilled at the idea of having company.

"Chances are, they're in danger too, and we don't have the resources right now to send them elsewhere. No one knows they're from the Vault, and the Captain wants to keep this under the radar." Miles rubbed the back of his neck. "I would just prefer them at a different location. We can't even do background checks without any identification or real names. Our facial-recognition software can't find either of them—just like you guys."

"Trust me, the only thing creepy about Frank is that he seems a little delusional." Chloe put her arm around me.

"That, and Harper was the only one that would talk to him, anyway."

I looked at Chloe. "What do you mean by that?"

"He only talked to you. No one else dared to talk to him." Her arm dropped from my shoulder as she leaned closer to the phone. "I think they should come here. You already established the city wasn't safe, and this is the perfect spot to keep them under the radar."

"I agree." I wanted to see Travis and even Frank.

"I'll talk to Brandon and let you know." His concerned dark-hazel eyes held mine. "I don't think it's a good idea, but I don't know if there's an alternative. I know Travis is your friend, but it's been a week and a half, and they show up now." He sighed. "I'll let you know."

I nodded and handed the phone over to Brandon. I ushered Chloe outside, despite her resistance. I wanted to stay too, but they needed privacy.

Chloe and I paced outside, hoping their discussion was leaning toward them coming to the cabin. About ten minutes later, Brandon walked outside.

"You guys are in luck. With a little convincing, Miles said yes." He smirked. "They'll be down in a few hours."

"You won't be outnumbered now, Blondie." Chloe laughed, using her new nickname for Brandon.

The fact that Travis and Frank were coming made her chipper, and I couldn't deny my excitement either. It had been tempting to leave and search on my own, but with Travis around, it should help that feeling subside for a few more days.

We mulled around for an hour, trying to pass time, until Chloe suggested we should make dinner. Brandon took us to the store to get ingredients for spaghetti, and of course, Chloe wanted more ice cream, so we grabbed two containers. We were on our way to check out when Chloe stopped walking in front of me.

"What is it?" I asked worriedly as Chloe froze and stared off into space.

"What's going on?" Brandon walked over in front of her when she didn't answer.

"Eggs," she muttered.

"What?" Brandon raised an eyebrow.

She looked up at him and then turned to me. "I remember."

"What do you mean?" I asked.

She grabbed my shoulders, smiling. "I remember eating meatloaf with hard-boiled eggs." She let go of me, rubbing her forehead with one hand. "I was at this table with a peach, laced cloth. I don't remember anything else. Just eating meatloaf that had hard-boiled eggs in it with spaghetti. There were plates to my left and right, but I can't remember anything else. It's like a small clip of a memory, and I can't play the rest." Her eyes brightened. "But it's a memory! We should get eggs for tonight, even though we don't have meatloaf."

"Seriously!?" That was promising news for both of us. It meant we might remember, *eventually*. "That's awesome!"

"Well, let's go get some more eggs." Brandon turned the cart around and headed toward the dairy section. After we grabbed a carton of eggs, we checked out and rushed to the car so we could get dinner done in time.

The trip home was longer because Brandon took a couple of extra turns to make sure no one was following us, so we had just finished adding the hard-boiled eggs to the sauce when someone knocked on the door. A grin escaped my lips as Brandon gave us the hand signal to stay put. He checked out the window and opened the door. Miles walked in first, carrying two bags, with Travis and Frank right behind him.

Travis dropped his bag and strode toward me. I met him halfway as his lanky arms wrapped around me, swinging me in a circle; his touch didn't bother me.

"I thought you didn't get out . . . or worse." I sighed with relief into his shoulder.

"You can't get rid of me that easily." He pulled back with a big grin and pinched my cheek. "I couldn't let my little sister down."

"You're younger than me." I batted his hand away and rolled my eyes.

"And the sibling bickering starts," Chloe chided from behind us.

"And she speaks." Travis's blue eyes lit up as he held out his arms. "We can't escape a dungeon and not hug."

I glanced at Miles and smiled in thanks. He nodded, his face impassive. Frank stood behind him in khaki pants and an argyle sweater vest. His grey stubble had turned into a short brown-grey beard. I wasn't a hugger, but I urged myself to walk over and give him one. This had to be hard on him also.

"It's, uh, good to see you too." Frank let a small smile show.

"Same. Come eat, we have a lot to catch up on." I waved him over to a chair, and he followed with his normal hobble.

"Travis, how did you get out of that mess?" Chloe asked once everyone had a plate.

"Shortly after you guys left, I ran out of bullets." Travis shoved a fork full of spaghetti into his mouth. "Man, this is good." He was wearing khaki shorts and a forest-green long-sleeved shirt that complemented his shaggy blond hair. I was used to seeing him scarf down food but not used to seeing him in normal clothing.

"I made a run for the door, took a left, and then ran down an alley," Travis continued. "A few followed, but I lost most of them when they split. One stayed on my trail, but I was able to hide around a corner and socked him good."

"Then where did you go?" I asked.

"I hid in the city," Travis replied.

"For over a week?" My eyes widened.

He set his fork down. "I circled back in the morning to check things out. Once I saw you guys outside the building with the cops, I knew you were safe, but something was wrong. You guys didn't come out with anyone. So, I decided to see if I could find anything out on my own"—he grinned— "of course, exploring the city in between. Once I didn't find anything, I figured I would go to the cops and find you guys. That's when I found Frank. Poor guy was wandering around an alley with bums."

I glanced at Frank; he must have been so lost.

"Did you guys go straight to the police?" Travis asked.

"Kind of." I put down my piece of bread. "They were right on us, so we split up."

"More like you made yourself the bait," Chloe huffed. "She waited until they saw her after she sent me away."

Miles raised an eyebrow at me. In my statement I'd said that we had split up, not that I had waited so they would follow me and not her.

"They had the advantage of knowing the city." I bashfully shrugged. "Splitting up was the best option. Plus, they had orders to not kill me." I finished telling Travis and Frank the rest of my story, up to the part where we went into the Vault. I mentioned there had been an attack at the precinct but skipped the details—leaving out the beasts. Chloe told her side and that she had ended up crossing a bridge over the river, making her way to the Northeast Precinct.

After dinner, I asked Frank if he wanted to play chess, and he gladly accepted. We ended up playing on the couch while the others played cards at the counter. He seemed more relaxed after a few matches, and later, all of us ended up talking outside. At the end of a conversation, Miles stood and went inside. I excused myself, planning to go to bed after checking on him.

I found him filling up a glass of water and leaned on the island behind him. "You've been quiet. Well, not that you're usually a talkative person, but you're extra quiet tonight."

He turned around, pressing his lips in a flat line. "I don't like this. It doesn't make sense."

"What?" I asked, crossing my arms. "Them being here?"

"Yes. Both of them were missing for a while." He took a sip of water.

I sighed. "Travis told you everything; you have nothing to worry about with him. And Frank? He's just"—he was hard to describe—"a little messed up from the Vault."

"If what you said about everyone in the Vault being from their late teens to early twenties, why would they keep him around?" Miles asked skeptically.

"I don't know." I shrugged. "I don't think the treatment worked for him. He probably never went mad or changed, just a little traumatized from all the experimenting."

"I still don't trust either of them," he grumbled. "And I can only stay one night. Kat wants me back tomorrow."

Something inside me ticked. "Well, I trust Travis a whole lot more than I do you or *Kat*." I stormed to my room, despite my lie about not trusting Miles like I did Travis. I hadn't known him as long, but I felt like myself around him; I felt whole. Regardless of my curiosity about why Kat wanted him back tomorrow and what they were working on, I left.

My emotions had been kept under control the last few days, but I couldn't hold back my outburst. Going to my room was the best option, and I didn't want to cause a scene or get into an argument. I wanted to call Miles an idiot for not trusting Travis, but most of all, for not trusting me. Not to mention the fact that Miles hadn't even been telling me the entire truth before.

I lay in bed squeezing my eyes shut, trying to summon sleep. After a few minutes, I sat up. I had so much energy and wanted to run. Seeing how that wasn't an option, I opted to practice. I focused all my anger and energy toward my palms, which became tingly hot. Small bolts shot up at Chloe's bed above, shadowing the room with blue light. I quickly shut off the stream of energy as the room darkened again.

CHAPTER NINETEEN

"Aren't you a little warm?" The comment at Miles—who was wearing sweats, a hoodie, and sneakers—came off snider than I had intended. There was a slight brisk morning breeze, but nothing that warranted his attire.

"Aren't you up a little late?" He walked down the deck stairs and started stretching in the backyard.

"I actually didn't plan on running this morning." I narrowed my eyes at him.

He grunted. "Like you could go without running or pass it up."

I walked over and sat on the stairs, cocking my head and raising an eyebrow in defiance.

He walked over and sat down next to me, letting out a sigh. "I'm sorry you're angry, but I'm not sorry for doing my job."

"Lack of trust is a part of your job?" I crossed my arms over my chest.

"Well, yes, in a way." He curled his lip upward as I mentally slapped myself for that one; he couldn't just trust criminals. "It's not that I don't trust you. This entire situation is unique, so to speak. We've had no luck and are running out of compliance with the FBI. We're hoping we find something today."

"Like what?" I let my arms fall into my lap.

"I don't want to get your hopes up." He didn't elaborate further.

I sighed, resting my chin on my hands. The quietness that

followed allowed my mind to wander. A few minutes passed before I couldn't take thinking about the horrible things that could be happening to Liam, Maya, and even Ellie as I sat on the hard wooden steps.

"Fine, let's run." I was already wearing the appropriate running clothes with my shorts and jacket. "By the way, thanks again." *Ugh*. Why was I thanking him? I was still mad at him.

"For?" He eyed me as I moved to the grass to stretch.

"Do you have to ask?" I pulled my heel toward my back, stretching my hamstring. "For still helping us, even though the FBI doesn't want you to. And for believing us."

His half-smile lacked authenticity. "Kat believes this case relates to an old one. Her superiors are telling her to close this one, so she has been dragging on handing in her paperwork and has been working a lot off duty."

"What old case?" I asked.

"Nothing relevant yet." His impartial voice was almost a whisper.

I was about to ask more when Travis walked out onto the porch, wearing only boxers.

"Good morning." His eyes assessed us. "Going for a run?"

"Really, Travis? Where's the rest of your pajamas?" I rolled my eyes.

"These are my pajamas. We're free to wear what we want now. Just be lucky I'm not naked." He winked. "So, are you guys going for a run or what?"

"Yes, we are." I tried to hide my laugh but failed.

"Care if I join?" Travis looked between Miles and me.

"Not at all." I secretly wanted to practice, but I had missed him. I would also give him a full day to adjust before telling him about what I could do.

"Cool, I'll be right back." Travis disappeared into the cabin. I turned to Miles, who looked disgruntled, whether it was for Travis's lack of pajamas or for him joining us.

"What?" I shrugged.

Miles took a couple of steps toward the forest. "Are you still going to practice today?"

"No. I don't want to tell him just yet and freak him out." Though he hadn't freaked out about Liam when we saw him. "It'll be fun. He reminds me a lot of Brandon."

Miles seemed agitated the entire time we ran, but I doubt Travis noticed. He still didn't trust him. Chloe was anxiously waiting for our return, while Frank sat on the porch sipping his coffee. She asked Travis to join our training, and he gladly accepted the offer. Travis proposed that we have a match with the two of them against me, but I weaseled my way out of it by saying that we could tomorrow.

I trained with Chloe for fifteen minutes before letting Travis take over and joining Miles, Frank, and Brandon on the deck. Brandon had come outside shortly after Chloe and I started.

"I have to go." Miles got up and nodded goodbye at Brandon.

I got up and followed him inside. "Will you keep us updated?"

"Yes." He grabbed a small bag near the couch. "I'm going to shower first. I have to head into work from here."

Instead of sitting on the couch awkwardly waiting, I decided to start tidying up the kitchen. Miles showered and changed in five minutes before coming out in a clean pair of jeans and a grey, pocketed t-shirt.

"No uniform?" I asked.

"I haven't been on patrol that much recently, so I've just kept my badge on me." Miles grabbed his jacket off the back of the couch. "Plus, you don't want to ride a motorcycle in uniform while off duty."

"I guess that's true." I walked over to the other side of the island and leaned against it. "See you tomorrow."

His smile fell as he eyed the back door with an untrusting glare. "Promise me you'll stay out of trouble?"

I rolled my eyes and pulled out the phone. "Don't worry, I won't run alone, and I will always have this on me."

"You mean you won't go anywhere without Brandon." He eyed me before sighing, "Just be safe."

I leaned off the island as he pulled open the heavy wooden door and left. I let out a small sigh and went to take a shower. When I was done, I grabbed a bowl of cereal and joined the rest of the crew outside, sitting down by Frank.

"Did you want anything?" I asked him.

"No, thank you." Frank leaned back in his chair.

"How did you get out? Sentinels were everywhere."

He frowned as he glanced at me. "I went out the main door. They were too occupied in, uh, searching for you and your friends. It created a clear path."

Over the radio that night, we had heard them mention we were missing and that they needed to find us. I guess they'd probably thought Frank was the least of their concerns. "I'm glad you made it out okay." I paused. "Dr. Roulings was your doctor, right?"

Frank nodded.

"What was he like?"

"Umm, direct, prompt, and, uh, deceptive." Frank didn't seem bothered by the question.

"Aren't they all?" I frowned. "How come he was never around?"

Frank rubbed his beard. "I don't know. He always seemed like he was around to me."

* * *

"Guys, come here," Travis called from the kitchen as Chloe and I surveyed our options of board games, even though we already knew what was in the closet.

"What's up?" Chloe asked as we reached the kitchen.

"I have an idea, but—"

"Nope." I cut Travis off before he could finish. Three bottles of wine sat in front of him on the island.

"Just hear me out," Travis pleaded. "Let's convince Brandon into taking us out tonight; you guys have to experience it. If he sees how much fun we're having here, it might work."

"Ha, that's a lousy plan," Chloe cackled.

"He takes his job seriously. What makes you think he would say yes?" Despite hearing about how much Brandon liked to go out, he wouldn't drink while on the job, let alone take us out.

"You said he was like me, and if that's the case, he would want to get you guys out of here and have some fun. Harper, it's supposed to be a fun day today." Travis winked.

I held up a finger, trying to move past his comment. "Nope, you're not doing this."

"What do you mean?" Chloe interjected.

"I'm just saying." Travis shrugged. "I think we should, but if you guys won't budge, we'll settle for drinking here."

"Umm, what did I miss—" Chloe stopped talking when Brandon walked in the front door from doing a perimeter sweep.

He took off his damp army-green cargo jacket and hung it up.

"Found the stash, have we?" Brandon walked over to the island, his eyes moving past each one of us.

"Well, we were wondering if you wouldn't mind if we had a glass?" Travis asked politely as Brandon glared at him. "You know, as a celebratory drink . . . for not being in the Vault."

"No." Brandon grabbed the bottles and walked over to the stove, putting them back in the cupboard above it.

"You knew there was wine here and you didn't tell us?" Chloe asked.

"Yeah, I found it the first day." Brandon closed the cupboard.

"We could have used a drink." Chloe's eyes narrowed.

I'm surprised she hadn't already climbed the counter and checked those cupboards out of boredom.

"You guys aren't old enough," Brandon commented.

"She's pretty close." Travis pointed at me as I rolled my eyes at him. "And you're telling me you didn't drink at our age . . . what . . . four years ago?"

"There will be no underage drinking." Brandon glared at Travis. "You know what, I'm going to put these somewhere else."

He grabbed the wine and walked over to the hidden hatch in the floor, lifting it. He paused as his cell phone rang in his pocket. Shuffling the bottles to one arm, he pulled out his phone and sighed when he saw the screen. "I've got to take this." He answered his phone and descended into the cellar.

"What do you think that was about?" Chloe asked.

"I don't know." I shrugged, wondering if it was Miles or the Captain.

Travis walked over and grabbed three large opaque plastic cups from the cupboard. Chloe and I stared at him curiously as he filled them with ice and reached into a cupboard below the island, pulling out another large bottle of wine.

"What are you doing?" My eyes widened.

"You guys deserve a drink."

"Where did you find that? I've been under the sink before," Chloe said.

"In a much better hiding spot than the other three." He pulled the cork off quietly with his hand.

"Eww, was that already opened?" Chloe scrunched her nose.

"I uncorked it earlier so I didn't have to try to finagle with it now. Plan B." He poured it in two of the three cups and slid them toward us. "Come on, you have to try it. It's pretty good."

"How do you know?" I slid the cup back toward him.

"I took a sip earlier. I had to make sure it was good." Travis pushed the cup back at me and glanced toward the cellar. "We're running out of time. Just one drink—well, two—in that cup. You've spent five years in the Vault; live a little. If not celebrating today, do it for Liam and Maya. They'd want you to."

"I guess we can't waste it. Who knows how old and expensive it is." Chloe tapped her cup with mine and walked away.

"Fine." I sighed, knowing he was right. I picked up the cup and swirled it as Travis went over and filled his with water. "Why aren't you having any?"

"I had plenty to drink since being out." He grinned as he set his cup down and disappeared with the bottle to the room Chloe and I shared.

"Where does he think he's going?" I waved my hand.

"I don't know, but this is pretty good." She took another sip.

I was about to follow him when I heard Brandon's footsteps coming up the stairs. "Yes, I will. Okay, take care. Ah-uh, yes. Okay, love you too. Bye." He hung up the phone and glanced at us as he reached the top. "What?"

"I take it that wasn't the Captain." Chloe smirked.

"No." He scratched his forehead. "It was my mom. Where did Travis go?" Brandon looked around.

Travis came around the corner and huffed. "I forgot he was still in there. I'm just going to go outside."

He squeezed by us and went outside. A few minutes later, he returned and grabbed his cup from the counter as Brandon eyed our three cups suspiciously. Travis started walking toward us, tripping on the carpet.

"Whoops! Sorry, good thing it's just water." He looked over at Brandon. "Do you have any paper towels?"

"Uh, yeah." Brandon grabbed the paper towels and handed them to him. Once he realized it was just water in Travis's cup, he stopped being suspicious of ours. He probably thought Travis would be drinking if we were. Brandon went to shower after an hour of playing games and keeping our cups out of his view.

Travis told Frank we would be right back and pulled Chloe and me into our room. "Okay, first off, I was wondering if I could stay on this third bed in here. Frank creeps me out."

"What, you're afraid of the old man?" Chloe mocked.

"No, he's just quiet." Travis's face reddened. "Plus, I don't want to sleep on the air mattress."

"That's fine with me." It wasn't like Chloe and I slept in our underwear. "But you have to wear shorts and a shirt." I paused. "Oh, and you can't judge him on being quiet. He's been in the Vault for a long time, and he's nice if you actually talk to him."

"That's what you've always said." Travis looked at Chloe. "You?"

"Pshh, I don't care." A slow smile crept on her face before she shot out her cup at Travis. "Refill?"

He laughed and grabbed the bottle hiding between the third bed and the wall. Chloe snatched it from him and started pouring herself more.

"Just a small one. We're going out," Travis warned before indulging in the details of his plan, despite my objections.

I argued with Chloe that we shouldn't go—she had said yes. Travis left us to change when she mentioned she would convince me.

It might have been the wine, but she ended up changing my mind. Our alcohol tolerance was low, and two glasses of wine were enough to encourage us. Her winning argument was that we weren't prisoners anymore and could do as we pleased.

Everything about this said it was a bad idea, but a part of me felt bubbly and wanted to do it. I didn't want to ruin their fun either. We were good fighters, I had powers, and I doubted we would come across any of those beasts. It would piss off Miles, and for some reason, that urged me to want to defy him. I was still grumpy about the keeping things from me situation.

After all, I'd promised I wouldn't go anywhere alone, and never answered his last remark about not going anywhere without Brandon.

CHAPTER TWENTY

"So, how do we get drinks?" Chloe raised her voice as we got closer to the bar with music blaring. "We don't have fake IDs or money."

"They won't ID us, and I got the other part covered," Travis said as he held open the door for the three of us. Frank had asked if he could join as we were about to sneak off with Brandon's car while he showered. I couldn't say no, even though Travis didn't want him to tag along.

Inside, people were spread out and some were dancing to the live band. In the city, the majority of the people had worn dresses and suits. At this place, almost everyone was in jeans. The band was a group of older men playing a mix of classic rock and country. There was a long rectangular bar to the right along with tables and red booths throughout. Various items from record discs to deer heads scattered the walls, and it smelled like beer and fried food.

"Come on." Chloe grabbed my hand. "We're going to the ladies' room. We'll be right back."

I followed her lead and laughed at her in the bathroom. "Must be the wine is going through you already?"

"No." She pulled out a miniature clutch from her pocket. "Just figured we should spruce up a little, especially if we're going to order drinks."

"When did you get this?" I looked at the few things of makeup.

"When we went shopping." She pulled out the eyeliner. "Let me do you first."

I went with it, closing my eyes. After she finished, I checked out her work in the mirror. The brown eyeshadow accentuated my light brown eyes, and the dull pink lipstick made my lips look fuller. The blush was dark and gave my cheekbones life against my blond hair. My face matched the nice jeans, sleeveless red blouse, and Chloe's ankle boots I wore. Chloe did an amazing job with hers as well, fancying up her floral V-neck shirt and dressy flip-flops.

After Chloe finished, we walked out and found Travis sitting at a table with Frank. I was already starting to get hot and took my jacket off, hanging it on the back of the chair.

"See, told you they wouldn't ID us." Travis waved his hand at the two drinks he had sitting at the empty seats across from them. I had no idea how Travis got ahold of money, but I didn't care at the moment.

I sat down and stirred the red drink with the straw. "What is this?"

"It's better if you don't know and just trust me." The corner of Travis's mouth twitched upward. "Just try it."

"Yum!" Chloe continued drinking hers.

I sipped my drink as my eyes roamed over to the people dancing across the way. Chloe insisted that Frank should at least have one drink, but he kindly declined her prodding each time.

"Lucky for him he looks older than what, eighteen?" Chloe laughed as Travis went to go get more drinks, despite ours not being gone yet.

"Nineteen. He turned nineteen in July." I felt bad we didn't get to really celebrate birthdays in the Vault. I felt my phone buzzing in my pocket and pulled it out.

"Crap."

"What is it?" Chloe peered over my shoulder.

"Two missed calls from Brandon and five from Miles." I stared at the screen.

"They've been calling me too." She pulled hers out, showing me the multiple missed calls. "See?"

My phone started to buzz in my hand as Miles's name popped up on the screen. "He's calling again."

"Just ignore it." Chloe tried to grab my phone, but I swatted her hand away.

"I'm just going to answer to tell him we're fine and then hang up." I hit the green button and held it to my ear.

"Harper, where are you? The tracker in your phone isn't working." Miles's voice roared through the phone before I could even speak.

"We're fine, don't worry about us." I rolled my eyes. *Wait!* Did he just say tracker in my phone?

"Okay, done. Let's go dance." Chloe grabbed my arm and tried to drag me away. I tried to put a finger up for her to wait, but she pulled me right off the chair.

"Harper—" Miles started, but I cut him off.

"Everything's fine, sir. I'll give you an update in one hour. Ouch!" I stubbed my foot on the leg of a chair, tripping, and laughed. At least I didn't faceplant.

"Are you drunk?" I could hear the irritation in Miles's voice.

"What? No." I glanced at Chloe and laughed again. "Okay, maybe."

"Harper, listen to me, you can't tru—" His words were cut off as Chloe grabbed the phone and ended the call.

"Come on, let's dance!"

I let her drag me to the dance floor. Miles would be fine, but I did feel bad for Brandon. I had left him a note saying we went out; I knew how much my notes were loved. We took Brandon's car, and I'd jacked the four-wheeler keys so we would have time. This was the only bar in the area, so they'd figure it out soon, if they hadn't already.

I wasn't sure how long we danced before we needed water and made our way to Travis at the bar. The tall brunette bartender Travis was talking with was very courteous and greeted us as soon as we arrived, serving us two waters.

"Another drink for you two?" the bartender asked.

"No, I think we're good." I put an arm around Chloe's shoulder and glanced at Travis. "Someone kept bringing us drinks while we danced."

"We danced out all of those." Chloe waved me off.

"Well, I hate to be that person, but I think Harper's right. You guys should probably stick to water and we'll head out shortly." Travis gave the bartender a wide smile. "It was a pleasure to meet you." He put a ten-dollar bill on the counter and walked over to our table, where Frank sat. I went to ask where he got the cash, but I got distracted when cold water seeped down the back of my leg.

I turned to see Chloe gasping. "I'm sorry! Let me get some napkins!"

"It's fine." I couldn't help but laugh, which in return made her laugh. "I'll just go grab paper towels from the bathroom. I'll be right back."

I left them and headed to the bathroom, nearly bumping into a lady on the way in. She smiled politely at me and continued walking. I grabbed a wad of paper towels from the dispenser and soaked up what water I could from my jeans. I tossed the paper towels and looked at myself in the mirror. My face was beet-red and my hair was slightly disheveled, but surprisingly, my makeup had stayed intact. The sharp pang of betrayal struck my chest as bile rose in my throat. I quickly ran to the stall as the drinks and my earlier dinner came back up.

I was pretty sure the alcohol caused my nausea, and not the guilt of betrayal. Nevertheless, it still made me sick to think that I had just gotten drunk while Liam and Maya were still trapped. I flushed the toilet and walked over to the sink to rinse my mouth.

I reached for my phone, figuring I should let Miles and Brandon know we were okay and heading back shortly. My screen showed multiple missed calls, voicemails, and text messages. I opened the text messages first.

Harper, please pick up your phone, now. —**Miles**

That message had been sent a little less than an hour ago, and the next one had been sent shortly after.

You can't trust Frank. He's not who he says he is. He is Dr. Roulings. —**Miles**

Panic instantly shot through me as fear and disgust crawled up my spine. I squeezed the phone in my hand, swearing to myself before running out of the bathroom. I started scanning the crowd when Travis appeared in front of me, grabbing my shoulders. The sudden movement made me nauseous, but I held it down.

"We have to grab the other two and get out of here." His voice was alarmed.

"What do you mean 'grab' them? Where's Chloe?" I peered around him.

"She needed fresh air and went out back with Frank. I was waiting for you until I vaguely felt them." Travis steered me toward the back door.

"Chloe's with Frank?" I shouted. "We have to get her away from him!"

He stopped and turned to face me. "Wait, why?"

I held up my phone, which still displayed the message.

Travis's face went white when he read it. "Let's go."

As we weaved through the crowd, what he'd said earlier finally unscrambled in my brain. "What do you mean you 'felt them'?"

"The others," was all he said as we ran out the back door and into a small, dark alley.

Through the mist and fog, I spotted Chloe and Frank to my left. Chloe had her hands against the wall as if she had just finished getting sick, and Frank appeared to be comforting her.

"Chloe!" I jogged over to her side, knowing that with Travis there too, Frank was not a threat. "Are you okay?"

"I think so. Everything's spinning." She leaned off the wall to look at me.

"Come on." I helped her away from the wall and away from Frank. Travis came over and helped when I stumbled under her weight. We headed toward the parking lot on the side of the bar, ignoring Frank behind us. If he didn't know we knew about him, we could get away and leave him behind. Travis froze and shuddered as a dark figure rounded the corner in front of us.

"We can't go this way." He turned us back toward Frank who hadn't moved.

I thought I was going to be sick when I felt a faint tingle in the back of my mind, but I never did. Travis let go of Chloe and took a deep breath while stepping forward. He held out his arms at his sides with his palms outward. I wasn't sure what he was trying to accomplish, but he tried it again.

"It won't work." Frank's voice had completely changed. "I slipped an inhibitor in your water. You can't morph, Travis."

"I will kill you." Travis snarled as he backed up, aware of the person behind us.

"What's going on, Frank?" I questioned.

"You are already figuring it out, dearie." He took a step closer.

"Stay where you are," Travis warned.

"You guys are a little weak right now." Frank frowned. "If you haven't figured it out by now, Harper, your friend here has already gone through the change to become a Hybrian. That is the real reason he was gone for a week and a half, wasn't it?" He eyed a growling Travis.

"It was an easy choice on who to give the inhibitor to." Frank's eyes shifted to Chloe. "Her body hasn't accepted the treatments yet—if it does—and you"—his dark eyes shifted to me—"your . . . abilities will be suppressed from the alcohol.

By the way, how have they come along?" I didn't answer, confused at how he knew. "You did something to Ellie and our team at the precinct, something we didn't expect you to have. It seems Liam's fight with the sentinels and your fight with Adam did its job."

"You mean the fight where Adam tried to have us killed? That was you?" I stammered, frozen in my tracks.

"Adam's instructed to train and teach you guys, but I guide him if I want something done specifically. And you guys being killed was never on the table, just a scare tactic. You weren't changing, and we couldn't wait any longer. I needed a different stimulant, and fear has an unfortunate, yet astounding, effect on the brain and body." He frowned again. "Putting Liam's and your life falsely on the line was the stimulant the four of you needed. It worked, even though Maya was already starting to show signs of change, but then you guys escaped. Your father would be proud."

"My father?" My voice dropped as I shifted Chloe's weight against me.

"Yes. He is the reason Hybrians are possible." He waved his hands as two figures appeared behind him. I squinted in the dark as one emerged into the light. Fangs snared from her mouth, amber cat eyes reflected, and claws erupted from her fingertips. Something about her was familiar, like I had met her, but I couldn't place it.

I attempted to reach the small thud of electricity in me, but there was nothing. There wasn't even a spark. I tried a couple more times, but nothing came forward. Two other figures emerged next to Frank, and I gasped as soon as their faces came into view.

Maya stood next to Liam with black pants, a denim jacket, and her hair slicked back into a ponytail. Travis and I shared a confused glance as trepidation and disbelief churned in my gut. I looked back at Liam, who stared at me with an unreadable expression. He wore jeans with a black unbuttoned shirt opening to a white T-shirt underneath, almost making him unrecognizable.

"It will be much easier if you three willingly come with us. We aren't here to hurt you, I promise. Once we explain a few things, you will understand, and Travis, you will remember everything soon." Frank attempted a warm smile, but I wouldn't fall for it again.

"Run!" Travis shouted.

We bolted through a small pathway on our right. If we could loop around the back of the second building and get to the side of the bar, we could get to the car. I would call Miles, and we would meet somewhere else now that the cabin was compromised.

CHAPTER TWENTY-ONE

Chloe let go of me and tried hard to hold her own. I was still pretty quick, but lagging. Both of us were slowing Travis down. We came up short as we rounded a corner; the man who had been behind us was now in front of us in his beast form—a Hybrian.

"You two need to go. I can handle him." Travis prepared himself.

"We can't leave you."

"You guys are in no shape to fight. You need to stay ahead of the others. Go." Travis lunged after the Hybrian, who easily avoided him.

Travis was right—if we stayed, we would make the situation worse, and would need help ourselves. I needed to get Chloe out of there. I grabbed her hand, pulling her around them.

"Keys!" Travis shouted, and I turned just in time to see him tossing the car keys in our direction.

I fumbled them as they hit my hands, causing them to fall to the ground. I quickly snatched them and started toward the parking lot. My stomach knotted as we ran. We'd left Travis behind, again, and each step felt like we were going nowhere. The sound of a motor roared nearby, and something hard knocked us down from behind. I barely caught myself on the asphalt and looked at Chloe next to me. Her eyes were closed.

"Chloe!" I reached my arm out and shook her, but she didn't wake. I rolled over onto my back to see the same

Hybrian that had first appeared next to Frank staring down at us with glowing amber eyes.

"Sorry for this." She aimed a gun at me as I got to my knees. I was about to attempt to disarm her, but a gun went off, causing me to drop to the wet cement. Through the stray strands of hair covering my face, I saw the Hybrian lying on the ground. I whipped my head around to see Brandon running at us with a gun in his hand.

"Are you guys okay?" Brandon's eyes went from me to Chloe on the ground. He dropped down and put two fingers to her neck before assessing the blood from her head where she'd hit it on the ground.

"Will she be okay?" I asked worriedly.

"She has a strong pulse. Let's get out of here." He shoved his gun into his belt and scooped Chloe up, cradling her against his chest. "Where's Travis?"

"Fighting another . . . person." I grabbed the Hybrian's gun, only to realize it was a taser.

Brandon started to jog. He didn't seem too alarmed by the Hybrian, unless he couldn't tell in the dark. "The four-wheeler is around the corner. I'm going to get you guys out of here."

"Wait, what? How did you . . ." I stopped talking; how he got there didn't matter right then. I was just happy he'd shown up when he did. "Would this be better?" I pulled out his car keys, dangling them.

"Yes." All joking from him was absent. He held out his hand, and I gave him the keys. He flipped his hand back over, holding the keys between his palm and Chloe's leg.

"We can't leave Travis," I stressed as we neared the parking lot.

"We won't. Miles will get him."

"How did you find us?" I asked, even though I had my assumption.

"Good guess. It's the only bar in the—" Brandon abruptly stopped and laid Chloe down. He reached for his gun, but was too late. It went flying out of his hand as a Hybrian kicked it. He had come out of nowhere, and I needed to pay better attention.

I aimed the taser, but he quickly disarmed me, knocking it to the ground. As he started toward Brandon, I sprang into action and threw a roundhouse kick to his back. Not only did it barely knock him off balance, but it made me dizzy. Brandon used the small window and punched him, but was quickly tossed backward after the Hybrian recovered. With my current state, there was no way we would win this fight and keep Chloe—who lay unconscious on the ground—safe.

"Hey! Dickhead!" I got the Hybrian's attention. "If Dr. Roulings wants me, then come and get me."

I ran the way we came—which was moronic—but I couldn't lead him to the car. I turned to make sure he was following and kept going. A small yard beyond the buildings presented itself, and I ran through it into another part of the town. I had a feeling he was going to catch up quickly, so I tried to run between and around buildings, getting farther away from the bar.

Eventually, I ended up in front of a closed-down gas station. I felt like my legs were going to give out underneath me as a lump formed in my throat and the nausea came back. I hid behind one of the gas station's pillars, which had a row of blue barrels next to it. I peered around the pillar and didn't see any sign of the Hybrian. I didn't see anyone. The street was eerily empty.

I couldn't clearly remember where I'd run and had no idea where I was. My heart raced as I started to panic, knowing I was useless to my friends if I was caught. After a few deep breaths, I realized I had my phone and pulled it out, calling Miles.

"Harper? Are you okay?" His voice sounded muffled.

"Yes." I stepped out from behind the pillar. "I'm at an old gas station. There's a—" I froze when a figure started approaching me through the thick fog from the other side of the lot.

Frank soon came into focus. He appeared to be alone, but I knew the others wouldn't be far behind. I started backing away, readying to run.

"Harper, please don't. Aren't you curious about yourself, about your father?" He worked his way toward me, his limp completely gone.

"Yes, but not if it gets me killed—or, worse, captured." I scowled as I lowered the phone, making sure not to end the call.

"It's just you and me." He waved his hand at the phone. "And whoever is on the other line, but I have a feeling you don't care if they hear our conversation. I'm betting it is Officer MacLand."

"Why should I even listen to you?" Sweat started to drip down my neck.

"Because I have the answers you seek, and I am not who you make me out to be." He now stood about fifteen feet away.

"That your real name isn't Frank? I figured that much." As much as I knew I should run, he was right. I wanted answers, and that urge kept my feet planted. "What answers?"

"You have a specific marker in your DNA that makes you special; you were the second Hybrian created." He stayed where he was. "Your mother became ill when she was pregnant with you. Her treatments were failing, and she was slowly dying, something your father hid from her. He did not want her to carry the burden of knowing she was going to die, especially before you could be born."

Frank sighed. "Your father was a brilliant man. We were working on a serum to help create superior, stronger soldiers to protect our country. At first, we were making remarkable progress, until we realized what our serum could do. Our first test subject changed into a hybrid: part human, part animal. There was one issue—the rage. The subject presented with severe emotional disorders and outbursts, even killing a few of our staff with no remorse.

"Once your father learned of this, he destroyed the only vial we had, and all of the work that went with it. Without his help, I was at a loss to create a new serum without the negative side effects.

"He discovered he was going to be a father, and five months later, your mom fell terminally ill." Frank took a breath. "When all hope was lost, he resorted to the last thing he could think of—a different serum. The serum we'd created had healing properties, properties we could not research further after we lost our first subject and the original serum. He created something new with similar markers and told your mother it was a trial of vitamins and enzymes created to attack the illness. After multiple injections of the serum, your mother slowly recovered. A month later, there was no sign of her illness, and less than a month after that, you were born; both of you were healthy.

"Your mother didn't have the rage, nor did she physically change. Around the age of five, you fell sick to the same genetic illness, but you were only ill for a couple of weeks before recovering on your own. She didn't have any markers, but you did. When you were in your mother's womb, the serum had passed through the barrier. Neither of you ever knew. It runs in your blood and is in your DNA. Something we have not yet been able to completely extract. That's why you are different than the others." He stood there studying my dumbfounded face.

"Why should I believe any of this? What happened to my parents . . . How did I end up in the Vault?" I tried to hold my voice steady while comprehending everything he had just said.

"Your father became a subject of interest. Especially his work, which at that time was to find cures. He died shortly after people found out about you." His voice dipped.

"My mother? Is she still alive?" My voice wavered. This

entire time I had hoped that when I got out, I could return home to my family.

"That's enough information to process for now." He stayed still as Maya appeared behind him. I heard a noise behind me and turned to see the Hybrian that had been chasing me was now standing behind me with another. The three of them started to close in.

"I got her." Maya sneered at the others. "Hi, Harper. It's been a while."

"Maya? What are you doing?" I stared at what had once been my best friend.

"Taking you in, but I know you'll resist." Her beautiful smile was filled with venom. "We had it all wrong. Alcorp is good. They created a better life for us—one where we can make things better."

"Maya, you need to wake up. They're brainwashing you. *They* are the reason this happened to us. They took us from our families. They experimented on us."

"They saved me from my family." She inched closer.

"What do you mean?" I couldn't fathom how she classified what they did as saving us.

"I didn't have something you'd call a real family." She continued to creep forward.

"Maya, please. You still aren't yourself." I begged for the Maya I had known, but she stayed buried.

Maya broke her slow pace and attacked. I was slow but quick enough to evade her and counter, sending her to the ground. My body responded to muscle memory, the only good thing I had going in my inebriated state.

"Maya!" Frank's voice was a sharp warning. *How sweet.* He was worried she was going to kill his precious experiment. My eyes burned with anger.

Maya stood, flipping her damp hair out of her face—the fog acting as a wet mist despite being under the covering of the gas station. This time, when she looked at me, her eyes transformed.

The sound of tires burning out on the wet pavement and the roar of an engine interrupted our stare down. A single headlight pierced through the fog as my stomach cringed and danced at the same time. Part of me felt relieved to see Miles, but the other part worried for his life. They wanted me alive, which was not the case for him.

Frank pulled out a phone he'd somehow conjured and took off. The sound of a low growl turned my attention back to Maya. Her body morphed, with similar features to the others. She attacked again. This time she was too fast, and sent me flying into the blue barrels. I thought I heard a gunshot, but it could've been the sound of my body smacking into the barrels filled with sand. At least it wasn't the cracking of my head on the pavement or a pillar.

Maya was already on top of me, pulling me to my feet. In the haziness behind her, I saw Miles's motorcycle on the ground, along with a Hybrian. The other one had managed to knock his gun free and they were locked in a fight. Miles held his own for now, but he wouldn't last against the Hybrian's strength.

A sudden rush of adrenaline rose, and I kicked Maya in the knee while landing a punch to her chest. She dropped me and I fell. Curse the clumsiness of my own two feet right now. I stood, steadying myself.

I backed away, trying to put some distance between us. As fast as the adrenaline rush had come, it had left, and my power wasn't anywhere to be found. I tried to glance at Miles, but Maya blocked my view.

"Maya, please. We know each other. This is what we were afraid of becoming. You can fight this." I pleaded for any sign of her to be in there, just like Liam had to me back in the Vault.

A gut-wrenching howl came from behind her. She turned, moving enough that I could see Miles pulling out a knife from the Hybrian's stomach. A low growl rumbled from Maya. Instead of going at Miles, she turned on me. I got in a weak punch before she tossed me to the ground, knocking the wind out of me. Out of the corner of my eye, I saw Miles pick up his gun and aim in our direction.

"Miles, don't!" I shouted as loud as I could, regardless of the lack of air in my lungs. Miles hesitated and looked at me before slowly steadying his left hand, aiming at Maya. "It's Maya. This isn't her," I croaked.

I saw the trouble in his eyes as Maya bitterly laughed and grabbed my shirt. "You're coming with me."

A gunshot sounded and my heart stopped. The next thing I knew, Maya was no longer standing over me. Everything started to become white as my mind pictured Maya bleeding out.

"Maya." A low, untroubled voice I would recognize anywhere broke through the air as my eyesight adjusted.

"Liam?" I scurried to my knees and slowly stood. Liam took his hand off Maya's shoulder. She didn't have any signs of being shot. He must have pulled her out of the way just in time.

"You were supposed to wait for me." Liam's soothing voice faded. "Let's get her home." Liam held one hand out after Maya had turned away from him, telling Miles to hold.

"You know I'm impatient." Maya took a step, but was yanked back when Liam wrapped his arm around her neck and began choking her, his eyes morphing.

"Liam, what are you doing?" I started toward them.

"Shhh, it'll be okay," Liam calmly whispered to Maya before looking up at me. "Harper, she'll be fine," he grunted as Maya struggled against him.

Seconds later, she stopped fighting and morphed back to her normal self, and so did Liam. She looked peaceful as Liam slowly laid her on the ground, her chest still rising and falling. He stood and looked at me. He let his guard down for a fraction of a second, and I could read every emotion on his morphed face: remorse, grief, sorrow, and anguish. His face became impassive as Miles started in our direction, raising his gun.

"He won't hurt me!" I yelled to Miles before looking at Liam. "Is Travis okay?"

"He's fine. He's with Chloe in the car with the other cop." Liam glanced at Miles who had lowered his gun. "This must be his partner."

"Yes." I had so much to say, but only a single word came out.

"He seems like he can handle himself." Liam's eyes examined the two bodies on the ground behind him as remorse flashed across his face. "Stay with him for now."

I looked at Maya on the ground.

"She will be fine. We thought she could control herself, but she wasn't ready yet. I'll take care of her." He glanced at Maya and then back at me.

"We should get moving," Miles beckoned as he reached us.

"Both of you should come with us." I held back the tears that welled in my eyes.

"We can't. I don't have time to explain things right now, but it will make sense soon. I promise." He grabbed a damp loose strand of my hair and tucked it snuggly behind my ear.

"One more thing," he said as he leaned in, softly kissing my lips. "Happy birthday, sunshine."

Surprise froze my bones in place as he swiftly turned and picked up Maya before disappearing into the fog. Confusion whirled through me as my stomach fluttered from either excitement or embarrassment. I never thought we would have a first kiss, let alone that it would be like that. Last I knew, he had feelings for Ellie.

I wanted a redo, one where my breath didn't smell like alcohol and vomit, and one where I would kiss him back instead of freezing. I wanted to be able to explore what true emotion came forward. With the thought of alcohol and my mind spinning, I suddenly felt sick. I turned to steady myself on the pillar as I hunched over, reliving what I'd done earlier in the bar's bathroom. I officially hated throwing up more than running suicides.

"You're going to be okay." Out of nowhere, Miles was next to me, moving my hair so it lay on my back. "I'm going to get my bike. I'll be right back."

"I'm never drinking again," I mumbled as he walked away.

In less than a minute, he was already back. He put his helmet on me and lifted the lens so I could get air, leaving the spare hooked to the back of the motorcycle. "Do you think you can hold on? The car's only a few blocks away." I nodded in response, climbing on after him.

"I'm sorry . . . for everything," I mumbled into his back, unsure if he could hear me. The familiar scent of leather and pine offered comfort as I wrapped my arms around his firm torso. Miles started the motorcycle before clamping his right hand around mine and shifting his legs out so mine tucked underneath his, which I assumed was because he didn't trust me to hold on. I didn't either.

After a few blocks, we arrived at a convenience store, where Brandon, Chloe, and Travis were. I shivered when I got off the bike and away from Miles's warmth. I wished I hadn't left my only jacket at the bar. Miles noticed and shrugged off his jacket to give to me. I climbed into the car, and, once I saw they were all okay, I laid my head against the window and passed out.

CHAPTER TWENTY-TWO

I rolled over and tugged the comforter over my face. My eyes squeezed tighter at the pounding in my head, and my entire body ached. The events of last night came rushing back: the dancing, everything Frank said, Maya, Liam kissing me, throwing up in front of Miles, and the reason I felt this way. I was never drinking again.

The last thing I remembered was passing out in the backseat of Brandon's car. I opened my eyes to the haze of a dark-blue comforter when I felt someone stir next to me. I bolted upright, relaxing when I realized it was just Chloe. The sudden movement sent a sharp throb across my forehead, instantly making me nauseous. Hopefully, my healing would assist my hangover.

Pine and a hint of leather reached my nose, and I realized we must be in Miles's bed. Heat rushed to my face, even though it was Chloe next to me and not him. It was probably the next safest place for us to go to last night. I looked around the toasted-grey painted bedroom. Not much filled the room besides a chestnut dresser with a TV, one nightstand, and a full laundry basket in the corner.

I heard hushed voices on the other side of the sliding barn door and quietly slid out of the bed, not wanting to wake Chloe. I tiptoed to the door and snuck out, shutting it behind me. Miles was standing at the end of an island, while Agent Foster sat on a barstool at the other end. She stood when she saw me, her tight black curls bouncing with the movement. Her black slacks made her look slim and tall despite wearing flats, and her blazer with a deep purple blouse underneath finished off the "I'm an FBI agent" look.

"This is your . . ." I left my question open as I noted my surroundings, a living room furnished with a grey couch and recliner. A TV hung on the wall behind me next to the barn door, and light shined through the tall windows lining the entire left side of the apartment. The kitchen was straight across from me and had white countertops with dark walnut cabinets and stainless-steel appliances.

"My apartment," Miles answered. "Do you remember what happened last night?"

"Surprisingly, yes." I rubbed my eyes as I walked over to them. The light didn't help my headache, making me want to retreat to the bedroom with its black curtains.

"Drink this and take this." Miles grabbed a glass of water and a pill that was sitting on the counter before walking around the island and handing them to me. My eyes scanned over his taut white T-shirt and then down to his jeans. My sluggish self took a moment to realize I was checking him out as he stood right in front of me. I cleared my throat and grabbed the pill and glass as my cheeks blushed.

"What is this?" I examined the pill.

"Something that will help you feel better," he said, suppressing a smirk.

Despite not wanting anything in my stomach, I took the pill and gulped it down with water. I set the glass on the counter and went to lean on it when I noticed what I was wearing.

"Umm, how did I get into these?" I tugged at the plain baggy T-shirt and baggy sweatpants. I looked up to see Miles attempting to hide another smirk behind his hand as he leaned against the counter.

"Don't worry, I'm the one that changed yours and Chloe's clothes last night. They were soaked and those were the only spare clothes Miles had that worked. You still have your undergarments on." As Agent Foster spoke, I couldn't help but admire her beautiful, glowing skin, and there I was looking like a teenage boy who never showered.

"Thank you, Agent Foster." I should at least say thanks for not letting me stay in soaked, smelly clothes, though I think I would have preferred it.

"You can call me Kat." She smiled genuinely and held out her hand. "I don't believe we officially met."

"Is Travis here?" I reached over and shook her hand before looking around for another bedroom.

Miles frowned as he pulled out a folded piece of paper from his pocket. "No. He left last night, but he left this for you."

I took the paper, unfolding it to Travis's chicken-scratch handwriting:

Harper,

Sorry I left without saying goodbye. I put you guys in more danger and should have just stayed away. I hope you and Chloe can forgive me. I can't sit around waiting for the cops to find them while they hunt us down and trick our friends. I'm going to see if I can find them before they get far. Stay safe and don't worry about me. As long as I don't drink, I can always go into beast mode. ;)

—Travis

I smiled at the winky face he drew next to beast mode, but my lips fell. I didn't blame him for leaving, but maybe he would have taken me with him if I'd told him what I could do. He couldn't take them down by himself. Part of me felt better that he could change to protect himself, but that didn't stop me from worrying.

"What's the plan?" I tossed the paper on the counter, looking from Kat to Miles.

"Right now, it's for you to shower and change so we can discuss this when you feel better," Miles said.

"I'm fine. Did any of them get arrested last night? Fra . . . I mean, Dr. Roulings?" I must have looked like crap if he was telling me to go shower.

"No." Miles swallowed. "There were no signs of an attack, and everything was cleaned up—just like the precinct."

"And the Vault." I sighed.

"You should shower, and when Chloe wakes up, we can go over a few things." Miles stood up and grabbed a protein bar, tossing it my way. "Eat this. The bathroom is down the hall and there're towels in the closet at the end."

"Oh, and don't forget these." Kat walked over and handed me a small bag. "I picked them up this morning and guessed on sizes."

"Thanks." I took the bag, deciding I probably smelled like vomit and was nose-blind to it.

After eating the protein bar and showering, I opted for a T-shirt and a pair of jeans from the bag. I appreciated her skill at size-guessing and felt instantly better, even though I smelled like a man from Miles's shampoo. I used some mouthwash and brushed my teeth with my finger to help with my putrid breath, which would have to suffice.

When I emerged from the bathroom, Chloe was sitting on the couch with her legs tucked underneath her. She had a bucket next to her on the floor, and her face was very pale. I was lucky I didn't feel that bad. The shower, plus the pill, had helped my headache turn into a dull throb.

"You look rough." I sat in the chair.

"I feel worse than rough." Chloe closed her eyes.

"You should shower. It might help." My speedy healing must have aided me.

"Nope. I'm not moving. I'm just going to sit here and let the pain reliever kick in." Chloe wrapped her arms around her stomach and shot Miles and Kat a look. "Will you guys please just tell us what we need to know?"

"It's a lot to take in, especially for you, Harper." Miles paused before continuing. "Besides who was there, it's as if last night never happened. The bar's surveillance was down, so they don't have a recording of Dr. Roulings being there. All the information we had on him in our system disappeared, along with his picture we took the other night. We didn't want to raise awareness of Travis and him, so we created a small, separate file. Your transferred statement was also erased."

"Someone went to great lengths to make sure he didn't show up in our system and deleted any record we had of him. We're not completely sure if we were hacked or if it was an inside job," Kat interjected.

"I had a camera on my motorcycle," Miles said as he leaned off the counter, "but it's too dark and foggy to make out any faces. It's being investigated, so they can't toss your case yet."

"Miles called me last night. He knew something was off and asked for photos from an old case I was looking into. I remembered hearing about the case, and it had similarities to yours." Kat grabbed a folder off the counter and walked over to us. "Miles came across this photo and recognized Dr. Roulings. This picture was mixed in with an old military case, but there was no name or info on who he was. He was a ghost." She handed me a photo of two men, nicely dressed, with their arms around each other. They were clean-shaven, with grins from ear to ear, and looked like buddies.

"That's Frank." My eyes narrowed in on one of them, who looked like a much younger, healthier version of Frank with dark-brown hair. The other man looked familiar, with his dirty-blond hair and bright-blue eyes, but I couldn't place it.

"I was about to contact you guys, but Brandon beat me to it, telling me the three of you stupidly snuck off with his car and Frank." Miles sternly looked at us as I swallowed and averted my gaze. I had felt so crappy earlier that I didn't think about how angry and disappointed he would be. "Something was blocking the signal to the trackers in your phones. I couldn't locate them, and I imagine Dr. Roulings had something to do with that."

"So, you did put trackers in our phones?" I wouldn't put it past him as I unintentionally make things complicated.

"There's more," Miles continued, ignoring me as his face softened. "After your conversation with Dr. Roulings last night, I did some digging. Your father and he were partners. Dr. Roulings mentioned your father had passed away, and that is the same with the other man in that photo. His name was Benjamin Westbrook, and that photo was from twenty-three years ago."

Kat looked at Miles, who nodded. She pulled out a folded newspaper and handed it to me. She had it open to the obituary page. Miles walked over and knelt in front of me.

"He had a daughter. Our records say she passed away almost five years ago." He pointed to one of the photos. "Harper, her name is Isa Grace Westbrook."

Chloe sat up and leaned over. "Whoa."

It looked like me—younger, but it was me. My blond, wavy hair was the same, but shorter, and my eyes were the same light brown, but my face was softer. I had to be about thirteen or fourteen in the picture. "How did you find this?"

"I did some research and found out when Benjamin's daughter died. No other photos of you exist online—just in the newspaper, and that Isa Westbrook had passed away on December fifth five years ago. I was able to pull it from the archive in the library. They managed to make it so no one could look you up and facial recognition software wouldn't recognize you," Miles said softly.

"Whoever Alcorp is, they're good at covering things up." Kat took a couple steps back to give me some space. I wondered how she'd heard about Alcorp, but then realized I had mentioned it during my statement, and she had probably been filled in by Miles. Miles had been listening through the speaker in his helmet last night, and I wondered what exactly he had filled her in about that, too.

"The Smith guy said that they bought the building twelve years ago. If that was the case, why does it have my father's name on it, if he was dead?" I felt like a deer in headlights.

"Your father founded the company. Kat and I assume Alcorp is using it as a front and had bought the building before turning it into a research facility." Miles stood up.

"What are we going to do?" Chloe's voice was barely audible.

Kat straightened up and cleared her throat. "We're going to put you guys into witness protection. That's the only thing we can do to keep you both safe for now."

"Do you know where my mother is? *Who* she is?" I glanced at Chloe, who had gained back a little bit of color.

"We are going to reach out to your mother and have you meet. The news is going to be a lot to take in for her and your stepfather. We'll—"

"Stepfather?" I cut her off.

"Yes, you had a stepfather for a while before you were taken," Kat continued. "We'll inform them of what happened and our plans to put you into witness protection. We'll have an officer or agent keep an eye out for their safety in case Roulings decides to use them to get to you."

"Do you think he'd send his . . . men after them?"

"At this point, no. But it's better to be safe than sorry. From the little bit we could see from Miles's video and from what Miles has said, his men are well-trained." It didn't sound like she knew, and if she did, she would know one officer was not enough protection. I guess Miles hadn't shared everything with her.

"Wait . . ." Chloe's eyes bulged as she looked at me. She must have just realized what she had seen last night. I discreetly shook my head. Thankfully, she got the hint and didn't ask about the Hybrians. "I'll take that protein bar now, please."

Miles nodded as Kat gave her and me a strange look.

"I'm not going into witness protection." My statement got Miles's attention quickly. "I want to help find my friends, and we have a better chance if I'm not hiding."

"You don't really have a choice," Kat said, and I knew Miles was thinking the same thing.

"You're saying I don't have the right to deny witness protection?" I questioned her.

She sighed and put her hands on her hips. "You know the risks and dangers."

"More than you." She had no clue what was actually out there.

"And what about you?" Kat asked Chloe, disregarding my unintentionally harsh comment.

"Same." Chloe curled back up on the couch, trying to stomach the protein bar Miles had handed her. "I'm staying. Maybe we'll find out who I am. I had another memory last night. I was on a hot sidewalk with a buttload of people around and the sun beamed off skyscrapers. I was feeding my chips to the pigeons." She smiled at the memory.

"Chloe, that's awesome!" With each memory, we were closer to finding out who she had been.

"This is putting your lives in danger. You guys should really consider witness protection." Kat looked at Miles for help.

"It'll be safer in witness protection. You can still help, just from farther away." Miles crossed his arms.

"No, and this is something I won't budge on." I shook my head.

"Yeah, nope." Chloe agreed.

Miles sighed. "So, it looks like we have to figure out what we're going to do with you two. I have a feeling trouble is ahead."

"That's all you got?" Kat murmured to Miles.

"There's no persuading these two. Especially that one," he mused as he waved a finger at me.

I brought the picture of my father and Frank to the front. Benjamin Westbrook was my father and I was his daughter, Isa Grace Westbrook. My real name sounded foreign to me, and the more I stared at my father's picture, the more I saw the resemblance. His rosy cheeks and dimples matched mine, but I must have gotten my fair skin from my mother. I had always thought that if I saw a picture of my parents, it would stimulate a memory; I was mistaken.

CHAPTER TWENTY-THREE

"Did you eat lunch? We can grab something once we get out of downtown," Miles asked, even though it was two o'clock and we were stuck in traffic. His motorcycle sounded nice right about now instead of his red truck.

"Thanks, but I ate at the café," I lied. I didn't have breakfast or lunch because I was too nervous about going to spend the weekend with my mother and stepfather.

I was relieved to be getting out of the city after living in a small apartment with Chloe in downtown Portland for the last two-and-a-half weeks. I had done some research at the library regarding Canby and the surrounding area where I grew up. Canby wasn't a small town, but it was minuscule compared to Portland.

"You said your grandparents have land?" I glanced over at Miles. He hadn't mentioned exactly where his grandparents lived when he had invited me to stay a night after staying at my old house this weekend.

He nodded. "They live on a farm."

"Is that where you grew up?" The privacy and abundance of land would be a warm welcome to release my powers—the reason Miles had suggested it.

Miles hesitated before answering, "Yes. My grandparents raised me. My father was in the Army and my mom passed when I was little. My father died while serving when I was fourteen. That's part of the reason I enlisted to become a Navy SEAL as soon as I could at seventeen."

"I'm so sorry, Miles." My unanswered questions regarding him were starting to make sense.

"Unfortunately, it's life. Everyone gets dealt a different hand." There was resentment in his voice.

Once we weren't stuck in traffic, the drive was a little more than half an hour, and my lip was chafed from biting it so much. I had briefly met my mother and stepfather, Joe, at the precinct two weeks ago, the day after the bar incident, but the warm welcome hadn't jarred any memories and had left me feeling empty.

Miles constantly checked the rearview mirror the entire drive. We turned into a nice community with two-story houses and medium-sized yards before pulling up to a sage house with white trim, black shutters, and a partially stoned wall around the front door.

"Here we go." I shoved the anxiety riddled on my face deep down. Miles looked over at me as he parked the truck.

"You can do this." He didn't shut off the ignition yet, and I half expected my mother to come running out the front door, but, thankfully, she didn't.

"I've longed for this moment, but . . ." I didn't know how to define it.

"It's a part of your life that you should remember, but don't." His voice softened. "No one expects you to jump right back in where you left off. A lot has happened, and they understand. Take as much time as you need."

"I've had five years." This was the easy part, right? It was easier than being in the Vault, or at least it should be.

He reached for the keys in the ignition and turned off his truck. We both got out, flipping forward our seats. Miles reached across the truck and grabbed my bag before I could.

I glared at him. "I'm more than capable of carrying my stuff."

"I know." The corner of his mouth curved upward. I rolled my eyes and went to shut the door but stopped when he spoke again. "Open the plastic bag."

I looked down to see a bulky plastic bag. I reached down and pulled out a black leather jacket in my size.

"I figured you haven't gotten a jacket yet, and I know how much you loved shopping for clothes," he joked as he shut his door and walked around to the front of the truck.

"Thank you, really." I shut the door, smiling as I shrugged on the jacket. "It fits perfectly." I had put off getting a jacket the last two weeks as fall approached. Kat had set us up with bank accounts and IDs. Harper West was my fake name, and I preferred it over Isa. Working at G.A.H.O, Brandon's parent's café, had helped put money in our accounts.

I took a deep breath when we reached the front door and rang the doorbell. My mother immediately opened, her blond hair pinned back and a white apron covering her Carolina-blue top with rolled-up sleeves and khakis.

"Hi! Come on in." She beamed as she waved us in. "This is your home too. You don't ever need to ring the doorbell."

I stepped into the decent-sized foyer.

"Hi, Isa." Joe took up most of the archway leading to a cozy living room. "Hello, Officer MacLand, nice to see you again. Let me take your guys' bags and coats."

"Thank you, sir, but I don't mind carrying the bags." Miles gave him a polite nod.

"Isa?" Joe held out his hand, and I shrugged off my jacket, giving it to him. He hung it up in the closet while my mother cheerfully hugged Miles.

"Nice to see you again, Mrs. Westbrook." Miles repressed a smile as beeping rang from the other room.

"I should check on the pies." She smiled before heading down the hall. My mother and Joe had married when I was thirteen, but she had kept our last name.

Joe led us up the stairs to show us where we would be staying. The last photo on the staircase wall stopped me from ascending the final step. It was a picture of my mother, Joe, a younger me, and a Chocolate Labrador Retriever mix. I wanted to know the story behind the love and happiness in it; I wanted to remember.

"You were twelve in that photo." Joe pivoted on the landing to look at me with joyful mocha-colored eyes.

"Who's this?" I rubbed my finger over the spot where the dog was.

"That's Taco. You named him when you were seven. He took good care of you." Joe smiled in admiration. "You loved tacos. That's actually what your mom's making tonight."

"What happened to him?" I studied Taco's white chest, which had longer fur than the rest of him.

"He passed away a couple years after you, uh, were taken." He attempted to mask his frown. "He lived a good, long life. You guys rescued him from the shelter when he was two."

I swallowed. Those were two things in my life that I would never get to see again: my father and my dog. Joe continued, and I followed him with Miles in tow. He walked down the hallway and stopped in front of a closed white door.

He opened it, stepping aside. "This is your room."

Miles handed me my bag, and I stepped into the mint-green painted room—definitely had a teenager feel. A cloud-white comforter was neatly tucked over a full-size bed with a matching armoire and vanity off to the left. Next to the vanity was a double set of closet doors, and across from me was a huge double window with a bench and a telescope on its stand.

"It didn't feel right to change anything. Your mom came in here once a month to clean an untouched room." Joe sighed. "Anyways, we'll leave you to settle in, and I'll show Officer MacLand his room. It's across from yours, not that you'll need to know where he's sleeping." Joe's cheeks flushed against his umber skin, not meaning to say the last part out loud. "The bathroom is across the hall, and we're on the opposite end if you need anything."

Miles spoke as Joe turned. "Actually, Mr. Burns—"

"Please, call me Joe," he interrupted as he smiled, face still flushed. He definitely acted like a father figure. Miles was there on duty, but anyone could notice he was young and handsome.

Miles smiled in acceptance. "I was wondering if you wouldn't mind if I stayed on the couch. I can hear more if anything were to happen."

"Certainly. There's a sunroom downstairs with a pullout couch that would work. It's near the back door next to the kitchen. There's a half bath down there, so if you want to shower, you'll need to use the bathroom up here."

They went back downstairs as I tossed my duffle on the floor and sat on the bed. Nothing was ringing a bell, despite its homey feel. I lay back on the bed and laughed at the glow-in-the-dark stars stuck to the ceiling. They weren't glowing right now, but they would tonight.

A couple of pictures resting on the vanity caught my attention, and I hopped off the bed to walk over to them. One was a picture of my father, bright and cheeky, as he held up a drawing. Underneath the blue-eyed stick figure with yellow hair was signed with sloppy handwriting, *To Daddy, Love Isa.*

Tears swelled in my eyes. I didn't understand why it hurt so much to have lost someone I didn't even remember. Even though he was the reason this had happened to me, he was also the reason my mother and I were still alive. It sounded like he had wanted out and not to be a part of what Frank was doing.

My memories weren't returning, and I didn't want to be in my old room anymore. I wiped the brim of my eyes and headed downstairs. Miles was helping my mother and Joe set up the table outside on the spacious back deck. If it weren't for the privacy fence and the tall bushes, I doubt we would be able to sit outside for dinner. No one else was supposed to know I was alive.

My mother and Joe shared stories during dinner as Miles

genuinely enjoyed them. The stories were interesting to me, because they were my past, but I thought they would've been boring to anyone else. We each had a small sliver of the three different-flavored pies my mother had thought that four people needed before going inside.

Miles sat on the pale almond-colored sofa while I looked at the pictures on the wood mantel over the fireplace. There was one of my father, which meant he couldn't have been a bad person, *right*? Either way, it was reassuring that my mother kept one of him up in the living room.

"Unfortunately, the cookies aren't fresh. I made them yesterday." My mother walked in with a plate of cookies and placed them on the oak coffee table. "Did you guys want milk?" She put her hand to her mouth as her cheeks turned to rose. "Or anything else to drink? Isa, I know you just turned twenty—you can have a tiny glass of wine? Oh, if that's okay . . ." She nervously glanced at Miles, as if she had just remembered he was a cop and the legal drinking age was twenty-one.

"I'm okay." I had flinched at my name, but thankfully, she didn't notice.

"Miles?" she asked.

"That's okay, thank you." Miles leaned back into the couch, crossing his ankle over his knee.

Joe came in and took a seat in one of the chairs, sighing at the plate full of cookies as my mother went back into the kitchen. "She bakes when she gets emotional. She's a wonderful baker, though."

"I'm sorry. This has to be difficult for both of you," I said.

"Don't apologize." Joe sat up. "There's nothing in this world we wanted more than to have you back. And here you are—that is everything we could have ever wished for. There're no words to describe how happy your mom and I are. She's just trying not to overwhelm you. She's nervous she's going to scare you off."

"I may not have my memories, but you guys are family; her cooking would never scare me off," I managed to joke. At least one thing that I've learned from the Vault was that family was everything—even if they weren't blood.

My mother walked back in with two large green photo albums and sat in the chair next to me.

"I dug these out of our closet in case you wanted to look through them." She set them down on the coffee table. "If you don't want to, sweetie, you don't have to."

"I think it would be good." I blankly stared at the closed albums that carried fragments of my missing life inside.

I leaned forward and opened the photo album on top, angling it so my mother could look with me. There were photos from when I was a baby to my disappearance, along with other family members. I guess I had a few relatives, but they lived in different states. When I started the next album filled with pictures of my mother and father, she mentioned that they had met at Michigan State University. I flipped the page and saw one of my father in a military uniform.

"Was he in the military?" I asked her, glancing at Miles, who casually looked our way while Joe and he talked.

"He helped with molecular biology research at a base in New Mexico for a year before we eventually moved out here. He founded a research facility here in Oregon that soon turned into a corporation. It works on discovering ways to manage and cure terminal diseases." She took a deep breath. "He always had a heart for helping others."

"So, he was in the military for only a year?" I raised an eyebrow.

"Yes . . . and no." She reached over and touched the photo. "He already was when I met him during his studies. After a year on base, he had to travel a lot. Eventually, he landed here, and I moved here with him." She wrung her hands as Joe watched her sympathetically. "A cure he was working on failed, but he ended up creating a medicine that helps relieve certain symptoms for multiple diseases. When something failed, he was hard on himself, so I didn't want to upset him further with questions about the cures."

"Do they still research cures? At his old corporation, that is," I asked.

"I think so. After your father passed away, another research company took over the corporation. I was never really involved with any of it."

"What about you? What do you do?" She looked with-drawn, so I decided to steer the topic away from my father, despite my curiosity. She didn't need the added stress, nor could I tell her about the situation and why I needed to know. Not only would it crush her, but I wasn't supposed to say anything yet.

Kat had told her I had been held in a facility with other young adolescents, and they weren't allowed to know more at this time to protect me until they caught the perpetrators. My mother and Joe had promised to keep my being alive a secret until it was safe. In reality, it was more to protect them.

My mother perked up when I had asked, and she said that she was an occupational therapist. She told me about her work, along with more stories, and when we got to a stop-ping point, I glanced at the clock on the wall. It was already ten.

"I think I'm going to head upstairs. Thank you. Every-thing was delicious." I stood awkwardly.

"It's so good to have you home." My mother stood, giving me another long hug like she had at the precinct, except this time she didn't need Joe to pry her off.

Joe stood and gave me a quick hug with a noogie. "It's good to see you, kiddo."

"I'll walk you to your room." Miles nodded to them before following me to the stairs. I sensed Joe's urge to protest, but he kept quiet as my mother shot him a warning glance.

"How are you holding up?" he asked once we were in front of my door.

"Good. A little awkward, but this feels right, like this is where I should be." I chewed the inside of my cheek.

"But?" He raised an eyebrow.

I sighed and lowered my voice. "I should be out there doing something about Frank and the Hybrians. Not to mention figuring out what my father did." I stared at him, waiting for him to tell me that I was thinking irrationally and should let them do the searching.

"You should get some sleep. It sounds like they have plans to show you the area tomorrow," he said instead.

"You're okay with me leaving this house?" My eyebrow raised.

"Goodnight." He smugly smirked before leaving.

A couple of hours passed as sleep evaded me. I tossed and turned trying to get comfortable, despite the coziness of the down comforter. I stood and went over to the window seat, where grey cushions and mint-green pillows greeted me as I looked out the window. Worn spots where the window closed and the locks slid caught my attention. My finger ran over the tattered track underneath the locks before flipping the latches and opening the window. Cool air washed over my face and goosebumps rose as I leaned out, surprised there wasn't a screen.

There was a coral robe on the back of the bedroom door, and I decided to throw it on so I could investigate. Its softness cradled my body as I climbed out onto the roof, leaving the window open a crack behind me. I carefully sat down in the middle of the roof and huddled my knees against my chest while covering my feet under the robe. The stars were breathtaking in the clear sky, and I was able to identify Ursa Major easily, along with other constellations.

The sky suddenly shifted and the air warmed around me. I looked down to see that I no longer wore my blue, plaid pajama pants and yellow shirt, but wore shorts and a different shirt instead. I heard the window creak and looked over to see an unfamiliar figure climbing through, hidden in the shadows of the light shining from my bedroom.

"I've got the chips. I couldn't resist buying different kinds." The unfamiliar figure spoke as I tried to make out the details of his face.

"Harper?" This time a familiar voice spoke, and I jumped as a hand landed on my shoulder.

My eyes flew open, and I propped myself up from being curled on my side, still on the roof.

"Was I asleep?" I shivered and looked down at my robe as Miles knelt next to me.

"Yes. I heard something and went to check on you. I knocked, but you didn't answer."

"Oh." I must have fallen asleep fairly quickly.

"Everything okay?" He shifted and sat next to me, resting his arms across his knees. The slanted roof made it so the angle didn't interfere with his injury, and I shivered just looking at him in shorts and a T-shirt.

"Yeah," I said as I pulled the robe tighter around me. "I think I came out here often. Apparently, I know some constellations."

"I didn't think you'd climb out here to sleep when it's fifty out," he gently teased. "You seemed confused when I woke you. Were you dreaming?"

"I think so. It was short and felt real, but it wasn't my reoccurring nightmare." My eyes widened as his brows furrowed. He didn't know about my other dream, the one that now included him lying lifeless outside the death pit on blood-soaked grass, smoke rising from his body. "You must be cold—we should go in." I went to stand, but he put a hand out.

"I'm fine. If you're cold, we can go in. But if you're not, you can inform me of what's what." He pointed to the sky.

"Umm, okay." I bit my lip and settled back down. I started to point out the different constellations and stars from the knowledge that I didn't remember learning, which I'm sure he already knew.

CHAPTER TWENTY-FOUR

"Pick a hat." Miles held out two hats in one hand and a pair of sunglasses in the other. I eyed the sunglasses and raised an eyebrow. I glanced out the window behind him at the foggy weather.

"Just keep it low." He pulled back the sunglasses, knowing the weather was colder and gloomier today without having to check.

I took the army-green hat with a sepia American flag on the front because it looked smaller and went with my white sneakers, jeans, heather-grey V-neck, and leather jacket. After I chose, he put on the plain blue hat with a black American flag on the back.

"You brought hats?" I questioned him, trying not to stare at how attractive he looked in a hat.

He shrugged. "Five years can be a long time, but when you're not a kid, appearances tend not to change as much."

"Fair enough." I headed to the garage, where my mother and Joe sat in the silver Volkswagen Atlas.

Miles opened the rear passenger door for me, and I climbed in, sitting on the tan leather seats. He shut the door and climbed in on the opposite side. His jawline twitched, hating the fact that he wasn't the one in the driver's seat. Sometimes his control inclinations were a bit much.

"We'll stop at the school first. We can't go in, but we can walk around the outside," my mother cheerfully said from the passenger seat.

I shot Miles a look, unsure if it was a good idea to go

looking around my old school. Disgust rose in my chest at giving satisfaction to Alcorp by keeping up with my fake-death charade, but I couldn't put anyone else in danger. My mother only knew I was alive because she had the right to know once I'd found out who I was. I took a breath, calming my emotions. They hadn't spiraled out of control in a while.

"I went over their plans with them this morning." Miles noticed my glance. "We checked the schedule; there are no events scheduled at the school. The weather is also in our favor. Just keep your head down, and if anyone asks, we are distant cousins who are visiting."

I nodded and looked back out the window as we left my old neighborhood of cookie-cutter houses. As we reached the school, we drove around to the back, parking in a small parking lot across from a gated football field.

"You were a freshman. Football games weren't your go-to on Friday nights." My mother's voice wavered after we climbed out of the car.

"That doesn't surprise me." The thought of freezing out there didn't appeal to me.

"You spent most of your free time with Dylan." She gulped.

"Dylan?" I raised an eyebrow.

"He was—is"—she looked down—"I'm sorry, I don't know . . ." Her voice trailed off.

"It's okay." I reached out and put my hand on her shoulder. "It can't be easy for your daughter to come back from the dead, especially a crazy daughter like me, who happens to have amnesia." That got a small laugh out of her. "You can tell me your narrative however you want. I promise I won't be upset." I lowered my hand.

"I see you still act so grown up." She continued, "Dylan has been your best friend since elementary. You guys did everything together—rode bikes, played games, watched movies, had sleepovers . . ."

"Stargaze?" I added as she went down memory lane.

She chuckled. "All the time. You would take your telescope out on the porch. We could never get you guys to come inside." That explained how I knew the constellations.

"We should get started. Let's walk around." Joe waved for us to follow.

Nothing jump-started my memory after four hours of exploring the town. My mother and Joe did their best to hide their disappointment, and so did I as we pulled into the garage.

"Thanks, Joe. We'll meet you inside." I stopped at the bottom of the stairs leading into the house as Joe held open the door. He nodded and went in, letting the door close behind him while I turned to face Miles.

"Are you all right?" His hazel eyes studied me.

"Do you always do that?" I said without thinking.

"What?"

Crap. "Study me. Study people. You're always analyzing everything."

He cocked his head. "Of course. It's my job."

"I don't mean it in a bad way." I shook my head. "Anyways, I'm glad you're here, and wanted to thank you. You're always helping me out." I smiled and quickly turned before he could see me blush. My intention was to thank him while we were alone, instead of sounding like a babbling idiot.

In the kitchen, my mother and Joe were already busy prepping the chicken alfredo for dinner. Right as we sat down to eat, the doorbell rang.

"Were you expecting anyone tonight?" Miles stood, pushing back the chair.

"No, but we have a lot of friends and neighbors that like to stop by." My mother shrugged as Joe turned his head to look at her.

The doorbell rang again, twice.

"They'll go away." Joe took a bite of pasta.

"Not if it's the Galsiminas." My mother nervously rolled

her eyes. Miles narrowed his eyes at her when the doorbell rang again.

"I don't think they're going away, and we don't need them looking around. Harper, go in the sunroom." Miles stood, pulling his gun from a hidden holster tucked in the back of his jeans. My mother's and Joe's eyes widened.

Miles walked over to the living-room window and peeked through the curtain. "It's a young man."

Joe walked over and discreetly pulled back the curtain. "It's Dylan. What's he doing here?" He looked at my mother, who shrugged.

"Who's Dylan?" Miles's unbreakable expression made my mother and Joe both swallow. I don't think he realized how much his solidity and seriousness stunned them.

"He's a kid from around the corner. We've known him since he was little." My mother rubbed her arm.

"The one you mentioned earlier?" Miles's eyebrow raised.

"Yes."

Miles sighed and put his gun away. "Okay. Go ahead and answer it. If he wants to come in, tell him you guys are sick and not up for company."

Rushed knocks sounded from the door this time. Miles ushered me into the sunroom with the curtains drawn as my mother and Joe went to answer it. After I was out of sight, he hid behind the wall across from the sunroom. The spot provided him a good visual down the hallway to the front door, while also maintaining eyes on me.

I couldn't see anything as I heard the front door open.

"Oh, hi, Dylan. What brings you by?" My mother's voice faltered at sounding cheerful.

"Just thought I'd stop by for a visit." I heard a confused boy's voice after a long pause.

"Oh, dear, Joe and I don't feel good. We aren't really up for visitors," my mother said. Hushed whispers sounded, and Miles glanced at me, shaking his head in annoyance.

"Maybe we can chat in a few days when we feel better?" Joe added.

"I'm sorry. I know she's here, and I need to see her." Rustling sounded, and Miles steadily drew his gun.

"Dylan, wait . . ." Joe called.

It sounded like the boy had checked the living room and now moved down the hallway in our direction. Miles put a hand up at me as the footsteps got closer. He stepped out from behind the wall, gun drawn.

"PPD, don't take another step." Miles's voice sent shivers down my spine, and I could only imagine the fear coursing through that boy.

"Holy crap!" The boy's voice shook.

"He's okay, he won't do anything," Joe said with concern.

"I'm as harmless as they come," Dylan interjected.

"Why are you here?" Miles aimed his gun steadily down the hall.

"I, uh . . ."

"Don't look at them. Look at me."

"To see Isa."

"Isa Westbrook? Their daughter?" Miles paused. "She's dead."

"Oh crap, sorry, I didn't mean to look at them," Dylan said nervously. He'd probably subconsciously looked at my mother and Joe for help.

"Mr. . . . Officer . . . I mean, sir," Dylan stumbled, "I know she's alive. I know I wasn't supposed to come here while she was here, but I couldn't resist. I need to see she's okay with my own eyes."

Something he said struck me. I slowly emerged from the sunroom, revealing myself around the corner. Dylan's auburn eyes widened behind his glasses when he saw me.

"Harper . . ." Miles growled.

Dylan shook in his black Converse shoes with his hands in the air as sweaty, dark circles dampened his armpits through his blue peacock button up. He was tall and slender, with curly black hair, and his pale skin suggested he did not spend much time outside.

"What did you say?" I asked, ignoring Miles's warning.

"Who, me?" Dylan nervously put his hands on his chest, but quickly put them back up in the air. He looked harmless, but on the other hand, I'd learned not to judge a person by their appearance and even initial demeanor.

"Yes." I took a step forward, standing next to Miles.

"I have to see you?"

"No, before that."

"Um, I knew that you were here and I couldn't resist," Dylan answered.

I couldn't resist. I had heard that in my dream with the same voice. "My mom said we would stargaze on the porch. Did we ever on the roof?"

His auburn eyes shifted behind his black-framed glasses from Miles to me. "Uh, yeah. Yeah, all the time."

"What?! You guys snuck out onto the roof?" my mother exclaimed as Joe nudged her with his elbow.

I couldn't hide the small smile that spread across my lips. "You're the chip guy. You're also in the photos I saw last night." A bunch of the photos that my mother had shown me were of me and a young boy with wild, curly black hair and glasses. The boy who stood in front of me was considerably more grown up and not a boy anymore.

"Mhmm. Could you please tell James Bond to put the gun down?" Dylan sucked in a nervous breath.

"He's okay." I put a hand on Miles's arm until he lowered his gun.

"Oh, man." Dylan rubbed his sweaty hands on his jeans. "I thought you were going to shoot me."

"Just because I didn't doesn't mean I won't." Miles tucked the gun back in his holster. "What are you doing here?"

"Uh . . ."

"I told him." My mother nervously rubbed the back of her hand.

"Why would you do that?" Frustration crossed Joe's face. She turned to him. "I thought he deserved to know. This entire time, he blamed himself for not saving her."

"Can I talk to you both in the kitchen?" Miles looked between my mother and Joe. They nodded and walked toward the kitchen. Miles's stern eyes told me not to do anything stupid as he walked by.

"So, you're alive." Dylan wore a sheepish smile.

"I am."

"I'm sorry for the scene. I didn't realize you'd have a T-800." He itched his forehead.

"It's fine. He can be a little overbearing." I laughed at the *Terminator* movie reference and wondered if I had watched it with him.

"Yeah. I hope I didn't get your mom in trouble," he added, frowning.

"I'm sure she's secretly happy you showed up." I didn't doubt she'd known who it was on the first ring. "What did she tell you about me?"

He shrugged. "Just that you were alive and lacked your memories. You were taken and held with others. It has to be kept a secret to keep you and anyone you know safe because the bad guys are still out there."

"That's it?" I asked.

"That and you can't remember anything before the night you were taken. It's like a Jason Bourne movie." He was funny, and I was surprised I understood most of his movie references. I could see how we were friends.

Miles walked in with the other two right behind him. "Congratulations, Dylan, you can stay for one hour." He leaned up against the wall, crossing his arms over his chest. He wasn't a fan of surprises, and Dylan was a surprise.

"Good." I went to sit in the living room and the others followed. Miles wasn't happy about the situation, but so far, the only thing I had remembered was a dream that Dylan was in. I needed to talk to him.

We sat in awkward silence as Miles scowled at Dylan, who fidgeted on the couch next to my mother and Joe.

"I have so many questions." Dylan anxiously looked among the four of us, breaking the silence.

"They can't be answered," Miles said dryly.

I frowned at Miles and stood. "Tell you what: Dylan and I are going to the sunroom so we can talk without him being scorned."

"I don't think so." Miles stood.

"And you don't control me." I held my ground and wasn't going to let him order me around. "Part of the reason we came here was to help get my memories back, remember?"

Of course he remembered. His face remained hard as he grumbled and waved his hand toward the sunroom. "I'll be in the kitchen—*after* I do a perimeter sweep."

CHAPTER TWENTY-FIVE

Dylan scurried right behind me as I shut the French doors to the sunroom. There were a couple of cushioned patio chairs and a brown futon with a neatly folded blanket and pillow on top.

"That was rough." I led Dylan over to the chairs.

"It sure was," he agreed as he sat.

I looked down at my folded hands in my lap. "So, we were best friends?"

He raised an eyebrow—I assumed at my use of the past tense. "Yeah, we did everything together and knew everything about each other. I knew who you had a crush on and you knew who I had a crush on." He chuckled.

I forced a smile, wishing I could remember. "And we snuck out onto the roof a lot?"

"Yeah. We could see more sky." He talked so casually about our past.

"My mother said you blamed yourself for not being able to save me the night I supposedly died?" I felt bad for going right in, but I doubted Miles would give us long.

"It was . . . difficult. I didn't know you were alive. I would have looked for you." His eyes were somber. "I'm so sorry."

"It's not your fault. It sounds like they covered up my death and practically all of my existence very well." I paused. "How did I die?"

No one had explained to me how I had supposedly died; they had only said that I was reported dead almost five years ago. He frowned in response.

"If you don't mind me asking," I quickly added.

He fiddled with his glasses and sighed before his eyes became bright again. "No, I don't mind. I thought someone would have told you."

"Nope. They think I'm this fragile person that needs protecting." That came out more rashly than I intended.

"That's far from true. I'll tell you all that I know." His cheeks puckered for a moment until he released the air. "The night you died . . . well, when everyone thought you died . . . we were having a movie night at my house while my parents were out. It was comedy night. Most Fridays and Saturdays we would have movie night and rotate between horror, action, rom-com . . . you name it. You were picking the movie while I grabbed the snacks and soda."

"You seemed to have liked your snacks," I joked, thinking about the memory I had where he had brought multiple bags of chips out onto the roof.

"I still do. You did too." He chuckled. "Anyways, you were downstairs and I was up in the kitchen. It was weird. I remember an odd pinch in my neck and then getting dizzy before passing out on the kitchen floor. Our furnace had malfunctioned and was leaking carbon monoxide through the vents before catching on fire. It was in the basement—the same room you were in.

"When I woke, I was outside being loaded into an ambulance." He sighed. "They found me in the front yard, but I don't remember how I got there. They said I must have dragged myself outside while I was disorientated and just don't remember because of the fumes. I kept telling them you were in there—they told me they were working on getting to you. The entire house was engulfed in flames behind them." His head hung low. "They couldn't get to you before the house collapsed. It wasn't until the next day when they . . . found your body . . . unrecognizable and charred." His eyes pooled with tears.

"That wasn't me." My heart ached. How could anyone hurt people like this? Alcorp had no boundaries.

"Thankfully." He shook his head. "I don't want to know whose body they found."

"Me neither. Hopefully it was fake." Shivers ran up my spine.

"The body matched your DNA, so the autopsy had to have been falsified, but that doesn't rule out if it was another person or a fake," he said gravely.

"You got to see the report?"

"Uh, yeah. I couldn't believe that you were dead. Everything just seemed . . . fishy. So, I hacked into the police server and found your autopsy report." He took a deep breath. "It looked convincing."

I raised an eyebrow at him. "Sounds about right."

"Our furnace wasn't even that old; my parents couldn't believe that it happened. They were distraught," he continued. "Once your mom told me you were alive, I started to dig some more." He paused. "Do you mind if I ask you a question?"

"Go for it." I wanted to know what he'd meant by 'dig some more.'

"What did they do to you . . . and to the others?"

"What do you mean?"

"You don't hold hostages under a research facility and not do anything to them." He timidly shrugged.

"I thought my mother didn't know where we were kept?"

"Oh, she doesn't." His head hung low. "She thinks it's more of a trafficking situation, even though the police reassured her it wasn't."

Her poor heart. I guess I had never put much thought into what she believed had happened to me the last five years. I had thought that her not knowing the truth would protect her, but it might be haunting her even more.

"The police were right. I didn't know that she thought

that . . . is she okay?" She was battling a lot more than just her back-from-the-dead daughter visiting.

"She's tough, like you. Your visit makes her happy, and I think seeing you healthy helps. After all, she is a mom. They usually think the worst, but she'll be just fine."

"So how do you know that, then?" I asked curiously.

"I know things." He grinned from ear to ear. "I'm good with computers."

"That never went into a police record, though."

"No, but a random inspection that clears out a branch of your dad's old business for two days and then you resurfacing shortly after isn't suspicious or anything." Dylan rolled his eyes.

The public had been told that Westbrook was closed for a couple of days because of *something* they'd found during an inspection. Everything had been deemed safe shortly after. Those who knew the truth were furious, but the others, who believed it was a bunker, had been asked by the FBI to remain quiet. It hadn't been publicized to keep citizens safe from attempting to sneak down there. Yet the investigation wasn't officially closed—at least, that's what I had been told. He looked at me with eager eyes, wanting to know more, but remained quiet.

I sighed. "Don't tell Miles I told you this"—he nodded in response—"but they pretty much ran test trials on us. They gave us injections daily and watched what we ate and made us exercise." Exercise was an understatement.

That little tidbit was probably too much. After Frank, I wasn't sure who I could trust. Could I trust my old best friend whom I used to sneak out onto the roof to stargaze with or watch movies with? I hoped so, but the truth could also put him in danger.

"I—" Dylan looked off behind me, and I turned to see Miles barging through the French doors.

"You guys have five more minutes." Miles looked between us both and left.

"Miles can . . . he can take his job seriously." Part of me wanted to say be protective.

"He's terrifying—hot terrifying." Dylan looked from the doors to me.

I raised an eyebrow and he laughed, knowing what I was questioning.

"Sometimes we had the same crush in school." He winked.

I had a gay best friend. That explained a few things. I imagined Joe wouldn't have let me hang out alone with a boy as teenagers, even if we had been best friends since we were little. He was having a hard time with Miles there as a cop.

"Hey, Izz." Dylan's tone leveled as he used my former nickname. "I missed you. I hope we can see each other again soon."

"Me too. And if it's not too much, do you mind calling me Harper? As long as my mother and Joe aren't around." I couldn't take three people calling me Isa or Izz. Not until I could remember who I was.

Dylan smiled. "Sure thing. I like that name."

"You don't find it weird?"

"Nope. I don't find much weird." He laughed and walked over to the desk in the corner, grabbing a piece of paper.

"Here's my number if you need anything. I'll be in Portland next week for work." He handed me the paper. "Not that I know that's where you are, just taking a wild guess," he quickly added with a smile.

"Thanks. We should go before he comes charging in here and kicks you out. I don't think he's happy that someone else knows about me who wasn't supposed to."

"You think?" He grinned. "It seems like it's more than a job to him."

* * *

We left shortly after eight in the morning and would arrive at Miles's grandparents' around ten. I didn't think any of us had slept well last night. My mother was up early with Joe, making eggs and bacon. She kept apologizing, and, of course, Miles was up. I was starting to think he never slept.

After half an hour of driving, I decided to break the silence. "So, you didn't like Dylan, did you?"

"It's not that." He curled his lips inward.

"Then what is it?"

"It's not safe."

"Besides from you and your gun?" I teased.

"No. And you know from what." He side-eyed me. "It puts you in more danger. And not just you—Chloe, your family, even him . . . everyone who knows. We don't know what we're up against."

"True, but I trust he won't say anything." Dylan knew more than my mother did, but I'd save that conversation for later.

"Just like you trusted Frank?" His voice lost its rough edge.

"Good point. But it's different. He's . . ." I didn't know how to explain that it felt like I still knew Dylan without remembering him.

"Gay?" He raised an eyebrow.

"What?" I shook my head, cursing myself for leaving my sentence open.

"Please don't tell me you trust him because he's gay?"

"No! I . . . wait . . . you know he's gay?" I looked at him, confused at how he knew.

"When I was with your mother and Joe in the kitchen, your mother mentioned that he was a good kid and would occasionally stay the night or you would stay at his house. She said she wouldn't have allowed it if he was a bad kid. Then Joe quickly added that he was gay, defending the fact that they had let a boy stay the night. It was comical—despite the circumstances." Miles glanced at me, his smile turning genuine. "To Joe, you're his daughter and he cares about you."

"I could feel it." I smiled, knowing that I did have people outside of the Vault who cared about me. "At least I knew Dylan before the Vault, unlike Frank, and we were best friends."

"Do you *really* know Dylan?" Miles engaged.

I inhaled and let out a breath. "Not really." Besides one memory and what he said last night, no. I looked over to see his smug, jubilant expression. "If we're talking about trusting people I've met," I added, "then how do I know I can trust you?"

Even though I did.

A smile played at the corner of his mouth. "Good point."

CHAPTER TWENTY-SIX

We pulled off the quiet highway and down a long dirt drive lined with trees wrapped in white bark and bulging brown notches. Their branches bloomed green leaves that canopied the driveway as fields roamed beyond them on both sides. A white farmhouse with a wrap-around porch, black shutters, and a detached garage revealed itself when the trees ended.

The weather was a complete flip from yesterday as the sun hit multiple red barns shadowing the house. Fences surrounded the property, and pine trees bordered the edge of the field in the distance as the mountain behind continued to climb.

"Wow." My eyes widened at the beauty. "This is where you grew up?"

"Yes." He let a small smile show as he pulled off to the side of the drive, turning off the truck. "It's not too late to turn around."

I laughed. "We aren't turning around. Your grandparents don't know me, and I don't know them. This will be a piece of cake."

"Just remember, I gave you the chance to opt-out multiple times." He quietly chuckled. "I'll get the bags if you're ready."

I nodded as I got out of the car and soon followed him up the porch steps. Though the house was beautiful, it showed signs of age. The paint was chipping on the spindles and staircase, sections of the vertical siding were worn, and areas of the gutters were unhinged.

"Can I take my bag now?" I chided and stood off to the side as he knocked on the frame of the screen door.

"Nope." He rocked back on his heels, more relaxed than I had ever seen him. His eyes were still constantly on the move, but he wasn't on edge.

A small lady with powdered-white hair, wearing a white blouse and blue trousers opened the red door. Her green eyes brightened when she spotted Miles.

"My Macky! Rusty, Mac Jr.'s here!" She opened the screen door and hugged him, giving her a clear sight of me. "Oh my, she's beautiful. You must be Harper." She smiled from ear to ear as she pulled away from Miles and hugged me. *Okay*, maybe I wasn't ready. "I'm Miles's Grandma, Rose. And the crotchety old man inside is Russell."

"Grams, no need to scare her off before she even gets inside," Miles said.

"If anyone would have scared her off by now, it would've been you," she joked with a hint of factuality.

Pattering came from inside on the wood floor, and a second later, a merle Australian Shepherd emerged. His entire butt wiggled as he rubbed against Miles's leg.

"Hi, Chase." Miles knelt to give the dog a warm welcome. "This is Chase. He watches my grandparents when I'm gone." Miles winked at his grandma.

"What's all this fuss about?" A burly old man with glasses appeared in the doorway. "Mac, good to see you, son." Russell held out his hand as Miles cheerfully shook it.

"Rusty, this is Harper." Rose waved at me. "I know it's beautiful out, but let's get you two inside." She ushered us to follow.

Russell stepped aside, and I followed Rose into the entry-way, which led to a narrow foyer with a set of stairs off to the left. At the bottom of the stairs was a small library. Built-in wood shelves holding an abundance of books lined one wall, and in the center was a floral couch with matching chairs that accented the sage walls.

"Oh no, dear, you don't have to take those off. You can leave them on." Rose stopped me as I went to take off my sneakers. "Mac, you can set those upstairs while I give her a tour."

"Yes, Grams." Miles leaned toward me as a witty smile appeared on his lips. "If she tries to take you to the basement, don't let her."

Rose reached up and lightly slapped Miles on the back of his head while rolling her eyes. "It's been months since he's stopped by, and he thinks he can talk like this?" She chuckled. "All right dear, follow me."

Rose led me down the foyer while Miles brought the bags upstairs. She stopped at a large doorway leading to a living room with white-washed shiplap walls and a brick fireplace. Russell slid by, planting himself in one of the grey rocking chairs.

"Don't mind him. After the cows this morning, he's ready for his nap." Rose steered me back down the foyer, which led to a huge open kitchen.

The white cabinets and farmhouse sink brightened the desert-sand walls and wood countertops. To the right were a large, rectangular rustic table and a small arched doorway that led back to the living room. She led me out the back door to a covered porch with a gravel patio and fire pit at the bottom of the steps, along with chickens that pecked at the grass. I walked over to the radio on a wicker end table that sat next to a porch swing and smiled. It had to be beautiful to sit out there on a clear night listening to either music or the crickets.

"Mac keeps a stash of his favorite CDs in the top drawer under the window in the library. He hasn't listened to them in ages." Her blushed dimples popped as she leaned closer. "We used to bring him to the local tavern when he was a boy. He'd join in on the line dances and dance with this adorable little girl. He looked so cute in his cowboy hat and boots."

The back door swung open as Miles walked through, and I tried to picture the hardened man before me in a cowboy hat while line dancing. That would be a marvelous sight to see.

"Speaking of . . ." Rose straightened. "I'll have Mac show you the barns and the rest of the house, dear." She went inside before Miles could get a word out.

Miles rubbed the back of his neck and sheepishly grinned. "I guess we'll start with the cows? There's only four. There used to be more, but it's hard for my grandfather to take care of them along with the horses and chickens." The grin he wore subdued as he put his mask back up.

Miles showed me the barn where the cows were held as Chase followed. There were about twenty stalls, but only a handful of them were full of bedding and had water. He briefly showed me the chicken coop next, and then the horse barn with four stalls.

When we were in the pasture, he put his fingers to his mouth and whistled. Less than thirty seconds later, two horses came running over a small hill. One went straight to Miles.

"This is Colonel. She's an American Paint." Miles ran his hand down her brown-and-white-spotted neck. Her face was brown with a white stripe, and there were brown spots splattered all over her white body.

"She's beautiful. They both are." I looked at the other dark-brown horse that stood behind Colonel.

"That's Pineapple Express. She's a Quarter Horse. My Grandfather named her after the weather." He moved his hand to Colonel's brown mane with white wisps.

"After the weather?" Pineapple Express was a term used for the heavy, torrential rain that hit the west coast. It caused dangerous weather conditions, such as floods and landslides.

"You know what that is?" He raised an eyebrow.

"I guess so." I shrugged, shocked that I knew what it was,

but hadn't thought of it before. It would have given me a clue that I had most likely lived on the west coast.

"Yes, she's named after it," he continued. "Pine wasn't easy for my Grandfather to break. She's still stubborn at times." He looked from me to Colonel. "But this one here is one of the calmest horses I've ever met. I rode her as a kid."

"Is she yours?" I stayed behind him, staring at the beautiful creatures.

"Sure is. Got her when I was nine. She's named after my father." He paused at the mention of him. "She's nineteen, but Pine over there's twelve."

"They seem to listen to you well." I was surprised a horse would come to a whistle.

"For the most part." Miles left Colonel and went over to stroke Pine. She let him for a short while until she took off into the field. "Go on." He waved at Colonel, who had waited for his command to leave.

We went back inside, where he showed me the upstairs guest room. I imagined this farm had many untold memories, with its five bedrooms and two-and-a-half baths. Miles asked if I was ready to let off some steam as we descended the stairs, and I excitedly said yes.

"Grams, do you mind if we borrow the side by side? I want to show her some trails and maybe go for a hike—the city's very crowded," Miles asked his grandma from the doorway to the living room.

"Of course not, but you should eat first. How about some sandwiches and chips? Do you like turkey, dear?" Rose stood from her chair and tottered past us into the kitchen.

"Grams, I'll make the sandwiches," Miles protested.

"I can make them just fine. Besides, I don't get to see you often." She ushered us to the table. "Now sit."

Miles shook his head in my direction, saying that there was no arguing with her. I now understood what Brandon had meant by saying that his grandmother was the only one who could tame him. Miles wasn't one to take no for an answer, and I saw where he got it from. Rose made us the sandwiches, as well as one for her and Russell, whom she coaxed to the table to eat.

"How about they take the horses instead?" Rose looked up from her sandwich at Russell.

"Colonel is his horse and he knows Pine." Russell looked at Miles from behind his glasses. "If you decide to hike, you know how to tie 'em up."

Miles glanced at me, grinning. "What do you say, want to ride a horse?"

"I don't know how." I nervously looked at him. I was positive if I had ever ridden a horse, I would have known something about it.

"You can wear Elizabeth's boots." Rose stood from her chair. "Your feet look to be about her size."

"That'll be safer than sneakers." Miles smiled, but I saw a hint of sorrow behind it when it clicked in my head. Rose was going to let me wear her daughter-in-law's boots—Miles's mother.

"Oh." I set down my sandwich, which I had decided to eat like a normal person. "I'll be fine in sneakers."

"Don't be silly. They've been sitting in the closet collecting dust." Rose left and came back with a pair of beautiful brown cowgirl boots with teal stitching.

"Oh, they'll fit you perfectly." She slowly bent over, placing them next to my feet. "Go ahead, try them on."

I gave Miles an apologetic look as I slowly took off my shoes to put on the boots, tucking my jeans inside. He gave me a reassuring smile, any hint of sorrow undetectable.

As Miles and I walked to the barn with Chase in tow, I tried to figure out how to apologize for wearing his deceased mother's boots. It did not feel right to be wearing them, but before I could bring it up, he did.

"She was right, they fit you perfectly." Miles was looking down at his mother's old boots as he clutched a saddlebag in his hand.

"I don't even need to wear shoes." I stopped walking and balanced on one leg to take them off.

"No," he snorted as he stopped me, "they look good on you."

I lowered my leg as Miles started walking again. It took me a minute to move my feet. It was like the wall he always had up was dropped, and it took me off guard. I enjoyed seeing this side of him, but I felt awful about the boots.

Miles prepared the horses, explaining as he went. He pulled out a gun in its holster, two extra loaded magazines, and a pocketknife from the saddlebag. I cocked my head to the side as I watched him.

"One magazine's for you. We'll take the side by side out later so you can shoot." Miles clipped the gun and holster at his left side with the grip facing forward. Lifting his shirt revealed another gun on his left hip with the grip facing the right.

"Do you mind if I ask why you put them on the same side?"

"No." He kept his green shirt tucked behind the guns. "This one," he said, pointing to the one at his back hip, "is easy for me to grab with my left hand. And this one," he said as he gestured to the one on his side, "is easier for me to draw with my right hand from across my body. The rotation's easier on my shoulder, and I can shoot from my hip if needed."

"Oh, sorry."

"Don't be. But if you have to carry and the holster is on your back, make sure the grip is facing the opposite of your strong hand. Don't reach back like the movies; instead, reach with your palm facing your back. It's easier to get your finger in position, and you'll naturally aim the muzzle away from yourself," he said as he showed his draw.

"Hopefully, I can just shock whoever I need to."

"I know you like to electrocute people"—he grinned—

"but being prepared to protect yourself in many different ways is vital."

"Yeah, yeah, yeah. Thank you for teaching me." I let out a sigh and smiled helplessly at his stupid smile.

Once we were on the horses, we rode down the path.

"Do you feel comfortable?" Miles looked back at me when we had a little bit of field left until the evergreens.

"I think so." I glanced down at my white-knuckled hands gripping the reins, and when I looked back up, Miles was wearing a huge grin. *Uh-oh.*

"Hold on tight and relax. If you want to stop, just say 'whoa' and pull back on your reins."

I went to protest to whatever he was about to do, but he made a clicking noise, and Pine started in a canter. Colonel followed on cue, and I tensed as my hands started to slicken with sweat. I quickly told myself to relax and let my body flow with Colonel's movements.

Miles looked back at me and studied me for a moment, his amused grin reappearing. He made the clicking sound again and tapped his heel on Pine's side. She broke into a gallop and, of course, so did Colonel. My heart started to race as Colonel picked up speed. I found myself enjoying it, just as I had when I was on the motorcycle; it was invigorating. I felt the static build at my core and dissipate as we slowed at the tree line. I let out a laugh as Miles spun Pine around to face us.

"You seemed to have enjoyed that. I'll take it easy on the trails." Miles grinned as he turned Pine back around.

We rode until we reached a clearing at the edge of a hill. The scenery was stunning with its rolling evergreens. Miles climbed off Pine and tied her to a nearby tree as I swung my leg behind me and climbed off Colonel.

"You got down pretty easy." Miles came over and took the reins.

"I'm told I can be a quick study." I thought of Frank; he had told me that after a chess match.

"You are," Miles said as he tied up Colonel.

I was thankful for the boots as we walked through the prickly grass and uneven ground in the field. Miles found a relatively flat spot that was far enough from the horses so I wouldn't spook them.

"Okay, let loose." He crossed his arms.

"You're not going to have me start small?" The last few times at the cabin, he'd had me work my way up with pushing the electricity out farther each time and then try to isolate it to a certain area on my body, which I have yet to be successful with.

"Start wherever you want."

"Okay. You should back up, though." Even though I wasn't able to push the bolts far, I still worried about controlling them.

"I'll be fine." He had more faith in me than I did.

I closed my eyes and focused on the idle static inside my chest. I could feel Miles a few yards away; his presence helped me relax and gain a little more control. Instead of little sparks sputtering uncontrollably, I had control over small electric bolts.

I held out my hand with my palm up. I felt the ripple of energy trickle from my chest and down my arm to my palm. I opened my eyes just as a blue bolt shot straight up. It lasted a couple of seconds before fluttering out. A few weeds nearby served as targets until I attempted to hit a tall blade of grass about eight feet out, but it didn't quite reach. This time I held out both hands, palms slightly angled toward each other. The bolts merged, striking the grass as a victorious smile spread across my face.

The blue sky and beautiful weather added to my cheer, when suddenly my dream occurred to me. My dreams had started in a field similar to this, with blue skies, knee-length grass, and the sun shining down—except the field was endless. That had been a long time ago. Now they were dark, petrifying, and filled with death. Images flashed through my mind as I saw the bloody faces of my friends and family, most of their bodies charred and covered in blood. Liam always had stab wounds to his chest and burnt hands as I gripped the bloody knife.

I shut my eyes, trying to shake the images out of my head, but the new image of Miles's lifeless steel eyes bored into mine as smoke drifted off his body. Death surrounded me, and it was all my fault. I was a ticking time bomb. I thought I heard my name but dismissed it as my head started to ring. I grabbed my head, doubling over.

I heard Miles move closer, but it was too late. It felt like my skin exploded, relieving the pressure in my head and the burning in my veins. My eyes flew open to the blue haze I had only seen once before. The ringing dulled into silence as it dissipated, and reality hit as I knelt on the ground.

No. I quickly pivoted on my knees and saw Miles lying motionless on the ground. I pushed myself to my feet, running to him.

"Miles!" I cried out as I shook his shoulders. "Miles, please wake up!" I went to bring my fingers to his neck to check for a pulse when his eyes fluttered open.

He let out a cough as he sat up. "That was impressive."

I sighed in relief, blinking away tears. "I thought you were . . . I thought I killed you."

"You think a few shocks would take me down?" He attempted to reassure me, but all I could think of was his life-less body lying on the blood-soaked grass, still smoldering. He frowned. "Hey, it's okay. I'm fine, see?" He stood up and held a hand out toward me.

My teeth worried my lip as I took his hand. Mine felt small in his callused one as he gently hoisted me to my feet.

"I could have seriously hurt you." I pulled my hand away. His hands could be lethal, but mine were with a single touch. Nothing about what I had just done was okay.

"I promise, I am perfectly fine. I've been hit with a lot worse." He turned and waved me to follow.

My adrenaline was pumping, so I didn't feel the exhaustion like I normally did after practicing, but I would soon—especially after what had just happened. Miles led me to a small creek whose bank had a few bare spots at the base of the trees lining it. I sat down, leaning against the tree as the fatigue began to wash over me.

"You must have had a lot of built-up energy." He sat next to me with his left arm resting on his propped knee while his right lay across his sprawled leg. "The only time I've seen you do that was at the precinct the night we first met."

"Yeah," I said as I rubbed my forehead. "I'm worried I won't be able to control it."

"That's why we're practicing." He gave me one of his cute half-smiles.

"Doesn't it frighten you?" I tried to ignore how his smile made me feel; for once, when I needed serious Miles, he was nowhere to be found.

"No," he said casually as he studied me, his face becoming a little more serious.

Finally.

"If you want me to yell at you, it's not going to happen." His grey eyes softened with green. "I don't understand everything that's going on, but I trust you."

"I don't trust me." I did want him to yell at me, because scolding myself internally wasn't enough.

"You'll learn to control it."

"And if I don't before someone gets hurt? I can't get the images out of my head . . . everyone I care about dead . . . scorched . . . bloody." I held back the pent-up tears from my repetitive dream. The more people I met, the more who were added to the pit as my internal struggle deepened.

He cocked his head. "Your nightmare?"

"Yes," I whispered. There was no point in lying. A few moments of silence passed. "You aren't going to ask about it?"

"If you want to talk about it, you'll talk when you're ready." A flicker of recognition flashed across his face.

A few seconds passed before I spoke. "Everyone's burned or stabbed, and I'm holding the knife. Every time someone important enters my life, they're added to the pile. I recognized my mother and Joe, and even the back of my father's head. You're among them and I—" My words faltered as a tear ran down my cheek. Miles gently put an arm around me, and I let my body give in, leaning against him. His warmth and familiar scent brought security as I stifled a sob.

"It's hard to talk about." I sighed after having my moment of weakness and mentally telling myself to toughen up.

"That's understandable." He leaned his head back against the tree and looked at me. "What can I do to help?"

"Unfortunately, there's not much." I shook my head. "I thought that getting out of the Vault would help, but it's only gotten worse. I'm worried it will come true."

"Things don't always go as expected." His words were soft. "But as far as it coming true, it won't."

I snorted at his confidence. Frank wasn't in control of me anymore, but I couldn't let my power control me either.

"How are you feeling?" he asked, even though I should be the one asking him.

"A little tired." The exhaustion had started weighing down my arms and legs, but I was not as tired as I'd thought I would've been. "And you?"

"Great. A million times better than hell week on four hours of sleep."

"A week on only four hours of sleep?" I asked bewilderedly.

"Well, five days. And you train the entire time." He was starting to open up as he distracted me from my turmoil.

Miles talked about a few drills he had gone through during Navy SEAL training. In one, they had swallowed a pill that monitored their temperature as they entered freezing water. They'd kept them on the brink of hypothermia, and if their core temperature fell below the cut-off, they would pull them out just long enough to get back above hypothermia. I stared at him in admiration at the strength and endurance it took for him to become a Navy SEAL, or anyone to become an elite soldier.

We sat in silence for a few minutes after he finished.

"There's something I need to tell you." I sat up and fiddled with a blade of grass that sprouted through the fallen leaves. "I heal quicker than normal. All I know is that my wounds and bruises heal in about half the time, but I still get scars if the injury's bad enough." His eyes landed on my throat where Maya had once sliced it open. I didn't elaborate on the healing, because I didn't really know anything else.

We started our ride back down the hill shortly after.

"I was thinking about that night at the bar." Miles kept his eyes on the trail. "I know we argued about it, but I never apologized. I'm sorry for shooting at Maya."

His apology took me by surprise. I didn't think he'd ever apologize for trying to save me, and I didn't know if I would have forgiven him if the bullet had hit her and she'd died.

"Apology accepted." No damage was done. I would have done the same thing, even if it had cost our friendship, in order to save his life.

He glanced at me as I frowned at the thought of Maya. "We'll find them."

"I hope so." I pushed down the hurt in my chest. "I don't understand why Liam didn't grab her and run when he had the chance."

"Sometimes there's more to the story."

"True, but he always used to be upfront with me."

"You two seem pretty close," he stated coolly.

"We are." Liam and I had left things rocky in the Vault, but that didn't mean we wouldn't do anything for each other.

"Are you guys together?"

"Umm, not that I'm aware of." My eyes shot to Miles, caught off-guard by his question.

"I don't think he knows that." He let out a small chuckle as I slowly realized he must be talking about the kiss.

I blushed and wished that Miles had not seen that. "I thought he was with this other girl, Ellie. He didn't talk to Travis or me for a month and only talked to her, but now I think he was planning the escape and dealing with changing into a Hybrian. I had no clue. I thought it was because they took Maya, but I don't know what to think anymore." My face became even more flushed. "I'm sorry, I don't know why I just said all of that."

"Usually I have the opposite effect on people." He grinned at the truth in his words. Besides Brandon, most people stayed quiet around Miles. He had this formidable power that emitted off him. "So, it's complicated?"

"No, we aren't together, and yes, it's complicated." I didn't know how to describe Liam's and my relationship—especially to Miles. "Why are you asking?"

"Besides the alcohol, you seemed pretty confused the night he kissed you." Miles rode ahead before I could respond.

I thought back to Chloe's and my conversation a week ago in Washington Park, where we loved to go on sunny days if we got the okay.

"Are you sure you don't want to go?" I had asked Chloe about going with Miles and me to my parents' as we lay in the grass—before Miles had offered to visit his grandparents.

"Yes. I'm having fun here, and I'm close to remembering who I am," Chloe had replied. "Plus, it gives you some alone time with Miles."

"What?" I had looked over to see her smirking. "He's only going because I supposedly need to be chaperoned."

"Uh-huh. That's why Kat's not going instead, right?" she'd jested.

"It's not like that," I had reiterated. "You know how he is. And he's older."

"You're right, I do." Chloe had sighed. "But you can't blame me. You guys get along *really* well, and five years isn't that much of a difference when you're older." She'd teasingly reached over and nudged my arm.

I'd taken a deep breath. "Liam kissed me."

"What? When?!"

"The night they attacked us at the bar," I had admitted. "I don't know what to think of it." I had been drunk and my emotions were already blurred.

"So, Miles was there?" Her eyes had beamed with curiosity.

"Why should that matter?" I had known why. Deep down, I had feelings for Miles, but I wasn't exactly sure how I felt about Liam; my emotions had been haywire then from the change.

CHAPTER TWENTY-SEVEN

Rose and I sat on the back porch swing while Miles helped Russell fix something in the barn before dinner.

"So, I know I'm not supposed to ask you questions, but I have to ask how you and Mac met. It was through his work?" Rose held her coffee cup snugly on top of the knitted blanket drawn across her lap. She had offered me a blanket, but it was plenty warm out. The sun was shining, adding to the cooling start of fall.

"Yes." I grinned at the memory.

"Must have been memorable, judging by that smile." Her voice bubbled.

"It was." I laughed. "You have a very kind grandson."

"He's a very sweet good-hearted boy, just like his mother. But he's also a little hard-headed, like his father." She joked casually in remembrance.

"Thank you for letting me wear her boots. They were lovely." I looked down at the sneakers I now wore.

"It's good they get some use." She patted my leg, and I, surprisingly, didn't flinch at her touch. "Her death was hard on the boys. Mac was so young, and my son engaged himself in the Army. Everyone mourns differently."

"I'm so sorry."

"Oh no, dear, I'm sorry. I shouldn't burden you with this grief." Her cheeks pinched upward. "Have you had the pleasure of meeting Brandon? He's a saint to Mac."

"I have. Certainly is a pleasure." Brandon had been nothing but kind, even after Miles told him about Hybrians during our stay at the cabin. I'd had no clue he knew until the night we snuck out.

"After Mac's incident in the Navy, Brandon visited him at the hospital and during his recovery. He's the reason Mac's an officer. The captain was looking for another man to join his force."

"Miles knew Brandon before they worked at the precinct?" I had only known that they were partners. I was starting to feel like Miles knew everything about me, and I knew little about him.

"Yes. Their fathers were friends."

"Richard was friends with Miles's father?" Neither Charlotte nor Richard had mentioned anything about that at the café.

Rose nodded. "They both served together. It was ironic they only lived a couple of hours away from each other. When Mathew was home, he had Richard, Charlotte, and Brandon over all the time from the city before Elizabeth's death. After that, Mathew was rarely home, but Charlotte would often visit with Brandon. It was good for Mac to have someone to play with. He barely hung out with other kids anymore." Her eyes saddened the more she explained. "When Mac got hurt, he shut everyone out. His brothers died right in front of him. It wasn't his fault, but he blames himself. Brandon didn't let Mac's insolence and temperament push him away."

"I had no idea." I had known Miles was fighting something internally, but I'd had no idea what.

"That's okay, dear, he doesn't talk about it. He shuts people out." Her cheeks lifted. "But it sounds like he's talked to you."

"I guess he's opened up a little, but not much." He had told me about his arm, that his parents died, and other little things here and there, but nothing in detail.

"More than most. He hasn't brought a girl here since his junior prom date," she bubbled.

I doubted he hadn't had girls over to his loft or a girlfriend Rose didn't know about. Yes, he was a little command-ing, but he was still kind, a gentleman, smart, handsome . . . I inwardly rolled my eyes. I may as well wipe off the drool from my chin.

"I know what you're thinking, dear." Rose spoke as I blushed. "If he's talked to any girl since then, it wasn't one important enough to bring home." Miles could read me like an open book, which I started to think was another quality he'd inherited from her, and the only reason he'd brought me was to expend energy that I couldn't in the city.

Later that evening, Miles and I sat outside by the fire. It was a clear night and the stars shined above. I sat in one of the Adirondack chairs with my knees pulled to my chest and a blanket wrapped around my shoulders. The fire radiated heat through my jeans and onto my shins. The chamomile tea that Rose had made provided additional warmth as I held it close to my face.

Miles sat in the chair next to me with his ankle resting on his knee. The fire shadowed his black stubble and flickered against his hazel eyes, along with his jeans and leather jacket. He held his empty coffee mug and appeared to be too focused on whatever he was thinking to notice me staring at him.

Boy, was I wrong. His eyes darted to mine as he raised an eyebrow.

"You looked like you were deep in thought." I kept my eyes on his instead of looking away, not wanting to look guilty for ogling him.

"Nothing more than usual." His eyes shifted to the mug I held close. "Are you cold?"

"I'm actually comfortable." The air had cooled once the sun went down. "I'm starting to think you never get cold, though."

"This feels balmy to me." The fire flickered across his grin.

"The fire's balmy; the air, not so much." I smirked, aware my dimples were in full force.

He let out a laugh.

"You've been much more relaxed since we've got here." I took a sip of my tea.

"It's good to be home." He pressed his lips together, letting a minute of silence pass.

I bit my lip and set my mug on the ground next to the chair's leg. "I have an idea." I pulled the blanket tighter as I stood and walked toward the porch.

"Where are you going?" Miles asked.

"I'll be right back." I didn't look back as I went inside.

I asked Rose if I could borrow one of Miles's CDs she'd mentioned earlier, and she excitedly said yes before going upstairs and grabbing Miles's old hat. She handed me a pecan felt cowboy hat with a chocolate leather band.

Miles was watching me as soon as I stepped onto the porch. His eyes narrowed at his old hat clutched in my hand. I went over to the radio and put in the CD. It buzzed as it started spinning and a song started playing, sounding like a mix of country and rock. I took a deep breath and tried to calm my nerves. I wasn't sure if what I was about to do was stupid or going to be downright embarrassing. I descended the stairs and made my way over to Miles.

"I heard you were quite the line dancer. Care to show me?" I grabbed the brim of the hat and placed it on his head.

Miles suppressed a smirk and stared at me from his chair. "Did Grams put you up to this?"

"No, she just told me where your CDs were and gave me the hat." I shrugged.

"Uh-huh." He stayed sitting.

"So, what do you say, cowboy?" I stepped back and waved my hands.

"Fine," he grumbled as he stood. He walked over and stood next to me, letting out a stifled laugh.

"What?" I didn't like the sound of his laugh.

"You asked, so you have to dance, too." He didn't hide his smug smile this time. "Do you know who this is?" I had no answer. "It's Steve Earle. *Copperhead Road* is a classic. Just follow me."

Miles showed me a series of steps and kicks followed by a stomp, turn, step, and another stomp.

"Is this all you do?" After each turn, you repeated the steps.

"Pretty much." He continued as I copied him.

After a few more rotations, the song picked up, and Miles picked up with it. I tried to keep up but failed. I took a step back and stopped to watch him. The light from the fire flickered across his grinning face, and his hazel eyes were bright with green. After a few more spins, he stopped and looked at me.

"What? That's all you do," he mocked.

"Okay, okay, that got more difficult. I have to admit, dancing in circles can be fun," I teased, but it was the truth; I was having a lot of fun.

The next song that came on had more of a country feel and was upbeat. I must not have listened to country, because I had no clue what song it was.

"All right, how do you do this one?" When he didn't move, I added, "Come on, one more?"

"Fine, but this is a partner song." He held out his hand as I diffidently took it. "Just follow my lead."

He led me through a shuffle, with one hand wrapped around mine as the other rested on my hip. I accidentally stepped on him, making a fool out of myself, but he only let out a small rumble of laughter and kept going. About halfway through the song, I caught on, and toward the end, I felt like we were just dancing along, and not following any pattern.

At the end of the song, he spun me out and then pulled me back in. I landed against his chest with his hand at the small of my back and the other still holding mine. His hazel eyes wavered with conflict as his gaze dropped to my lips.

My lips parted but froze under his gaze, my mind swirling as no words came out. I soaked in the fresh pine and leather as my heart thudded against my rib cage. My stomach fluttered but felt comfortable—different from the nervous fluttery feeling I had with Liam. This was excitement with anticipation, and not just jitters.

A noise sounded from the back door, causing me to jump and look in that direction.

"It's just Chase." Miles's warm breath ran against my turned cheek while his arm stayed wrapped around me. Sure enough, Chase had come through the doggie door. I looked back at Miles. He had never taken his eyes off me and was grinning at my jumpiness. I swallowed and took a step back as Chase trotted to our feet.

"Do you know why his name is Chase?" Miles casually knelt to pet him.

I shook my head no as I fumbled for words and tried to catch my breath.

"He used to chase the horses and cows around as a pup." Miles rubbed Chase's chin and stroked his neck. "It's a miracle he never got kicked."

"How old is he?" I finally was able to make my mouth form words.

"Eight. The horses and cows eventually took a liking to him once he grew up."

"He seems attached to you." If Chase was eight, then Miles would have been in the Navy and at Portland for the majority of Chase's life.

Miles gave the dog one last good rub down. "He was my buddy during my recovery for a couple months. He wouldn't leave my side."

"He sounds like quite the companion." I pictured Miles lying on the grey couch in the living room with Chase snuggled between his legs.

"Sometimes dogs can be more humane than humans." His eyes looked longingly at Chase.

I absentmindedly rubbed my palm. "Well, I guess I should get to bed. I have a very important task in the morning."

"Yes—milking cows. It can be strenuous," he joked back. I had offered to help Miles with the chores in the morning, and my offer had earned me brownie points with his grandfather.

"Today was great. I don't remember the last time I had this much fun." I had forgotten about all of the bad that was going on outside of the farm. Part of me felt guilty for it, but I felt less weighed down.

"What about the night you snuck out to the bar?" He raised an eyebrow. "You sounded like you were having lots of fun ignoring me—that was, until the others showed up."

"Even with the good parts of that night, it wasn't as fun as today." I smiled. "Thank you."

"No problem." His smile was sincere. I turned and headed inside before my face blushed even more.

* * *

"I'm going to miss the company." Rose dried the plate I'd just finished washing after lunch the next day.

"I'll miss you guys also. Thank you for having us."

"Anytime, dear!" She gave me a warm smile and glanced at the to-go bag containing Miles's favorite dessert. "Don't forget the blueberry slump, and please feel free to come by whenever, even if it's without Mac." She put away the plate as her smile grew. "It's been a while since I've seen my grandson this happy. He wouldn't stop by with just anyone—even if he was in the area for work."

I handed her the last plate that needed to be dried and stared out the window, pretending to admire the beautiful day. I thought about last night and how close Miles and I had been. I wondered if his breath had caught, his heart rate had increased, his palms had become sweaty, and excitement had stirred in his stomach. Besides the hint of conflict in his eyes, he had been unreadable. Rose had no idea the real reason why we'd come—for me to be able to practice in solitude. I was a little remorseful at the deception, even though Miles had enjoyed seeing his grandparents and vice versa. I had never seen him this happy. He had let his walls down, something I hadn't thought was possible.

CHAPTER TWENTY-EIGHT

I sat on the couch in the apartment flipping through the stations on the TV. I had gone back to the café Tuesday, and Miles had been slammed with work. We'd barely talked the past couple of days. Brandon had the evening shift most of this week, and Chloe was in NYC, leaving me to spend the afternoon and evenings by myself in the apartment.

A memory had come back to Chloe while I was gone. Her disappearance was still a mystery, but she had remembered living with her grandparents and her name: Chloe Livingston. She had gone to NYC with an FBI agent, a friend of Kat's, to visit her grandmother. Kat had regretfully found that Chloe's grandfather had died a year ago. She'd asked for just her grandmother's new address and not to inform her, wanting her visit to be a surprise. They'd arranged everything so she had been able to leave yesterday, which was Wednesday.

My stomach growled, but all we had was condiments and Chloe's coffee stash. I should have gone grocery shopping when Chloe was around. What I really wanted was takeout from down the street, but unfortunately, they didn't deliver.

After another fifteen minutes, I made the decision. I called in my order before going to my room and putting on the army-green hat—which I had forgotten to give back to Miles—over my bun. I threw on my leather jacket and grabbed one of the two umbrellas Brandon had graced us with. He'd said it was our "housewarming" gift. It had been raining on and off all day, so no one would question the umbrella. People even carried them on sunny days in Portland.

I pulled out my phone and turned off the camera outside our apartment door from the app. It had a motion detector, so every time someone came or left, a text alert was sent to Miles, Brandon, Kat, Chloe, and me. Very tedious, but thankfully, it wasn't battery operated, which abetted my plan.

Once it was down, I booked it out the door and down the blue-tiled floor toward the stairs. The red stairwell sign next to the wooden door was bright against the white walls, marking my exit. The stairs didn't have cameras and were quicker than waiting for the elevator. I would have taken the fire escape, but it wasn't in working order, and would be a long jump to get down to where I wouldn't be able to get back up.

I turned the camera back on once in the stairwell, and not a second later did my phone start ringing. I slowed my breathing—the short run wasn't the cause for my rapid breathing, but the thrill and nervousness were.

"Everything okay?" Miles sounded tired.

"Yeah, the power keeps flickering. I think it messed with the camera." I kept my voice calm. "I wouldn't be surprised if it keeps doing it. I could go wave to the camera each time," I teased. He paused, deciding whether or not he should be concerned.

"No, that's not necessary." Thankfully, he decided the latter.

"Tell Kat that she should have set us up in a better apartment," I covered with a joke.

"I'll be sure to do that," he said flatly. The happy, laid-back Miles I had seen at the farm was gone.

"Well, you two have a good night," I kindly said and hung up the phone before he could respond. Luckily, he hadn't called my bluff. I felt guilty for lying, but the other part of me thought illogically. He should trust me enough to go out on my own.

Once I was on the main floor, I pulled the rim of the hat down. Keeping the umbrella closed, I put it across my shoulder so it hid the side of my face from the cameras that the FBI monitored—though who knew how much they were actually monitored with all the resistance on the investigation? I pushed open the apartment building door and turned right down the sidewalk. As soon as I was out of sight of the front door, I relaxed, dropping the umbrella.

My socks started to get damp as water seeped through my sneakers from the unavoidable puddles. The damp socks were agitating, and I'd have preferred to be barefoot if it were socially acceptable. As I walked, the odd tingling sensation rose in the back of my mind again. It had been happening whenever I left the apartment since getting back Monday.

Once I had the bag of takeout from Cheng's in my hand, the dull sensation was easily ignorable as I quickly headed back to the apartment. The sweet and spicy aroma wafted from the bag as my stomach grumbled.

"It's a bad idea to get takeout alone." A voice made me jump as a hooded figure came out of nowhere, brushing my shoulder with his. My free hand automatically shot out and sent a quick zap to his side.

"Ouch! What the heck . . ."

I looked at the hooded man as soon as I recognized the voice. "Liam?" I pushed him into a nearby alley. "What . . . are you okay?"

"Yeah." He took off his hood, causing his brown tousled hair to be even more erratic. His chestnut eyes searched my hands. "Did you just tase me?"

"No, I shocked you. You're lucky I barely did." I shook my head. "Never mind that. What are you doing here? Are you okay? Where's Maya?"

"We're all fine. Travis too," Liam said. "Seriously, though, what just happened? Your eyes flashed blue."

"Like how you guys morph—it's what happens to me." I took a deep breath. "Travis is with you too?"

He hung his head and looked at me. "You don't morph, but can shock people?" He completely ignored the Travis part.

"More like electrocute, but yes. I guess that's my version of morphing." I was still understanding my blue-eyed beast.

"Do you have the amplified strength and heightened senses?" He raised an eyebrow.

"What? Umm, I don't know." I'd only practiced calling forward the static that I could feel. "You guys have heightened senses?" I had assumed the strength, but not the senses. No wonder they were so difficult to fight.

"Yes, when morphed. We can partially morph, where only our eyes change and we have partially heightened senses and strength, but it takes practice. It intensifies our vision, hearing, smell, touch, and I don't know about taste, but we have a sixth sense when others are nearby that triggers when we aren't morphed. I would think you could partially morph, but you're a little different."

"I'm too focused on the static when I practice." I had tuned out all the noise to concentrate.

"That's interesting." He glanced toward the end of the alley where we had come from, and then up at the sky as it started lightly raining. "We need to be quick. We've been following you since you got back Monday. You aren't safe."

"Wait, you've been following me?" The wheels started turning in my head.

"One of the days I had to leave, so Maya and Adam were on the lookout."

"Maya *and* Adam?" My voice rose in astonishment.

"Maya's back to herself." Liam's face remained impersonal, just like he'd usually kept it while in the Vault.

"Clearly not." If she was partnering up with Adam, then there was absolutely no way she was herself. "We can sense other Hybrians?"

"Yes, but we can't tell how many or where. And we can't precisely tell how close." He scanned my confused face. "Could you sense us?"

"I thought it was something else, but now I think otherwise." I shrugged. The odd sensation I felt in the back of my mind was them.

My eyes widened as I suddenly realized I could hug him without consequence. I tucked under his arms, wrapping myself around him. He pulled me close for a minute before pulling away, his natural sage and vanilla scent sticking to me.

"I can explain more later, but we *really* don't have much time. I'm sure someone will realize you're gone soon." His warm hands were on my shoulders as large rain droplets fell from the sky. "And like I said, it's not safe. You should come with me—we can protect you." Liam stared at me for a moment. "Ah, screw time." He pulled me back into a hug.

"Liam," I said, letting him hug me a little longer before being the one to pull away. "I don't know what Frank has done to you, but I can help. Just come back to my apartment with me."

"We were wrong about Dr. Roulings."

"Yeah, sure." I searched his eyes for the truth. "If you're trying to have me come with you now, why didn't you the night at the bar?"

"Maya wasn't ready for you to be there yet; it wasn't safe for either of you. She needed to return to herself first." His eyes briefly turned pleading. "Dr. Roulings is trying to help you."

"By being a victim to his lunatic experiment? Have you heard of Stockholm syndrome?" I rolled my eyes and grabbed one of his hands, leading him out of the alley as the droplets became more frequent. "Come on, we can talk more at the apartment."

"This isn't that." Liam grabbed my other hand and spun me toward him. "We're the good guys. You need to be with Hybrians who can protect you. *I* can protect you."

"It's not protecting me by bringing me straight back to what I'm evading." Even though I wasn't completely hiding from Frank by going into witness protection, I didn't want to be captured again either. "He's in your guys' heads."

I was thoroughly aware of his hands wrapped around mine as he pulled me closer. "I can't always keep you safe if you're with them."

Them must have been Miles, Brandon, and the FBI.

"Hypothetically, if I go with you, what about Chloe?" I mused over the delusion that Frank had put in his head.

"She's not a Hybrian, and she's currently safe in New York City. When she comes back, we'll get her." His lips pursed together.

My brow furrowed. How did he know she was in NYC? I went to question him, but my voice hitched as he pulled me closer and brought his face to mine, stopping only inches away. We had a lot to catch up on.

"You can't fight them." His warm voice trickled against my skin as he leaned even closer, avoiding the rim of my hat—Miles's hat. "I'm sorry for how I left things in the Vault. I would never do anything to intentionally hurt you."

Empty words caught on my tongue, but my face gave away my apprehension.

"Sunshine . . ." he whispered.

My eyes dropped to his lips, but something in my gut tugged me away. I pulled my hands out of his grasp and started toward the sidewalk. I stopped and faced Liam, whose eyes flashed with pain as he stood where I'd left him.

"I don't know what Frank has done to you, all of you, but I will figure it out. I will get you back." My voice wavered at the thought of them being free from the Vault, but still being manipulated by Frank.

I walked away, knowing that I couldn't reason with him. I would find Frank and take him out myself. It started to pour, and I clutched the takeout, which I no longer had an appetite for, to my chest. My hand felt for the button on the black handle to the umbrella. It shot out and provided cover from the rain, which I didn't care to be protected from.

I made it back safely to the apartment with only a text from Miles after the camera alert. My hair bounced out of its bun as I removed the hair tie and lay down on the couch, still damp. I lay there for a good fifteen minutes until I heard a knock at the door. I sat straight up as my hands felt for my phone until I realized it was on the counter next to the hat. I stood up to check the monitor in the kitchen and sighed in relief when I recognized Miles. My sigh turned into a gulp when I noticed his set jaw and fierce grey eyes staring into the camera.

"Be right there!" I yelled as he knocked again. Miles, Brandon, and Kat all had a key, but they had promised to respect our privacy.

I hastily shoved the takeout into the fridge and tossed out the receipt with today's date.

"Miles?" I slowly opened the door.

He eyed me up and down, the fierceness fading from his eyes. I was thankful my clothes were almost dry and the damp spots were undetectable unless you felt for them.

"Come in." I waved. "I'd offer you a beer, but I don't have any," I rambled as I made my way to the couch.

"Where did you go?" His voice was uncharacteristically nonchalant as he shut the door.

"What do you mean?"

He reached over and picked up the umbrella. *That,* however, was still wet.

"The agents might not be able to recognize you, but I would recognize you and my hat anywhere." His eyes landed on his hat on the counter.

My jig was up, and there was no way around it.

"You caught me." I walked over, picked up his hat, and held it out to him. "I'm sorry I forgot to give it back." His eyes went from the hat to me.

"Keep it. Seems like you get more use out of it than I do." He put the umbrella back down.

I set the hat on the counter, unsure why he wasn't yelling at me yet. "How did you know?"

"Conveniently timed power surges and the length of time between the camera going off were suspicious enough. I made a call and had the entrance recording of that timeframe sent to me. And there weren't any reports of power surges on this block." His eyes narrowed. "So?"

"You want to come in or stand in the entryway all night?" I walked over to the fridge. "I have Cheng's." I pulled out the brown paper bag and set it on the counter.

"Cheng's? You risked yourself for Cheng's?" His voice started to rise, but he took a deep breath and relaxed. I started to notice the bags under his eyes and that his five o'clock shadow was coming back after being clean-shaven Monday. He hung his jacket on the rack next to the door and kicked off his boots.

"I was really hungry." I stared at the bag, which held enough food for three people.

"You didn't touch it." He eyed the stapled-shut bag.

"No." I had to tell him what happened, but I wasn't sure how to explain that my friends weren't being held captive, but were under Frank's influence.

"All right. Let's eat together." He went over to the cupboard and grabbed two plates, along with two forks.

I divvied up the orange chicken, fried rice, and lo mein. We sat on the couch to eat, and I stared at my plate, slowly gaining my appetite back. I wasn't sure if it was the company—surprisingly calm company—or the sight of food that had made me start to relax.

Miles watched me as he sat on the opposite end of the couch, barely touching his Chinese. I had a feeling he'd only offered to eat because he wanted me to eat.

"I ran into Liam." I finally blurted out when he didn't question me. "Well, more of, he ran into me, and then I zapped him."

"You zapped him?" His eyebrow raised.

"Unintentionally. He surprised me."

Miles repressed an amused grin. "And?"

"He wanted me to go with him. Him and the other Hybrians . . . and Frank." I frowned.

"What?" Miles's voice was hard as he stiffened, all traces of amusement gone. That was more of the response I had expected.

"He didn't make any sense. He said I was safer with them." Liam had seemed like himself, not crazy, like Maya had been. "I think Frank somehow brainwashed him."

"Where is he now?" He asked firmly, setting his barely touched food on the coffee table.

"Probably gone. I don't feel him," I partially lied. I didn't feel Liam, but I'm sure he was lingering. I didn't want Miles to go looking for him. "I've had this weird feeling in the back of my mind on and off since we got back. It turns out we can sense when other Hybrians are near. We just can't tell exactly how close, where, or how many."

"He's been here all week?" Something told me that he would have been okay with the extra protection until he found out Liam was trying to get me to go back to Frank.

"Not just him—Maya, too. And Adam."

"Adam? The instructor who tortured you? I thought he wasn't a Hybrian." His forehead creased.

"He's not. At least, I don't think he is." I took a breath. "He said Travis is fine; I think he's with Frank also."

"Did he say anything else?" Miles questioned.

"Not really." I thought about how my lips had been only inches away from Liam's. For some unbeknownst reason, I felt guilty, like I had betrayed Miles, even though we weren't together and Liam and I hadn't kissed.

"I'll stay on the couch tonight. Just to be safe." Miles stood and pulled out his phone.

"No, you've slept on enough couches and pullouts recently." I shook my head. "Liam won't hurt me."

"I can stand guard in the hallway if you're more comfortable with that," he joked, but was also serious as he looked up from his phone.

"It's fine, I promise. I won't leave, and I'll keep the door locked," I reassured him. "If they wanted to grab me, they would have by now. Liam only wants to protect me."

"That's what I'm afraid of." Miles looked back down at his phone.

"I promise, Liam won't let any harm come to me." His lack of response and typing into his phone told me that I had to go about this a different way. "If you trust me, you'll trust that I trust him and will be fine."

He lowered his phone to look at me, rationalizing the situation.

"I know I have bad judgment when it comes to trusting people, but I've learned." I had known Liam for what felt like my entire life. If I couldn't trust him, then I would give up on the world.

"I trust you," he finally responded. "But that doesn't mean I trust anyone else."

"I'll take it." I rolled my eyes and teased, "You still didn't say if I can trust you."

"I think you trust too easy." He couldn't help but smile.

"That's something we both agree on." I needed to keep my guard up, but I could always trust Miles and Liam. I just needed to figure out what hold Frank had on Liam.

CHAPTER TWENTY-NINE

I received a text from Chloe early in the morning. I was surprised she was up, but then I realized she was three hours ahead of Portland. She said that she was visiting her grandmother and trying to get to know her but also mentioned that we needed to talk soon.

I finished checking a lady out at work and went to take the order from the next person in line. Once the lady stepped aside, I looked up to see troubled, faded hazel eyes that belonged to a handsome face.

"Miles?" He normally waited off to the side if he needed to tell me something.

"Can I talk to you?" There was a hint of uneasiness in his voice.

"Um, sure." I glanced behind him to make sure no one else was waiting and turned to Jasper, my coworker. "Hey, do you mind watching the register for a couple of minutes?"

Jasper looked up at Miles, then back to me. "Yeah, no problem."

Jasper had no issue with covering both and was more than happy to. Somehow, the added job made him work even faster, and being a barista was his calling. He was exceptionally good at it. I walked out from behind the counter and followed Miles over to a corner where no one was sitting.

"I have to go out of town for the weekend." He kept his voice low. "There's been multiple disappearances from clubs and bars in Seattle the last two nights, along with sightings of people wearing wolf masks. I don't think it's a coincidence. We want to try to catch them before they skip town."

"We? Are you and Kat going?" If this had something to do with the Hybrians, I wanted in.

"Kat and two other agents are going; we fly out at one. I don't want to leave you, but if this is *them*, you're safer here." He sighed. "I think I'm going to have to tell Kat."

Kat still didn't know about the Hybrians. We had wanted to protect her as long as we could, even though they were involved in her investigation. After the night at the bar, Miles and I had agreed that she was safest if she didn't know, but if it came down to it, he would have to tell her the truth. She also wouldn't believe us without evidence, and I wasn't ready to expand the list of those who knew what I could do.

"Let me go with you. I can help." I'd rather be doing that than taking orders all morning and sitting on my couch all evening.

"No," he said, shaking his head, "it's too dangerous. Brandon is going to patrol this area and take you home at three."

"Isn't he on night shifts?"

"He's not on duty." Miles glanced at the door as a customer walked in.

"This is what I was trained for, what I'm made to do. Please let me help." I was different, and it was time I accepted that part of me.

"You're not going." His jaw set. "Call Brandon or the captain if you need anything—they'll be closer." He took a breath and relaxed his shoulders. "Please call me if anything happens."

"That's not fair." I ignored his benevolent change in attitude. "I should be going with you, and you know it."

"It's bad enough that there are Hybrians *watching* over you." He stared at me. "It's hard for me to leave you, but I'm not going to put you right in the middle of it. I'll keep you updated if we find anything out."

He walked away and out the door. I was fuming with anger. We had just talked about him trusting me last night. If he truly had, why wouldn't he trust me enough to go? I was more than capable of handling myself, and I *was* their best weapon. Well, Miles was a weapon himself. The others didn't even know what they would be fighting! I turned and stormed back behind the counter.

"He seemed nice," Jasper retorted as he glanced at the closed door Miles had intensely exited. The espresso he was making matched his taper-fade haircut and was sharp against his taupe skin.

"He's just having a bad day." *Why did I say that?* I had no clue why I was defending him.

I took my spot at the cash register, even though there was no one to wait on. I dreaded the thought of staying while they went to Seattle. I hadn't felt the presence of a Hybrian on my walk this morning, and I wondered if Liam was also in Seattle. *I need to go.*

I thought of ways to get to Seattle on my own, and as soon as I started conjuring up a plan, I had no time to waste.

"Would you be mad if I asked to go home? I know it's early in the shift, but I don't feel well," I asked Jasper.

"Not at all. It's a walk in the park. You go home." He probably thought my red face was due to holding back tears, and I was going to let him think that it was boy problems.

"Thanks." I forced a smile and walked back to the office where Charlotte was.

"I'm not feeling that great—do you mind if I head out early?" I asked Charlotte. Grey emerged from her roots in her thick bun, and her jeans hugged her wide hips as she sat.

"Of course not!" Her green eyes softened behind her glasses. "You're flushed. Go home and get some rest."

"Thank you. I appreciate it."

I grabbed my bag and replaced my apron with my jacket. I walked a couple of blocks over to the closest library. Once inside, I paused to admire the beautiful interior and take in the smell of old books before telling myself I needed to get going. I used the computers to look up the bus times from Portland to Seattle.

I assumed they were taking a private helicopter, especially if Kat was involved. I could have used my phone, but this was much quicker and easier. The bus would take about three-and-a-half hours, and a helicopter would take about an hour. The next bus left at ten, which was in five minutes, and there was no way I would make it. The next scheduled departure wasn't until twelve-thirty, which would put me there long past two. It took almost an hour less by car, and I knew there was no way I could convince Brandon to take me.

I pulled out my phone and searched through my contacts. My finger hovered over Dylan's name for a brief second before hitting the call button.

"Hello?" A confused voice answered.

"Hi Dylan, it's Harper." I blushed at the embarrassment of using my "new" name.

"Oh! Yes, hi, Harper! I'm glad you called!" He didn't stutter with the name change.

"I hate to ask this, but does that 'call me if you need anything' still apply? It's a huge favor." I stood to leave.

"Uh, duh. There's no such thing as huge favors between us." He acted insulted.

"If you aren't busy with work, do you have time to take me to Seattle? I just need to be dropped off." I could take a bus back if I couldn't find Miles.

"I would love to! When?" He sounded ecstatic.

"Now?" I questioned, unsure if he would still be chipper after that detail.

"Certainly! Where do you want me to pick you up?" Nope, still chipper.

I gave him instructions to meet me at a parking lot down the street from my apartment in twenty minutes. I scurried down the back way toward G.A.H.O.—the café—and called Brandon.

"Harper! Didn't expect to hear from you so soon." Brandon answered on the second ring.

"Hi, Brandon. I'm not feeling so well, and was wondering if you could stop by that little antique shop down from G.A.H.O. to pick me up. I started walking to the apartment until I realized Miles wouldn't be happy with me." I didn't lie often, so I prayed he didn't notice the waver in my voice and chalked it up to me not feeling well.

"Sure thing. I'm right around the corner."

I thanked him and hung up. I scurried down the alley and made my way to the antique shop. I didn't want to be picked up at the café, where there might be questions about my whereabouts for the last twenty minutes. Brandon arrived a few minutes later, and I kept the talking to a minimum as he asked me what was wrong. I mentioned that my stomach felt off and my head hurt. Little did he know that I rarely got sick.

"So, you're my go-to while Miles is flying out?" I joked while rubbing my head, pretending it throbbed.

"Hey, I'm always the go-to man." He winked.

I let out a brief laugh. "Must be important for them to take a helicopter. Unfortunately, he's leaving his go-to man behind."

"Someone's gotta watch out for you, especially with your second half gone." He was talking about Chloe, and boy, did I miss her. She would have been one hundred percent down with going with me to Seattle. Brandon's lack of correction of my comment had confirmed that they were taking a helicopter, but I didn't want to give up my intentions by asking where they were flying in to.

"Do you need anything?" he asked as he pulled in front of my apartment.

"Just rest, thank you." I put my hand on the door handle.

"You know, I should walk you up to your room."

"Yes." I glanced around, pretending to search for a parking spot. "I think I need to get to a bathroom, though."

"Okay, just this once." He surprisingly let me go. I think my face was still flushed or pale from trying to pull it off.

As I got out of his car, he pulled out his phone—probably informing Miles. I rushed to the elevator but casually strode down the hall to my apartment. As soon as I shut the door, I ran to my room and changed my shirt. I shoved some clothes into my duffle and donned Miles's hat; he would recognize it, but Brandon might not if he happened to drive by. The sneakers I wore would do. As I swung the duffle over my back, my phone buzzed in my jeans pocket.

I pulled it out and looked at the fluorescent screen.

Hope you feel better. Sorry for upsetting you.—**Miles**

At least it was an apology and didn't say anything about staying put. Last I checked, he'd said that *he* didn't want to put me in the middle of it, and nothing about me going on my own. I hoped he wouldn't try to check on me before he left, but I imagined he was busy and would know I'd try to weasel my way into going.

While I had my phone out, I messaged Dylan to let him know I would be there in five. I went over to the living-room window and opened it. My hands gripped the windowsill as cool mist washed over my face. Once I went down the fire escape and attempted the long jump to the ground, I wouldn't be able to climb back up and retreat. I inhaled and climbed out, shutting the window behind me. There was no going back.

CHAPTER THIRTY

M y duffle hung over my shoulder as my hands stayed dry in my jacket pockets. Dylan pulled into the parking lot in a blue Subaru sedan and parked next to me, rolling down the window.

"Come with me if you want to live," he said in a deep monotone voice, causing my eyebrow to raise. "*Terminator?* Come on, I know you know that one."

"Ah, got it." I laughed as I put together the joke.

He popped the trunk and stepped out of the car. Droplets of water from the fog stuck to his curly black hair as he walked around and opened the trunk the rest of the way. He shut it after tossing my bag in. We climbed into the car and started driving.

"Where to in Seattle?" He glanced at his phone, which was on the dashboard being used as a GPS.

"Honestly, I'm not sure yet." My impromptu trip wasn't thoroughly planned.

"So, keep going north. You got it." His auburn eyes gleamed at the thought of adventure.

"You're not going to question what I'm dragging you into?" I studied his bubbly demeanor.

"Nope." He shrugged. "When you have an idea, it's usually a good one. Sometimes a bit wild, though." His eyes wandered into the past.

"Sounds about right," I mumbled. "Thank you."

"Anytime, Captain." He pretended to salute. His nerdiness entertained me.

I pulled out my phone, planning to search maps for nearby airports in Seattle. I imagined they would use a small or private airport to land the helicopter. I tapped the frozen loading screen and let out a low grumble.

"You want to use mine? It has its own hotspot, no gigabit cap, and the data's not shared." Dylan's eyes focused on Route 5 as we made our way out of the city.

I assumed all of that meant his phone was faster, and I had no idea what we had, besides that Chloe was constantly on her phone using up the data. He reached over and pulled his phone off the mount, handing it to me.

His phone loaded impeccably, faster than mine and even the library computers. I did a quick search and found two likely candidates that were about half an hour from each other. We couldn't chance missing Miles. We would arrive around one thirty in Seattle, and Miles would be getting there around two—if they didn't leave sooner than planned.

"Do you know any low-key airports around Seattle?" Maybe Dylan would know.

"Hmm, not off the top of my head. Is that where we're headed? Are you flying away?"

"What? No!" I didn't want him thinking I was running away. "I'm trying to meet someone."

"Don't worry"—he chuckled—"I was joking. You don't run away from anything—not even Miranda Graves."

"Who's that?" I relaxed.

"I guess it's a good thing you don't remember her. She was the queen bee of middle school and high school. She stepped all over everyone," he scoffed.

"Oh." Things like that seemed so trivial.

"Anyways," he continued, "where's this person coming in from? That might help narrow it down."

I bit my lip, unsure whether to tell him the whole truth, the partial truth, or just flat out lie. I just needed him to get me there, and didn't want to put him in any danger.

"Flying in from Portland. I'm just trying to beat them

there. They'll be in a helicopter," I said as he glanced at me with raised brows and a smirk.

"Okay, something low-key, huh?" He was dissecting the partial truth.

"Yeah."

"Well, I'm just going to speak my mind here, and please stop me if I'm wrong or you want me to shut up." He spared a glance at me. "I'm betting you're trying to intercept Mr. Hunk, who is on a work trip that you were not invited on, at an airport hangar."

"How did you . . ." I trailed off.

"We're best friends. Just because you don't remember me doesn't mean I don't remember you." He shrugged again. "That, and this was a very last-minute request and you don't exactly know where to go. So, it only makes sense."

"Uh, yeah." I guess I would tell him *most* of the truth. "So, remember how we talked about the hostages at Westbrook?"

"Yep."

"Well, this has something to do with that. It might involve some of my friends who were held there with me. Miles didn't want me to go, but I have to."

"No one tells you what to do. You're the Captain America to Iron Man." He snorted. "So, does this have anything to do with those things that've been attacking?"

My head snapped in his direction. "How do you know about that?"

"As I said, I'm good with computers." He grinned.

"But you said those *things*—you mean the people in masks?" Miles had said wolf masks, so the news would have said that too.

"Sure," he answered rhetorically.

"Okay, spill," I accusingly demanded.

"Remember when I said you don't just hold people hostage underneath a research facility without doing anything to them?"

"Yeah?" My forehead creased.

"Well, I hacked them. I know they were trying to make Hybrians—whatever that means. I got booted before I could dig into it further and made sure they couldn't trace it back to me." He glanced at me. "I'm sorry if they experimented on you."

My mouth gaped open. How could he find all that out, yet no one had been able to find out I was alive for the last five years and that there was a huge underground facility underneath the city? I guess no one would have been looking for a dead person.

"As soon as you mentioned Seattle, I put two and two together." He went from being bubbly to somber. Okay, I guess I was going to tell him the whole truth.

"You're right about it all." I sighed. "Miles, an FBI agent named Kat, and two others went to Seattle to check it out. I guess there're reports of attacks all over."

"It seems like they're mostly in major cities," he added. "It's easier to hide and blend in with a higher victim population." He wasn't wrong about that.

"Miles told me to stay in Portland, but I can help if something happens."

"Are you . . . a Hybrian?" He raised an eyebrow.

"Sort of." I shook my head. "Dylan, it's not safe to know any of this. Once I find out where, I just need you to drop me off and you need to head out."

"Even though you can't remember, you're forgetting something." His eyes gleamed again. "I'm just as stubborn as you when it comes to adventures and investigating."

I rolled my eyes and took a deep breath. He practically knew everything, so why not tell him the rest? He'd find out himself anyway. I filled him in on almost everything, and boy, did he have a million questions. We spent the next two hours talking about the Vault and everything after it. I told him a dull version of what I could do. That I could electrocute people through contact with my hands, which was the only part that seemed to astonish him—not the brute strength, increased senses, or body-altering features.

When we were close to the city, he said we needed to find out what direction to go. With all the Vault and Hybrian talk, I had almost forgotten where we were headed. I still had no clue which airport we needed. He pulled over to the side of the road and put on his hazards.

"I have my backpack with my laptop in the back, but it'll work on my phone." Dylan motioned for his phone and got to work right away.

"Are you going to track their helicopter or something?"

"Ha, no!" He snorted. "I'm going to see what local airports the Feds normally use."

"How are you going to do that?"

"It's a lot easier than trying to find a random helicopter."

His fingers moved quickly across the screen. Not even a minute had passed before he found something.

"Here we go." He tilted the phone toward me so I could see a name and address on the screen. "Was Bill's Shop on the map?"

"No." I didn't remember seeing it. "That doesn't sound like an airport."

"It looks private." He plugged the address into maps. "Definitely has a runway and an area for a helicopter to land, along with two hangers. It's just southwest of Seattle."

"How do you know that's where they'd go?" I asked.

"It looks like the Feds use it to fly into Seattle from all over. They have it in their records. Bill's Shop must have paper records, because I couldn't find anything from them." He sounded certain as he started the directions. "We would arrive at one forty. Do you want to try it?"

"Sounds promising. Let's go." It was our best lead.

He pulled back onto the road. We had half an hour, and now that I had spilled about me, I wanted to know more about Dylan, even if I technically already did.

"How did you get so good with computers?"

He smiled as if I should have already known. "I messed around with computers when I was young and played a lot of online games. I taught myself and learned from others online. After high school, I got my bachelor's in cybersecurity, so that's what I've been doing this year for a big corporate company. Most of the time I can work from home—well, my parents'"—his eyes rolled—"but they send me into Portland a lot."

"Your bachelor's? Aren't we the same age?"

"Yep. We are. I graduated a year early in high school and got my bachelor's in two and a half with an accelerated online program." His smile flipped. "I didn't see the point in staying in high school if you weren't there."

"I'm sorry." That must've been rough, thinking his best friend had died.

"It's not your fault someone faked your death and kidnapped you." He inhaled. "We were each other's sidekick. Without the other, school sucked. There was too much drama, anyway."

"At least most of me is back now."

"Yeah," he said as a big grin washed over his face, "and now we're practically vigilantes."

"Umm, not even close." I laughed.

After a little longer, we turned onto a paved side road with brooding pine trees on the left and a wood fence on the right. Soon the airport appeared on our right as we pulled into a decent-sized parking lot with a handful of cars. There were two large metal hangars and a small office on the opposite side with a connected area of floor-to-ceiling windows. Behind the hangers stretched a flat-smooth dirt runway and hazy riveting mountains that were a perfect scenic backdrop.

Dylan went to unbuckle his seatbelt after we parked, but I stopped him and frowned. "You don't need to come in and can head back. I'm not sure how this is going to go."

"What if it's not the right place? Then you're stuck out here." He waved his hands in front of him.

"If Miles finds out I got a ride from you or what I told you, he is going to be furious." *Worse than furious.* "I'm going to tell him I took a bus and then a taxi. With me already being there and knowing Brandon wouldn't take me, he won't look farther into it."

Dylan pursed his lips as he thought. "Yeah, okay. I really don't want to see Mr. H turn into the Hulk. But I'm waiting here until I know this is the right airport and you're at least with him."

"Fine, I can agree to that. But make sure Miles doesn't spot you. He's always on the lookout."

"Got it. I'll be incognito." Dylan slouched down in his seat and pressed the button to pop the trunk.

Before I got out, I turned to him. "Thank you. I wouldn't have gotten here in time if it wasn't for you."

"Sure thing, but let's make sure this is the right place before we celebrate." He smiled as I climbed out of the car.

I grabbed my bag and started toward the office, praying this was the right place. The fog had lightened up, but the skies overhead had an overcast of grey. When I reached the door, I took a deep breath and pulled it open.

I instantly regretted my plain T-shirt and wished I wore something a bit more professional that made me look older. I took the hat off, letting my hair down, and ran my fingers through it. No one manned the wooden counter so I walked over and rang the bell. A middle-aged man with a recessed hairline and a medium-length beard emerged from the door behind the counter. He walked over to a large notebook on the counter.

"What can I do for you today, Miss . . ." the man asked as he glanced up from the notebook to me.

"Uh, West." *Crap.* I probably shouldn't have used part of my real last name or my fake name, but I didn't want to give him my first name—either of them.

"I don't see anything scheduled for you, Miss West. This

is a private airport, and we schedule in advance," the man kindly iterated.

"Yes, I am actually meeting someone here. Agent Foster is due to arrive soon." I went straight for the nail on the head.

"Oh, I see. She didn't mention she'd have anyone waiting for her." His eyes shifted to the glass waiting room, where you could almost see the entire runway. "She should be here anytime now."

He walked from behind the counter and led me to the waiting room. "You can wait in here if you'd like. I'll tell Jack to let them know you're here when they arrive. She usually skedaddles right away." The man waved at the first hangar.

"Thank you." I took a seat facing the runway in the middle of the room and set my duffle on the chair next to me. He pulled out his phone and went back into the office behind the counter.

I put the hat back on and checked out the room around me. Two vending machines, one for food and one for drinks, sat in the corner behind me. Chairs—besides the row I was in—lined the windows on two of the sides. There were three doors in total: one facing the runway, one toward the parking lot, and one back into the office.

I took out my phone and sent a quick message to Dylan to let him know we were in the right place. My phone buzzed with his response—a thumbs-up and a smiley face. About fifteen minutes later, my chair started to vibrate as a loud humming grew. I left my duffle on the chair and walked over to the tall windows.

A black helicopter came into view and landed next to the front corner of the hangar closest to me, off the runway and clear of the hangar entrance. My heart pounded in my chest as my anticipation rose. Miles was going to be livid, but that was something he was going to have to live with. This was my problem before he ever met me.

The blades slowed to an eventual halt. The cockpit partially faced me, and I could tell that the two in the front were removing their helmets but couldn't make out who they were. Two tall men climbed out of the back wearing ordinary clothes, one with dirty-blond hair and the other with black. Kat descended from the passenger side of the cockpit and stood off to the side, waiting for the pilot. Seconds later, a man wearing black jeans that fit him perfectly, a leather jacket opening to a green shirt, and cowboy boots stepped out. My jaw dropped. Had Miles really just flown that?

Kat and Miles walked over to a man who came out of the hangar to greet them. The man talked to them for a minute before pointing in my direction. *That must be Jack.* Kat and Miles both looked this way, but I doubt they could see me. Miles held his hands out toward Kat and shook his head. He turned and started storming in my direction, looking like he was walking down the aisle to a wrestling ring.

I heard a door from the other room and turned to see the guy I'd spoken to earlier leaving the building. He headed toward the hanger and waved to Miles as he passed. Miles wore a fake smile and nodded. I walked over and stood next to my bag. At least I was there and he had no choice but to let me help.

Miles pulled the door open, refraining from ripping it off the hinges as his storm-grey eyes met mine.

"What are you doing here?" he asked through gritted teeth.

"Being your backup, obviously." I arched an eyebrow at his unreasonable rage.

"You don't listen!" He closed his eyes and took a deep breath. "How did you get here, and how do you even know where *here* is?"

"I took the bus and a taxi." I shrugged. "I have my ways." I held his glare, not backing down.

He brought both hands to the back of his neck. "It's not safe for you here."

"Nowhere is *safe.*" I started to pace, trying to calm myself down.

"I gave you orders to stay in Portland," he snapped as he lowered his hands. "I should've had Brandon lock you up at the precinct while I was gone."

I stopped dead in my tracks.

"No, you don't get to say that." My voice hardened as I bit back tears. "I was locked underground for five years. I'm not getting locked up anywhere."

I thought I had seen him flinch, but the Miles I saw now made me think otherwise.

"This is more than you." His voice was still on edge, but he had better control over it.

"Whether or not you like it, this *is* me."

He held my stare. "You're going back to Portland."

"You don't get to tell me what to do." I jabbed my finger into his rock-hard unmovable chest. Despite my childish action, I pressed on. "There're more Jects out there who are being tormented and mind-warped. We can end it. It's going to take a team to do that—one that knows what they're up against." I felt my eyes burn with tears of hurt and anger, but I wasn't going to let any fall. "Let me help."

Miles's eyes glossed over with confliction. "We'll give you a ride to the bus station. I'll let Brandon know where you are and that you're going back to your apartment."

He reached around and grabbed my bag. A sigh of frustration escaped my lips as I watched him walk outside. He went over to the others and said something before grabbing another bag and heading to the parking lot. Holding my breath, I glanced at Dylan's car, releasing it once I realized he was hidden.

Miles waved me on. I sulked out of the glass waiting room and followed him to the black Suburban parked on the opposite end from Dylan. He set the bags in the trunk and held the door open for me to climb into the back. *Great, I get the backseat, too.* He shut the door after I got in and hopped into the driver's seat, sitting in silence as Kat and the other two agents loaded their bags. Kat climbed into the passenger's seat, while one agent sat in the far back and the other sat next to me.

I ignored Miles's constant glances at me in the rearview mirror as he drove. I'm sure I wasn't the only one who noticed; he wasn't very subtle. The two agents introduced themselves after a little while. The one with spiked dirty-blond hair was Calvin, and the older one with short, curly black hair was Jared. Calvin had to be the youngest-looking FBI agent out there and was very chatty, keeping Jared plenty busy.

I needed to tell Dylan that I was fine and pulled out my phone, keeping it low against my leg. I sent a message saying thank you for the ride and that I owed him. What I did not mention was where they were taking me or the fact that I was not going to get on the bus. I did a quick scan of the SUV and saw that no one had noticed.

I stayed quiet and focused out the window as we drove into the city. We pulled over to the curb near an intersection where people rushed around the concrete sidewalks.

"I'll be right back," Miles denounced as he climbed out of the vehicle. He grabbed my bag from the back and opened my door.

"Can I at least carry my bag?" I rolled my eyes as I jumped out. He was being arrogant, and I didn't want to let him be chivalrous.

His silence answered me as he strode across the street toward an orange bus. I swore under my breath and followed. He stopped near the bus door and turned to face me.

"It's scheduled to leave in five minutes and will take you to Portland." He handed me my bag and held out a wad of cash. It felt like there was more than necessary for just a ticket.

I reluctantly took it. Miles stood there, waiting for me to get on the bus like I was a child. Anger rose to my cheeks at the way he was acting. I turned and stepped up on the first step. *So much for not getting on the bus.*

"Harper." My head hotly jerked back at the sound of Miles's voice. "Please be safe."

I ignored the shadow of guilt in his eyes and got on the bus without saying a word. I found an empty seat and sat down with my bag. I stared out the window and watched the black Suburban drive off. As soon as it was out of sight, I stood and quickly strode down the aisle.

"Ma'am?" The bus driver's gruff voice called as I got off, but I ignored her. The clicking of the door told me it had shut after I got about ten feet away. The bus roared to life and the brakes squeaked as it started to move.

I jumped when I felt my phone go off in my pocket. I quickly scanned the area and saw no sign of the black Suburban as I reached for my phone. Dylan's name lit up on the screen.

"Dylan?" I started to cross the street.

"Head north to the corner of Jackson and Fifth. There'll be a bus parking lot—I'll meet you there." I could hear the joy in his voice.

"How do you know where I am?" I started heading north—at least, what I thought was north.

"I followed the van."

"*Ugh*, you could have been caught!"

"Not the way I followed them."

"You were supposed to head home." I sighed, not understanding what he meant. "Fine. See you soon."

I wasn't the only one who was awful at following orders. I weaved through the busy sidewalk on Jackson Street until I saw the parking lot on the corner at Fifth, where Dylan was waiting in his car. I tossed my bag into the back and climbed in.

"Where to, Captain?" His ecstatic energy radiated off of him.

"Who said you were coming with me?" I eyed him.

"Who got back into my car?" He shrugged.

"Touché." I forced back a smile. "I suppose I could use

your help, but are you sure you want to do this? It could be dangerous."

Miles had done enough ordering me around for one day, and I wasn't about to do the same to someone else. That, and I had to admit—Dylan was good at finding things out.

"Dangerous is my middle name." He smirked.

I rolled my eyes.

"So, where are we off to?"

"The Fowler Hotel." I'd heard Calvin chatting about it. He was elated that they would be staying in a nice two-bedroom suite and not some run-down motel. I pictured Miles and Kat sharing a room, and quickly shoved the thought aside—it wasn't like that.

CHAPTER THIRTY-ONE

Dylan and I got a room with two beds a floor below Miles and the others. Dylan had said he could get his own room, but I said it was fine. I had a feeling we weren't going to get much sleep anyway.

He had hacked the lobby and hallway cameras to the hotel and found out what room they were staying in. We kept our distance and checked in once they were settled in their suite. I watched Dylan hack the cameras in less than a minute. By the pure joy on his face, you could tell he lived for this kind of stuff. We both knew what we were doing was illegal, but we believed it was for the greater good. What had been done to me was illicit and no one had been prosecuted for it and more were getting hurt. It had to end.

Dylan sat at the desk with his computer while I sat criss-crossed on one of the beds and toyed with the hem of my pants. Dylan was in the middle of a story about how he'd accidentally tripped and his pizza had gone flying onto Miranda Graves's white pants when my phone buzzed.

I looked down and opened a message from Brandon.

Spoke to Miles. I can give you a lift when you get here. I'll just be a little late.—**Brandon**

"Crap." I forgot about Brandon. They would be worried if I didn't get off the bus and would know if I wasn't at the apartment because of the camera. Miles would track my phone and find out where I was. I was surprised he hadn't already tracked it to make sure I'd stayed on the bus. *Stupid.*

"What's wrong?" Dylan asked.

"They'll know that I didn't go back to Portland. Brandon, Miles's partner, wants to give me a ride from the station to my apartment." I bit my lower lip. "There's also a camera on my door and it sends alerts when there's motion. They'll know I didn't go back, and I'm pretty sure Miles will track me through my phone."

"Hmm." Dylan rubbed his chin for a moment. "I've got an idea."

* * *

I silently cursed as we pulled out of the hotel garage. There was no way we were going to catch up, let alone find them. The city was huge, and they could have gone in any direction.

"Don't worry," Dylan said as we stopped at a red light.

He gestured for me to hand him his laptop. I was about to ask how he still had Wi-Fi when I remembered he had mentioned earlier that his phone had a hotspot. He wouldn't want to use public Wi-Fi anyway for the things he was doing.

"There," he said as the red light finally changed.

He handed me back the laptop, and I squinted at the screen to see a black Suburban amongst other vehicles.

"How did you find them?" I asked.

"I'm using tracking software that scans for their license plate." He acted like it was a no-brainer. "That's how I followed you guys earlier."

"Isn't that type of software only accessible to the authorities?"

He raised an eyebrow at me.

"Why does that not surprise me?" He had hacked the police records, so why not their software? "Ooo, they're moving." A different camera popped up with them on it.

"Where does it say they are now?"

"I don't know." It took me a second to notice it said what intersection the camera was at in the corner. "Oh."

He laughed. "Later, you should drive, so I can man the computer."

"Hey." I glared at him. "I'm figuring it out—well, not the hacking part. They're moving along First Avenue. Plus, I don't know how my driving is."

"Atrocious." He laughed again. "No, it's not that bad. Mary just worries too much."

My gut pinched at hearing my mother's name. It sounded familiar yet estranged.

"How would . . ." I stopped myself. He probably had seen me drive in a parking lot or heard stories from my mother or Joe. They probably had let me practice a few times before I was taken that December.

We followed the SUV to a run-down industrial area of Seattle. They checked out an abandoned warehouse before leaving and parking near a nightclub. When they were let into the closed nightclub, I assumed they were checking out the locations where the kidnappings had happened.

The software did most of the work tracking them, but it couldn't locate them near the abandoned factories where there weren't any cameras. I bet there had been a secret rave at the warehouse. Most nightclubs were twenty-one and older, not that teens couldn't have fake IDs. Jects were in their late teens or rarely early twenties, so a rave would be more ideal to find candidates.

"Ready to go shopping?" Dylan asked after they entered the club.

"What?"

"Looks like we're going out tonight." His eyes looked over my attire. "And you cannot wear that."

"I won't be able to get in. I'm not twenty-one," I added.

"I'll contact a friend." Dylan pulled out his phone.

Moments later, Dylan had found a strip with multiple stores. We had to park far away to find an open spot. I found myself trying on a blue sequined dress at Dylan's request. It was the eighth dress I had tried on, and the second store. I was done refuting all of the dresses I tried on, and Dylan finally approved.

It was beautiful but not my style—that I knew of. The royal blue went well with my blond hair, and silver sequins mixed in with the blue around the v-neckline and the cuffs of the long sleeves. It fell mid-thigh, and it could have used more fabric to reach my knees. As I looked in the mirror, I couldn't help but think that I looked anything like a Ject or a Hybrian. I still looked fit, but I looked feminine. I hadn't worn anything like this in the last five years.

Dylan purchased the dress and a pair of black ankle boots before I could deny his gesture. He said that he wanted to, and I told him that I'd pay him back. I asked him why we weren't looking for him, and he mentioned that he had clothes in his bag from work that would do.

On our way back, we stopped at an apartment complex. Dylan had me wait in the car while he paid the meter and ran in. When he came back, he handed me an ID.

"Do I even want to ask?" It looked legit and had my age at twenty-one.

"I know some people out here." Dylan shrugged. "Don't worry, they're just geeks like me," he answered my concerned look.

"Batman, really?" I glanced back at the ID where it said my name. Grace Wayne.

"Good ol' Bruce Wayne. It was either that or Rogers."

It was almost eight by the time we got back to the hotel. Most clubs didn't open until nine or ten, so we planned on heading out around nine thirty. Miles and the others got back to their suite around eight and left shortly after nine.

"You should really stay here. You could use your laptop from the hotel," I mentioned to Dylan as we walked to the car. We could have walked and taken a taxi so we wouldn't have to struggle with finding parking, but we had both liked the idea of having the car nearby.

"Nope. I already told you, I am all in. I'm your Robin." Dylan laughed at his Batman joke.

Miles and the others had pulled directly behind a row of nightclubs. There weren't any cameras in that specific area, but the cameras hadn't seen them leave. We parked in between both locations with nightclubs. Dylan pulled out his phone and did a few things before we got out and started walking in the opposite direction of Miles. No need to cover the same area or risk running into them.

A foggy haze floated between the buildings, but thankfully, the rain was holding off. I wished I had my leather jacket, as a chilled breeze swept through the street, but was at least thankful the dress had long sleeves and a hidden pocket for my phone.

"Did we go to the city a lot when we were kids?" I asked Dylan, not feeling like this was my thing.

"No," he snorted, "you would dance in the privacy of your bedroom or my basement, though. It was quite the scene." I elbowed him. "We were quite the introverts."

"You seem to know your way around the city." We rounded the corner as neon lights from the nightclubs greeted us.

"Yeah, work also sent me to Seattle a few times. They have a few good gay bars here, and fake IDs are easy to make. I would've made yours if I had the resources." He frowned. "I kind of had a rebellious stage after you . . . *died*." He motioned quotation marks at died.

There wasn't a line at the front, and the bouncer let us in without a second glance after checking our fake IDs. Music blared as fog washed over us with colorful beams of light reflecting in every direction. Despite the lack of a line, the club was plenty full, and my dress suddenly felt more modest. Dylan blended in with his khaki skinny jeans and a tucked-in blue button-up with small white triangles. He wore contacts instead of his glasses, and I noticed a few girls checking him out.

"Let's dance," Dylan yelled over the music after forty minutes of scanning the crowd.

"I'm okay," I shouted back at him, sitting on the couch. We had stayed on the balcony with our two sodas, eyeing the crowd below. I was hoping I could sense if a Hybrian was near, but the feeling never came.

"Come on!" Dylan grabbed my hand and dragged me down the stairs to the dance floor. "We have to blend in if you want to find the bad guys." Dylan turned and started bouncing from side to side. "All those shows and movies we watched taught us that."

I rolled my eyes and tried to relax my body into a natural sway with the upbeat music. After a few songs, I finally relaxed, and was surprised to find myself having fun while keeping an eye out. Dylan was ten times better at dancing than I was, and after twenty minutes, a cute, petite brunette who couldn't be older than nineteen walked up to him.

"What's your name?" she purred into his ear.

"Dylan." His eyes averted to me, asking for help as she started to dance with him.

"Nice to meet you. I'm Samantha." She turned so her backside was against him as she faced me with a smile. "Hi!"

I nodded at her, continuing to dance on my own. I felt bad for Dylan, but this was payback for dragging me out onto the dance floor. Once the song was over, Samantha grabbed my hand and pulled me toward them. I almost dislodged her arm and punched her from the contact but told my reflexes to cool it.

"You two should come to Grath's rave tonight."

"Grath's?" I asked.

"Yeah, he switches locations and you never know where he'll be until the night of. Here's the address." She pulled out two small tickets and handed them to Dylan. "It's a secret, and only people like us get invited."

"Like us?" Dylan asked this time.

She giggled. "Yes, silly. Young and beautiful. I hope to see you two there."

She walked away and found her next mark—a girl who also looked too young to be there.

"That was strange." I leaned over Dylan to look at the tickets.

"It doesn't surprise me." He turned them so I could see. "They have people recruit the type of crowd that they want at a rave all the time. It usually has underage drinking, so they try to be quiet about it."

"Telling two strangers, that's not so quiet." I started walking off the dance floor.

"It usually works in their favor. The people they target in the clubs are usually looking for fun and not to call the police," he said, following me.

"Well, shall we go?" I found an opening near the wall. "It says the doors open at eleven."

"We shall." He smiled and held out his arm like a prince. I rolled my eyes and took it, not wincing at the touch.

The rave was in the same area that we had followed Miles to earlier, except in a different building. It would have looked abandoned if it weren't for a few cars along the far side of the old warehouse where we parked. The ticket instructed us to park on the far side, away from the entrance, if we couldn't get dropped off.

It was a treacherous, cold walk in this short dress and these boots. The music and thumping from the bass wasn't heard or felt until we were close. Right inside the door was a large, burly man holding a flashlight. My eyes winced as the bouncer shined the flashlight in our faces. He checked our tickets and scanned us for weapons before waving us through.

A small thrill ran through me as we walked down a barely lit hallway into a ginormous room with brick walls and boarded-up windows. The building's worn-down features accented as décor. Something about this excited me more than it should have, and I wished Chloe was there; she would have loved it.

A packed bar was to our left, and straight in front of us on the back wall was a raised platform with massive speakers and a table. The DJ behind it wore a glowing bandana over his face, black sunglasses, a black hat, and headphones. Three bouncers guarded the platform surrounding the DJ, and everyone appeared to be under twenty-five. It had a similar feel to the nightclub, with the fog machines and lights, but with more of a daring edge. Whoever this Grath was, he sure knew how to throw a rave.

"Have you ever been to one of these?" I leaned over to Dylan.

"No, I've just heard about them." His eyes were wide and his mouth gaped as he checked it out.

Dylan mentioned that the Suburban had left and headed toward the other strip of nightclubs. After scoping things out while dancing for a little bit, he added that the tracking software had lost them and was searching for them. I had a feeling they were on their way.

I became thirsty but didn't dare to drink anything, even if it was alcohol-free. As I motioned to get Dylan's attention to tell him I needed a break, something pricked the back of my mind. *Hybrians.* I grabbed Dylan's armed and pulled him off to the side.

"They're here." My heart rate picked up.

"Who?" His eyes bulged once it clicked. "Oh!"

"Stay behind me, and don't leave the crowd if we get split up." I scanned the area, not noticing anything out of the ordinary.

We had made it to a less-crowded area when an unguarded hallway toward the back caught my attention. If I were going to take someone, that would be the perfect spot to drag them away. I brushed past people and headed in that direction, with Dylan right behind me. A hand landed on my shoulder when we reached the hallway, and it wasn't Dylan's, as he was on my other side. I couldn't risk using my power this close to everyone, so I reined it in.

"Harper?" a voice said as I turned.

"Travis?" I gasped.

He pulled me into a hug. "What are you doing here?"

"I could ask you the same thing." My eyes narrowed, trying to figure out what his intentions were; Liam had said Travis was now with *them*.

His eyes glanced behind me. "Who's this?"

"I was going to ask that also." Dylan pressed his lips in a thin line.

"He's an old friend." I ignored Dylan.

Travis raised an eyebrow. "You have your memories back?"

"No, not yet." I sighed. "Dylan, this is Travis. Travis, this is Dylan."

"The Travis? The now-Hybrian Travis?" Dylan exclaimed.

"In the flesh," Travis grumbled, not thrilled that Dylan knew about Hybrians.

"It's an honor." Dylan held out his hand and Travis reluctantly shook it.

"Why are you here?" Travis's blue eyes turned to me.

"There have been kidnappings in this area." My eyes narrowed. "You wouldn't happen to have anything to do with them, would you?"

"What?" His eyes widened. "No. Why would you say that?"

"Oh, I don't know, because you're with Frank now," I snapped.

He took a deep breath. "No, I have nothing to do with the missing people. That's actually why I'm here."

I went to interrogate my friend's motives when a faint scream echoed down the hallway. Travis and I shared a knowing glance while Dylan stared at us confused; he wasn't able to hear it.

"Stay here," I yelled at Dylan as Travis and I took off down the dark hallway.

I could barely make things out once we got away from the rave's strobe lights, but my slightly enhanced vision must have helped. I glanced over at Travis and saw his irises glowing a shade of burnt yellow, not his normal crisp blue.

Liam's words came back to me—he had mentioned that Hybrians could partially morph to somewhat heighten their senses. I think our senses were naturally heightened in general, but it was very minuscule. I brushed the thought off as we came upon a turn. I needed to keep my mind clear and prepared, something Adam taught us. Oh, great, now I was thinking about my cruel old trainer. I shook my head. *Focus.*

As we entered the T, another muffled scream sounded, along with the closing of a door to our right. Travis and I ran down the hall and came to a metal door with an exit sign above it. Travis looked over at me with his normal blue eyes; I knew what he was thinking and I nodded. There was trouble on the other side of that door, and he was asking if I was ready. My stomach swirled with fear and a dash of excitement.

I pushed through the doors, and was greeted by a bone-chilling breeze as I took in our surroundings. A man was about to round the corner of the metal-sided building as he dragged a kicking girl. The girl's efforts were futile, as the man acted like she was just a mere annoyance.

Travis and I started in a sprint. The man spotted us and was shocked at our sight, but it was replaced with excitement as his lips curled into a wry smile. He disappeared around the corner, and my feet pushed harder against the ground—as fast as they could in these boots. I was not going to let him take her.

The air around us smelled like the wet pavement we ran on. We rounded the corner to see a different man finish shoving an unconscious girl into the side of a large white panel van. He had turned to look at his partner, the one we had followed, when he spotted us and stepped in our direction.

"Let them go." A growl escaped my lips as we slowed.

"I don't think so," the man moving toward us snarled. He was easily half a foot taller than Travis and almost triple his size.

"There's no reasoning with them." Travis took a fighting stance.

"He's right." The man's face transformed as his body grew bulkier, if that was even possible.

"Get the girls!" Travis's eyes changed, morphing as the Hybrian lunged at him.

I nodded and went after the guy we had followed. He had finished shoving the girl he'd kidnapped into the van, and the bit of fight she'd had was gone as the man tossed a syringe inside and shut the door. He faced me and bared his teeth, already morphed.

The corner of my mouth rose into an inviting grin. I looked like an easy target, but as the energy rose within my chest, my glowing eyes said otherwise. The Hybrian faltered as he barreled toward me, surprised. I ran at him and dodged his attempt to send a right hook to my face. My foot found his knee, barely sending him backward.

Normally I stayed defensive, but not tonight. I looked at Travis to see he was holding his own. Part of me knew I could take him down with a quick electrified palm to the chest, but I wasn't sure if I was ready to show whoever they were what I could do.

Travis and I could take them down. They were strong, but appeared to rely on brute force, while we relied on years of training and used our heads. I stayed in his pocket, throwing punches and kicks while dodging his. I cursed the short, tight dress for restricting my movements and riding up with each assault. I had pulled it down a few times already before giving up.

Movement out of the corner of my eye caught my attention as a girl not much older than me came out a back door to the building with a young man. She cursed and punched the panicked look off the guy's face when he saw us. He fell to the ground, unconscious. My glance caused a hard blow to my stomach, but I recovered quickly.

Out of my peripheral vision, I saw the woman glare at the brawl. She strode toward us, her eyes changing to amber as her claws erupted from her fingertips. Her cheeks sharpened as her jaw set in a hard line.

"Travis!" I shouted, alerting him of our new company.

Travis glanced at her. "Three against two. This oughta be fun."

She paused.

"Are the packages in the van?" Her voice came out in a snarl.

"Yes," the man I was fighting gritted out as he threw a punch.

His fist just grazed my face as I leaned back. I dipped low, sending two short punches to his stomach, then backing out of his pocket. I peered over to see that the woman was no longer coming toward us, but toward the van. She was going to take the girls.

At that moment, it didn't matter if they found out what I could do as long as those girls were safe. I ducked past an engaging arm and sent my palm into the Hybrian's chest. Blue sparks flew around my hand as he grunted and staggered backward. It wasn't enough to knock him out, but enough to render him frozen.

I leaped into the air and brought my fist down into his rabid face, finishing the job. Hunched over with my hands on my knees, I peered up at the woman, who kept her wide eyes on me.

"It's her. Take her alive," she ordered to the Hybrian fighting Travis—both of them had stopped to stare at me. The blue sparks must have caught their attention. The man disregarded Travis and came at me, but Travis pulled him back.

I looked back at the woman, who had opened the back of the van and quickly wielded a gun. She aimed it right at me and ordered Travis to stop fighting. Travis listened while I held up my hands. She was too far away for my powers to reach her.

"Brass, get the sedative. She's coming with us," she said, her voice laced with poison.

"You're not taking her or the girls," Travis snapped.

Headlights flashed around the corner behind the woman as a honking blue Subaru drove at us. She cranked her head to see what was going on. *Thank you, Dylan.*

"What the—" The woman was cut short as I took a few steps forward and reached both hands out in front of me, sending what looked like blue lightning into her chest. The gun dropped as she fell to the ground, her chest rising in slow, rhythmic breaths. At least that one was powerful enough to knock her out.

Travis rammed the other Hybrian into the van and bashed his head against the hood twice before he fell unconscious to the ground. Travis looked at me, nodding as I nodded back, telling him I was fine.

"Liam told me you were strange, but not that strange." He winked. I shook my head at him and waited for the Subaru to stop in front of me as Travis went to check on the two girls.

Dylan climbed out of the car with a worried expression. "Are you okay?"

"I'm fine," I reassured him. "Are you?"

"Holy Batman! That was insane." Dylan took in the scene, ignoring my question. "You didn't tell me you could shoot lightning bolts! You're like the God of Thunder. You just got promoted from Batman to Thor."

"Did you just call her a god?" Travis laughed as he bowed at me when he walked by and headed toward the unconscious guy next to the door.

"Harper!" A gruff voice edged with worry rang through the chilled air. It sent both warmth and trepidation through me. I turned to see Miles and Kat rounding the corner, holding their guns out in front of them.

"SNAFU," he muttered when he reached us, lowering his gun. "Is everyone okay?"

Miles's hazel eyes scanned over me in worry, the green barely visible. His breath hitched. I wasn't sure if it was at how disheveled I looked or the fact that I wasn't in my normal attire. I unconsciously tugged at the bottom of my dress, even though it had stayed after my recent adjustment.

"Perfectly fine." My voice was bitter, but I couldn't help the small swirl in my stomach as his eyes fawned over me. The swirling seized when his eyes turned storm-grey with frustration.

"We'll talk later." His jaw set. He holstered his gun and turned to Travis, who was carrying the unconscious man. Travis gently laid him on the ground next to us.

"There are two girls in the van. They're okay," Travis answered before they could ask.

"How did you two take these three out?" Kat asked Travis and me as she sized up the bruised, burly men on the ground.

"How do you know Dylan didn't help?" I asked as both Kat and Miles glanced at Dylan.

"I ran into them," Dylan piped up. "I followed you guys, but when I saw you go outside, I figured I should go get the car, so I turned around. You know, in case you guys needed a getaway or if I needed to hit someone."

I raised an eyebrow at him.

"What?" Dylan shyly shrugged. "I didn't want to be helpless, so I figured maybe I could run them over or something."

"Or something." Travis glanced at me. He didn't want to mention what I had done and wasn't sure who knew.

"I ran into them—well, more so, into the brick wall," Dylan said as he glanced from Kat to Miles, "as I was almost through the crowd. I pointed them in the direction of the hallway and ran to get the car. I figured going out the front would be the quickest." He frowned and looked at the small dent in the front of his car. "I had to drive through a fenced gate to get back here. They must have gotten their van in a different way or—"

"Or locked it after they came in so no one else would drive back here," Travis interjected.

Kat walked over, opened the van, and shuddered. "I'm calling the others. And I'm getting this rave shut down."

"I wouldn't do that," Travis remarked as Kat pulled out her phone. "If they take these guys in, it'll cause trouble. They're ruthless and will do whatever it takes to get out, even killing whoever gets in their way. You guys aren't equipped or prepared to deal with them. We can take care of them for you. They'll be locked away and won't ever be a threat again."

I went to question Travis on who he meant by "we," and where he planned to lock them away, when Kat let out a rhetorical laugh.

"Oh, you're being serious." Her laugh fell short as she glanced at Miles, who was still staring at Travis. She went to dial, but Miles placed a hand over her arm.

"He's right," Miles agreed.

"You can't be serious!" she stammered, pulling her arm away.

"They did things to us," I quickly added as she went to dial again. Miles nodded when I glanced at him. "Down in the Vault, underneath Westbrook, they experimented on us . . . injected us with a serum. It changed us, altering our appearances and enhancing our senses and strength. They call us Hybrians. If we get angry enough, the beast comes out, or we can summon it." That was the best way I could describe it, even though my beast was electrical. "If you take them in, when they wake up, your people will get hurt or killed. They're like nothing you've dealt with."

Kat stared at me, dumbfounded, not believing us. I nodded at Travis, who took a step back. His body morphed quickly as he transformed fluidly, unlike most TV shows where werewolves transformed, their bones breaking—though we also weren't werewolves. Kat gasped, and he let her take him in before morphing back.

"So cool," Dylan said, elated. I shot him a look and he sucked in his lips.

"The reports said they were being taken by men in masks—they weren't masks," Miles said gently. "I know it's a lot to take in, but Travis is right that people will get hurt. Though, I don't suppose we can trust Dr. Roulings, can we?" Miles turned to Travis. "And how exactly do you plan on taking care of them?"

"I already called for clean-up." Travis looked at me. "Liam's right; we're the good guys. What's happening here doesn't have anything to do with Doc."

I opened my mouth but closed it when a black Ford Expedition zoomed around the corner. Miles hovered his left hand over his gun but slowly lowered it when Travis told him they were friendly. I watched as the car parked, and my heart stopped when Liam got out of the driver's side and Maya out of the back. Liam surveyed the scene and then looked at me. His mouth parted as if he was about to say something but faltered at my expression.

I stiffened when a tall brawny man with short brown-russet hair and an auburn beard stepped out of the passenger side. A face I'd seen almost every single day over the last five years. A face that infuriated me and made me tremble at the same time.

"What is *he* doing here?" My hands clenched into fists as Miles took a few steps to stand next to me.

"Adam's with us." The words flowed casually out of Travis's mouth, but I couldn't process them. Sure, Adam had helped me during my spat with Liam, but that didn't change what he had done to us—done to me.

"I told you we should've had him stay in the car." Maya's voice was different. It wasn't laced with anger or hatred. It was the voice I was used to, her voice.

"Sunshine." Liam gave me a smile that said everything was okay, which I couldn't see how it was. "How many?" he asked Travis.

"Three and three," Travis answered. "They're sending more Rogues and taking more people at once. I think they would've grabbed more if we hadn't intervened."

Liam nodded. "I doubt they would have sent three Rogues just to capture three people."

"Rogues?" The question was on the tip of my tongue, but my mouth stayed clamped as I glared at Adam; Dylan was the one who had asked.

"They're the Hybrians we're after." Liam kept his voice calm. "And who are you?"

"Dylan—apparently, a friend of Harper's," Travis answered.

"What is he doing with you?" I restated. Their first response had not been good enough.

"I will explain later; first we need to take care of this." Liam waved toward the unconscious Rogues. "And I think the agent could use your help." I didn't need to avert my glare to know that Kat was still in shock, but so was I. Seeing them in person side-by-side with Adam was infuriating.

"You said that the last time I saw you. It's later." I took my eyes off of Adam to see a flash of hurt on Liam's face. Our little meeting the other day had not gone as he'd hoped. I took a deep breath and looked at Kat, who was white as a ghost.

"You're all . . . those things?" She looked Miles up and down in question.

"Not everyone." Miles pointed between Dylan and himself. "We aren't. And she's"—his eyes found mine—"she doesn't change like they do." Kat didn't need to know the details on what I could do; it would only freak her out more. She needed to process the other information first.

"And him." Travis pointed at Adam with a smirk. "He's one hundred percent Scottish human."

"Okay." Kat shook her head and composed herself, all signs of fear and bewilderment gone. "Let's clean this up and get medical help for these three." She gestured at the girls in the van and the guy on the ground. "Once you get the other . . . *Hybrians* . . . out of here, I am calling these kidnappings in and shutting this rave down. Miles and I interfered, and the perps left them behind so they could get away."

That was why she was in a leading position. Kat's assertiveness in authority was impressive as she composed herself quickly, even with learning about something that should be unfeasible. Technically, she was in charge of Miles, but that was loosely. He was a different force of his own.

I watched Adam help Travis, Liam, and Maya load the Hybrians into the back of the white van after they took the girls out. They acted like he was one of them, especially Maya, as they bantered back and forth.

"Want to drive the bodies? They need to be sedated and cuffed first," Liam asked Maya.

"Duh." Her eyes lit up as Liam tossed her the keys.

I watched Adam as he grabbed a briefcase out from the Expedition and headed to the back of the van. He injected something into the Rogues' arms. Silky black hair flashed in front of my face as Maya popped out of nowhere to hug me.

"I'm so sorry. I didn't mean any of it," Maya whispered in my ear. She quickly turned, giving me no time to react, and practically skipped to the driver's side of the white van. My glare flitted to Adam, who gave me a sympathetic smile as he climbed into the passenger's side.

"It was fun teaming up with you again. Can't wait for next time." Travis slapped the side of my shoulder and hopped into the Ford.

"You can call it in now," Liam told Kat and turned to me. "I promise I'll see you soon."

Liam walked over and climbed into the driver's side of the Expedition. His eyes held mine for a moment longer before he drove off.

CHAPTER THIRTY-TWO

I had scarfed down the roadhouse burger, which had been neatly displayed with a wooden pick pierced through it. Dylan hadn't had any problems finishing his burger, either.

"Wow, you guys must have been hungry. Can I get you two anything else?" The brunette server smiled as she grabbed our empty plates. She scanned Dylan and me up and down, shocked that two people our size could finish ginormous burgers in a matter of minutes. Dancing, fighting, and using my powers had made me work up an appetite.

"I'm good. Did you want anything?" Dylan looked at me.

I quickly gulped down the chocolate malt milkshake that I just started chugging. "No, thank you." When the server left, I started chugging the delicious, thick dessert again. "This is so good."

"Chocolate malt was always your favorite." Dylan laughed. "You better slow down so you can taste it."

I chucked my straw wrapper at him as he grabbed his plain chocolate milkshake. Dylan had said we used to visit a retro diner in Canby similar to this one. Apparently, we'd gone there often as kids, and even more often once we were allowed to go on our bicycles. I guess burgers and milkshakes had been one of our favorite pastimes.

Dylan had asked if I wanted to get something to eat before we headed back to the hotel, and I'd decided that was a good idea. Miles was going to be busy for a while, and I was famished. I may not have remembered Dylan, but it still felt like I'd known him my entire life. He was so easy to be around, and there was never any awkward silence.

"We should probably get going," I said after he finished his milkshake.

The server came over with our check, and I snatched it before Dylan could. He told me I didn't have to pay, but I argued that I liked to pay my own way. Plus, I owed him more than this dinner had cost for the dress and shoes, which were a bit overkill for the diner.

Once we got back to the hotel, we took the elevator to our floor. I came up short as I rounded the corner to our room. Miles leaned against the wall next to our door with his jacket clutched in his hand. A grey crewneck sweater had replaced the green T-shirt he wore earlier. He spotted us and leaned off the wall. I hesitantly walked over with Dylan, who slowly trailed me.

"Can we have that talk now?" His eyes stayed focused on me.

"I'll, uh, be in here if you need me." Dylan pulled out his room key and disappeared into the room. I wished he'd stayed or that I could have disappeared into the room also. Miles was not thrilled about my deception.

Miles started walking down the hallway, and I sighed as he led me to the stairwell. I imagined he'd chosen it because it was cold outside and provided privacy for the conversation we were about to have.

Once inside, he turned to face me. His eyes quickly glanced at my dress and back up. "Go Hybrian hunting afterward?"

"No, we went to get food." I studied his face after he used my own words against me. He was trying to keep his composure, but the vein pulsing in his neck gave him away.

He closed his eyes and took a deep breath. "You never took the bus or a taxi."

"No." I lowered my eyes to avoid his gaze. "How's Kat?"

"She's handling it well. We talked while we waited for

backup to arrive—the others don't know. She's putting the pieces together." He paused. "And Dylan knows everything?"

"Yes." I swallowed and looked up at him, knowing our twenty questions were nowhere close to being over. "I see you found our room."

"You aren't the only one who can find things out. So, how did you find the airport, our hotel, the rave, and manage to have your phone trace back to Portland? Which is still saying it's there, by the way."

My hand flitted to my pocket, where my phone was. I'd have to remind Dylan to change that. I'd thought our plan was going to be ruined when Brandon had texted me earlier, and I knew Miles would track me. I could have turned my phone off, but that wouldn't stop them from worrying, and apparently, it could still be tracked. Even though I was upset with Miles, I hadn't wanted him to think I was taken.

Dylan had proposed a plan, and it appeared to have worked brilliantly. He pinged my phone's GPS off a few cell towers along the bus route and then near my apartment at my supposed arrival time. I texted both Brandon and Miles saying that I would make it home myself when the bus should have arrived in Portland. The entire block my apartment was on managed to have a power outage for an hour, thanks to Dylan. He was dangerous with a computer. Miles wouldn't suspect me if the entire block was out, and I'd ignored Miles's call and told Brandon that I didn't want company and was fine. I had lied in the text message I sent Miles to seal the plan:

I made it back fine. The power's out. You can check with your buddies—it's not me this time. I don't want to talk, just leave me alone. Happy Hybrian Hunting.—**Harper**

I had ignored his next call and knew he would track my

phone if he hadn't already. I didn't receive another call or text after that, so I assumed he had bought it.

"Dylan's good with computers and phones—"

"So, he's a hacker?" Miles raised a thick brow.

"Umm, sort of." I probably shouldn't have admitted that. "He was able to change my phone's location, create a small power surge, and we guessed on the private airport."

"You guessed?" He knew I was lying.

I didn't want to tell him Dylan had hacked into the FBI database, although he probably had his suspicions, so I passed on his question. "We found out about the rave while we were at one of the clubs. We were approached by a girl who looked younger than me. She was handing out tickets and said it was invite-only." Which made me wonder how they'd gotten the location. They had to have snuck in. Miles wasn't the kind of guy you would walk up to and invite to a rave where the bouncer scanned for weapons. Their presence would have busted up the party right away. "How did you guys learn about the rave?"

"Saw a young man targeting people to give them a ticket. I asked him nicely for one." Miles swung his jacket over his shoulder.

"Sure you did." I went to smile but ceased when I thought about the reprimand I was about to receive.

He noticed my apprehension and frowned. I waited for him to say something, but when he didn't, I couldn't be quiet anymore.

"You said that you trusted me." I glanced up at him. "If you did, you wouldn't have sent me away."

"I do trust you, but that doesn't mean you can go off on your own."

"I wouldn't have if you had let me come with you." I crossed my arms. "Kat is a great FBI agent, but she can't do what I can. And even now that she knows, she still wasn't trained to fight them."

"And you were?" His storm-grey eyes narrowed in on me.

"Yes . . . technically, no." I lowered my head. We hadn't trained against Hybrians in the Vault, but I was positive it was part of the intent.

"I need you to listen to me, and if that means to stay home, then stay home. You could get hurt."

"Why have you been helping me learn how to use my ability, then? I'm sorry, but I'm not going to stay on the sidelines or be locked up in the precinct." I looked away, lowering my arms. "You aren't the only one worried about someone getting hurt. I guess we won't figure this out together. This was my problem before I ever met you." I had turned to go out the door when his hand gently wrapped around my arm.

"Harper . . ." He dropped his hand when I looked back at him.

His eyes swirled with different hues of grey and silver, scarcely any green. He rubbed the back of his neck and grabbed his jacket from his shoulder, clenching it as he strode over to the stairs. He sat on the top step and leaned forward, resting his forearms on his knees.

His jaw clenched as a muscle ticked in his jaw. I hadn't thought he would ever drop his barrier more than he had when we were at the farm, but right now, he did not attempt to barricade anything. Fear, anger, remorse, and other emotions I couldn't recognize flickered across his face like a flipbook. I sat next to him, waiting for him to speak.

"My brothers and I were on a mission." He studied my face before dropping his gaze to his hands. "It was supposed to be a routine sweep of a presumed vacant village. We weren't expecting to find anything, but you can never assume that. The thing was, nothing was there. I should have known something was off and gotten them out of there. The abandoned village was on a river. We left our boat downstream and entered by water, so we would be undetected, to be safe." His hands shook, barely perceptible.

"Multiple RPGs hit us from a neighboring building. None of the buildings nearby picked up any heat signatures." He took a moment to compose himself. "I lost four brothers that day. I lost one of them two days later in the hospital bed next to me. I was the farthest away from the blast zone. A piece of shrapnel ricocheted through my shoulder and rubble fell on top of me. But that was nothing. My brothers were hurt far worse; only one was still breathing."

"How did you guys get out?" I gently asked.

"His legs were crushed, so he couldn't walk. We had no idea if they were going to see if they'd finished the job, so we needed to get out. We got to the water and then to the boat. We drove a while before help arrived. They eventually were able to retrieve the rest of my brothers."

"I am so sorry, Miles." I couldn't imagine what he had gone through and was currently going through.

"I couldn't protect them." His face hardened.

"There was nothing you could have done. It sounds like you did everything you were supposed to do. It was unexpected."

He looked at me and spoke through gritted teeth. "I could have trusted my instincts, despite everything saying it was clear and retreated . . . not to continue . . . gotten them out of there so they could be alive today." His jaw relaxed as he looked back down. "Expect the unexpected."

I laid a hand over his shaking ones. "You can't blame yourself. It will only eat you up inside." His grandmother was right. "It's not your fault. Just because you survived doesn't mean you can blame yourself."

"I should be the one dead." He had survivor's guilt. I didn't know what that felt like, but it had to be a million times worse than the guilt I'd felt when I was freed from the Vault and not my friends.

"Nah. Who else would be helping my crazy ass right now?" I gently smiled as he peered up at me, the corner of his mouth slightly raising.

"I've lost so many." He moved a hand out from under mine and placed it on top. "I can't add you to that list."

I bit my lip. It was crazy to think how important someone can become to you in just a couple of months. "I can't lose you either."

* * *

After my dinner for one, I patiently waited for Chloe to arrive back from NYC. Soon enough, a knock came from the door. I checked the monitor to see Chloe and Brandon opening the door.

"Harper!" Chloe squealed as she tossed her bag down and ran over.

My chest could hardly move as I laughed in her tight embrace. "I missed you too."

Brandon strode in behind her, carrying her other bag. She hadn't planned on coming back this soon, and had taken most of her clothes.

"Well, I'll let you two gals catch up." Brandon set the bag down and went to turn around.

"Did you just say 'gals'?" Chloe chuckled, stopping Brandon mid-turn. They stared at each other for a moment as Chloe's cheeks started to blush.

"Maybe. I'll catch up with you *gals* tomorrow." Brandon grinned and left. He was back to dayshift tomorrow and had insisted on driving her from the airport instead of the agent who had gone with her.

I looked at Chloe with narrow eyes and a smirk. "Is there something going on between you two?"

"What? No!" she exclaimed.

I grinned but stopped myself from telling her I thought otherwise. Brandon always joked and Chloe bantered back, but I'd never seen Chloe blush like that, nor had Brandon ever said "you gals."

We brought her bags to her room, setting them on her bed.

"Want help unpacking?" I asked her as she started to put clothes away.

"Thanks, but that's okay. It won't take me long." Her happy eyes turned somber as she looked up at me. "Can we talk?"

"Of course. What's wrong?" I sat down on the edge of the floral bedspread so I was out of the way but not looming over her.

"My, uh, grandma . . . it didn't work out." Her eyes dropped. Unfortunately, I had figured that, or else she wouldn't have been back so quickly. "My grandma is in a nursing home. It looks like she went there about a month after my grandpa passed away. I guess she didn't handle losing him well. She doesn't remember me and has dementia."

"Oh, Chloe, I'm sorry." That must be dreadful to meet your family, who were supposed to be the ones who remembered when you couldn't.

"It's okay. At first, I was devastated, but then thought at least they didn't have to go through the panic and worry about me missing." She brushed a strand of her brown hair out of her face.

"True, but that doesn't mean it doesn't hurt," I consoled her.

"You're right. I was excited to see them and get answers." She walked over and put a handful of clothes in a drawer. "I don't remember any of that. One of the nurses recognized me. She thought I'd stopped coming because I couldn't bear to see my grandma like that anymore. I'm also pretty sure she thought the agent was my boyfriend." She let a small smile escape her lips. "The nurse knew more than I did. It sounded like she'd kept my secret about staying on my own for a month-and-a-half. I had to stop asking questions when she gave me a concerning look about my mental health."

"Apparently," she continued, "I avoided the foster system for the next month until I turned eighteen. They're the only family I had, and I was living on my own in our old apartment after that. That's all I found out. My grandma thought I was a stranger and didn't care for my company. It was heartbreaking to see her like that."

I stood and gave her a warm hug. I could feel her body start to shake as she sobbed. We stood there for a few more minutes until she sniffled and pulled away.

"Enough about me," she said as she wiped away her tears. "I want to hear about your trip."

"Chloe, it's okay. We don't need to talk about that. There's not much anyways." She didn't need to hear how caring my mother and stepfather had been.

"Oh, come on." She elbowed me. "Spill. I want all the details on everything—your family, your house, Miles . . . you and Miles had an entire weekend together." She grinned. "It would be a good distraction," she pleaded.

"Fine. I'll tell you everything." I started with my old house and ended with last night. She had known about my powers since after the cabin, and I filled her in on my progress. I didn't mention what Miles had shared with me last night, though; that was his and his only to share.

CHAPTER THIRTY-THREE

Chloe and I exited the front door of the café after work and waited for Miles. A few minutes later, a red truck stopped in the road. I waited for Chloe to climb into the back before I got in the passenger seat.

"Hey, Miles!" Chloe said.

"Hi, Chloe. Brandon filled me in. I'm sorry to hear what happened."

"It could be worse. I just get to annoy you all more." Chloe had apologized last night for telling Brandon before me, but I'd told her not to worry.

"I think that's a privilege for Brandon." Miles smiled.

"Yeah, Miles is too serious, and I just give them heart attacks." I grinned.

"Your little *escapades* are going to be the death of us," Miles grunted. He had been calmer since our talk at the hotel two nights ago.

"I won't lie—I kind of wish I were a part of those," Chloe added.

Miles shook his head just as his phone started to ring. He fished it out of his jeans pocket and held it to his ear.

"Yes," Miles answered and paused as the person on the other line spoke. "Harper and Chloe are with me, hold on . . ." He held out his phone and pressed a button. "Okay, you're on speaker. Where are you?"

"The Union Yard." Brandon's voice was full of apprehension.

"How many are there?" Miles pressed his lips together.

"At least three."

"Hang tight. We'll be right there." Miles hung up and glanced at me next to him and then at Chloe in the rearview mirror. "Looks like you might get to get in on the escapades, if you guys are up for it?"

"Yes!" Chloe answered, but I was too shocked to speak. Was he actually asking?

"I could use your help." Miles glanced at me. Before, he would have kicked us to the curb and not have put Brandon on speaker.

"Of course," I managed to say.

Miles turned his lights on and whipped the truck around at an intersection. I had been in this truck for hours. How did I not notice the hidden lights on the top rim of the windshield?

"And, Chloe, you are fully aware of the danger?" Miles kept his eyes on the road.

"Duh. Finally, I get in on the action." Chloe grabbed the back of my seat as Miles weaved through cars. I was thankful we had changed our shirts at work and no longer wore our embroidered G.A.H.O. shirts.

"Brandon said there were two girls with them." He turned off his lights as we neared the trainyard. "They didn't spot him, so we still have the element of surprise."

We pulled into the yard and down the dirt drive. Cargo containers, train cars, and train tanks were scattered into rows, some on tracks and some off. Miles pulled next to Brandon, who was standing by his police cruiser, the rows of cargo trains providing cover. I quickly climbed out of the car with Chloe right behind me and walked over to Brandon.

"They separated. Two of them took the girls toward the docks, and the other one went that way." Brandon pointed.

"How do you know they're Hybrians?" I asked.

"One didn't look human." Brandon inhaled. "I got a call that someone heard a couple of screams down here, and when I investigated, I saw the three of them. Only one was changed."

"It's a safe bet all three of them are, then," Miles added. "Chloe, you and Brandon stay near the vehicles. Make sure the other one doesn't double back. Harper and I will go get the girls."

"But—"

"He could have told you to wait in the car." Brandon cut Chloe's rebuttal off. Chloe sighed and nodded.

"Call me if you have anything." Miles reached into his pocket and made sure his phone was on vibrate as I did the same.

"Did you want me to call for backup?" Brandon asked.

"No, it will only make things worse." Miles rubbed the back of his neck. "Call Kat and let her know. Let's go."

I followed Miles as he drew his gun. We kept our heads low as we ran across the uneven rocks and gravel. The carts provided color to the dreary trainyard and intermittent cloudy day. Surprisingly, no one was around, despite it being three in the afternoon.

"Why did you have me come with you instead of Brandon?" I whispered.

"It's a good idea to keep you and Chloe split up." Miles glanced my way. "I could also use your fighting skills. You know the enemy more than we do."

"Maybe." A small thrill shot through me.

What I did know was that Miles trusted Brandon. They had grown up as friends because their fathers had served together. They were good partners and had each other's back, which also meant that they knew how the other one operated. I was glad to know Chloe was safe with Brandon. She could fight, but she wasn't a match for a Hybrian.

"Don't show them what you can do." Miles led me closer to the docks, where more train cars and cargo containers were lined up in a conglomerate maze. "We don't know who we're dealing with, and I don't want you to pique their interest."

I nodded and froze. "I think I hear them."

"Where?"

I pointed in the direction where I'd heard muffled voices. We snuck between two oil cargo tanks and down a row of carts. Miles held out his hand and I halted as he pressed himself to a blue cart. He peered around the side of it and waved me to take a look. I peered my head around the corner and quickly pulled back. Two men were pacing in front of an open container that had two girls inside on their knees, their mouths taped shut and their hands tied. I noticed a dock a short distance away.

"Do you think they're going to get them out of here by boat?" I kept my voice low, knowing they probably had good hearing.

"More than likely." Miles studied me as I scrunched my nose. "Are you okay?"

"I don't sense anything." I had thought maybe I couldn't sense them because we weren't close enough, but now that I could physically see them, the familiar tingling had never risen. "Maybe they aren't Hybrians." I doubted Brandon would have seen things, though.

"Just stay alert. Expect the unexpected." He gave me a sincere look.

I nodded in response. "What's the game plan?"

His lips curved into a mischievous grin. "How's your acting?"

* * *

"Go with pink. It looks so good on you!" I let out a bubbly laugh into my phone as I spoke to my fake friend. "Yes, it'll make him go crazy." I twirled my hair—which I had taken out of my ponytail—around my finger. I casually walked by the cargo container where the men stood. I looked up and froze, pretending to be in shock when I saw them and the two girls behind them. "I'm going to have to call you back."

I shoved my phone into my pocket and held up my hands while slowly backing away.

"What are you doing here, little girl?" An angry man with a Russian accent strolled toward me as the other one closed the container doors.

"Nothing . . . I was just taking a shortcut." My voice quivered with false fear. "I didn't see anything, I promise."

"Stop!" The man's bloodcurdling voice echoed through the trainyard. I froze. Just his voice made this place feel like a graveyard.

Beyond the guy barreling toward me, I saw Miles on top of the container the girls were in. He crouched down and waited for the other guy to be positioned far enough away so he could make his stand. Once he was, Miles leaped down behind the guy and held his gun out, standing between the man and the container.

"Don't move." The edge in Miles's voice sent thrills down my spine. "Portland Police."

The man at the end of the barrel dropped his jaw in fright as he faced me while the guy headed my way stopped. His mouth curved into a sneering smile, causing the scar slashed across the corner of his lips to twitch.

"Well, well, well. What do we have here?" The man closest to me turned just enough so he could watch both of us, his eyes scanning me up and down. "Is she a part of your diversion? You know, it's not easy to sneak up on us. That's a bit impressive for a beat cop."

"No one has to get hurt if you let us take the girls." Miles threatened as he steadily aimed the gun at the back of the other man's head. Miles knew we had to make sure they couldn't use the girls as leverage and had suggested getting the jump on them. He was itching to simply shoot them, but his cop side held him off.

"You're outnumbered." The guy in front of me sneered.

"Miles!" I shouted but was too late.

A flash of silver soared toward him, but he was quick.

He dodged the knife as it pierced the car to his right. A third man had rounded the corner, eyes glowing. A Hybrian. *Why didn't I sense him?*

A growl brought my attention to the man in front of me as he partially morphed. He faced me with glowing yellow-orange eyes and clawed hands. Liam had said that could only be accomplished with practice and concentration. We could've been in trouble.

He let out a laugh after sizing me up. "You didn't bring a weapon?"

Oh, I had. I was the weapon. I glanced past him to check on Miles. The other two were attacking him, and his gun lay on the ground across the yard. The Hybrian who had been at gunpoint had seized the opportunity when Miles dodged the knife to disarm him. Miles was holding his own, for now. He moved with such force, speed, and calculation. The other two relied solely on brute force and the enhanced senses from the beast, just like the Rogues at the rave. I prayed Miles's skills and acuity were enough. They had been so far.

I feinted right as a clawed hand came barreling toward my face. He came at me again with the opposite arm, and I dodged it so my back was to him. While grabbing his wrist, I elbowed him in the gut and slammed the back of my fist into his nose. He backed off, grasping his gushing, bloody nose.

"You—"

"What? I thought I didn't have a weapon?" I couldn't help my smile. I loved the look of surprise when my opponent realized he or she had underestimated me.

He let out a roar and attacked again. I dodged him and sprinted toward Miles. The gun was too far out of reach, and I would get cut off before I could get to it. Miles saw me coming and shoved the Hybrian attacking him to the ground as he kicked the other one back, leaving me an opening. We had a better shot if we were side by side.

"You guys don't seem shocked by our appearances." The man I had just fought strode toward us, his black hair slicked with sweat across his forehead and sides of his face. His eyes receded to their normal black as the other two flanked him; he must be their leader.

"You don't seem to care that we aren't." Miles's voice was low and deep.

"It just makes things easier for us," he mocked.

The three of them simultaneously morphed. My eyes shifted off to the side, where the gun lay out of reach.

"Miles . . ." With all three fully morphed, we would have a hard time taking them on if I didn't summon my beast or if we didn't get his gun.

"Only if you need to," he said through gritted teeth.

I nodded. Miles and I kept our backs to each other as we fought. We were holding our own and managed to receive only a few blows. I couldn't help but think Miles and I made a great team. It was like we knew what maneuvers the other was going to perform so we could fight with a similar tactic. It was effective at keeping the Hybrians back. As my kick collided with the Hybrian who had thrown the knife, I couldn't help but think about Chloe and Brandon. Were they okay? Was he the third one Brandon had seen?

"This ends now." Their leader seared with anger as sweat evaporated off his skin. He reached for his pocket, pulling out a switchblade.

"You can't handle us without a weapon? Where's the honor in that?" I snipped. Out of the corner of my eye, I saw Miles attempt to hold back a grin while also giving a disapproving head shake at my remark.

The Hybrian grumbled and attacked. Miles dodged the first swipe, and on the second, he was able to disarm him and retrieve the knife. However, the other Hybrian came in and hit him hard, taking him down while I was too busy with the third to stop him. I felt anger pool inside me as Miles hit the ground.

"Whoa." The Hybrian in front of me froze, staring at me. I used his hesitancy against him and delivered a hard blow to his face, knocking him to his knees. I turned to see their leader leering at me as a sinister grin spread across his face.

"What the—" The other Hybrian was cut off as Miles knocked his feet out from underneath him.

Miles hoisted himself off the ground as the hum of a motor caused all of us to turn our heads toward the docks. A small speedboat approached with a single man on board, and less than a second later, Brandon's cruiser came soaring from around the corner.

"Let's go." The scarred-faced man ordered.

"But the girls?"

"They aren't what we're looking for." He bolted for the docks with the other two at his heels.

I went to follow when gunshots sounded. Miles stood, grabbing my jacket and pulling me back as bullets zipped by our feet. He pulled me behind a container and shielded me. My heart began to thud against my chest at his closeness. I looked up, meeting softened eyes and a tense jaw. Miles swallowed as my body froze in time.

For a brief moment, I had forgotten about the shooting until reality kicked in that Brandon and Chloe were still in the crossfire. I looked over to see Brandon taking cover near the front of the hood, shooting back. I didn't see Chloe but imagined she was staying low.

Miles's eyes stayed on me until the firing stopped twenty seconds later. His eyes hardened again as he reached for his gun and took off toward the docks. He aimed at the boat, but it was gaining distance and was too far away. He silently swore as he lowered his gun and jogged back over to us.

I went to the front of the container and started opening it after looking over to see that Brandon was okay. Miles joined me as we heaved open the doors. Light shined into the containers, revealing two girls huddling near the back corner. They both had blond hair and were about my age.

Shuffling sounded from outside near the back of the container, and Miles brought a finger to his lips. Miles made his way around the corner with his gun drawn, but lowered it and relaxed his shoulders. I rounded the container and almost gasped.

Miles looked from the girl on the ground to me with an afflicted expression. The third man who had showed up was actually the fourth, and he'd had another young blond girl with him. They were looking for someone blond, average height, and young. They were looking for me. It couldn't have been Frank—he had to have known where I was if Liam, Maya, and Adam knew.

Miles put his gun away and softened his expression, making himself look less intimidating as he walked over to the girl.

"You're going to be okay. We're with the police." Miles showed her his badge and then took out the Hybrian's switchblade, which he had pocketed, to cut her hands and feet free. Her feet must have been tied up when the Hybrian heard the commotion.

"Keepsake?" I eyed the switchblade in his hands that he detained from the scarred-faced Hybrian.

"Just until I can return it." He pocketed it again. "And get mine back from the captain."

"Did he confiscate it?" I raised an eyebrow.

"No, just borrowed it this morning. But right now, I regret letting him." He patted his jeans pocket, where it normally would have been.

"Do you always keep it on you?" I waved for the frightened girl to follow as we walked back to the front.

"Usually."

"Harper! Are you guys okay?" Chloe jogged over and hugged me. Brandon cut the other two girls loose in the container behind her.

"I'm good. Are you?" I pulled away to look her over.

"I'm going to get these two to the car." Brandon showed the girls past us.

"We'll join you." Miles escorted the other girl behind them.

Chloe and I walked over and stood about twenty feet from the cruiser, giving them space. They were probably more comfortable with Brandon, who was in his uniform.

"Looks like dinner will be delayed," Brandon remarked as they strode back over to us once the girls were in the cruiser.

"I'm sure we'll get plenty more nights at Mel's," I joked. We had gone to Miles's and Brandon's favorite bar a few times for pizza and wings.

"It's not like we get to save lives every day. Although, I didn't really get any action." Chloe glanced over at the docks.

"How did you guys know when to show up?" I followed Chloe's gaze to where the boat had been moments ago.

"We tried to see if we could find the other guy." Brandon glanced at Chloe, his look suggesting that by "*we*" he'd meant "*she*." "He got on a boat, and we guessed he was going to pick up the others. I tried calling, but I see why you didn't answer." He looked at Miles. "Sorry, I didn't know there were four of them."

"I'm betting he had just arrived with the other girl." Miles sighed. "I'm sure we'll still have time tonight. I don't think it will take long. Do you ladies mind a detour to the precinct?"

"Umm, not at all." I was surprised Miles didn't try to order us to stay in our apartment indefinitely after realizing what they were looking for.

"Nope. Not if it means on top of saving three people tonight, we get to have my welcome-back dinner also." Chloe grinned cheerfully.

I chewed the inside of my cheek; we hadn't caught the ones responsible, though.

CHAPTER THIRTY-FOUR

I wiped down the empty tables while thinking about Mel's last night, thankful it was a slow morning at work. We had shared some laughs, and I think the normalcy had helped ease Kat, who had joined. She seemed wary of me the most. We told her Chloe couldn't morph and that I was only partially affected. She asked questions about the Vault, and I answered. When we had gotten back to our apartment, Chloe said she was amazed I wasn't angry at how close Kat stayed to Miles.

"It's not like that. I mean, I might be a little jealous of how gorgeous she is, but that's not how it is. I think it's a purely platonic coworker relationship," I had told her. After all, they're working on an investigation that benefited me.

"He definitely has eyes for you, and you like him," she had replied.

"And how do you know that?"

"Because it's obvious. The way he looks at you while you're not looking . . ." Chloe had a huge smirk on her face.

I had finished wiping down the tables and went to take my position at the cash register when something pricked at the back of my mind. I hastily looked up, checking my surroundings. I didn't see anyone outside the windows, and no one new had come in. I turned to Chloe and pulled her away from the front counter.

"They're here," I whispered. It took her a second to realize what I meant.

"What! Where?" She looked around.

"I don't know, but I can feel them." I looked down the

hallway and saw the back door was still locked. "I don't know who it is. I couldn't sense them yesterday at the trainyard."

"Really?" Chloe was about to say something else when the bells on the front door chimed.

We both turned our heads, relaxing when an older gentleman walked through. My body went rigid when I did a double-take. I inhaled sharply, forgetting to breathe. I didn't take my eyes off his, which were more blue than grey today. His face was stubble-free, and his hair had been cut and smoothed out compared to its normal crimp. It was styled similar to George Clooney's haircut, which I had seen on the front of a magazine a couple of days ago, but with brown hair. His black peacoat wrapped around a dark-blue sweater and hung over his grey slacks.

"What are you doing here?" I snapped, keeping my voice low to not concern the customers in the café. I pulled out my phone and sent a quick text to Miles as Chloe tensed next to me, realizing who he was.

Frank is here.—Harper

"Texting your boyfriend?" There was amusement in his voice.

"You should leave." I strode over to the register where he stood.

"I would like to order a regular French vanilla coffee, please."

"You can get it elsewhere." My hands clamped into fists at my sides.

"Your friends are right outside—it is quite all right." He kept his eyes on me as I glanced around him at the front windows. Sure enough, Liam, Travis, and Maya were standing there. They looked like they were a couple of college students just hanging out.

"One regular French vanilla coffee, please." He pulled out his wallet and handed me a ten.

"Fine. Chloe, can you make one French vanilla coffee, *please*?" I took his money and started to count the change.

"Keep the change," he added. Chloe walked over with the cup of coffee and handed it to me. She must have wanted him out of there pronto because that was the quickest coffee she had ever poured.

"Here, now leave." I wanted to wipe the smug grin from his face.

"Thanks, dearie." Frank grabbed the cup and took a sip. "Mhmm, scrumptious. Harper, would you care to join me and your friends outside for a chat?"

Chloe shook her head, but I turned to Frank regardless. "You have ten minutes."

"Harper . . ." Chloe warned.

"I'll be right back. Liam and Travis will be there," I reassured her, taking off my apron and setting it on the shelf below the counter. I followed Frank out and glanced at our customers. They were too engrossed in their computers, phones, or conversations to notice the tension radiating off of Chloe and me.

"After you." Frank waved at the door. A low grumble rose in my throat. His charisma did not faze me, as I saw through his act now. I took a deep breath. If I let my anger get out of control, my eyes would glow.

Just as I started to step through the door, I heard a motorcycle. Miles parked in between two cars in front of us and ripped off his helmet, closing the distance between us.

"We should probably step away from the little coffee shop's entrance. I'm sure this amount of hostility would scare off potential customers." Frank let the door close behind him as he took another sip of his coffee and walked down the sidewalk. Liam, Maya, and Travis trailed behind him. I shared a look with Miles as we followed.

"It is not safe for you here anymore, Harper. It would be wise if you came with us." Frank stopped and turned to face me when we were in front of a brick wall and not a store window.

"You should listen to him," Liam said, keeping his eyes

on the passersby. Travis was also scanning the area, while Maya wore sunglasses on this cloudy day, so I couldn't tell where she was looking.

"You already told me that once, and I gave you my answer." I looked from Liam to Frank. "And how would I be safer with you? You tried to have all of the Jects killed. *Them* killed." I waved a hand at my friends.

"I would never have any of you killed. Our members would not do that to each other. I knew you had a sentinel's radio, and I hoped my commands would scare you into surrendering. I could not have you guys running around talking about the Vault, or you out in the open." Frank smiled. "You guys still managed to escape. A remarkable feat."

"Yeah, sure. Why isn't it safe here, the Rogues? And what do you mean 'each other'?" I wasn't buying his lies.

"It is the truth, dearie. And precisely due to the Rogues, but even more so, their leader." Frank acted as if I didn't hate him.

"Who's their leader?" Miles asked.

"The reason Alcorp exists, to protect the world from him and others alike. He is the definition of evil with no mercy, someone everyone should fear." Frank's smile faded as he looked from Miles to me. "Someone who scared your father more than anyone else."

I swallowed. "Did he kill my father?"

"He wants your DNA, Harper." Frank used my fake name like he'd never known my real one. Even when *he* said it, it felt real to me. "A serum with your DNA has the potential to be modified to create abilities like yours. He speculates you might be alive and theorizes you carry the serum in you that your father created. He might not know about your ability, but he knows your father's serums are unique, have a higher success rate, and are nearly irreplicable. Right now, you are the most valuable thing to him. It's the reason you were in the Vault—to hide you from him. If he gets what he wants and you don't cooperate afterward, you'll be disposed of."

"Disposed of how?" I don't know why I asked that.

"There are many things he could do to you that would technically kill you." Frank's lips fell flat.

"How did you *dispose* of the sentinel Liam killed and the ones Travis shot? Or the ones shot by Brandon or Miles?" Or stabbed. I thought about the night at the bar. "You say that you didn't want to hurt any of the Jects, but what about them?"

A flash of guilt and hurt crossed Liam's face. I shouldn't have brought it up, but I needed to prove a point.

Frank swallowed and dropped his nonchalant act for a moment. "It is with deep sympathy that we lost one of our own. I take full responsibility for Pearson's death and any injuries, as I had let the situation get out of hand both times. As far as the others, we were able to save them and help them recover. No one was supposed to get hurt. The guns are meant for an attack, not for the Jects."

I scoffed, glancing at my friends, who also looked hurt. Dr. Cole had mentioned the Sentinels were there to protect us.

"We are fighting a silent war most of the world doesn't know about. Their leader is on a dangerous path, and we need to fight back with similar power—without using his heinous methods. A few of our acquaintances in the FBI have been trying to close Agent Foster's investigation, but she is stubborn. A good stubborn, but we need to keep Alcorp a secret. She would be a good recruit now that she knows."

"Heinous? You are the definition of heinous." My words hurt Frank as he lowered his eyes.

"Jects were recruited, and we knew what we were getting into. We are members of Alcorp. The serum has a side effect of short-term memory loss until you change or stop receiving the treatments. That's why we didn't know until after the fact. It takes a week or less after the change, but it is different if the serum is stopped or your body doesn't accept the change." Liam held my questioning eyes.

"Except for you and Liam. We are wondering if it was

something to do with your relationship. Most Jects don't form a strong bond, and the mind is a powerful thing," Frank added. "And we were only trying to extract what is inside you to create an antidote if your DNA were to be weaponized."

I opened my mouth but couldn't force out the millions of questions and retorts that rested on my tongue. Liam and I were close, and we had always been there for each other. It was all overwhelming. A few moments of silence passed.

"We guessed right." Miles looked at me as he thought. "That's why they tried to take those girls yesterday."

"What girls?" Liam snapped his head back toward the conversation.

"These . . . Rogues . . . were trying to take three girls at the yard yesterday." Miles's eyes fell on me. "They had blond hair, average build, and were in their late teens."

"They must suspect you are here, then," Frank denounced. "We were not sure if he knew."

"Speaking of yesterday, I didn't feel you near." I looked at Liam. "And I couldn't sense the Hybri—Rogues."

"We were still in Seattle, taking care of things." Liam's eyes flashed a burnt yellow as he briefly looked around. "We can't sense Rogues, and they can't sense us, either—we don't know why. They must've followed you back."

"If they had, they would have known what she looked like and known where she was staying." Miles's voice hardened. "But that doesn't mean they didn't decide to look into where we're from. And with Kat's investigation, it would seem logical that Harper would be here."

Frank nodded in agreement.

"Those Rogues have tried to take a guy, and those girls looked nothing like me," I said.

"They were recruits." Frank took another sip of his coffee. "They may have had others nearby and saw Agent Foster's team there, so they didn't engage."

"They saw your eyes," Miles said.

"Who did?" Liam asked.

"The Rogues from yesterday." Miles glanced at me.

Realization hit. I had been angry when they hit Miles and felt a small surge, but I hadn't realized my eyes had changed. I should have known better. I glanced at Frank when he didn't question what was different about my eyes.

"He knows what I can do?" I snapped at Liam. *Great.*

"Yes, he—"

"I can't believe you!" I cut Liam off, saying it a little louder than I'd intended as a passerby looked our way. I took a step toward him, but a hand gently wrapped around my wrist.

"Another time," Miles said as Liam's gaze landed where Miles's hand wrapped around my wrist. I closed my eyes and took a deep breath.

"Why do they want me?" I asked as Miles let go and took a step back.

"You know why," Liam stated.

I did, and I was sure Miles did too. Even though he had been on his motorcycle, I'd had him on speaker when Frank had told me about what my father had done to my mother. The difference between her and me was that I had been born with the serum inside me and it had altered my DNA.

"You should come with us." Liam took a step closer. "They'll find you. They're resourceful, but so are we."

"We aren't bad," Travis interjected.

"You can trust us. Trust *me*." Liam stared down at me with his doe-brown eyes.

I let out a hysterical laugh. "I trusted Frank once, and he lied. And now, because of him, I just don't know. Part of me says I should go, but the other part of me tells me to run. How do I know this isn't Frank messing with your heads? For crying out loud, look at our tattoos, and what, his was fake?" I glanced at the barcode tattooed on my arm—a constant reminder of my captivity. Outside of the Vault, people had thought Chloe's and mine were friend tattoos.

"Mine is quite real," Frank said as I let a low grumble escape my lips.

"There may be someone out there worse than you, Frank, but that doesn't mean you're good." I pivoted and started walking back to the café without sparing a glance at my friends. I paused to look behind me when Miles didn't follow.

"In case you hear anything." Miles handed Liam his card with his number on it. I started walking again and heard Frank murmur something to Liam.

"We will be around when you change your mind," Frank shouted after me, but I didn't turn around.

"Why did you give him your number?" I asked Miles when we reached the café. I glanced down the sidewalk, but they were gone.

"In case they need to alert us." Miles let out an inaudible sigh. "I don't like what we're up against. And I don't know if *I* have the resources to protect you."

I smiled. "I'm not a damsel in distress."

"You are more than capable of holding your own," he said, grinning, "as long as you don't do something stupid."

"Hey!" I nudged him and went into the café. "I've been good."

"For all of a few days." He raised an eyebrow as he followed me in.

"We both know if Dylan and I hadn't been there, those people would have been taken. And probably Travis too." I doubted Travis would have been able to handle all three Rogues, especially by the time Miles or Liam would have gotten there.

"Yes, but that doesn't mean it wasn't reckless." Miles turned me to face him, and I knew he had set all joking aside. "We're going to be truthful with each other, right? That's all I ask."

"As long as the truth doesn't harm anyone, but I promise not to lie to you." I wanted the truth, but sometimes it was best to keep your mouth shut. If I told my mom the truth about what I knew, it would break her heart.

He opened his mouth, but then shut it and nodded. "Honesty and no lying. I can settle with that . . . for now."

I nodded. He knew better than anyone that the truth could hurt. We stared at each other as heat crept into my cheeks. His light grip on my arms felt hot as heat radiated from his chest, drawing me closer. I felt him lean in as his eyes briefly dropped to my lips.

The sound of glass shattering broke us apart as we turned to see Chloe beet-red behind the counter.

"Sorry, I didn't mean to drop the pot. Please continue." Chloe waved us on as she bent over behind the counter to clean up.

Miles cleared his throat, hiding a smile. "I'm going to make a call to the captain and Kat. I'll be outside when your shift is done."

* * *

Miles stayed nearby for the remainder of work. I had taken him a blueberry muffin and black coffee, just how he liked it, after a couple of hours. I had chastised him about not visiting Charlotte and Richard, and he ended up saying hello. They were thrilled to see him, and I think Miles secretly was too.

Later that night, Brandon brought pizza to our apartment, and I was able to convince Miles to come in from being on watch outside. We sat down on the floor and played cards, just like the days at the cabin. This time, I was a little more relieved, knowing my friends were no longer in the Vault, despite them being allies with Frank.

Chloe asked Brandon to come up with a name for sensing other Hybrians, and he delivered with the *beast beacon*. It was suiting.

I gnawed on the inside of my cheek; I had a group of people watching out for me, and that was something I didn't want anyone to have to be burdened with.

CHAPTER THIRTY-FIVE

I hung up my green apron and donned my leather jacket after my shift. It was sunny and fifty-five degrees out, which felt cool compared to the eighty-degree summer. Chloe and I left work and headed to our apartment.

I was surprisingly relieved when I sensed a Hybrian nearby, same as that morning. The captain had needed Miles and Brandon in the office for a private meeting, and Kat was going to be there as well. They also had paperwork to catch up on from the trainyard.

Chloe and I had only made it a block when a scream interrupted our walk. The jolt of Chloe's head and the disturbed look she wore told me she'd heard it too. Another scream echoed down the long alley. No one around us seemed to have paid any attention. We both shared a look that said we couldn't just walk away, and soon we were jogging down the alley.

A fence blocked our path when we got to the middle as another scream sounded. I climbed the cold, rusty fence and landed on a flat cardboard box on the other side with Chloe on my heels. A wide alley appeared on our right, leading to a dead end with more dumpsters and a single door with no windows.

My heart stopped when my eyes landed on a pair of legs peeking out from behind one of the dumpsters. I guardedly walked over and noticed a young woman lying on her back with her eyes shut. She didn't have any noticeable wounds as

I knelt next to her. I was about to check for a pulse when I heard a burst of slithery laughter.

I shot upright as the girl on the ground's eyes flew open. She sneered and stood up, brushing herself off. Chloe and I backed away from her and the oncoming threats from our only exit. I inhaled sharply when I recognized one of them. Her deep-red, almost ruby hair and blue eyes couldn't be mistaken.

"It's been too long, little sunray or whatever," Avery hissed as she stepped closer with an accomplice and the girl from the ground, who had walked over to her side. I didn't think Avery was a Hybrian.

"What do you want?" I demanded.

"You, evidently," she barked.

"How'd you find me?" I gritted my teeth.

"We got lucky." She shrugged. "Saw you walking out the back of that little café while scoping the area for you. He told me he suspected you might be what he needs; you are either a rumor, or a new serum was created." A malicious grin spread across her face.

"Did Dr. Roulings put you up to this?"

She let out a cackle. "Of course not. Dr. Roulings is way too soft. My body rejected his serum, and I was left with empty promises. I was approached by someone else. Someone whose vision is influential and true. It comes with better promises, as long as he gets you. There was no other way I would have stayed with Dr. Roulings that long if I weren't spying. You were his favorite, and I heard you might be a little different."

Not only did I take in her words as she spoke, but I took in our surroundings. Chances were, the door behind us was locked, and every other option that didn't include Avery and her friends was a brick wall.

"So, if it's just me you want, then let her go." I gestured toward Chloe.

"Harper . . ." Chloe argued. I knew she wouldn't want to

leave me behind, but if they just wanted me, she didn't need to be involved.

"Uh, I don't think so." Avery narrowed her eyes. "She can be your motivation to cooperate."

She pulled out a tranquilizer gun, and as she did, the man and woman beside her morphed. *Rogues.* If she shot me with that, I wouldn't be able to get us out of there. I let the energy surge through me and summoned my beast. Avery fired, and I dodged the tranquilizer by half a foot.

"If there's an opening, run and call Miles." I looked at Chloe as she nodded. Where was Liam, or whoever I had felt nearby? My beast beacon had gone silent but picked up again.

"I won't miss next time," Avery declared from behind the Rogues, who ran at us.

Chloe readied her fighting stance as they approached. I fended off the guy who came at me and sent the girl flying backward with a roundhouse kick. The only thing able to stop me other than an inhibitor or sedative would be a knife to Chloe's throat.

I couldn't risk it, and went over to Chloe's side, luring both of them closer to each other. Once both of them were in reach, I shoved one hand into the guy's chest and extended the other at the girl, who was only inches away. Blue sparks flew from my hands and found their marks. Both of their bodies shook as they hit the floor.

I turned to Avery, whose jaw dropped. She raised the tranquilizer, firing twice, and missing both times as I ran at her.

"Just a little different, huh?" Even though she'd probably meant my DNA, she seemed surprised at my powers. I raised my hands and blue lightning sailed through the air, striking her in the chest. The force sent her flying backward, skidding across the pavement.

"Come on. Let's get out of here," I said, pulling out my

phone as Chloe and I passed Avery's unconscious body. We started in a jog toward our apartment, but I slowed to a stop.

"What is it?" Chloe asked.

"We shouldn't go back to the apartment in case they're tracking us."

"Good idea," Chloe agreed.

"Let's go to that playground that's a block away." We had passed it multiple times when we went to Washington Park. We started in that direction, and I hit the call button on my phone while clutching my bag with my other hand as it hung across my shoulder.

"Harper? What is it?" Miles answered on the second ring.

"Rogues attacked us on our way home—"

"SNAFU," Miles muttered into the phone.

"But we escaped," I continued. "We're fine and are heading to the playground on the corner of Fairview and Harrington."

"Don't hang up. I'm on my way." He said something that I couldn't make out along with shuffling in the background. I imagined he had informed Brandon, and pictured him grabbing his jacket off the back of the chair and storming out the door. I put the phone on speaker as I kept it in my hands and ran with Chloe at my side.

"Holy crap!" I yelped, nearly running into Liam.

"Are you guys all right?" Liam's eyes were filled with worry.

"Yes, we're fine," I answered.

"Liam?" Miles's voice crackled through the phone. It sounded like he already had his helmet on.

"I'm here," he answered. "What were you guys thinking? You were walking home and then all of a sudden decided to run down an alley?"

"We fell for a trap." I stepped around him and continued to jog toward the park. Miles would be there soon, and I wanted to distance myself as far from Avery as I could.

"How did she trap you?" Liam caught up to me, and so

did Chloe. We looked like an odd trio; two of us ran with jeans, while Liam wore a black long-sleeved shirt and black cargo pants.

"We heard a woman scream," Chloe replied. "Got the best of us."

"You said she—how did you know it was Avery?" I questioned.

"I was staying back, trying to not draw attention, when I saw you guys take off. When I finally figured out where you guys went, I found her and two others lying there." Liam glanced at me.

"Yes, I zapped them," I answered his eyeing look.

"No, you 'zapped' me. You electrocuted them."

I shrugged at Liam and slowed down as we neared the park.

"It looks clear for now." Liam surveyed the area.

"Almost there." Miles's voice resounded through the phone.

"Avery said she wasn't working for Frank, so who is she working with?" I asked Liam.

Liam looked at me, his eyes filled with disgust. "The man Dr. Roulings was talking about yesterday."

"I gathered, but who *is* that?"

"Dr. Killian Krauss." He spoke the name with hatred.

"Great, another doctor," I murmured.

"He sounds evil," Chloe commented.

Liam went to say something, but stopped at the sound of a motorcycle approaching. Miles rode toward us and parked on the edge of the road. He flipped the kickstand down and set his helmet on his bike.

"How did they know where you were?" Miles asked when he reached us. He had heard how they'd lured us in over the phone, but neither he nor Liam knew what Avery had mentioned.

"Avery said they were scoping out the area and got lucky

when they spotted me leaving work." I sighed, putting my phone in my pocket.

"I don't remember seeing anybody when we left, but then again, I wasn't really looking." Chloe rubbed her arm. She knew this meant our cover had been made, and we couldn't work at the café anymore.

"Do you think they'll go after Brandon's parents? Avery likes leverage," I said. Avery's tactics worried me. She had wanted to use Chloe as leverage, and had used Maya to do her bidding in the Vault. The leverage there was that I wouldn't kill my friend no matter what. Krauss must not have wanted me then.

"So does he," Liam muttered.

Miles typed something in his phone. "Brandon's on his way there now. He's going to stay with them."

"I'm sorry I failed to be alert." I was kicking myself. Awareness had been part of our tactical training in the Vault.

"Don't apologize; you wouldn't have known," Liam placated me.

"Don't coddle me. I know better, especially with all the warnings," I retorted, a bit harsher than intended. I took a deep breath. I was taking my anger out on Liam, and he didn't deserve that, but now wasn't the time to act like I was a delicate flower.

"What do we do now?" Chloe asked.

"We get you guys somewhere that's not compromised," Miles answered.

"And that would be with us. We have to get you both somewhere far away from the city." Liam pulled out his phone.

"No. I spent my life trapped, and I'm not about to spend it running." I closed my eyes. There had to be another way.

"He's right," Miles claimed. My eyes shot open, giving him an incredulous look. "It's not safe in the city anymore. They'll have scouts everywhere. We need to get you guys out of here and regroup."

"I don't trust Frank," I declared.

"I don't either," Miles said, glancing at Liam, "but *he* wouldn't let anything happen to you."

"And if I want to stay with you?" My stomach clenched at the thought of being away from Miles.

"It won't be forever." His eyes swirled with grey. "If they're on to Kat, they're on to me."

I let the unspoken words his eyes told me sink in. Avery could easily find out where Miles's grandparents lived. She could use them to flush him out if he left with me, the same with Charlotte and Richard.

"I could become a ghost, but chances are, they already have all the necessary information on me," Miles answered as he read my thoughts. "If their resources are as good as Liam says, it could be bad."

"Krauss may have his suspicions, but they don't know who you really are yet." Liam read between the lines. "Frank never told Avery, and your files with the FBI will be nonexistent once we get Agent Foster's papers. Your obituary photo was taken down also. We'll send members from Alcorp to keep an eye on everyone who knows you. They'll be safe, but only if we don't give them a reason to go after them."

"Safe for now." I swallowed. "Are there a lot of these *members?*"

"Yes." Liam smiled softly. "Alcorp has members all over the U.S. Not everyone goes through the Ject program—it's optional. Alcorp is truly a secret organization that is trying to protect our country."

"I'm not sure of what to think of everything, but I never did thank you." I gave Liam a sincere smile, realizing I had never given him the appreciation he deserved. He had done a lot. I missed him and wanted my best friend back. I was tired of being angry.

"We should get out of sight. Do you have anywhere that's not compromised?" Miles acknowledged.

"Yes." Liam nodded.

I glanced at Miles as our eyes met. My heart stilled, and his face told me he felt it too. We knew we would soon have to say goodbye, but it wouldn't be forever.

CHAPTER THIRTY-SIX

M y arms wrapped snuggly around Miles as we rode behind the Ford Expedition. The hum of the motorcycle's engine did little to drown out the reality of what was happening. My location was blown, and now I needed to hide to keep the ones I cared about safe, despite my tenacity against running.

We followed Liam, Travis, and Chloe north alongside the river until we reached our destination. A fallen, illegible sign overgrown with grass and weeds lay near the entrance. Liam hopped out of the passenger's side and unlocked the gate. My arms tightened around Miles as he followed the SUV over the bump. The electricity in me was dormant, but warm sparks reached for me wherever Miles and I made contact—even through the leather.

An old fishery revealed itself on the edge of the river after driving around the bend of pine trees. We were near the edge of the city, where no one would venture unless they were mischievous teenagers. At least the entire place appeared to be fenced off, with No Trespassing signs. The building had an attached garage with three large bays big enough to fit moderately-sized boats. I was shocked when one of them opened, expecting the rusted doors not to be functional.

Miles parked inside and killed the engine. I swung my leg behind me and hopped off. My ponytail needed adjusting after removing my helmet, and I did a half job at fixing it. It never looked like the movies, where luscious locks fell out after removing a helmet—my blond hair just looked frizzy and sinuous.

Another SUV was parked to my right, with an empty spot on the other side. The outside looked worn, and so did the areas inside that hadn't been recently set up. Equipment and furniture were scattered throughout, transforming the large space into a secret temporary base. A few couches sat around a TV with a coffee table in the middle, and a kitchenette was situated on the far side. A table with a few computer monitors and a chair also sat near the couches. There was a hallway leading to a dark abyss and an old office near the kitchen.

Multiple box-shaped heaters made a perimeter around the couches, along with one next to the chair by the computers. All the electronics were plugged into surge protectors leading to the outlets on the beams throughout the garage, making me skeptical they'd pass a safety inspection.

Miles went to make a phone call to fill Kat in after answering Liam's glare that he wasn't going to share our location. My restless feet wandered to the back and soon found myself exiting a door that was barely hanging on its hinges. A covered wooden deck built over the gravel beach that extended to the water greeted me.

"Neat place, isn't it?" Liam's stealthy approach caused me to jump.

I nodded and glanced at the boat tucked inside the boathouse at the end of the dock. "Does it run?"

"Yes. It gives us access to travel by water, or an alternate route to escape." Liam glanced from the boathouse to me.

"Is this where you've been staying?"

"Beginning of that week you snuck out for Chinese." Liam grinned, but I saw the hint of hurt our meeting in the alley had left in him.

"How'd you know I went to Canby, and where our apartment was? Travis only knew where Miles lived."

"I didn't know where you went, until now." He smirked. "Dr. Roulings assumed you had gone to visit your mom, but we weren't positive. And it was easy to find you—we have friends in the FBI. Miles managed to lose us when we tried to tail him, so it was easier to just get the address. One of the guys monitoring the apartment building was ours."

"Wonderful." I rolled my eyes. That would be the reason Kat was receiving resistance on her investigation.

"Come on, I'll fill you in on some things, and we can talk about what we're going to do."

We headed inside toward the others gathering near the couches. Miles had already finished his call, and his grey eyes, which were once full of green, found mine, showing a hint of uncertainty.

A noise sounded, and all of our heads jerked to the third garage door as it opened.

I halted. "Who's that?"

"Maya." Liam kept walking, and I hesitantly followed as a Ford Expedition pulled in. "With dinner."

How could Frank afford all of this? Dumb question— he could afford a vault. The engine turned off, and Maya hopped out of the driver's side. The tinted windows provided too much cover to see through. Two more doors opened, and Adam hopped out of the back while Frank emerged from the passenger's side.

My body tensed and my breath caught. I had known they would be there, but seeing them made me relive everything I had gone through in the Vault—all the lies. A scowl left my lips, but it was overpowered by a shriek.

"Holy crap!" Chloe yelped, but not out of fear. "I think I need to sit." Chloe walked over to one of the couches and sat, running a hand through her hair.

"What's wrong?" I jogged over to her.

"Nothing's wrong." Her soft brown eyes lit up as she smiled. "I remember."

"What?" I tried to stay calm at her excitement.

"Everything."

CHAPTER THIRTY-SEVEN

"You remember everything, dearie?" Frank walked over and stood just outside the enclosed area created by the couches.

"I do." She beamed. "It all makes sense now."

"I don't know why you ever doubted us." Travis winked. "We wouldn't be hanging with this old man if we didn't have a reason."

"I can't believe I remember," Chloe said.

"Took long enough. Normally, you get all your memories back in about a week or less after the change." Travis walked over and grabbed a sub from the bag Maya had put on the table next to the computers.

"But I didn't go through the change." She raised an eyebrow. "I'm not a Hybrian."

"If your body doesn't accept the change, your memories come back slowly. They were jumbled puzzle pieces floating through your mind and needed to be put together. You did not have time to reach your potential number of treatments, so your memories returned differently," Frank explained. "That is why we inform you of everything beforehand, have full consent, and have you record the videos of yourself stating everything you know."

"I remembered seeing you get out of the same type of vehicle before and it all came rushing back." She pursed her lips and looked at Frank. "Just, I guess there's one thing I don't get, even though you tried to explain it before you took me in. Why did everything have to be hostile? You couldn't have just shown us our videos?"

Beyond Frank, Maya was listening to the conversation as her hand reached out, grabbing Adam's. *If I weren't wrapped up in what was going on, I would have gotten up and zapped him.* Miles noticed what I was glowering at as both he and Liam were intently watching my reactions to the information Frank dished out.

"The serum has a better altering rate when the person does not know what they are becoming. It's as if the anticipation slows it down or halts the change completely, and the video would have told you too much. Fear is a good motivator, whereas the change is triggered by strong emotions. Besides the unintentional side effect of memory loss, it is better to have a clean slate until the second phase."

"I mean, I guess it sort of makes sense." Chloe laughed and my jaw dropped. *What was going on?* I glanced around the room; all of my friends, except Miles, were calm with all of this.

"None of this makes sense!" I stood.

"This is what I was going to fill you in on." Liam walked over into the enclosed circle of couches.

"Well, there needs to be a lot of filling in, because she just went from hating him to . . . I don't know what." I looked from Chloe to Frank, and now to Maya. "And she's holding hands with him!"

"It's okay, sunshine." Liam walked over, gently grabbing both of my shoulders. "We went into the Vault of our own free will. Dr. Roulings gave us an opportunity to do something good, something to fight for . . . a purpose."

"There's no way he'd do that," I bit back.

"It's true." Maya dropped Adam's hand and stepped forward as Liam lowered his from my shoulders. "He saved me from a bad situation. My mom abandoned my father and me when I was a baby. Things got tough, and he . . . he drank and took his anger out on me. I ran away at fifteen to try to make better of my life. I didn't. I was sixteen when Dr. Roulings found me, and I wish it had been sooner."

"I'm sorry, Maya, I didn't know." My bones wilted, filling some of the stifled anger with sorrow. Her words from the gas station came back to me: *They saved me. I didn't have something you'd call a real family.*

"It's okay. You didn't know." She gave me an understanding smile, as if she had come to terms with what happened. "I'm sorry, too."

"You don't need to be." I wasn't sure if she meant the time she had cut my throat or at the gas station. I presumed both.

"All of it." She stepped closer and grabbed my hands. "I . . ." She glanced at the scar on my throat, and her eyes began to pool with tears. "I'm so sorry. The change brought out an anger I couldn't control. I was jealous Adam always paired with you in training, and then again later, when I found out you had family who loved you. But that was stupid of me. I promised Dr. Roulings I wouldn't hurt you the night outside the bar, but the rage controlled me. I was in the backseat and it took the wheel." She took a breath, getting ahold of her emotions. "I now know why. Adam worked with you the most because you need to be the strongest. I guess I had a crush on him that I never really admitted."

"You always did comment on how hot he was." I attempted an eye roll, but she still saw how weary I was.

"It's hard to accept, but I promise Adam is good. Dr. Roulings isn't so bad, either." She smiled at him and slid her hands out of mine, going back to stand with Adam.

I turned to Frank, who was watching us like we were playing a game of chess. "You said you never intended to kill me or hurt me, but why all the pain and torture? Just being in there created strong enough emotions."

"I am truly sorry for all of that, Isa—"

"Harper," I corrected.

"My apologies, Harper. You are an exclusive individual.

Everything you experience is new to us, too." Frank's eyes gleamed in admiration. *Okay, that's weird.*

"Did I make one of those videos? Did I know . . . Did you?" I looked over at Liam.

"I did," Liam answered.

"And you're okay with how they treated us? How *he* treated us?" I pointed at Frank.

Liam briefly closed his eyes and inhaled before re-opening them. "Like Maya, Dr. Roulings found me. I was in the hospital when I was initiated. When I was fifteen, my parents, sister, and I were on our way home from dinner one winter when a drunk driver failed to stop at a stop sign. I was the only one who survived. He gave me the option to join something that would help people. I had no one left. You guys became my family."

"I'm sorry, Liam." He hadn't directly answered my question, but that didn't make me any less remorseful. "You don't have any other family?"

"No." He shook his head. "My mom had a sister, but I never met her, and she never bothered to meet us. We lived in Ohio and she lived in California."

"She didn't come looking for you?" I frowned.

"No. She thought I died in the hospital." Liam smiled gently. "I 'died' from the injuries I sustained from the car crash. Alcorp covered up my death so it would be easier for me to join them."

"Were you aware that you might not have become a Hybrian?" I asked.

Liam nodded. "Yes. If I didn't become one, I would still have learned how to fight, like Adam did." It was starting to make sense, yet it was still incomprehensible.

"Precisely," Frank said. "Adam started the second phase, but his DNA never accepted it. Same with Avery." His eyes briefly dropped at the mention of her name. "He was one of the toughest fighters and had a strong will. I knew he would be a great teacher for the Jects. Adam took over for Dodge, a friend of your father's and mine, so we could use his help else-where." He glanced at Adam, who raised his sleeve to show me his barcode tattoo; he had always worn long-sleeves in the Vault. "All of our initiates—Jects—they knew what they were going to be put through. Once initiated, we wiped all traces that they existed—if possible—and said that they had died, or gave them a cover story."

"Except me?" I narrowed my eyes at Frank.

"We need to address our current situation at hand. We will have plenty of time to fill in all the details for you and Officer MacLand." Frank turned to Miles. "We will discuss this at length, and I am sure you will respect our mission with the utmost discretion."

"I want to know one more thing." I turned to Travis, hoping for a good answer. "What life did he take you from?"

"I was initiated while visiting abroad in Ireland with friends." Travis swallowed the bit of sub he was chewing. "I was going to join the military when I got back, but this piqued my interest. I told my parents I fell in love and was going to study abroad."

"Wouldn't your parents notice your absence the last few years?"

"Nah, they're workaholics. I knew they wouldn't even at-tempt to visit, and they're pretty loaded, so I already had my own bank account. They haven't even noticed that I wasn't pay-ing for college, and if they somehow did, they would just think I had dropped out and was living there. Plus, it wasn't supposed to take years for the second phase to start. Doc"—Travis ges-tured toward Frank—"sent them messages and pre-taken pic-tures while I was in the Vault. They don't bother calling, either."

I chewed on my lower lip. His family was alive, but they didn't sound like they were interested in being in his life. I was glad they hadn't been forced into the Vault, even though I didn't agree with the ethics of it.

"Now, why don't we all have a seat and grab some food." Frank gestured at the couches. "We have much to plan and the night is coming to an end."

CHAPTER THIRTY-EIGHT

I sat next to Chloe, not bothering to grab a sub. After the information overload, I felt a little light-headed and imagined the next conversation wasn't going to help. Only Maya, Adam, and Chloe ended up grabbing a sub while Travis took a second. Liam twitched as if he were going to sit next to me, but then thought otherwise and sat next to Travis, leaving Miles to be the only one standing.

Liam always thought about my well-being and safety. He had looked out for me in the Vault, made sure I got out, protected me at the bar, watched over me in Portland, and even protected me now. He didn't want me to feel uncomfortable, so he was giving me space. Despite teaming up with Frank, he was still the Liam I had become close with over the five years in the Vault.

His eyes drifted to mine, and I quickly averted my gaze. Things shouldn't feel awkward between us, but they did. We needed to talk. I looked over at Frank, who had already been talking for a minute, but my mind had been preoccupied. I had to focus on what he was saying to bring me back up to speed.

". . . other locations are not compromised. Harper and Chloe should go to one of those locations with Liam until we can manage things here. And hopefully, catch Avery."

"I'm glad you didn't share Alcorp's secrets with that psycho." Maya rolled her eyes. She sat with her legs crossed, wearing black leather pants and a black denim jacket.

"We can leave tomorrow," Liam added.

"What about all of our clothes?" Chloe asked.

"I can get them tomorrow," Travis offered.

"Umm, no, you're not going through my underwear drawer," Chloe remarked.

"I could get them." Maya shrugged.

"The FBI is still watching the apartment. Even if one of them is in league with Alcorp, it would raise a red flag." Miles kept his voice composed, maintaining its normal level of authoritativeness.

"Then it's decided, Harper and I will go get our own clothes."

"Neither of you should go, either." Miles looked from Chloe to me. "They know where you work, which is only a few blocks away from the apartment. They will have eyes everywhere, and more than just Avery knows what the two of you look like now."

"Harper, you are Krauss's prime target. He would use all of his resources and personnel to get you." Frank nodded. "What you have to offer is a dangerous weapon. You are his diamond in the rough."

"Haven't you been trying to replicate the same thing?" I crossed my arms.

"Yes, but as a defense mechanism in case he ever creates anything similar." Frank folded his hands in his lap. "An antidote."

"Why not try to destroy it so no one can replicate it?" I asked, causing Liam to blanch.

"That would mean destroying you," Frank said, inhaling, "and that is not an option."

"So, what do we do? Wait here until we leave tomorrow?" I shivered and sank back into the couch. My powers would be dangerous if they fell into the wrong hands; I couldn't let that happen.

"Yes," Liam answered.

"I'll call Kat again and have her pick up some of the clothes and meet her tomorrow." Miles looked at me, waiting for my okay to step aside. I nodded as Chloe frowned at the "some of the clothes" comment.

"Can we have a quick conversation before your call?" Frank asked Miles before walking out the front bay doors.

Despite it being drafty in the oversized garage and the temperature dropping outside, I left the cocoon of the heaters and stepped out back to get some fresh air. I walked along the rocks toward the water until a lonely log caught my eye. I sat down and rested my head on my hands. My sneakers shifted through the gravel, shuffling the stones side to side. The sun's dull orange glow bounced off the water as it peeked through thin clouds; it was almost sunset.

I was not fond of the city, but I wasn't ready to leave the small life I had created behind. I would miss the Kovars, the small-but-nice apartment Chloe and I shared, going to Mel's Pub, visiting my mother and stepfather, regaining Dylan as a friend, Brandon, and most of all, Miles. Sure, I would be with Liam, Maya, Travis, and Chloe, and I was happy about that, but I couldn't shake the void in my chest.

"Here." Liam emerged out of nowhere, draping a fleece blanket around my shoulders.

"Where did you get this?" I tugged it tighter and glanced up, noticing he had thrown on a black cargo jacket.

"We don't all snuggle up on those couches." He grinned. "We have rooms with beds and heat. They aren't the greatest, but it beats the cement."

"Thanks." My smile faltered as he stood there, waiting. "You don't ever need an invitation to sit next to me." I slid over to make room.

Liam sat down and rubbed his hands together. "It's nothing like our nights in the Vault."

"Definitely not seventy-two degrees with no wind." I laughed and then frowned. "It's not what we hoped for once we got out."

"But it's also not the worst." Liam nudged me with his shoulder.

"Nope." I bit my lower lip. "I'm really sorry about your family."

"It will always hurt, but I have come to terms with it. Doing what I do now, helping the world, it kind of keeps you occupied."

"You're always so kind and selfless, something I secretly envied about you in the Vault." He snorted at my remark, and I raised an eyebrow at him. "What?"

"That's ironic, because everyone would say that about you."

It was my turn to snort. "Yeah, sure. You jumped down from that air vent to save Ellie, knowing you wouldn't make it out if you did. I made it out; I left you behind." I wanted to ask where Ellie was, but at the same time, I didn't want any more information. Not tonight. I held back the tears threatening my eyes as I stared at the stones.

"Hey," Liam said softly as he wrapped an arm around me, pulling me close. I was about to protest and then realized I didn't have to. "You didn't leave anyone behind."

"I did, and when I went back, you guys were gone." Guilt, which had been led by false pretenses, had tormented me.

"You did everything you could. Besides, we weren't in any danger." Liam tightened his arm as a single tear flowed down my cheek. "*Your* selflessness and determination are two of the many things I love about you. Even though you really should think about yourself more often."

I looked at him. I truly believed I may have had stronger feelings and an attraction to him once, but it was different from what I felt around Miles. I didn't have the urge to kiss him, nor was I jealous when I thought about Ellie anymore. My emotions were more under control, but they were nothing compared to the last month in the Vault, where every emotion had been heightened.

"When you went through the second phase, did you think you were going insane?" I asked.

"Yes. My brain felt like it was on fire, and I was angry all the time."

"You hid it well."

"It wasn't easy." He looked off toward the river.

"The night you fought those sentinels, was that when it happened?" I thought about how that day had changed him.

He nodded and looked back at me. "It was like a switch went off inside me. I thought they were going to kill me, and when . . ." he said, hesitating, "when I looked up and saw the worry on your face, I knew I couldn't let that happen. I couldn't leave you guys."

"I couldn't either," I whispered, thinking about Adam's hands around my neck right before I had snapped.

He averted his eyes and shifted. "If only I knew it was a damn test."

"You didn't know. You believed what they wanted you to believe. So did all of us."

"Is that when you felt it?" He brought his eyes back over.

"I thought so, but it felt like a switch was flipped multiple times, not just once. I think it manifested differently in me."

"I think so too. Travis had a hard time with the rage, just like Maya," Liam added.

"It only took Travis a few weeks?" He had been MIA for a week and a half after the escape and was fine at the cabin. Maya had still been amped up a month later.

"He hid those two nights with you well. We found him practically seething with hatred when he was looking for us. He had gone through the change a few days before that, and got his memories back shortly after we found him."

"Were you angry with me in the Vault? Is that why you avoided me for a month?" Anger was the strongest emotion I had felt, and it was one of the most uncontrollable.

"No." His voice was soft as he grabbed my chin and turned my face to look at him. "I was never angry with you. I never have been." He dropped his hand. "I didn't want anyone to know that I was changing. They would have sent me away."

"I saw you morph when we were escaping—you knew what you were. Aren't your memories supposed to come back in a week or less?" I asked.

"Yes, but for some reason, they didn't." Liam shrugged. "Dr. Roulings is still trying to figure that one out." He took a deep breath. "If they had, things might have been different. I wouldn't have worked on a plan that ended up hurting you and putting you in harm's way. You and Travis knew me best, and I couldn't risk you guys learning the truth and them finding out. I thought that was the best way to get you guys out of there."

"The closet," I murmured. Ellie had known how to help. The day I had found him kissing her in the closet, he'd thought I was someone else. It was a cover-up so they wouldn't find out what they had really been up to.

"I never meant to hurt you."

"Don't be sorry. I was blind, and my rampaging emotions clouded my judgment." There was a moment of silence. "Did you have feelings for me when we were in the Vault?"

"In the Vault?" His voice held. "I still do."

I shook my head. "I don't mean like family or a best friend, I—"

"I don't, either."

I pulled back the tiniest bit so I could get a better look at him. He was telling the truth, and I had to be honest with him. I may have had those feelings for him in the Vault, but it hadn't been anything like the way he was staring at me now. It was something I had wanted, but it was also a spark that had been ignited by my change.

"Liam . . ." I swallowed. This was hard, harder than the first day in the Vault. "Liam, I—"

"Don't reciprocate the same feelings." He gently smiled. "I know."

"I am so sorry, Liam. I believed that there was something

there," I said as I pulled away and looked in the other direction, hiding my face, "but it's not what I thought. I still love you . . ."

He let out a small laugh. "Like you said that I don't need permission to sit next to you, you don't need to hide from me." He pulled me back in, wrapping both arms tight around me. "I understand."

"How do you do that?" I mumbled into his chest.

"Do what?"

"Be so stoic and composed."

He chuckled in response, making me smile as we stared at the now-blackened river.

I had thought I was trapped in the Vault, but it turned out it had been protecting me. And, now, I was going to run to prevent anyone I cared about from getting hurt and prevent my DNA from being used as a weapon. Shying away from a fight wasn't my thing, but this was a war. A war that I needed to be strategic with, and my best strategy was to let Alcorp take care of Dr. Krauss while keeping the weapon inside me hidden from him. A war that would meet its end in time, and if my memories hadn't returned by then, I already knew who I was without them.

I was Harper.

Continue in *The Alliance*—
the next book in *The Hybrian Series*

ACKNOWLEDGMENTS

Special shout out to my wonderful husband for always believing in me, even when I don't. Thank you for putting up with your crazy wife and helping with our little munchkin when I needed to meet deadlines. You are my rock.

I'm eternally grateful to have had such wonderful beta readers whose feedback were gold mines—you all are amazing!

Special thank yous are in order to the professional editors and interior designer who've helped shape *The Vault*, getting it where it needed to be.

Last but not least, thank you—the reader—for coming along on this ride. If you enjoyed it, please take a moment to share a review.

ABOUT THE AUTHOR

L. Wood enjoys living in the countryside of the Great Lakes Region. When she's not writing or working with animals as a veterinary technician, she loves spending time with her family, playing volleyball, and hiking. If a sparkling pool, lake, or pond is nearby, it's hard for her to resist the urge to jump in—much like her dog. And, of course, there's always room for ice cream, no matter the time of day.

Please visit authorlwood.com
and find her on social media for more!